The Ark of the Blessed

By: SCOTT NEALE

Book I of the Starlight Series

Prologue

"First, let me welcome you to Alliance Studies 451 – "A Perspective of Alliance History".

So you have taken this class to find out about the history of our glorious Alliance and how it was formed, eh? Of course you did, and good for you as this knowledge will make you a better citizen!

Well, I could give you a rough idea of our entire history in about two minutes and you could skip this entire class – which I am sure many of you would love, right? Sorry, it's not going to be so easy!

Well in a nutshell, our history started at the same time that the planet was changed dramatically during what came to be known as the Hemispheric War. 2028 was the year when everything changed – the bombs were launched and the world started to become one big mess...and we caused this mess ourselves by launching those damn bombs against our own allies! Of course after that, our friends in the southern hemisphere couldn't trust us up here in the north...and eventually the two halves of the planet collided in the big one – which started in 2031.

If the planet was not already messed up enough before the two halves started throwing smart bombs at each other...well, it became an even bigger mess after we stopped the bombing. Because, when the bombs stopped working, we started throwing other things...weapons, and then people – our troops -- at each other. The central part of the globe around the equator became the new war zone. I swear one could – provided they could take off their protective suit and actually breathe the air – could smell the death that emanated from Central America if they stood where the Rio Grande used to flow. If that wasn't bad enough, we had to take our spat out into space! The moon became a floating pile of rocks and debris – thank goodness we no longer have a real ocean, as the tides...anyway, I digress. This was all just in a matter of years – the ground and space wars started as soon as the bombs stopped falling – that was in 2034.

Eh, well enough with the historical numbers – what is even more important is what happened right here on our crispy planet...inside of our government, all of which resulted from those bombs and wars.

The President became the Supreme Commander and he took over and created the Council of Order. They took care of us war beaten citizenry – they set up the domed cities and decommissioned the four military services and created two new branches – the Secret Service and the Ground and Space Battle Commission. The latter was eventually separated into the Alliance Ground Force and the Alliance Space Force and Patrol.

This allowed them to continue warring with our enemies in the south while keeping order here in the homeland. Also, with the war effort came progress – major gains in technology and science which led to many wondrous discoveries...and some not so wonderful. As an example of the latter, our government began experimentation into mutations of the human body – you have to wonder what they have created that is hidden away in some laboratory somewhere, don't you? They also started practicing selective breeding and genetic enhancement – now THAT -- brought us the Blessed.

And there you have it...the history of the Northern Alliance of Order. Really, do I need to even go on from here? Haven't I covered all of the history? Actually, I hope you are now even more interested.

I guess what you should be asking yourself at this point is what exactly is history? Is it what happened in our past, or is it what we think has happened? Is what we have been told to be fact, or conjecture, or is it a flat-out lie?

I will tell you that when I am not with you here in the classroom, I have been spending all of my time out in the radioactive mess in search of this answer – to find the truth. There is evidence about what really happened, and someday I will find that evidence.

Ah, you are probably saying to yourself that I am headed for a death camp with talk like that! Possibly...that might and probably will happen someday. But for now I will use my position and the safety of my position to talk about it – to bring up questions and conversations about our history. To raise doubt and produce deep consideration and thought about where we came from and why...and perhaps discover where we are going."

Professor Simon Piccolo, Alliance Historian

Opening lecture, Spring semester – 2054

Alliance University of Sector 5

The Ark of the Blessed

Starlight Launch Time Minus 72 hours 25 minutes

Jaime Bordeaux:

Jaime tapped on her computer pad adding some buttons to the design of a dress uniform. *"Hmm...It still needs something else."* She bit her lower lip while she contemplated her fashion design. She needed to make this outfit special as this party was going to be the event of the year, and possibly of her life. There was going to be an announcement of many major appointments and promotions throughout the Alliance Space Patrol and she knew she was up for one of those promotions. She made a few more adjustments to some of the piping around the edge of the blouse. She gave the screen another long look. *"There, perfect! This will knock them dead at the launch party."* She smiled and nodded at the now completed image of her dress uniform. She placed the computer pad on the desk then walked over to the window.

Her cabin was located in the flight officer's section of the massive starbase grid. From her vantage point, the various red tones of the Earth were directly below her. The grid was currently floating over the southern part of North America and upper isthmus of Central America as it ventured on its orbit around the poisoned Earth. The terminus of daytime had crept onto the surface below -- it was already evening in much of the North American Alliance proper. She stared at the dying planet, a large ion storm swirled across the surface of what used to be Texas. The slight glow of the shielded cities showed through the storm clouds. The surface of the planet flickered different shades of red as the soil itself constantly burned – the bombs had done their worst to the planet and now Mother Earth was showing her rage. Where the ocean's vast currents once flowed, large masses of polluted red radioactive water now sat – no natural water was fit to drink. As she looked toward the lower part of the world, she could see in the distance the domed cities of their hated enemies in the southern hemisphere.

As she peered at the enemy cities, she was reminded of the on-going war, and of what one of her instructors once told her while in battle school *"Those who control the air win the war – thus, we must control the air!"* No one really controlled the air down there, except nature. She looked down again at the burning

5

planet – the swirling, shifting currents of heat, and the constantly roving ion storms as large as Europe. No starship could maintain any amount of prolonged flight in that swirling, radioactive, super-heated, atmospheric soup. The ion drives used on the ships of today were rendered useless by the charged electrical forces in the planet's angry sky. Only a chemical or fission powered rocket could make the trip now, and it did not happen often, except to shuttle people and supplies to and from the surface in quick dashes through the atmospheric chaos. She chuckled to herself as she wondered if that old fart of an instructor still gave that line of malarkey.

As a trained fighter pilot, she had the knack to see motion even far away. Using that ability, she caught a number of slight glimmers from the southern part of the planet below. *"Did I just see something ascending from the planet?"* As if being answered by some mystical force, her communication device buzzed on the side of her head. She tapped at the small button behind her right ear and spoke normally "Alpha Wolf Pack Commander Bordeaux here."

"Alpha Wolf Pack Commander, this is Alliance Star Patrol Control. We have multiple Southern Fighter bogies approaching Earth apogee orbit and are headed this way. Your squadron is to destroy them."

She was confused at this order. "Why me? I have been placed on reserves and have not flown combat or patrol in months."

"Alpha Wolf Pack Commander, I have direct orders from Star Force to send the most experienced pilot and wing we have. You ARE the most experienced, and Alpha Wing is the best we've got. Now, please respond to your orders."

"Star Force eh?" She wondered why the Alliance Star Force would get involved with a low Earth orbital issue as that was not in their jurisdiction. "Very well, I will prepare. Have my Wolf Pack gathered and prepped for battle. I will be there in ten minutes" she ordered and tapped at her communication device to deactivate it without waiting for a reply. It had been years since there had been an air or space battle with the Southern fleet. She wondered why the South would suddenly become aggressive in the skies again. Nonetheless, she now needed to prepare for battle once again– to start her preparations she walked over to the computer cleansing bay and removed her clothing.

Before stepping into the device, she took a moment to reach back and take hold of her long strawberry blonde hair. She softly and gently stroked it. *"Shit, it took so damn long to grow this…"* Her small mouth puckered downward and a slight bit of tearing came to her eyes as she continued to admire her long locks. Finally, she dropped her hair and let it fall down across her naked breasts before she commanded to the machine "Computer, prepare the cleansing bay…"

The computer screen queried "State level of cleansing."

Her face became stern and her lips tightened as she barked out the hurtful order "Complete cleaning, prepare me for flight – shave me."

She stepped into the cleansing bay, and upon activation an array of lasers arced across her body – the small precise beams removed dead skin, soil, germs and every small and long lock of hair on her body. Fans removed any smoke from the laser's work and a light mist of fragrance coated her body. Within moments of stepping into the cleansing bay she emerged completely clean and totally shaved. Not a hair remained on her entire body. She stopped at the mirror as she examined her totally nude body -- the freckles on her shoulders and cheeks were the only marks that provided any coloration to her alabaster skin. Her gaze returned to her now bald head. *"Damn, it is going to take hours of growth stimulation to get any of that back!"* She ran her hand across the smooth skin that made up her scalp. *"I guess I will be adding a hat to my dress uniform…"* She shook her head in disgust as her hand moved to rub her now naked eyebrows and she let out a small chuckle of frustration.

As she gave up on her lost hair, she stepped into another computer bay that provided her with a flight suit. She entered commands into the console and the computer responded by opening a drawer filled with a number of dark colored vinyl items of clothing. She took out a flight suit and slid it over her body -- the tight material snapped into place, seams self-sealed as soon as she bound the edges of the suit opening. She inspected the suit – it was a dark black, one-piece, skin-tight item of clothing. Silver ribbing flowed down her arms, legs and torso along the sides, front and back – the ribbing gave off a slight phosphorescent glow.

She placed a black skin-tight cap on her now bald head which molded itself while linking to the main body of the suit – ribbing on the cap began to glow as it too joined the main suit body. She took a pair of tight, flat heeled boots and stretched them onto her feet, then a set of gloves all with matching silver ribbing going along each digit. Each item of clothing she put on merged like melted plastic into the main part of the suit, which encased her in a thin layer of black shiny acrylic. The silver ribs each took on the glow of the rest of the suit as they merged with the main suit body. Finally, she reached into a drawer and obtained two patch badges – each had the image of a snarling wolf embroidered onto the plasticized fabric. She slapped a patch on each shoulder, once again the material instantly bonded with the rest of the suit. On each of her shoulders, she applied the Greek letter Alpha – her rank insignia.

She then reapplied her ear communication device, then tapped it to activate "Alpha Wolf Pack Commander Bordeaux here, ready and on my way to the flight line. Have my Wolf Pack ready for my arrival" she ordered.

"Yes Alpha Wolf Pack Commander!" snapped the voice which sounded as if he had jumped to attention at the sound of her voice. She could have sworn she even heard him click his heels at her command as she raced out the door of her quarters and down the hallway. From there, she ran the short distance to the lift that took her to the launch hangar.

When she arrived at the hangar bay, there was a flurry of activity – much of which was due to confusion and disorganization. It had been quite awhile since the crews had to prepare the Wolf Pack Star Fighters for actual battle and they were showing how out of practice they had become. Preparing for a patrol was nothing compared to getting a Wolf Pack prepared for actual space combat. A pair of crew chiefs were discussing – actually arguing over the correct armament configuration when she approached them. She cleared her throat and softly said to the pair as she leaned over their shoulders from behind "So, have we forgotten everything?"

The two men jumped to attention -- one of them attempted to conceal their confusion. "Umm, no Alpha Wolf Pack Commander! We were just discussing proper protocols..."

She smiled and whispered "I know it has been awhile since you have prepped me for battle. How close are we to being ready?"

"We are ready, Alpha Wolf Pack Commander!" he replied quickly and saluted. He then added "Well almost...we need another moment..."

She gave a warm smile "Very well, prepare the ITZee for me please.'

The two men scampered their fingers over a bank of computer switches. With a quick swoosh a door opened in front of her. She grabbed a clear acrylic helmet from a shelf next to the hatch, and then gave a brief light thump to her chest and a sideways salute to the two men who returned similar salutes – as was the protocol in the Alliance Star Force and Star Patrol. The men immediately returned to their configuration – and their bickering as soon as she entered the chamber.

Once inside she walked down a catwalk and approached a black, wheat kernel shaped pod turned upright and resting in a metallic cradle suspended above the hanger launch portal floor – the catwalk extended to the top of the pod. The pod was encased with thousands of miniature-hexagon shaped external sensors. In the launch portal below the pod, mechanical arms loaded and configured various armaments and ammunition to the waiting Star Fighters.

Stepping to the edge of the walkway she flipped a switch on a console attached to the walkway rail and the tip of the pod opened. As she flipped another switch a trapeze style bar was lowered down to eye level. She placed the clear acrylic helmet over her head and it immediately bonded with the rest of the suit. A slight hiss escaped as the helmet pressurized – the back of the helmet shrank and contoured to her skull, the front of the helmet tightened but provided plenty of room for airflow to her nose and mouth. She took a few breaths of air to ensure the suit was working properly, then grasped the bar and pushed a button mounted on the bar. The winch on the bar lifted her into the air and moved her body over the opening of the dark pod. She flipped the switch the other way which then lowered her slowly into the pod.

The pod, known as the Immersive Tactile Command module of the Wolf Pack Class Star Fighter, provides its pilot with vision to see in every direction as if flying without a craft. With its tactile controls enabled, the pilot can control all movement and weapons fire by thought, voice, body motion, hand movement, and leg motion. The pilots refer to the pod as ITZee even though the official designation is I.T.C.

She released her grip on the trapeze allowing herself to softly drop onto a small clear circular disk in the middle of the pod. She now looked around the pod, and examined the small glimmers of the thousands of image-emitting diodes that made up the inside shell of the pod. The diodes twinkled in the dim interior light being provided above her head. The entire interior of the pod was covered in these diodes. They not only provided an image of the space outside, but also projected virtual controls and displays for the pilot's information. There were also individual sensors that detected control signals given by the pilot. She made sure everything looked proper in the pod, and then waved her hand over a small sensor mounted on the disk immediately below her. This activated a number of visual control readouts. She quickly checked the readouts appearing on the space screen in front of her. Finally she moved her hand across a sensor above her which activated servos that closed the hatch. That sensor went dark and a green light appeared in front of her.

"All systems check green, filling pod with sensory gel" she signaled. She received a small beep tone from the on-board computer as she waved her hand over the green light sensor.

The pod began to fill with a thick clear gel. The gel itself is a protein based cellular substance, close to being its own single cell life form. The gel provided a connection from the pod's thousands of sensors to the nervous system of the pilot via the special ribbing of the flight suit. The head cap merged with the helmet and the rest of the suit which provided a total body neural connection to the gel. The ribbing allowed the gel to detect movement of her body.

As the gel hit her suit she gave a slight pleasurable moan as the connection took place. Jaime was no different from any of the other Wolf Pack pilots -- she thoroughly enjoyed stepping into the pod and experiencing the feeling of becoming one with her ship. Not only does the pod provide the tactile connectivity to the ship, but it also provided a pilot with atmosphere and nutrition through the thin suit. A pilot could survive for quite a long time if they found themselves adrift in space -- as long as the pod's shell remained intact. Carbon dioxide received by the gel as waste gas from the pilot is utilized in the same way as the foliage of a plant and is then returned in an almost perfect ratio of oxygen and nitrogen and provided a safe breathing environment for extended periods of time.

The development of the interface was the one reason the Northern Alliance had won the air and space war. It was the reason they maintained superiority above the planet. It was the reason the South had given up trying to take over outer space – until today.

When the pod finished filling, the interior center disk moved back and away from the pilot which allowed her to freely float in the center of the pod. Upon her command, the pod lowered and locked into the fuselage of the fighter. The fighter was long, thin and shaped like a stiletto, providing a small profile that made it hard to hit in a dogfight and helped to avoid blasts from planetary weapons. In addition, its black colored coating made visual sighting difficult and this same coating contained a layer of stealth sensor deflecting polymers to help in avoiding SCADAR scans. There was a single ion accelerator engine attached to the back of the ship. Small P-accelerator beam weapon ports were located in the front point. The tips of the small partial wings and upper and lower tail fins hosted photon cutter beams. Concealed atomic-charged particle rail gun launchers were located in the underbelly. The front of the ship tapered to a sharp point, which if engaged in atmospheric battle provided a sleek aerodynamic profile for speed. Internally stored wings can be deployed which gave the ship additional atmospheric lift and maneuverability. Unfortunately, since the total devastation of Earth's atmosphere – flying near the surface of the homeland has been impossible by a fighter craft -- at least until today. The only time in recent past that the Wolf Pack Star Fighters had seen atmospheric battle was in fighting for Mars. That too ended once the South gave up on obtaining other planets of the Solar System.

She motioned her hands over virtual switches that had appeared in the gel. Power began to flow through the body of the ship. Through the tactile interface she actually felt the ship come alive. She felt power flowing through her own body as the ship coursed ions through its conduits. "ITZee, are you there?" she queried of the interface. She received a small beep and a few blinking lights that told her the computer was on-line and with her. She received ready signals from her squadron, then validated that the space dock was clear of human life. "Power...One-hundred percent. Engines are go, all pups are powered up and ready, imagers active. Starbase, evacuate launch bay atmosphere, open space doors and prepare for Wolf Pack launch."

After a moment of depressurizing, the space doors opened on the massive fighter space dock module of the starbase, the remaining air escaped with a slight hiss. Jaime could see stars through the launch bay doors, and as she thought about increasing engine thrust, at the same time she extended her arms out toward the open door as if she was pulling the ship through the doors and into space. Immediately the ship followed her command and increased thrust, moving the ship slowly at first, then as she thought of more motion, the engine provided one strong short burst which moved her and the ship quickly out through the bay and into open space.

As the ship cleared the space dock, the pod walls appeared transparent as the remaining imaging diodes activated and provided display throughout the pod. She was surrounded by the universe and the depth of outer space. For a brief second, she took in the sights and feelings she was experiencing. It had been awhile since she had been outside the starbase and even longer since she had flown in a Star Fighter. Below her was the Earth, charred reddish-brown and glowing red like hell's fury. Above her were the remnants of the moon – three fourths of it still intact, the other quarter floated above the surface like a dusty, ragged ring of Saturn. She spun her body around moving the ship at the same time. She looked to each side and saw the outline of her eight pup drone ships.

Each Wolf Pack pup ship was an exact copy of the manned vessels. The only difference between her ship and the pups was the pod. Her ship was the only one in her pack with an I.T.C. The pups each had an identical kernel shaped pod which contained a complex computer brain. These computers were matched to the mental frequencies of the pack pilot, which provided full mental control over every aspect of their flight and battle. The black ships followed her every move like obedient children. She placed her pups in a circular formation as she did not want the enemy figuring out the controlling spacecraft.

The number of pup ships a pilot could command also identified the overall strength and ability of the pilot. In addition, the more pup ships a pilot commanded, the stronger a pilot actually became. When a new pilot was assigned to a Wolf Pack, they were given a single pup – as that is the maximum number a green pilot could handle and control. As they became stronger and more experienced they would be rewarded with more pups. The strongest and most advanced pilots had the largest number of pups. Jaime's abilities were very obvious to any other pilot, as she commanded eight pup ships – no other pilot in the Alliance Fleet commanded as many or more.

"ITZee, please play Idano's Toccata 1558 in ultra-sharp please." A rapidly pulsing, electronically chorded instrumental started playing inside the pod. "Ah yes, perfect!" she softly murmured as the music pulsed through the pod and into her body.

Small red dots of light appeared to her through the gel. ITZee's sensors were detecting the enemy ships which were headed straight for the space station. Above her, three green lights indicated a matching number of friendly ships – more of her Wing. She spoke to the lights. "Den Mother to Force… Check in."

A man whose face was obscured by a dark helmet appeared in the gel from the ship on the left. "Perfecto here, and ready to rumble. Great to be in battle with you again, Den Mother. I hope you have not gotten out of shape – or do we need to start sparring again?" She smiled and nodded at the hidden-faced man whom she had fought beside for so many years and through so many battles. His voice indicated fatigue even as he attempted to show enthusiasm. She knew the war had finally gotten to him and he had become tired of fighting. She hoped he still had enough spark to stay focused and strong during this fight.

"It's good to see and fly with you again my old friend!" she replied. "Don't worry -- I am in perfect shape as our enemy will soon find out!"

"Messiah here, ready to take another victory, Den Mother!" spoke an older man projected into the gel from his position above her. He had many scars – on his lips, above his left eye and a large former gash across his cheek. He had seen his share of battle and she had fought alongside of him many times both on land and in the air. She felt comfort with him being on her Wing.

"Hello Messiah, it has been so long...and yet you still defy authority with that name. They have not shot you yet for that?" she replied.

"Ah, I am too good of a pilot for them to do that. Besides, I think these southern barbarians will do that for us Den Mother."

"That or old age will finally catch up to him" said the image of a young woman appearing below her in the gel – the baby face of this pilot made her look as if she was barely out of her teens. Her eyes were bright green and she still showed excitement and energy.

"Star Child! I should have guessed they would put you with us old-timers. This makes the pack complete. Still have not gotten that second pup yet eh?"

Star Child was the name given to every new pilot when they first leave flight school and get their first fighter duties. Only when have they obtained enough kills and prove they have become strong enough to be assigned their second pup are they allowed to take a real flight handle. The young woman shook her head in the negative. "No, but I am hoping that this will be the battle that will get me one."

"Me too, good hunting..." she replied. She changed to a serious tone and ordered "Ok, let's get to work. Alpha Wing, take up battle formation L-38. We have a space station to protect...and I have to take revenge for ruining my hairdo for the party." Not like she needed a real reason to be revengeful as she found she still enjoyed the thrill of battle.

The twenty-four fighter craft formed a tiered, triple-layered, circular formation: Jaime's ship and eight pup drones, Perfecto who had control of six pups, Messiah who had five and Star Child as the youngest pilot only had her one pup drone craft. Jaime looked at her heads-up status display and saw they were completely out gunned as the enemy fleet contained seventy-five craft.

She kept her scanning radar watching the oncoming fleet. The South had sent up older Century-class model air-to-space fighters to take on the Wolf Pack. These ships had delta wings for atmospheric travel and resembled older aircraft of the twentieth and early twenty-first century – although their weaponry was modern and as lethal as the Wolf Pack's. The ships' silver skins reflected the sun as they flew through space, giving off bright sparkles of light that were the exact opposite of the almost invisible black Wolf Pack star fighters.

Jaime examined the returns of the scans on the ships. "So, they're all old styled, liquid fueled, rocket propelled, fission hybrids. That's how they were able to ascend through the atmospheric mess below. How old fashioned..." A brief shock came upon her as she read more of the sensor readings coming in. "My god, every one of those ships is manned!"

Messiah interjected "Just more pilots the South will lose today. I guess their lack of air battles has made them forget."

"Let's hope so..." she replied. She was curious however as to why they would launch such a large manned fleet at this point in the war. As they approached the invading fleet, she studied their attack vector and the realization of their maneuvers hit her like a brick. "Dammit, they're after Starlight!"

"Then what are we waiting for?" asked Perfecto.

"Nothing, let's go...Alpha Wing, attack!" she yelled out.

The small force's super-fast engines engaged and within seconds were upon the larger fighter force. The older fighters shut down their chemical engines and engaged fission powered thrusters.

"Man, these things are going to make a polluted mess when they blow up. Don't get too close to their asses unless you want to glow after the fight!" Messiah joked over the chat channel.

Jaime immediately engaged with the first group of ships, she looked at one of the enemy ships, tapped in the gel on the image and through thought commanded two of her pups with a simple word -- "kill". Instantly two pups broke formation and accelerated toward their target in attack mode while at the same time she targeted two other enemy craft and commanded three of her pups to engage those targets, while the remaining three pups stayed to cover her own attack. She precisely commanded each pup while at the same time selected her own target and fired her weapons.

Her body was in constant motion while she swirled and swam within the confines of the I.T.C. pod. Every motion and flex caused her ship to swerve and sway between the oncoming fighter ships. The gel was picking up her every thought as she both mentally and physically, through her motions, commanded her drones to fly and fight while she simultaneously fired her own weapons at her chosen targets.

Looking around the image in her pod she could see that all of her squadron had engaged and already had destroyed many of the attacking ships. She squirmed and moved her body like a sea snake gliding through the ocean as she maneuvered to approach behind yet another of the southern fighters. With a mere thought and the flex of her fist, she fired her weapons which provided yet another kill of the sortie. She moved in a shimmy that avoided the exploding ship and moved her ship into a position on her next victim. She sent three of her pups into a swarm of enemy fighters taking down an equal number of the enemy, all while she positioned herself for the next kill. She twisted and turned as she responded to the electronic beat that was being broadcast within her pod. The melody of death played on as she used the thumping sounds to glide and shimmy behind enemy after enemy – she moved in, then pounded them with the full force of her Pack's weaponry.

She quickly flew in behind yet another of the southern Century-class, delta-winged spacecraft and fired a full barrage of her beams and rail projectiles. The older ship exploded into thousands of pieces, which ejected the pilot with a violent force. As she avoided the debris of the explosion, the head and torso of the pilot floated into the path of her fighter. The partial body was totally naked as the force of the exploding spacecraft had cut, burned, and stripped the pilot's flight suit and helmet completely off. Because the body portions had no metal to indicate a threat to the computer, her proximity alarms never sounded. She knew nothing of the floating frosted flesh in front of her until the frozen half-dead human slipped in front of her craft. For a brief moment Jaime saw the remains of the pilot – his head was only partially covered with flesh. One eye was hanging frozen in a now bare socket, the other wide open in fear, and both eyes were bloated like small balloons, teeth exposed in the expression of a wide-open mouth, as the pilot must have screamed when his ship blew apart. His torso had entrails dangling through the point where he had been separated from his waist. The pilot's skin had deep gashes all across his chest. She saw the look of pain and terror on the face of the now dead pilot for that brief moment before the frozen body hit the pod with a heavy thump. A slight yelp escaped her lips as the body hit, then it immediately burst into a thousand small frozen bits of flesh, bone, and blood which scattered into the solar winds. She stopped her attack for just a second as she caught her breath from the surprise attack of the corpse – her ship's movement also slowed for that brief moment as she had lost her concentration, which in turn stopped her control of the craft.

Perfecto heard her yelp over the communications channel. "Den Mother, you ok?"

She took a quick deep breath before answering. "Yes, I was surprise attacked by a corpse. I really can't believe they would commit suicide like this. They aren't even good fighters – this is a blood bath!" She fired up her thrusters so she could swoop to the rear of yet another southern fighter.

"Guess they just wanted to give us some much-needed practice?" replied Perfecto scoring yet another kill.

She waved her hand and activated her ship-to-ship communicator. "Southern Fighter I have my weapons locked on you – why do you commit yourself to death in such a manner? Retreat now and save yourselves. Reply."

"Mercy?" asked Perfecto.

"No, curiosity...I think. I am hoping they will tell me why they foolishly fight us." she replied while she hoped that answer would quiet any further explanation. Something about that pilot hitting her craft had unnerved her demeanor. She was slightly hesitating and she needed to get her reason to kill back. She hoped for the correct response.

Within seconds a single message came through the translator circuit "Screw you Northern fascist..." He was too busy attempting to shake her pursuit to give a detailed answer – instead a flurry of curses flowed from the mouth of the pilot of the enemy ship ahead of her – that was what she needed to regain her edge. She sighed slightly while she lifted her arm, then shoved an extended hand toward the pursued ship which immediately fired her full barrage of P-accelerators and atomic projectiles from her rail guns toward the defenseless fleeing fighter. "Fucking bitch..." came across the translator before she heard the scream of the pilot being blasted to bits.

Suddenly, an electronic scream-like sound indicated a targeting-lock warning on one of her pups. She turned to see a fighter bearing down on one of the drones. She began guiding the unmanned craft through evasive maneuvers while she spun her body around so her feet now faced forward. She pushed her feet down as if digging into the dirt and her ship immediately stopped dead, then reversed. The attacking southern ship zoomed by her while in its continued pursuit of the drone -- she spun around reaching her arms out forward, then motioned down as if stroking through water. The ship hurdled forward in a burst of hyper-speed, moving in quietly behind the chasing fighter. It only took a second of flight at maximum thrust before she had acquired and targeted the fighter, then took it out with a single burst. "Whew! I was a tiny bit worried I had lost a pup for a second there..."

"Never lost one? Never?" asked Perfecto.

"No, there is a reason she is an eight-drone Commander and hero of the Homeland!" said Star Child.

"Never mind that, keep taking down this fleet -- they are getting closer and..." she was interrupted by a yet another warning indicator on her pod's heads-up display. "What the hell is that?"

In the distance, a mile-long, tubular rocket emerged through the atmosphere. As she magnified a portion with her visual sensors she was able to see a deep large pit which she assumed was the launching site of the giant projectile. It was powered by a mass of old twentieth century chemical rockets. It was flying at the speed of an old horse ready for the glue factory. It jerked and surged as it inched its way through the atmosphere, while it fought to escape the planet's gravity and reach apogee.

"Should we pursue?" asked Messiah.

"Negative, continue to protect the base and Starlight" she replied. "I am sure the base will fire upon that thing."

As if on cue, the starbase took aim and fired a barrage of photon cutter beams at the slow-moving ship. However, the beams simply bounced off the old-style rocket and traveled off into space. The base continued to shoot at the slow rocket with rail-fired, plutonium projectiles and a barrage of cutter beams and proton cannons. Massive arcs of plasma shot from the cannons and like the cutter beams, simply bounced off.

When the large ship had finally reached high Earth orbit, it started to break apart – the shell of the large rocket split in two – thruster rockets moved the shell away from the inside contents which allowed a totally different ship to slip out like a butterfly from its cocoon. The two halves of the old rocket shell continued to protect the emerging contents as they drifted apart. What came out of that shell was a modern starship. It had a long body with three large engine pods at the rear and two cylindrical pods in the middle of the ship which were slightly lower than the main engines to prevent thrust being blasted into the main power core in the rear. At the front of the ship sat a central command section. Between these two sections was a connecting hexagon-shaped central core that went between the command sphere and the hexagon-shaped engineering block that held onto the rear engine pods. Within seconds, as it cleared the booster rocket debris, the ship's skin lit up like a burning candle, blurred and disappeared.

For a second time in this battle Jaime was stunned at what she saw. "What the hell just happened? What was that ship?" a close explosion brought her back to reality. "Ok, let's clean up and go home." A small wiggle put her behind another ship that she quickly dispatched with a flurry of projectiles from her rail guns. She then arched her back to flip while she spun her body, rotating her weapons into yet another firing position against a fighter that was chasing one of her pups. Another squeeze of her left hand sent a barrage of P-accelerator beams at the hapless ship which tore it into pieces.

Within the next minute they had taken out the remaining southern fighters from the sky. Out of the seventy-five fighters that staged the attack, none survived. The casualties in the Wolf Pack – a scorch mark on one of the drones. Jaime and her pups took out forty-three of the fighters single-handedly. It would be reported on the Alliance News Network that the Alliance troops fighting below in Central America had one of the most spectacular fireworks shows – one that rivaled any of the Fourth of July shows of the twentieth century. The Alpha Wolf Pack made the light show and left a field of sizzling, popping space debris in its wake.

"Ok, let's get our pups back to…" she was interrupted by the scream of her sensor alarm. A missile had been launched and was locked on to her ship. "What the hell?" she questioned as she began evasive maneuvers. Her body wiggled and jerked to avoid the incoming weapon. She spun the ship around and released atomic chaff while she quickly turned again. The missile obediently followed the mistaken image created by the chaff, impacted and exploded. She smiled as she saw the missile hit its false target. Without warning, she was thrown across the pod and even with the gel slowing her motion, she slammed into the side wall as she heard the thump of an explosion on her ship's tail. Her ship was hit – it was only a minor hit, but she had been shot nonetheless. The ship sent a message through the gel providing Jaime with a tactile feeling of the damage it had taken. The gel transferred the message in the form of heat to the appropriate part of her body – she felt a slight burning on her right heel letting her know where the damage had just occurred. As she spun the ship around all she saw was an explosion in the debris field. Something had fired its last dying breath at her, and then self-detonated.

"Did they leave a suicide capsule to try to take you down?" Perfecto asked.

"Don't know...must have. Had to have been personal..." she replied as she struggled to maneuver the wounded ship "in any case, for the first time someone got the best of me. I can't believe I did not see the blast coming. My sensors did not even warn me..." She rechecked her controls and imaged read outs. She saw nothing unusual prior to the missile and the blast. "Well, guess I have to answer for the damaged craft. Let's get back to base."

The fighters returned to the starbase and parked within the docking bays of the fighter craft base module. I.T.C. pods were disengaged from their fighters and drained of their precious gel. The gel was deposited into a special vat where it would be regenerated and reused. The pod was then raised and turned so the top pointed down toward the catwalk. The top opened and the human contents slipped out of the smooth-surfaced pod onto the catwalk. Jaime hit the surface of the catwalk with a loud slushing splash. After it deposited the pilot, the pod closed and turned upright into a parking position.

Jaime laid on the catwalk unable to move as her body was totally spent. The launch bay hatch opened and the two technicians ran into the bay and grabbed a cable from the catwalk console. They popped a lid off of the cable and attached the end to the ribbing on her suit. Small amounts of voltage flowed from the cable into the ribbing of the suit, which in turn replenished her body with the electrical energy it needed to function. Within a few moments of power replenishing, she slowly propped herself up on her hands and knees, and after a moment could rise onto a pair of wobbly feet.

She removed her helmet and disconnected the power feed. "Thanks, I am fine now" she told the two technicians who snapped to attention and saluted. She first turned and looked down into the bay at the damaged tail section of her fighter then shook her head in disgust. The two men continued to salute but both had slightly pained looks on their faces – they had never thought she, of all people would be shot in battle. She gave a weak double salute then patted each one of the men on the shoulder as she walked out of the launch bay preparation chamber.

Still walking slowly, she headed back to her quarters for some needed rest. Her mind was totally blank except for getting herself back to her cabin to satisfy her need to sleep. Her mind concentrated on every slow step she was forced to take.

"So, once again the Queen of the Skies is given the chance to be the savior of the homeland I see. Ever thought of giving someone else a chance to be a hero? Oh, but wait...you allowed yourself to be shot." The low, gravelly voice behind her made her freeze in place.

She squeezed her eyes shut for a second and shook her head. She slowly turned to see a bald woman standing right behind her wearing a similar flight suit – she was shaking her head in disgust. The stubble on her head indicated that at one time she had dark black hair. Her face had some rough features, her chin was slightly square, her cheeks were sunken, and she had dark, almost black eyes. Eva Langolear – The War Bitch -- was only a few years younger than Jaime, but the years of battle had made her look much older. A single battle scar marred her long forehead. "Not now War Bitch! Now is not the time for this discussion!" she commanded to the woman. "Besides, is that any way to speak to your Alpha?"

"Oh, I am no longer your Beta. Haven't you heard? They upgraded me to an Alpha." A slight bit of shock came over her tired mind as her fuzzy eyes were barely able to determine that her insignia rank was no longer that of a Beta.

"WHAT?" she was sure it was her mind playing tricks. There was no way Space Patrol would make her an Alpha Wolf Pack Commander -- especially as long as she was still around. Sure enough however, her eyes were finally able to determine she indeed was wearing Alpha rank insignias.

"As a matter of fact, they just gave me your Alpha Wing. Don't know what they are going to do with you -- maybe they are finally putting you out to pasture?" she admitted with an evil smirk on her face. Jaime could tell she was relishing in giving her this bad news – that is, if it was true. "I have heard that the next assignment for you will be to fly a computer console at Starbase Control. Sounds like a good end for your career, don't you think? It is fitting – after all, you have been shot down."

"I don't believe you Eva. They would never take my squadron away, never..." she was much too tired to argue and started walking away.

"You'll see!" an evil cackle emitted from her throat which made Jaime cringe as she returned to her trek down the corridor -- slowly moving away from her tormenter.

Jaime stopped and turned as something she noticed finally hit her tired mind. "Eva, why are you in a flight suit?"

Eva stopped laughing and was quiet for a brief moment. "Well, I am about to go on patrol. Since the South decided to attack, Space Patrol has decided to send out more fighters to patrol and protect. Your squadron will be with me on patrol next shift as a matter of fact! They are mine, all mine!" Once again, she began to cackle.

"We'll see Eva, but not now..." she returned to her attempt to escape from the tormenting laughter, walking down the hall as fast as her tired body would allow.

She could still hear her laughing and chortling as she reached her quarters. She slapped her hand on the thermo-lock and quickly entered, then slapped the inside door control to shut out the hideous laugh. She was tired but had enough energy to remove her glove and tap her ear communication device.

"Yes, Alpha Wolf Pack Commander?" the voice queried.

"I was just told there is a change of command in my Wolf Pack. Is this true?"

The voice became nervous. "Umm, well...yes, I am afraid you have been removed from that unit."

"WHAT? What the hell is going on? Tell me now!" she ordered. Somehow she managed to find the energy to show anger.

"All, I can tell you is that you are to report to the Alliance Space Force Commander at the launch party and receive your new orders. I am sorry, that is all I can tell you." He quickly shut off the communication which prevented any reply.

"What?" Was all her voice could muster. She was confused and too tired to fight the battle at the moment. She barely had the strength to remove her flight suit, but her anger provided enough energy to throw it against the wall. She then used the remainder of her energy to throw her weak body onto the bed. Lying naked on the bed she felt her lip quiver and she mumbled some sad words of no meaning. As tears rolled down her cheeks, she finally lost the battle with fatigue and fell asleep. While she slept however, she saw that pilot's half-fleshed face -- his expression of fear and pain looking directly into her eyes the moment before it splattered across her view. The red of blood covered her vision as it hit, then replayed over and over while she slept.

The Ark of the Blessed

Starlight Launch Time Minus 61 hours 18 minutes

Dex Morgan:

Dex had not slept much last night. He was so worried about Jaime that when he started to actually drift off he would experience vivid dreams of her dying which startled him awake. All through the night, he wanted so badly to call her but knew she needed rest. Hours of sleeplessness drifted into morning where he couldn't take it any longer – he knew she would be awake and he could now call. He sat at the tele-vid and rubbed his sweaty palms together. "Jaime Bordeaux's cabin please" he requested of the computer.

When she answered the vid-line she still looked quite tired. Dex had never seen Jaime after a battle and was surprised to see most of her hair was gone. Only a small bit of stubble had grown back and he knew she had probably been working with the hair stimulation process to get what little currently showed. Still, he gazed at her image on the screen – her alabaster skin now even more pronounced without the hair. The skin on her face looked as soft as he knew it would feel when he touched her in person.

He stared at her thin face on the screen -- he admired her curving rounded chin, her soft high cheek bones covered with freckles, and her deep dark blue eyes. The only flaw on her face was a slight scar on the side of her left cheek – which was the result of a blast through the face from a southern sniper. The shot blew a hole right through the back of her cheek, through her nasal cavity and out the front between her nose and upper lip. If the beam had been wider, and she had not turned her head as he fired, she would have been dead. Luck was with her that day, and through her service she could spend the money to not only have full repairs performed on her facial bone structure, but also to have the scars reduced to the point where they were almost invisible.

This morning, she had almost a childlike look on her face as she pouted her full lips in embarrassment – he had never seen her bald before. "Good morning. Looks like you were able to get some of your hair to grow back" he told her hoping to ease her mind somewhat. He knew she was concerned about how she would look at the launch party this evening. The thought of her going to the party without him brought sadness to his heart.

"You're nice...I know it looks like crap however" she gave a weak attempt at a smile. "I am designing a hat right now...it should help."

He saw right through the façade however. "What's going on? I know it was not the battle yesterday – you were spectacular...well, except for that shot you took. Everyone is talking about your kills – it made the record books despite your being shot. Although, I was not happy to hear you were sent into battle again. Call me weak, but I always worry about you out there. I am just glad the enemy did not take you from me."

"Well sweetie, you will probably not have to worry about that any longer." She paused and took a very large gulp of air then blurted out "I was told they are taking my command away!" Tears started flowing down her cheeks and he saw her lips tremble as she held back falling into a sobbing emotional mess.

"No...why? Why would they do that? It can't be because you were shot. No one could have avoided that suicide capsule – it was too well hidden! Maybe it's just a nasty rumor. After all, you're the hero of the Homeland! I can't believe they would do that to a hero...to you!"

She regained her control but was still slightly sobbing. "Well, I guess I will find out for sure tonight. I'm to report to the Star Force Commander at the launch party. I hope they do not embarrass me in front of everyone – I don't know why they would. I figure they will publicly announce my retirement from the Wolf Pack to everyone. I will have no choice but accept graciously." The tears began to flow freely again.

"Bastards!" he realized his line was probably monitored and stopped his rant. "Well, we could look on the bright side. At least now you will be working a desk here and we can plan our civil union – or marriage if you prefer."

Her tears slowed and she gave a confused look. "But, I thought you were headed into deep space on Starlight? How can we unite if you are off in the stars? I refuse to be joined with someone who I may never see again!"

"Take a look..." He changed the display to an image of a government transmission.

"Applicant, the Supreme Commander and the Council of Order appreciate your willingness to sacrifice yourself in the expansion of Blessed mankind into the universe. However, the Starlight Star Explorer has a limited amount of room that can be used for Normal workers. At this time, we feel you are more valuable to the Alliance on our home planet and look forward to your contributions in the future. Hail to our Supreme Commander, Hail to Council of Order, Hail to the Northern Alliance."

"You know that they have filled that ship with Frogspawns..." Frogspawn was the derogatory term used for the hundreds of thousands of children spawned by the mating of the Supreme Commander, Council members, and high government officials with various genetically selected members of society. These children after being conceived are provided additional genetic enhancements in the hopes of forming the perfect human specimen. These perfected humans are known as "The Blessed" but are also called "Frogspawn" by many of the Normal population.

She shushed him immediately. "Don't talk like that please! You know what can happen...but that is horrible that they rejected you!" A realization then came to her and her tears stopped like someone had turned off the spigot to her tear ducts. "Sweetie, am I to take it you just proposed to me, and that you are staying?" She was now smiling.

"Absolutely!" he shouted. He was amazed how resilient she was. She went from sorrow to happiness in the blink of an eye. "As soon as you are done with this party and have been given your new assignment, I will arrange for both our civil union and if you like will order a tube for us."

"Umm, a child that quickly? Remember, I am still a career girl...although maybe not as much after tonight."

"Sure, why not...why take it slowly? We only have so many years -- let's get right on it, ok?"

"You know, I can't think of a reason not to either! Oh Dex...I really look forward to us being together!"

"Me too, my love. For now however, you had better get that hat finished and ready yourself for the party. I will watch the World-Net for the coverage of your big announcement!" They smiled at each other -- she blew him a kiss as she shut down the video image. He felt so warm and happy inside. *"Who could have known that such bad news would end up being so good?"*

Starlight Launch Time Minus 45 hours 27 minutes

Jaime Bordeaux:

Jaime looked in the mirror and fussed a little more with her hair. She had been spending as much time as possible regenerating her strawberry locks and she had managed to get another inch to grow back. She had the computer cut it in a short-ragged shag style. It was cute but not like it was before – although for the party it would have to do. She ran her fingers through the hair on the sides to fluff it a little more, and then put on a military garrison hat that would cover most of the top of her head. It was black with silver piped stripes along the side that matched the piping on her new custom dress uniform. On the left side was the raised fist insignia of the Northern Alliance. She adjusted it slightly which gave it a small jaunty tilt.

Her uniform was also a shiny black leatherette material with piping running down the front of the dark top then extended around the bottom of the blouse before it met up with the same piping on her skirt. This ran down the sides and then around the bottom of the short skirt. Her skirt was well above the knees and showed much of her trim, muscular thighs. She applied space protective transparencies on her legs then slipped on a tight pair of black boots with matching piping. The boots ran up to the bottom of her knees and had stiletto heels which gave her a slightly taller appearance.

Finally, she attached snarling wolf patches to each arm at the shoulder, a pair of Greek alphas -- rank insignias were attached to her epaulets, and finally she attached commander bars to the tight round collars of her top. She may lose her command tonight, but she would be damned if she was not going to show off her position and authority until then.

She admired her dress uniform. She had custom designed it just for this event and knew it would be the hit of the party. Everyone would notice her, and that was what she wanted. If they were going to demote her, she would draw the attention of not only everyone at the party but also anyone who would be watching on World-Net. She thought that if anything would attract attention, this uniform would do it.

She did one more check of her uniform, tightened her face slightly, then turned and walked out the door. She arrived at the shuttle deck and boarded the first shuttle to the Starlight Space Ark. As she took in the view from the shuttle viewports Jaime was amazed at how huge the ship had become over the past couple years of construction. It sat in its space dock, launch-ready at a moment's notice. It had become much larger than the original design as it was now over a mile long. She estimated the girth of the ship to be at least a quarter mile.

There were small navigation thrusters all along the sides, top and bottom of the craft to propel it in any direction needed at sub-light speed. At the back of the craft sat the three large subspace crawler engines surrounded by a semicircle of armor plating – a flat section of similar armor plating covered the area below the three large-hexagon-shaped engines. She wondered if the subspace crawler technique would even work – after all, it had never been tested except in computer simulations. The entire ship was a myriad of experimentation – many of the systems had never actually been used, such as the Pulsar magnetic drives located in smaller openings that surrounded the three large crawler drives. Everything in this ship was designed by computer simulation and had never had any in-flight experience – however, the Supreme Commander was in a hurry to get this ship launched and decided the risk of in-flight testing was worth taking the chance.

The craft was bright silver and had window ports all along the fuselage of the main body of the ship which could be covered for battle when needed. The main body was cylindrical and connected the engine section to the command pyramid. In the middle of this connecting structure sat a large semi-circular rack of sub-light ion engines. These would be used to propel the ship at near light speed when they were not using the crawler engines, the Pulsars or the Graviton propulsion system – the Graviton being yet another totally experimental theory turned hypothetical reality. Covering this bank of engines were large curved plates of hard shell titanium alloy armor.

The triangular pyramid at the front contained all of the command and control functions of the ship – which included the main bridge and command quarters. At the tip of the command pyramid were three large tubular beam projectors. These were the sub-space battering ram beam projectors – another component of the theoretical subspace crawler drive system.

These beams would be used to tear a hole in the fabric of space large enough for the ship to pass through into subspace. She also noted the many thousands of blaster ports that could be opened in the event of battle – this ship was ready to fight if needed. Her eye also caught a vast set of fighter launch bays which made her wonder why she would lose her command if there was a need for fighter pilots – they would need her as a force to protect Earth after they took all of the best fighter pilots. Her palms began to sweat slightly and her jaw once again became tight as she thought about losing her command. She shifted her thoughts instead to Dex, how she would be permanently stationed at the starbase and she could soon be joined with him. This thought soothed her and allowed her to relax, albeit ever so slightly.

Arriving at the space dock, the shuttle would deposit her in a specific location in the dock and she would be escorted by armed guards to the location of the party. No one except flag officers were allowed to wander the ship without an escort – not even the future crew. Once it was time to launch, the crew would be assembled and allowed to board. Not even the cargo loading docks would be connected to the ship until all security protocols were in place and the ship was virtually ready for takeoff. Security was extremely tight and she had never seen so many protocols. They were obviously worried about sabotage.

Her escorts met her at the shuttle port and guided her to the Star Force Commander's personal banquet room. The guard motioned her to the door she was to enter. When she attempted to enter the large room however, a large arm jutted out preventing her passage.

"Alpha Wolf Pack Commander" the voice controlling the arm boomed out "you must be announced before you can enter! It is protocol."

Jaime sighed and nodded. *"Oh shit, here we go..."* as the doorman announced her arrival.

"I would like to announce the arrival of a great hero, who was the leader of the attack on hill 231, victor of the battle of Chihuahua, defender of San Antonio outpost, awarded the Council's Medal of Valor for single handedly deploying mines in Central America during battle number 121 of the Panama Canal..."

Jaime blushed as the doorman went on and on spouting her accolades in no particular order. She wondered how long it

31

would actually take to finally be allowed to enter. She had forgotten half of what he was announcing as she had been through so much.

"Her actions led to the capture of the bomber of Paris…"

Her heart sunk when she heard that proclamation. "*My god, I was ten years old! All I did was to tell a policeman about…*" She had to put that thought out of her head – it was so long ago and it was something she always told herself to forget.

"10 kill ace in the battle over Phoenix, led an assault on southern Moon Base Sector 15, and killed fourteen southern enemies during the space battle for Eurasia…"

The announcements of her victories made her feel very old and tired. "*Perhaps my retirement will be a good thing? Perhaps it will be good to get away from the killing?*"

Agonizing minutes passed for her – it felt like hours. She never really added up how much she had done for the Alliance – how many lives she had taken in her short twenty-nine year lifespan. Fate was now showing her how much she had done and she realized that perhaps now it was time to ratchet her life down. She now felt more at ease over her retirement. Now, if only the doorman would let her in.

"…Led the bombing raid on Mars Base 45. Was the conqueror of Mars Southern Alpha Outpost 5, and just yesterday was injured in the battle for the Starlight Space Ark. May I present Alpha Wolf Pack Commander Jaime Bordeaux!"

By now, everyone in the room had stopped talking and had turned to look at the person who had done so much for the war effort. Jaime's face was blushing red as she faced the realization of standing in front of a large room of people hearing her accomplishments. She realized how uncomfortable it made her. The applause that followed his announcement made her blush even more.

She was quite relieved when the doorman finally motioned her to enter the room. She quickly stepped down the stairs and attempted to hide within the mass of people. Although hiding in the crowd was almost as bad. She fought through the shouts of "Thank the Lord for you Alpha Wolf Pack Commander!", "The Homeland is so proud of you!" and "Thank you for sacrificing yourself for our safety!"

She was saved by Boral Oldham the Star Force Commander, who with a wave of his arm cleared a path for her escape through the madding crowd. She approached the older man, his dark black uniform shined in the intense lighting that he always had above him – he liked the god-like effect it cast. He was sitting in a chair elevated above everyone else – yet another quirk of the Star Force Commander as he always insisted on being taller than everyone else, regardless of if he was sitting or standing. Thus, he always had a raised platform nearby.

His uniform had a number of gold cords on each shoulder, a red sash hung from his right shoulder down to his gold trimmed belt that held back the force of his large belly against his shirt – a large number of medals hung from the sash for various acts or perceived acts of valor to the Force. She noted that around his neck and exposed from his dress uniform hung a small platinum cable with a small platinum bead – on that bead was simply the number "1". The material of the bead indicated the parent's ranking in the Order – platinum was the highest ranking, followed by gold, silver, pearl and other less valuable metals, gems and materials. The number indicated the order of their conception. Boral was the first of the Blessed – he was the first son of the Supreme Commander and as such was given the highest position in the Space Military regardless of his abilities. He looked down at her with cold staring grey eyes before speaking.

"I guess we owe you quite a debt. After all, you saved everything we have worked for."

She blushed slightly "Thank you. I was just doing my job…"

"Well, speaking of that…now that you are injured…"

"Injured? No, my ship was damaged that is all."

"Your ship? Might as well have just gotten shot in the ass as far as I am concerned! Do you know how much it will cost to repair that ship?" he snapped. His face displayed bitterness for a moment. As soon as his eye caught sight of something across the room however, his expression took a complete one hundred eighty degree change as a large smile embraced his dry skinned mouth. "AH!" He waved as he summoned someone from across the room. His glance once again returned to Jaime and he looked her up and down before saying "Well, at least you know how to dress. I see you have taken your uniform cues from your superiors!"

Jaime was confused. She knew this was her design and no one else would have it – or at least she thought that until her eye caught a glimpse of Alpha Starship Captain Kip Gurrigan. She did a double take upon seeing him. The young man walked toward the pair – he sported a tight black leatherette dress uniform top, short skirt, knee high boots and a matching military garrison hat – a total duplication of her outfit. *"That bastard stole my outfit! He stole it from my computer!"* She was shocked that he not only stole her outfit, but somehow made it look good on him. She noticed his legs were almost as shapely as her own -- they were tanned to match his bronzed face and shaved silky smooth. She did find that the manly bulging muscular shape of his extremities did not look quite as good in the skirt as her smooth feminine legs -- that at least was a saving grace she thought.

"Ah!" shouted the Star Force Commander as Kip approached "I must credit you Alpha Wolf Pack Commander, you have taken to style yourself like a successful officer!" He waved his hands up and down toward Kip as to show off his dressing style. This infuriated Jaime -- however she kept the heat of her anger bottled up by squeezing her teeth together slightly. "Alpha Wolf Pack Commander, I introduce to you Alpha Starship Captain Kip Gurrigan."

"Pleasure to meet you Alpha Wolf Pack Commander. Bordeaux -- isn't that in the south?"

"Well, southern France...but that is above the Equator..." She was amazed how little any of the Frogspawn knew about geography and the layout of the Alliance's territories and even less of those of the enemy.

He then took a moment and looked her up and down. "Did you break into my computer? It appears you copied my uniform! Well, I am flattered nonetheless..."

Jaime's jaw was as tight as a vice grip. She relaxed her jaw just long enough to give a small laugh and fake smile. "I guess I must have done that...you caught me!"

"Yes, well I can understand wanting to imitate a Blessed one such as myself" Her jaw tightened again as she resisted the urge to make a very tight fist behind her back.

Boral broke up the tension "Well, in any case Alpha Wolf Pack Commander we have another assignment for you."

"*An here we go...*"

"Yes, we have been ordered...requested to promote one female non-Blessed officer to become a Starship Captain." Kip announced.

Boral added "We felt the best person to take this position would be you." He had a slightly disgusted look on his face again. Jaime could tell he was being forced into this decision.

"I don't know what to say..."

"Perhaps, yes would suffice?" answered Kip. "This is the opportunity of a lifetime for you. You will be a sub-Captain of the first Alliance exploration and colonization deep space vessel. This will be a chance for you to leave this burned planet and perhaps find a better life. You will live with thousands of the Blessed -- an honor in itself. Besides, it is not like you have a choice – the request came from my father, the Supreme Commander!" She noted that he too had a platinum bead around his neck, his had the number "66" engraved – a later model she surmised.

She felt a brief moment of excitement over getting on this ship and leaving the Earth. Then her heart fell from her chest into her gut. She realized what they were asking would take her away from Dex. "But, I was scheduled to be joined..."

"Joined?" Boral blurted out. "I hope you mean wed...as in a proper Christian wedding! Please tell me he is Blessed?" he snapped.

"Well, wedding of course...I really did not have a preference so I can understand your concerns and would abide – if he was able to join me on our journey. He is Normal...but please allow him passage with me."

"I suppose..." A heavy sigh blurted from his lips. "He is not part of the crew?" She nodded no and he sighed loudly once again. "Very well then, what is his name?"

"Dex...Dex Morgan."

"Alpha Starship Captain, do we have any openings on a duty roster?" Boral requested.

Kip tapped on his computer embedded into the skin on top of his left hand. A small holographic image appeared before him as he entered requests for listings of open positions for

Normal crew. "Yes, we have openings in Engineering, Housekeeping, Culinary…"

"Engineering, what do we have there?" Boral interrupted.

"We have many openings on the engine maintenance crews." he replied.

"Yes, tell me those."

"Vacancies are in engine crew numbers 2, 3 and 5"

"Crew number 5, assign him there" he ordered. Kip smiled and nodded as he entered the logging commands to make the assignment. "Anyone else that you need?"

"Actually yes. I would like my trainer Jeremy Ponds. He really is special to me."

"Ponds…Really?" Kip interjected and she nodded affirmation. "Well, I don't get why you use that guy, but I will make the transfer…with your permission Sir." Boral nodded to him and the transfer was ordered. Kip shook his head in amazement over her request.

"There, done! Now, Delta Starship Captain, I think it is time to make an announcement and have you take the oath don't you think, hmm?" Boral now had a small box in his hand as he looked down at her.

"Delta?" she snapped.

"Of course, you did not expect to come right in as an Alpha, did you?" he snapped back.

"No, I suppose not…"

"Besides, Starship Captain is a major upgrade even at a junior level. You will see an immediate increase in credit pay and privileges."

"How can I refuse?" she snapped to attention. "*Besides, what choice do I have anyway?*"

"Good, good!" He stood up and the room instantly became quiet as he cleared his throat. "Will the room now pay attention as we promote our next Normal leader." He looked down from his high platform and the intense light above him bounced off his partially bald head into Jaime's eyes which made her squint. "Jaime Bordeaux, do you take a pledge to serve your superiors --

the Supreme Commander, the Council of Order, and all Blessed to the best of your ability as a member of the Alliance Star Force? To uphold our edicts, give your life to protect the Blessed, and to worship our Lord and Savior?"

Jaime forced a smile and took a large swallow before finally answering "I will."

He lowered his platform until his face was a few inches away from her – his breath on her face was repugnant. He opened the small box in his hand and took out a pair of Delta shaped insignias – removed the Alpha insignias from her epaulets and replaced them with the Deltas. He then roughly pulled off the Wolf symbols from her arms and replaced them with two patches with the image of a shooting star – the symbol of the Space Exploration Commission. Finally, he removed her Commander bar rank insignias from her collars and replaced them with sun symbols indicating the rank of Captain.

"There! Congratulations Delta Starship Captain Bordeaux!" The crowd immediately gave a light round of applause – she could tell it was only a courtesy. "I think now you will need to socialize lightly then call it a night. You will need to be here early tomorrow to get fitted with command implants, command interface, hand computer and a command nerve induction gun."

Jaime shuddered at the thought of a nerve stimulation device being implanted in her spine and brain. But she knew she would need it to power her induction gun and the command system that would also be implanted. She nodded in agreement.

Kip raised his left hand and shoved it directly into her face then rubbed and stroked the induction gun attached to his left upper wrist. "You will probably not have the ability to fire this baby as well as a Blessed, but it will protect you and give you the ability to command by force if needed, at least."

She really wanted to roll her eyes. *"This guy's ego is way too big for his pea brain..."* She resisted and instead said "I will strive to become as in tune with my weapon as you. Hopefully someday I will at least get close." She wanted to throw up -- it was really hard for her to lie this much.

"I am sure you will, Delta Starship Captain, I am sure you will...at least get close."

A long hour dragged on for the former fighter pilot. She met and received praises from everyone at the party – that was until the Star Force Commander grew tired of her taking the limelight away from him. He ordered her home and at this point she was more than happy to follow his command. She bid farewell to the party goers as she left the party, was escorted back to the docking bay and boarded the next transport back to the starbase.

Upon her arrival, she found Dex waiting for her in her cabin. A large smile graced his strong face. "You already know?" she queried.

"I know that you got me a job on board the Starlight. Which means you also got on board – right?" He then noticed the Delta insignias? "A demotion? But you are also marked with a Captain's insignia..."

"I am a Captain, but only Delta level. But hey, it's a start...and it sure beats flying a desk!"

"So, will a lowly Engine Mechanic be able to join with a Starship Captain at any level?" he had a smile on his face, but she could tell he was a little worried.

"Of course, as long as it is a marriage and not a civil ceremony. The Star Force Commander made a strong suggestion."

His eyes lit up in excitement. "Oh yes...whatever he wants!" He shouted "Then once we are on our way we can perform the ceremony then? Should we plan for children while on board?"

She placed her hand over his mouth to stop his thoughts. "Ok, now that is too far, at least for the moment. Tell you what, how about we freeze our eggs and sperm as part of the ceremony then use them later after things get settled and we can tell where things are going with the voyage, ok?" she pleaded and he nodded agreement quietly with a smile.

She felt so comfortable with Dex, and for the first time was ready to totally devote herself to a man – to him. She had never felt this way about any man ever before – but she liked it. She decided now was the time to stop holding back. "How about we seal it with some pleasure? I think we have waited long enough. How about you get the Pleasure-Matic? It is in the closet. I think we have both waited way too long for this – I am so ready."

A huge smile came to his face which then turned almost evil. "Oh, I was hoping that now that you have some rank we might actually be able to physically touch - now THAT would be a great first time..."

"Well, I do now have rank...but let's not push the envelope -- at least not yet" she suggested. "You never know if they might be watching..." This comment caused him to sigh but then nod in agreement.

She quickly removed her uniform and stood in his gaze. "Besides, won't this be good enough? Haven't you wanted to see this since we met?"

It was the first time he had ever seen her naked. The sight made him gulp quietly. "Oh, no complaints here madam Captain!" He just stood there unable to do anything but stare at her. His eyes took in every part of her body and his hands reached out and followed everywhere his eyes went. She moaned slightly at his touch – it felt so good but was so illicit. When he looked at her lower torso, he noticed a scar on the right side. He touched it gently and gave a questioning sound.

"Heat sword from a Columbian terrorist..." she quietly told him.

"Hmm..." He moved his gaze to her shoulder where another scar blurred the freckles on her skin. "Blaster wound in the battle of Mars Southern Alpha Outpost 5." He found another scar on her arm. "Shrapnel from a sonic grenade in Central America..."

"And they were worried about you being shot down in space? This is like a history book...I bet I could read the entire war from your injuries!"

His comment reminded her once again how much war she had seen over the years and why she originally decided to transfer to the Star Corps. It also made her realize how very happy she was to be going into deep space, even more so since he would be with her.

"I have been poked, stabbed, shot, and blasted!" She placed her fingers under his chin and lifted his face enough so she could look into his green eyes and gave him a small but flirtatious smile before saying "Well, how about you stop reading that war novel and try a romance story instead? And while you are at it, why don't you go get the Pleasure-Matic, hmm?" She then kissed him – the taste of her kiss on his lips reminded him of berries he had eaten when he was young and the world was still alive, it was the most pleasurable flavor he had ever tasted until now. "Pleasure-Matic?" she asked again.

He quickly ran into the closet and a moment later returned totally naked and holding a small white cylinder in one hand and a number of wires in the other hand. The wires had electrodes on one end and connectors on the other that would be inserted into the white cylinder. He handed her a set of the wires – she looked at them with interest.

She reached over and grabbed her computer pad and started entering commands. "What, what are you doing?" he asked.

She put the pad down after a second and smiled. "I ordered some real wine. They will want to deliver it personally. Will you be a dear and meet them at the door?"

He nodded and put on his robe and started to walk to the door. As he reached the door he shouted out to her "We should have thought of this sooner. It might be a while for that delivery." He decided what was waiting for him in the other room was much more important than time spent waiting for wine. He went to the computer at the doorway, ordered and paid for express delivery service on her order. Within a few minutes the delivery robot arrived and appeared in the door monitor. Without waiting for the bell he opened the door and grabbed the two glasses of wine.

He quietly returned to the bedroom with the glasses of wine to find Jaime still looking at her computer pad. She had not realized he had returned -- he approached and startled her by his presence next to her. She gave a slight gasp as he looked down at her. "What's wrong? Is something going on?" he asked with concern. He then looked at the computer pad as she desperately tried to conceal the screen – he noticed the display showed the instruction manual for the Pleasure-Matic. He gave a slight chuckle and kissed her on the top of the head. "You mean you have never…"

She shook her head with embarrassment. "No, never…"

He smiled and kissed her again as he grabbed the bundle of cables. "Ok, let's start with this set with the green outline. See in the photo, they go on the temples." After he helped to apply the green electrodes, he proceeded to help her attach the other electrodes to her breasts, abdomen, and her inside thighs, then he also attached similar pairs of electrodes to himself.

She then held up two probes and looked at the screen image with frustration. Then after a moment of scrutiny she shouted "Really? 'F' and 'R'? You have to be kidding!"

"Well, sure -- you don't want to get them mixed up do you?" He had the evil smile of a prankster on his face.

"Hmm..." She grumbled slightly while she inserted the probes. At the same time, he slipped on a cable connected sleeve to his organ and added a matching pair of electrodes for each jewel.

They connected all the cables to the device then jumped onto the bed and stopped and looked at each other – both were breathing heavily in anticipation. She reached over to kiss him and he pulled back just as a small arc of electricity jumped from her lips to his face. "Ouch, what the hell?" she cried out.

"Didn't you read the warnings?" he asked. "Warning Number 3: When connected to the Pleasure-Matic, never touch your partner as this can result in severe burns or even death!"

"Sorry, I really don't know much about this."

"So, you have never used one of these ever – not even alone?" she shook her head in the negative. "Have you EVER even been touched by a man?"

"No, not ever – well, kissed, but that is it...always managed to avoid being touched, or if they did touch me they never lived to tell about it." She had a devious smile on her face.

"Umm, what exactly do you mean?"

"Well, the closest anyone ever came to having their way with me was when three southern soldiers found me alone in the battlefield. Thought they had found the sex jackpot..."

"Shit...really? They raped you?"

She chuckled. "Well, they tried...However -- when they got close enough I let each one of them feel the laser blade I had hidden in my hand. After I turned each one of them into a jigsaw puzzle I simply left them there to rot. I bet their bones are still out there undiscovered!"

He gulped, she giggled. "Don't worry -- you're not a southern bastard. You aren't, are you?"

"You should know that by now my dear."

"I do" she reached her head across the bed to give him a kiss and quickly realized her mistake by the small arc that floated between them. "Ah shit! We had better get this started before I accidently kill us!"

"What a way to go..." He smiled at her and stared into her deep blue eyes for a moment before he flipped the switch on the device. Once activated, the device began to stimulate all of the electrodes, sending the couple into a state of pure manufactured ecstasy. Their brainwaves passed between each other via the machine which allowed for mental satisfaction while the probes were actuated to give physical stimulation. The machine ran the couple through its pre-programmed cycle of love then shut down leaving them both satisfied and spent.

Now all they could do was lay on the bed barely able to move. Dex had started to drift into a slumber but Jaime was still wide awake and would have none of his untimely sleep. She turned and looked at the almost asleep Dex, and then mischievously reached over and let her fingers give him a slight zap of electricity onto his forehead which instantly woke him. She gave a small quiet giggle as he looked at her perplexed. She smiled at him and said "That was fun, how about we flip that switch again?"

Starlight Launch Time Minus 31 hours 8 minutes

Jaime Bordeaux:

Jaime awoke early this time cycle, as she was scheduled to receive her command implants. She felt bad having to leave Dex so soon and was already missing him after their wonderful night together attached to the Pleasure-Matic. She awoke this morning to find she was still attached to the cabling of the device. They had become so exhausted that they had not even bothered to take off the attachments before they fell asleep. While he slept, she awoke, got dressed, disconnected him from the machine, kissed him lightly on the cheek, and made her way to the Starlight shuttle.

She was feeling happy and energetic, more so than she had felt in years. She hoped that this new love of life would help her in getting through this procedure today. Being a flight commander never required the use of command weaponry and control as all of her ship's armaments were controlled through her flight suit. Now that she had been promoted to a flag command position however, she would be required to have the implants.

She was also to have a small micro-reactor implanted at the base of her neck. The reactor will provide additional electrical current to her nervous system. The additional current was designed to deliver electrical flow through nerve pathways that were to be enhanced with super conductive linkages. These linkages in turn will provide a high-speed pathway for current and the ability to handle the extra current that would be passed between the cells of her nerves.

Finally, an attachment module will be implanted at the point just a little above her wrist joint. The module will provide an attachment point for a wrist weapon apparatus. The wrist weapon can be used to fire pulses of static electrical discharges powerful enough to knock down the largest of men into unconsciousness, or if needed fire a variety of beamed weapons such as blaster rays or cutter lasers. Her body would become a deadly weapon if needed. The whole system was originally designed as a way to control the troops. With precise control, a field commander could induce pain into any soldier who was not producing in battle. If need be, that same soldier could be terminated to save resources and prevent mutinous actions by others.

In addition, her new high powered nervous system would provide control power and connectivity to the command console of the massive starship – allowing her to pass command functions to the ship's controls as needed. She still required the bridge staff to actually control and maneuver the ship, but with her nervous system in control of the bridge systems she could override or take control of the operations if needed. This ensured that the current Captain in control of the Bridge retained control in the event of a coup or mutiny. Without providing the command that released control, no one else could take over any of the functions of the ship.

When complete, she will have become quite powerful in an unique way from what she was accustomed to. Before, she was respected due to her abilities and sense of command. Now, she would be respected due to rank and fear provided by this new weapon. This brought her right into the spectrum of control via fear – it was the way of the Alliance on Earth, and it looked like nothing would change in deep space.

All she had to do now was get through this procedure. "How hard could it be? They are going to sedate me after all. I will not feel anything until afterwards..." No matter how much she worked at convincing herself, she was nervous and slightly scared. She never did like doctors.

Star Force Commander Boral Oldham:

Boral woke up in an extremely crabby mood as he was still mad at his father the Supreme Commander. Father had ordered him to not only promote a Normal to a command rank, but worse he told him to promote a woman. Now, he had this inferior woman as a starship Captain and would have to put up with her scatterbrained abilities probably for the rest of his life – unless he found a way to get her out of his hair. However, if he could not get rid of her he needed to at least find a way to break her.

Suddenly, he had a thought – if the procedure was as bad as she feared, perhaps she would resign if she was taught that command provided agony. *"Yes, she might just fall for that..."* he thought. At the very least, he felt it would weaken her mentally and cause her stability to be fractured, which would allow him to take control of her like a puppet. At least that was what he hoped.

He activated his tele-vid screen. "Doctor Jacoby, this is the Star Force Commander" he barked.

44

"Ah, yes great Star Force Commander! What can I do for you?"

"You have a patient coming in for a command nerve implantation correct? I would like to order the amount of pain killers and sedatives she will need."

"But, that normally is what I do. Don't worry, I will make sure she is totally out and will not feel anything. At least until afterwards, at which point…"

"Precisely! I want to tell you what to prescribe for her" he interrupted. "Can you put her into a state of light sleep only?"

The doctor had a confused look on his face. "Why yes, but we run the risk of her feeling some of the procedure."

"Yes, do that…light sleep only. Then half the pain medications you would give a Blessed during the procedure."

"Well, I will do what you command of course. May I ask why?"

"Well, she IS a woman…even worse in her favor -- she is Normal. She is lighter and weaker than the Blessed males that you are used to treating. I know you did not take that into consideration. I don't want her to die due to an overdose."

"Of course, you are correct." he said without showing any sign of disagreement. He would follow his orders explicitly.

"Then do as I command, tell me when it is done so I can put her to work." The doctor nodded and disconnected. A smile came to his face. "Yes, make it hurt…real bad…break her."

The Ark of the Blessed

Starlight Launch Time Minus 30 hours 45 minutes

Jaime Bordeaux:

As soon as she arrived at the landing dock she was quickly escorted to one of the medical bays. This medical facility was for exclusive use of flag command. The doctor greeted her with a partial smile. Judging by his tanned skin and perfect hair he was a Blessed. She then noticed a platinum wire choker with a small pearl bead with the number "199" on it. He introduced himself as Dartmouth Jacoby, which immediately confirmed her suspicion about him being Frogspawn as he was the son of a particular Council member who named his children after former large universities.

"If you are ready, we have a tight schedule and we need to start." She nodded in agreement and he pointed to a surgery table. She gave a slight gulp. "Don't worry, we will anesthetize you. Now, please disrobe and lay face down on the table."

She noticed there was not an area for her to change in privacy. As a matter of fact, she noticed there was no clothing for her to wear – she determined that modesty would not be tolerated on board this ship. She obliged his order and removed her clothing in the middle of the room and handed the vinyl suit to the waiting nurse. She peeled off her transparent space leggings and also handed those to the nurse. The doctor eyed her naked body for a moment which caused her to doubt her trust in this man. Finally, he motioned her to the cold stainless-steel surgery table. They strapped her head down, forcing her face through a small hole in the table. In addition, they strapped her arms and legs lightly to the cold steel table, and then prepared the equipment for the procedure.

They gave her the sedative and she started to drift into a light sleep as the surgeon began his work. Suddenly she realized she had not fallen into a deep sleep and was still aware of reality. She was aware of the conversations going on around her and she could feel the doctor making marks on her back with a marker at the point where the reactor was to be placed. She tried to make a noise, but was unable as her voice was neutralized by the drugs. She could not move either, that part of the drug was also working perfectly. The only thing not working was the numbing effects.

Suddenly massive pain wracked her skin as she felt the burning of the cutting laser on the skin of her lower back. The pain dug deeper and deeper into the flesh and muscle of her back. She could feel him separate her skin and muscle as he roughly dug into the meat of her back to reach her spine. She began to think maybe he was going to kill her. The cutter laser began once again to pierce through sensitive tissues as he reached her spine. The air on her spine sent shooting sensations all over her body. Then the wires were attached – jolts of electricity flowed through her back bone making her body convulse and jerk wildly. Through the pain and agony, she heard the doctor and nurse laugh slightly as he turned down the reactor output. Her body spasms matched with the output of the reactor -- which as he lowered the voltage her body finally stopped the simulated St. Vitus Dance.

The pain in her back felt like it lasted forever, but she knew it had only been a couple minutes. The mad scientist and his assistant poked and prodded their instruments into her, connecting electrodes and wires into her body while they roughly connected the various sensors and controls of the reactor. These sensors will allow her to mentally control the output of the miniaturized generator – provided she lived through this procedure.

Finally, they stopped and used a healer beam to seal the gash in her neck and back. She began to wonder if they were done when she realized that they had just stopped long enough to wheel a molecular bonding device above her. He took a small pen light out of his pocket and shined it into her eyes. "Are you doing ok Delta Starship Captain?" he asked. She knew he was totally cognizant of her state of awareness. "Let's begin the nerve bonding" she heard, dreading what she was about to experience next.

Before she even could imagine the next painful experience, she felt the burning and searing inside her brain. She did not realize they were now inserting molecular wiring into selected areas in her brain – all she knew was her head was on fire. She wanted to scream in agony but her mouth refused to move – she did manage to get a small squeak to expel from her throat. When Dartmouth heard the sound, he put his head down and looked at her, smiled then gave another small amount of sedative – only enough to ensure her vocal chords were totally silenced. He then went back to his bonding of power links into her brain. The burning continued for what she thought was forever, but then the pain started working its way down from her skull into the base of her neck and into her spine -- which was still on fire from his previous assault.

They were now "chaining" her nerves – this was the process of linking superconductive material between the synapses of selected nerves. This process provided a pathway for the flow of extra energy from the reactor to any of her extremities, and will provide power for her command weapon or for her to use her body to command the various systems of the starship -- provided she survived this.

Every time the doctor transferred and connected another superconductive link into a nerve cell she felt a sharp stabbing pain and a jerk in a muscle. She wanted to cry in pain but could not – those parts of the medications were working perfectly and the additional sedative he gave her actually prevented any way to provide a break from the constant pain.

For a brief moment, she would get a slight bit of relief between link connections. For each of those moments she forced a thought that would help her to prepare for the next jolt of pain. She thought about the revenge she would have on this man someday. She would kill him someday -- there would be no escape for him once they left the solar system. She someday would make him feel the same agony she was feeling right now – that was until she slit his throat or performed some other murderous act against him. Violence and revenge now coursed through her mind as she thought of the worst things she could do to him. Every jolt of the chaining provided more and more graphic visions of his death to her. Her mind then drifted back to the southern fighter pilot who died in that painful explosion she caused -- disemboweled, and naked. She saw him float toward her fighter's pod in slow motion. As he floated closer the face changed – it was now Doctor Jacoby. She envisioned herself pushing down her legs propelling her star fighter faster and faster toward the dead half body of the doctor. She aimed her ship and smashed into the dead carcass – the doctor's screaming face being pulverized into a mass of dust. She could hear the dead scream of the doctor as she smashed the remains of his body into atoms. She now saw that vision over and over as he continued to induce sharp pains across her body. They had worked from the top of her spine down her legs, even down to the tip of each toe. Now they were working on each arm, bonding the nerves down her shoulders, into her arm, down through her elbow and passing through the wrist finally completing a nerve bond with every finger. Once they finished with her right arm they proceeded doing the repeat of the procedure on her left arm.

An eternity passed for her, feeling the thousands of pains and jolts every second. She attempted to keep her mind busy thinking about her vision of the splattering man. When it was not the frozen torso of the doctor, she had visions of total violence dancing in her now delusional mind -- anything to try to ignore the pain of the never-ending procedure. Then, the inflicted pain suddenly stopped. Now, all she felt was the numbing, lingering pain of soreness and tenderness. Sparks travelled up and down her arms and legs, her entire body burned with painful fire. She wondered if her body had been totally mutilated by this fiend.

She started to think that perhaps it was finally done, that perhaps the torture was over. However, the nurse contradicted her thoughts by her next actions -- she felt the horrible assistant hold her left hand into the air and strap some tape onto the skin above the wrist. Then she felt the cold of metal against her skin – she knew more pain was coming. As if on cue, the pain began flowing through her arm as the wrist weapon connective electrodes were forcibly inserted into her skin. Then more poking and pain as they connected the electrodes into her chained nervous system. Another eternity passed as they connected and tested the system now inserted into her body.

They still were not done however as she felt an extreme burning pain in her left palm. They had cut into the skin, split it apart and then soldered a metal plate into the bone structure of her hand. Connective ports were then soldered into the plate and finally the skin was grafted back together and sealed. Finally a command control module was attached to the connective ports in her palm. This control unit would join with the command chair of the starship when it was time for her to command the massive craft.

They still had more to do and she had to endure a few more minutes of pain while they burned a small command computer micro-terminal onto the top of her hand. She would have access to the ship's computer network and database through this module. After everything she had endured to this moment, this final procedure hardly hurt at all. Or at least her brain was telling her this – she wondered if it could be that she was finally beginning to shut down from the intense and constant pain.

Somehow, she heard the words she thought would never enter her ears, the words that she thought she would die before hearing – ' Ok that is it, we are done." She hoped he would awaken her soon so she could kill him. However, he was not a fool and knew what thoughts were going through her head as he gave her a final injection. "This one is for pain -- it should allow you to go right to work. You only need an hour or so of rest at this point. Very well, I am done here. You will be able to get up in just a short few minutes and I am needed elsewhere." She could hear the footsteps of him actually running out of the surgery center and out of the medical bay into the main corridor, making a speedy escape.

When she was finally able to move, she slowly sat up and noticed that even the nurse had evacuated the center. They knew what they had done and did not want to be anywhere close to her when she was finally able to move. They were wise she thought to herself. She knew there would be plenty of time to kill both of them, she would bide her time and wait for the right moment. Besides, she could barely move without pain. Another lie from the doctor she realized – the pain medications he gave her are worthless. She felt nothing but pain.

She was barely able to tap her communication device and then somehow had gotten enough internal energy to let out a weak voice, despite the medications. "Jeremy Ponds..." A few seconds later she heard the familiar voice over the comm.

"Jeremy here...Jaime, is that you?"

"Jeremy, I need you...please tell me you are on board..."

"I am. Where are you?"

"Flag Medical Bay...Come quick..." She fell back onto the table. Pain wracked her body again as her now sensitive spine hit the cold table. She cried out in pain as the force of her body against the table caused pressure pain on both her back and body. The cold of the table felt like needles piercing her body.

It only took him a few minutes to reach her. He found her still face up on the cold steel table. "My god, what did they do to you?" She could not answer, she just mumbled instead. "Alright, let's get you dressed and then to a mineral bath. Then...and you might kill me for saying and suggesting this…but after a relaxing bath I want you to handle a multi-gravity session with me." Her eyes opened wide and she tried to speak but he put his large hand to her mouth, she obediently silenced her objection. "No, it is the best thing we could do for you. Only the pain of a serious exercise session will remove the agony you are in." He thought for a moment, before continuing "Then, I think you will need some help from someone other than me…"

He helped her stand and put a robe over her. He let her prop herself against his strong shoulders as he put his arm around her to steady and keep her from falling over. "Ok, let's start taking steps…" He made her take one agonizing step after another as they walked slowly around the room. She found that each step he made her take did actually help to strengthen her. Within only a minute or so she found she could slowly move on her own. It was like her recuperative powers had increased with the superconductive nervous system she now had. She always found she could recover fairly quickly – now however it seemed she was recuperating even faster than in the past. She could not explain it – every step she felt better and better, and she was not going to complain.

"There, now let's get you to the gym and get this pain out of your system. There will be plenty of time to plan revenge later…" he told her

She knew he was right. She knew that one day she would make that doctor realize his mistake. She now had so many ideas for how he would die -- she would make sure he knew that his death was designed to be slow and she would make sure he would experience everything that she experienced during his session of torture. Yes, he would discover every little pain she had planned for him. She would only have to find him when the time was right. Deep space would cover the screams of his murder.

With his assistance the pair walked from the medical center to the massive fitness complex of the ship – with each step she felt better and better until she was walking completely on her own. The facility had many individual gymnasiums. In addition to an enormous common workout area, there were multiple swimming pools and competition arenas. Jeremy had already reserved one of the gymnasiums for her recovery. He got her to the locker room, ran a soothing mineral bath that filled her body with healing warmth. After she dried off he got her to the gym and instructed her to sit on a bench just inside the door.

He handed her a bottle of water, a workout suit, and a towel "Get this on and drink some of this water, as soon as you're ready we will begin."

"You have GOT to be kidding me, right?" she barely had enough energy to spit out her protest. She felt pretty good, but fatigue was setting in – she was dead tired.

"Five minutes and I will begin regardless if you are ready or not. I would suggest you be ready" he warned.

She knew he meant everything he said. As soon as he left the room, she put on her workout uniform, chugged down the water and tried to mentally prepare herself. True to his word, after five minutes had passed the gravity in the room suddenly went from normal to less than Earth normal gravity. She struggled in her weakened state to maintain her balance and keep her feet on the ground. Within a moment however, the gravity raised slightly and she felt her feet stabilize on the gym floor.

He returned and stood in front of her wearing a black skin-tight workout suit. His large muscles bulged through the skin-tight material. He stood there holding a golden, odd-shaped, ball-like object – it seemed to be shifting its shape as he held it. He smiled then tossed the ball at her. She started to catch it then suddenly the weight of the ball changed from light as a feather to that of an elephant – at the same time, the shape shifted making the ball almost impossible for her to get a good grasp. Even in the light gravity she was unable to maintain her hold on the ball and it dropped with a thud onto the floor.

"What the hell?" she muttered.

"THAT is the command polyhedron" he answered. "It is the object of a game played on this ship called Command Tri-Polyhedrons. It involves that multi-dimensional polyhedron with its sneaky ability to randomly shift its weight. You have also probably noticed it has the ability for morph its shape at random intervals also."

"I noticed…"

"Anyway, since you are now a *Starship Captain*…" he said that with a slight bit of sarcasm "you will be required to play the game as it is a competition between only Starship Captains of all levels. If you win, you will move up in position or rank – however, I would suggest that for now you do not win."

"What the...why would I not want to win?" Her forehead had small lines from her crinkling the skin in confusion.

He reached up and rubbed her forehead to calm the muscles. "Watch the forehead, you don't want wrinkles yet!"

"Yes mother..."

"Humph...In any case, if you win too soon they will hound you and make your life a living hell – I think they already have that plan in your future anyway. So, you want to only move up in rank in very small stages. Move up slowly in the ranks of the Delta Starship Captains, then slowly work up to Beta rank. Don't go directly for Alpha – you do not want to show the Blessed up, at least not yet." She snorted in disgust and disagreement while pouting. "Please, listen and follow my directions on this. We both know you can best any of those wimps, but don't do it -- at least not yet. Save it for a special time. Besides, you will acquire a very large target on your back and every Captain will be after you in the arena. They will do anything to make you lose."

"Alright, I will try to not win too soon..."

He walked over to the computer console at the door. "Modify gym -- add Command Tri-Polyhedron features." Immediately the walls shifted as platforms formed along the sides, rings and loops also sprouted from the sides and up to almost the roof, and a long winding ramp formed from the bottom of the room to the top. "Good, now as you can see...there is a ramp that works its way up to the top of this gym. I will stand at the top and you grab the polyhedron and you try to get past me ok?"

"Sounds easy enough..." She waited for him to reach the top then went to pick up the polyhedron. It felt fairly solid and was now much lighter than before. She began running up the ramp when suddenly the gravity changed to 3 times that of normal Earth. Her still tired legs began immediately dragging and at the same time the polyhedron became quite heavy. She fought off the extra strain on her legs and attempted to run up the ramp toward Jeremy. As she reached him the gravity once again changed -- this time to normal Earth gravity. Suddenly, the polyhedron became blubbery and even heavier. Jeremy jumped up in the lighter gravity and swung a speedy roundhouse kick. She blocked the attack as best as possible, but he still landed the kick squarely onto her shoulder sending her spinning. The polyhedron began to slip and she struggled to keep ahold of the object. Jeremy spun around again and landed yet another solid kick to her other shoulder sending her slipping off of the ramp and landing on the floor with a heavy thud.

"Owww! Ok, that was a cheap shot!" she cried out.

"No, in Command Tri-Polyhedrons that is a totally legal shot. The gravity will change at random, the shape and weight of the polyhedron will change at random, and your opponents will gang up to prevent you from advancing. If you should happen to best any of them you will move up in the command order. Thus, they WILL do anything to prevent you from doing that -- including cheap shots and maybe even trying to kill you. There have even been rumors of weapon usage – although I have never actually seen that."

"Ok, I get the picture. Let's give it another go..."

She grabbed the polyhedron again and started running up the ramp. The gravity changed to less than Earth – quite a bit less. She jumped up as she reached Jeremy and proceeded to give him a speedy roundhouse kick when the gravity became four times that of Earth. She missed him and started to slip off of the ramp. He was still in normal gravity at the point where he was standing and moved in to assault her with a side kick when she jumped off the ramp and even in the heavy gravity was able to reach one of the many loops that were now attached to the sides of the room. She then moved the polyhedron from one arm to the other while still holding the loop then reached out with the other arm and grabbed another loop – then did the same maneuver shifting the polyhedron and grabbing yet another loop. She quickly found that despite the heavy gravity and her still excited, burning nerves, she was moving quickly along the wall. With a few more moves she managed to maneuver herself to a small platform on the wall. Upon reaching the platform she discovered that the gravity had once again shifted into a normal state. She stepped onto the platform then immediately launched herself off the platform back to the ramp.

Using the lighter gravity, she was able to obtain a good leap from the platform which allowed her to land squarely behind Jeremy on the top of the ramp. At that same moment, the weight of the polyhedron changed to four times its previous weight. She felt the change and instead of letting her arms drop, she instead extended her arms out and quickly spun her entire body around allowing the polyhedron to slam into Jeremy with an extreme force. He immediately slipped and fell off the ramp onto the gym floor. She spun around and saw a golden basket a few feet further up the ramp. She felt the gravity shift once again and her weight became extremely heavy. Despite her added weight due to the gravity, she forced her muscles to work quickly which allowed her to run up the remaining ramp and dunk the massively weighted polyhedron into the basket.

A buzzer went off and the gravity shifted to normal. She turned and raised her arms in victory, a large smile graced her face and cheer of victory left her lips. "Well, if that is it then this will not be a problem."

"This is only a small replica of the Command Tri-Polyhedrons field. The real field is much larger; there are multiple ramps, multiple platforms, various gravity change zones and every Captain gunning at whoever has the polyhedron. It will not be a cakewalk, even for you. Even with your advanced training in multiple gravities and various martial arts, you will have to keep developing your body to withstand as much g-force as possible, and we must keep it shifting so your body will never know what to expect."

She gave him a small pout. "In other words, keep practicing..." He nodded and tossed the polyhedron at her. She now realized she was really feeling pretty good – almost as if she did not just go through the procedure. The gravity and the weight of the object both changed to many times normal causing her to struggle against both forces. The polyhedron changed shape forming multiple points – each point digging into her skin and causing small drops of blood to form and drip onto the floor. "Hey, even this thing is against me...Damn!"

They spent the next hour jumping through the various levels of the gym hopping from one platform to another and on and off the ramp – while constantly fighting the changing gravity and the shifting weight of the polyhedron. When they were done, she felt tired but she also felt much better. She found that he indeed was right, the workout was just what her abused body needed -- that and her somehow enhanced recuperative abilities.

"Well, we have fixed your body, but we still have to fix your mind." He put his arm around her shoulder and guided her to the door.

"My mind is fine, it does not need any fixing" she said, slightly annoyed at his suggestion.

"Once again, listen to me as you know I am right. After what you just went through you have quite a bit of anger built up inside. I could not only sense it, but feel it in your attacks during our session. So, once again I insist...go find your new quarters. Your gear has been transferred from the station already. When you get there you will find someone who will be there to help."

With a confused look she turned and followed his command. Her body felt invigorated – perhaps she was fully recuperated, or perhaps it was due to the workout and perhaps also due to the flow of energy she was feeling in her newly enhanced nervous system. She jogged down the passageways, following her command computer's guidance until she found her newly assigned quarters. She unlocked the door, entered, and noticed in the far corner of the darkened room a woman sitting in a chair waiting for her.

The woman appeared to be the same age as Jaime. She had smooth white skin, dark brown eyes and dark brown hair – with the exception of two bright white stripes that she had pulled back from the temples to the back of her head. The way she had them pulled back made it look like she had skunk stripes.

"Hello, you must be Jaime." She stood up and extended a small hand. She was shorter than Jaime, slim, not muscular and was wearing a professional outfit consisting of a purple skirt, white blouse, matching purple jacket and large matching purple bow tied around her collar.

"Yes, Delta Starship Captain Jaime Bordeaux. And you are?"

"Doctor Catherine Harmony. I was requested to visit you by Jeremy Ponds -- he thought it would be helpful for you to spend an hour or so with me." She once again re-extended her hand to Jaime.

"Doctor of what?"

"Psychology -- I work with the mind." She pushed out her hand again. "I really will not harm you. On the contrary, I think that in an hour we can have you ready for anything. Trust me, please."

"I doubt you will be able to do anything in that little time. But since Jeremy sent you, I have to trust his judgment." She finally reached out and shook her hand.

"Listen Jaime, here is my plan. I will first find out what is troubling you. After that, I will simply put you into a state of hypnosis and I will place some suggestions that will hopefully help you to get over what is bothering you."

"Well, that is easy. I want to kill a certain Frogspawn doctor, his nurse and every commanding officer who set me up for the torture I just went through."

"Ok, I think we have something to talk about." She motioned Jaime to sit on the couch. She took a chair and moved it closer so she could look into Jaime's face as she told her story.

It did not take long for Jaime to tell Catherine enough to give her the exact reason for her anger. Catherine was shocked by her stories of battle, being shot in her last sortie, the embarrassment of being retired and moved into a lesser position, having her retirement announced to the entire world and finally the deliberate torture by the doctor. She was shocked but not surprised as she knew how evil and cruel the Blessed and the members of the Alliance could be. She wondered if there would be any help for her planet from the Supreme Commander and the Council of Order. She almost wished she was going to stay on board and leave this corrupted planet instead of returning to the poisoned world below.

Finally, Jaime finished her telling of the events. Catherine put a few more notes into her personal computer, and then looked deeply into Jaime's blue eyes. "Ok, I have a good understanding of what is going on. So, now I am going to hypnotize you and make a few suggestions. Then I will suggest some practices that will allow you to meditate and relax when needed, ok?"

"Ok, good luck with that. I doubt you will be able to put me under. I am really strong willed." She looked at Catherine and noticed waves in the air floating around her head – they were visible, but at the same time invisible. Her skunk stripes were glowing slightly. Jaime could not help but stare at the effects going on around this woman. After a few seconds, the stripes stopped glowing and the waves in the air disappeared. "Wow, I don't know how you did that, but that was really, really interesting! So, now what do we do to try to hypnotize me? I guess we can give it a good try."

Catherine smiled and gave a slight giggle. "I hate to break it to you – but you have been under for almost forty-five minutes."

"No shit?" she cried out.

"No shit..." she replied quietly. "I have given you a few suggestions to help you get over the pain you suffered and also gave you some subliminal training in meditation practices. When you need to relax, you will remember. I have to go now as you will need to rest before launch time."

"You are not coming?" she queried.

"No, I prefer to stay on Earth." She was not being honest with her, but for some reason she felt she needed to stay. "I will be catching a rocket back down in an hour. I would like to also grab a bite to eat while still on the starbase – the food is quite good up here!"

"Well, thanks for your help Doctor – although I don't know what you did."

"You will remember -- I did nothing that you cannot remember or made you do anything you would not normally do. It will come to you when needed. Take care of yourself Jaime -- I know you will be just fine. Use your strength and abilities to survive and excel." She extended her hand once again.

This time Jaime reached out and gave her a big hug. She squeezed the breath out of Catherine. "Thank you, Doctor. I will never forget you. I am not sure why, but even with our only brief meeting I feel like I made a friend."

She gasped slightly to regain her breath. "Knock the universe dead Jaime...always watch your back out there, ok?" Then backed up, smiled, and turned to leave. Somehow, Catherine got the feeling she would see her again but she had no idea why she felt that way.

Now by herself, Jaime realized she really was feeling better. Jeremy of course was correct in prescribing this for her. She walked to the communication center of her room and requested Dex. He was smiling until he saw how tired she looked.

"Wow, you look like hell!" he cried out.

"Gee, thanks. You know how to make a girl feel really beautiful."

"I'm sorry. You just look like you have been through a wringer, that's all. Are you ok?"

"Yes, actually I am fine now. I will tell you all about my day when you are on board and settled."

He had a surprised look on his face. "Didn't they tell you? I am already on board. I have to report to my engine maintenance crew chief in fifteen minutes for space walk and final departure engine checks."

"Really? So, I won't even get to see you before I take a nap? Damn! Promise me you will come to my cabin right after you're done?"

"I promise sweetie…"

"Thanks, Dex. I need to tell you…just how important you are to me. I have never felt this way, ever! I have so much to tell you…" Her face gave him a serious look "I know that I am a bit rough…but I know that you will smooth me out…"

The sound of a transport car stopping in the background interrupted her confession. "Damn, there is my transport. I want so much to hear your sweet words. Please, save them for me? I have to go…"

"I will love, until I see you later…" She blew a kiss to him as he disconnected, then sighed.

As she turned away from the vid-screen she spotted her bed across the room. She removed her clothes, dove onto the bed and almost instantly drifted into a calm quiet sleep as she felt happy and content once again. Visions of herself and Dex wandering through some new beautiful world entered her mind as she drifted asleep.

Starlight Launch Time 28 hours 32 minutes

Kip Gurrigan:

When Kip arrived at the loading dock it was filled with refugees. The dock was a large compartment vacuum attached to the body of the ship and used for loading of large items and large groups of people. Electrical fields had been activated in front of the group separating them from the ship's entry portal and kept anyone from entering without authorization. The dock was 1 of 3 – all are attached on the other end to the massive starbase grid via flexible passageways. There were passage airlock doors leading from the dock to the attached passageway. The doors were open and there was a crowd that filled the compartment all the way to the back entrance of the dock. The refugees were from all parts of the globe – some were the downtrodden from the main Alliance cities, many were southern defectors and others were just Normal citizens looking for a better life.

Kip stood twenty feet away from the crowd with his first officer and shook his head over the size of the mass of people – he ran his fingers through his blond hair in frustration. "Who the hell are all these people?"

Stanford Massey, his first officer checked his handheld computer. "All appear to have been granted passage by various programs set up by the Supreme Commander."

Kip tapped his communicator. "Star Force Commander. Sir, what do you want me to do with all of these people? Shall I let them in?"

Boral answered in a short tone. "Simply keep them there for the moment. I have other pressing matters." He disconnected immediately.

"Well, ok then…who leads this group? Or is there even a leader?" he asked Stanford.

He checked his personal computer gel. "According to the records, that man directly ahead of us has been designated a leader of this group." Stanford pointed to a tall, light-skinned Brazilian man. The man sees them looking at him and then began to wave to attract their attention. "His name is…Luis Cruz, a southern turncoat that was granted passage as a part of the Supreme Commander's "Reward our Southern Helpers" program."

"Great, like we can actually trust him" Kip sighed. "Ok, well we just need to keep them calm right now, so let's go speak with him."

Kip pressed a button on his command hand console which released the electric field just enough to allow a small opening wide and tall enough for Luis to step through. "Mr. Cruz, I am Alpha Starship Captain Kip Gurrigan."

Luis extended his large hand "Captain…"

Kip ignored the pleasantry. "That is Alpha Starship Captain to you, Mr. Cruz."

"Sorry, Alpha Starship Captain. My people were promised passage to a planet capable of colonization. We have seen many items of cargo, many Blessed, many officers, and many workers loaded onto this ship – but as of yet, none of our people have been allowed in. Sir, as you can imagine we are starting to lose faith that the promise made by our Supreme Commander will not be granted to us. I gave up a lot to help the Alliance -- I would hope that they would be willing to give up the small amount of room needed to house myself and the people that were promised a better life."

"Mr. Cruz, if the Supreme Commander promised a better life then it will be granted. You and your people will just have to be patient. Besides, we are hours away from launch. There is plenty of time – we can load you and your people onto the ship in a matter of an hour at the most. No need to worry, we can and will get you on. Now, if you will excuse me I have important matters to attend to. All we ask is you maintain control of the people."

Luis nodded knowing he had no choice. He returned to the other side of the barrier and started to speak with as many people as possible. He told them that they will keep their promises to them, and since they continued to make promises they must have faith in those promises. He attempted to promote a positive attitude to the crowd and tried his best to quell any discouragement.

Dex Morgan:

Dex arrived at the engineering section and was immediately provided a bright silver space suit. While reading the suit's manual, he stumbled into the suit, strapped on micro battery packs, tested his magnetic movement generators, checked

62

out his helmet, and finally gathered his work tools. He had only been on the ship barely an hour before he received the call to report to engineering – he almost didn't have enough time to even talk with Jaime for a brief moment. As soon as he arrived at engineering, his lead Crew Chief Sam Stombel instructed him to put on the suit and prepare for work outside the ship. Dex was apprehensive about immediately going out into space without any preparation or training. Sam assured him however that he would take care of him personally.

After he got his suit on, Sam performed a safety check for him -- made sure air hoses were properly connected and that all seals were working. "Ok, crew let's get out there and do our final engine check. Most of you know the routine – those of you who are fairly new stick with your team leads. Dex, you are with me – stay close." Dex nodded through his visor.

They entered the airlock. Dex panicked slightly when he heard the sound of the steel door close behind him with a loud thud. Sam reached over and adjusted his oxygen. The extra gas helped to put him a little more at ease -- he gave a smile and thumbs up to Sam.

Sam looked into Dex's eyes through their helmets with a stern look. "Now Dex, when we get to the engine you must remember to look inside the compartment and do not look out of the compartment until we are fully outside the engine. If you do look to the outside while we are on the engine components you will get star-struck – that is what we call it when someone who is on the rotating engine turbines gets dizzy from the spinning stars. So, don't look at the stars until you disconnect from the turbine and are not spinning – even if you have to close your eyes and jump off the turbine rings, ok?"

"Ok, don't look out when on the turbine rings -- got it." He hoped he would remember. Sam gave his helmet a slap.

The air finally finished evacuating out of the airlock and the door slid open. Sam took a step out and activated his magnetic movement field. By using magnetic repulsion, he moved quickly away from the body of the craft. He stopped when he determined he had travelled an appropriate amount of distance from the airlock. "Ok, Dex activate your magnetic fields and come on out."

Dex closed his eyes for a moment and took his first step out of the airlock. He floated just outside the door for a moment before he reopened his eyes. Realizing he would not fall, he activated his movement field and pressed the palm control to initiate motion. The field sensed the metallic body of the ship behind him and activated repulsion to push him away from the ship. As he approached Sam he stopped pressing on the control switch and he immediately felt a slight tug as his suit activated a slight attraction to the ship causing his motion to immediately halt.

"You're doing great Dex! Ok, we just need to head to engine number 59, check the fins on the turbine rings, look for interior damage, and then head back...simple, a cakewalk!" He checked the status display in his helmet to find engine number 59 amongst the center span of engines that made up the mid sub-light drive section, then aimed his hand to get a navigation lock on the engine then pressed his palm control. The computer determined the target and activated "magnetic attraction" in the forward magnetic field generators on his suit to initiate motion. He zipped quickly to the engine and stopped right at the opening of the large ion drive. He turned and motioned for Dex to follow.

Dex followed the actions of his mentor and travelled quickly to the engine. He gasped when he arrived – it was much larger than he anticipated. Its rear exhaust maw was over fifty feet in diameter -- he could see the shiny silver fins on the twenty rotating rings that lined the interior of the engine exhaust port. These fins helped to direct ion exhaust which would be used to steer the huge spaceship. A shaft took up the inside center of the engine – it also had small fins that rotated slowly as the engine was sitting idle – this assembly would provide the thrust output of the engine. Inside he could see the silver space suits of the rest of his maintenance crew – they were already deep inside the engine performing their assigned tasks. He then noticed the slight glow from the ion generator up in the front of the engine – seeing this gave him a slight feeling of foreboding doom.

Sam knew what he was thinking. "Don't worry, we will have plenty of time. Also, if for some reason that engine fired up there would still at least a minute before the thrust builds up to the point where it would be critical to us – plenty of time to get out before we would fry. Then all we would have to do is wait for space rescue to come for us. Now let's get to work before we waste so much time that they would WANT to take off without us." Dex thought about Jaime and how he would miss her so if that happened – he determined that he would be just fine and stopped worrying about that scenario.

They advanced to the opening and Sam instructed Dex to reach out and take hold of a passing fin. When he did he immediately achieved the same movement and speed of the turbine. He held on with white knuckles as he spun with the turbine ring. He maintained his vision to only the inside of the engine while hoping that Sam would soon help to guide him through this.

Sam jumped on the fin right behind Dex after he passed by him on his first rotation. He stood on the surface between two fins and grabbed Dex's arm and urged him to stand. Dex slowly followed suit and found he could easily stand upright on the spinning surface. "See nothing to it. Now, jump to the next ring…" Sam took a small leap and landed lightly on the surface of the next ring spinning in the opposite direction. He motioned to Dex, who followed with a light jump. He landed, not as spryly as Sam, but he made it. "Ok, let's move inward a few more rings and get our inspection started."

Now deep inside the engine, Dex found he no longer was feeling the fright he had when he first entered. He could maintain his balance and stand with confidence as he began running his inspection beam on each fin looking for stress breaks and factures. He announced on his personal communicator to Sam after a half hour of work "You know Sam, I think I am going to like this job!"

Jonathan Faraday:

He had slept through the waking chimes. He reached into a pouch attached to his bunk and pulled out an unusual pair of spectacles. He put on the strange glasses and looked at the clock. As soon as he saw the hour he awakened with a start. He had overslept and had been sleeping in a fully lit room while the rest of his workmates got dressed and left. They did not even bother to wake him.

"Oh shit!" he cried out as he realized he was over 45 minutes late for his duty post. He was scheduled to be on engine inspection duty and by the time he would get dressed and to the engineering section the crew would be out-ship and probably almost be done.

He would not be surprised if they just kicked him off of the ship. Now that he was so close to finally getting away from the crispy planet below he had blown it. He had ruined his chance to ever escape the Earth and all its hateful inhabitants. He had worked so hard to get past the preconceptions that everyone had about him and he had somehow managed to get signed onto the crew. Even as an engineering staff member he knew that he eventually would be able to secretly use his knowledge and talents to help this ship find a world where he might be able to live in peace. He hoped he would get the opportunity to get to a planet then sneak away where he could live a hermit's life alone and at peace. Except now he would probably be kicked off and sent back to Earth.

He threw on a pair of baggy black cargo pants, gathered all his "items of interest" and placed them into the pockets, and ensured that all of the pockets were securely sealed protecting the contents. He then splashed some water on his face, ran his fingers through his dark black hair, put his unusual spectacles back on, put on a blue engineering uniform shirt, and ran out the door.

"Crap, what if they space me?" He thought, and then considered that perhaps he could beg for forgiveness and they might keep him on board.

Starlight Launch Time 27 hours 7 minutes

Boral Oldham:

The bridge of the massive starship was now fully manned, the ship was loaded with needed supplies, most of the crew was on board, and the final prep work was being taken care of by the engineering crews. Everything had felt perfect and the timing of everything was just as it should be. Boral was feeling very confident and smug as he sat in the command seat on the main bridge.

He looked over his computer display showing the positions throughout the ship of key Blessed personnel -- they were where he expected them to be. He entered some commands into his computer console. He darkened the bridge lights slightly and increased the lighting on his command chair, thus highlighting him to the rest of the bridge crew. He activated his voice amplifier to boost his commands across the room. The booming of his amplified voice brought the room to a quiet murmur.

"Helm, what is our status?" he queried.

The helmsman, a dark haired Blessed man checked the controls. 'All is ready. We are at station-keeping Star Force Commander!" he shouted out.

"Very good, put the engines on standby. I have a bad feeling." The helmsman nodded and increased the output of the fusion reactor then gave a slight increase of generation energy to the sub-light engines. The extra energy produced a slight bit of output to each of the ion drive engines. It would not be noticed, but allowed the engines to be brought into travel thrust slightly faster than if cold.

"Bridge crew, give me status now." he barked.

"Helm at station-keeping, engines are primed and ready Star Force Commander" shouted the Helmsman.

"Laser sensors and SCADAR are on full scanning patterns Star Force Commander" communicated the Science Officer.

"Weapons are currently in non-battle mode Star Force Commander" announced the Tactical Officer.

"Crews are out doing final preparation checks on the engines, loading bays are still attached Star Force Commander" reported the Engineering Officer.

The communications officer looked over his console before providing his status. "All channels to the starbase are good, communication with Earth is established, Star Force Commander."

"Very good, maintain current status." Boral said in a softer tone. He smiled as he knew all was as it should be. His good feeling was interrupted however by an alert tone from the science console. This particular tone he knew would do nothing but give him bad news. "Report?"

The red headed Blessed man looked over his console, and then looked up with a worried look on his face before shouting out "Sir, SCADAR is showing we have a mass of bogeys rising from the surface of Earth, Star Force Commander." He looked down and continued to read the images on his display "100 – no, now 200 Southern fighter craft, Sir...Century Class Fighters. They appear to be loaded with nuclear weaponry and headed directly toward us!" he shouted in a panic.

Kip Gurrigan:

The mob in front of him was beginning to show their displeasure. When the alert klaxon sounded and the battle status alert lighting illuminated, the crowd started to go into a flurry. They were picking up items that they could hurl at the electronic field generators. Even their leader Luis Cruz was starting to shout and demand that they be allowed to pass through the barrier and board the ship. A crate was picked up by one man and hurled against the barrier. The barrier sputtered for a brief moment before shattering the plastic into thousands of small pieces. Kip took a jump backwards with the explosion of the crate and covered his eyes from the shrapnel that flew across the room at him and his first officer. A piece of the shrapnel put a small cut on his forehead and caused a flow of blood to dribble down his face.

He tapped his communication device and ordered up a channel with the Star Force Commander. "Sir, why are we in battle status? The crowd here has started to riot. I need troops to help quiet these people down!"

Boral spoke with a noticeable calm in his voice. "You and your command evacuate all loading docks and seal the hatches.

We are under attack and who knows what will happen. I don't want you in there. Get out...now!"

Without responding he turned and ran to the hatch. As soon as the two of them were clear of the door he activated the bolt drive closing and locking down the hatch. He gave a slight chuckle then wiped the sweat and blood off of his forehead with his fingers. He stuck his now bloody fingers into his mouth and tasted the mingled juices of the thinned blood and sweat then smacked his lips. He looked out through the hatch viewport at the crowd now in a state of pure insanity. He laughed again as he watched as they continued to throw whatever they could find – including themselves against the barrier. He pointed and called out at any rioter that he particularly enjoyed and cheered them on.

The area between the barrier and their hatchway was becoming stained with the blood and guts of the maniac crowd as they threw themselves and each other against the barrier. Kip would burst out clapping his hands, cheering and shouting with glee every time one of the rioters would hit the barrier – their bodies being cut into bits.

"I don't think I have ever seen such a bloody good time! Look at how those southern turncoats behave...like wild animals. This is a blast! Yes!" he shouted with laughter as yet another rioter hit the barrier.

The Ark of the Blessed

Starlight Launch Time 26 hours 55 minutes

Boral Oldham:

He knew it was time. The alert had closed and secured all of the open hatches into the ship. All weapons had immediately come online and were available for him to fire at will – all he had to do was give the command. Instead of deciding to immediately fight, he instead issued a list of orders. "Helm, fire up the engines. Engineer, disconnect the loading bays, we are leaving!"

The engineer yelled out "Star Force Commander, we have three engine crews outside the ship. We will need a minute to recover them…"

"No, we don't have time."

"Sir?" the engineer questioned.

The tactical officer cried out "Sir, SCADAR is now showing over 400 fighters – they are avoiding the starbase defenses and are headed right at us!" his fear had started to show in his voice, sweat now dripped down his forehead.

"Helm, continue with my order and fire up the engines to full thrust as soon as the docks have cleared the ship. This ship must escape this planet and find a new home where we the Blessed can multiply and thrive. Engineer, follow my commands or die. We have only moments to spare!" Boral aimed his wrist weapon at the Blessed engineer. He was surprised at the compassion for the teams outside – there was so much more at stake than a few hundred men. The engineer finally nodded and flipped the controls to disconnect the loading docks. The Helmsman saw the indicator lights and pushed the thrust controls on the sub-light engines.

Boral stared into the viewing portal at the stars ahead of him as he gave one final set of commands "Communications, notify the starbase we are departing. Helm, full speed ahead!"

Luis Cruz:

Even well before the claxon started to sound Luis had known that he and his group had been lied to. He allowed his emotions to get the best of him and decided to become as violent as the rest of the refugees. He now knew that they were not going to get on board the ship. When the claxons sounded, he should have realized that now was the time to go back to the station – but his rage did not allow it.

Instead he picked up a crate and hurled it toward the electronic barrier that was keeping them away from their goal of boarding the ship. As it hit the barrier, the plastic shattered into a thousand fragments. Some of the fragments hit Alpha Starship Captain Kip Gurrigan and his first mate. He saw a small amount of blood on Kip's face and that brought his blood lust into a total froth. He shouted and raised his arms in victory – he now needed to find something else to throw at the lying Blessed. He thought maybe he could find something small that might make it through the beams of the barrier.

As he searched for something else to throw, he turned and saw the two perfect humans run to the door. Kip was laughing as he reached up and flipped the switch quickly closing the hatch. Now his rage increased even higher. In the back of his mind, he thought about just leaving but his anger would not allow it. He needed to do more damage against the untrustworthy northerners. He had nothing else to throw at the barrier – his ears burned with the crying of a small child next to him. He turned, picked up the screaming child and threw him against the barrier. The small human blew into thousands of fragments as he hit the barrier -- splattering the deck on the other side of the barrier with blood and guts.

He shouted in victory, but then noticed a change in the temperature of the docking bay which calmed him for a moment. Then realization of his situation hit as he heard screaming behind him. He turned to see the rear hatch of the loading dock close. The mass of humanity was shoving into the back hatch pounding on the door and pleading for the people behind the door to let them out. The buzzing of the barrier also stopped ahead of him – they had shut it down. A moment later, he heard a hissing sound and realized the air was getting thinner.

He shouted curse words in Portuguese as the hiss turned into a whoosh and the bay suddenly let go of its death grip on the space ark. He grabbed onto a post for dear life. Refugees were flying out of the docking bay, freezing and slamming against the silver skin of the space ship now leaving. As the bodies hit, they shattered into micro-fragments. Each time a human would hit the skin of the ship, he could see Alpha Starship Captain Kip Gurrigan raise his arms in victory. He was thoroughly enjoying the plight of his fellow victims. Suddenly, Luis realized that the cold of space was freezing his body as his arm shattered into dust sending him flying out of the dock into the nothingness.

In the remaining seconds of his life he saw the ship quickly leave the bay exposing him and his people to the vacuum and cold of outer space. He quickly was sucked out into the vacuum and as he left the bay he felt the warmth of the bay turn into the quick-freezing temperatures of space. In what was left of his quickly fading life, he saw the bodies of the other refugees shooting out into space from the other two loading docks. They had all been deceived.

Dex Morgan:

He was so busy working on the engine fin that he did not notice that the control rings of the engine had stopped turning independently and were now spinning in unison. To the rest of the crew however, it was a different story as shouts of panic flowed freely over the comm-lines. Dex finally snapped out of his work when he heard one of the men say "Shit, the engines are hot firing!"

Dex knew that hot firing meant they had been placed in a state where energy had been applied in such a manner that the engines could be brought on-line and thrust applied within seconds. He also knew that meant he had just seconds to get out of that engine.

Sam also knew this fact as he announced over the crew comm-line "Everyone evacuate the engine, activate your distress beacon and hope that space rescue finds us!"

Dex looked up to see a mass of space suit clad bodies bounding past him as they ran out of the engine in "every man for themselves" mode. No one was helping anyone else – and he realized that he too was still in the engine! He reached down and activated his distress beacon. When he started to rise from the fin that he was working on, he felt a heavy space suit covered foot hit him in the small of the back sending him back to the surface of the ring. The force of hitting the ring sent his head into the visor of his helmet, dazing him. He tried to clear his head so he could evacuate – he shook his head trying to remove the cobwebs preventing him from standing. He started to rise onto his hands and knees but was too wobbly to stand properly. He started to realize he was doomed – there was no way for him to evacuate the engine in time. He thought about Jaime, how even if he was to escape he would be without her. Finally, he started to feel good enough to stand and slowly worked to his feet.

In his intercom, he heard "Dex, get out of here now!" Sam was screaming in panic.

"It's ok, I am losing Jaime so what does it matter." He now was totally on his feet. He looked into the engine and saw the blue flame beginning to flow down the center of the engine shaft. He knew it would only be a few moments now. He turned the other way and looked out the thrust escape way of the engine. The rings were spinning him quite quickly and as he took a step to the last ring he stopped and looked outside. The stars were spinning around and around. He felt the hypnosis they called being star-struck, he just stopped and stared at the sight. "My god, it's wonderful!" He said in a daze.

He swore he felt the heat of the engine start to pierce the protective skin of his suit and a force pushing him out like a hammer hitting him square in the back, but he didn't care anymore. "Goodbye, Jaime my love..."

Jonathan Faraday:

By the time he reached the engineering section he felt the surging of the fusion reactors and felt the thrust of the engine. He ran onto the engineering bridge – the duty chief Kate Grayson was standing in at the center console staring at the engineering displays. She did not even notice him enter the room – short of breath, panting, running with heavy feet, and sweating like a pig.

"Sorry Chief, I don't know what happened. My waking chime seemed to have malfunctioned. Please allow me to make up for my tardiness. Please allow me to continue working on board!" he pleaded.

She seemed not to notice he was there while he spoke. Then she finally realized he was standing next to her as she turned and looked down at him from the console platform. Tears were rolling down her cheeks and her eyes were swollen and red. "You missed your duty roster?" she said softly.

"Yes, please accept my apologies. Please do not kick me off..." He stopped speaking as his eyes caught the sight on the view screen.

"On Jon, thank god you overslept..." she sobbed and placed a hand on his shoulder as he stepped up to get a closer look at the view screen. "If you weren't so unreliable, they would have killed you too...thank god..." she squeezed his small shoulder while she softly spoke to him.

Jonathan could not say anything. The image on the screen had put him into a state of shock. He could do nothing but stare at the images. He watched as silver space-suited bodies were being ejected from the engines along with bright blue torrents of thrust. People he knew, his work mates and colleagues, some of them he might have someday been friends with were shooting out of the engines into space. They were being ejected into the cold and blackness of nothingness. Some were being dissolved by the thrust of millions of ions hitting their bodies. Some were simply being abandoned with no hope of rescue as the ship was leaving without them. Every member of the crew he was to be a part of, Engineering Engine Team Number 5 was suddenly gone right before his eyes. None of his team would survive or return to the ship ever again.

Jaime Bordeaux:

Jaime woke with a start "Dex!" She looked around and realized she was dreaming and was now lying in her bunk in the semi-darkened room of her cabin. She lay back onto the bunk and started to close her eyes once again.

A slight feeling of motion crept into her body. "Moving?" She looked at the ship's chronometer. "No, not time..." The ship's acceleration dampers were working perfectly as Jaime not realizing the ship was in motion fell back into a sound sleep.

She was awoken five hours later when summoned by Star Force Commander Boral Oldham. He personally told her of the death of Dex – she swore he had a slight smirk on his face as he broke the news to her. She showed him no emotion -- she tightened her jaw, straightened her uniform as she stood, saluted him, turned, and walked solidly out of his room. She did not show any emotion, did not shed a tear – until she returned to her darkened cabin. Alone and isolated, she spent the next two days locked in her cabin sobbing and crying until finally the suppressed meditation instructions placed by Doctor Harmony took hold. After she could calm herself she realized that life and the Alliance were not going to allow her any happiness – at least not without a fight.

Starlight Flight Time 32 days, 15 hours 8 minutes

Jaime Bordeaux:

The electronic reveille sounded -- Jaime slowly rose and sat up in the bed. Using her command module, she activated the view screen and focused on the ship's rear cameras. The Earth now only appeared as a small red dot in space. She was getting farther away from her former home and she found she was glad to be leaving the Solar System. She wished they could kick the engines and make the ship go faster to leave the system quicker – she so wanted to be away from all the sadness and sorrow she was leaving behind. However, she knew that the testing of some of the propulsion systems would take place as they passed by Mars, so she would be content with waiting.

She stood up and removed her sleep gown then walked over and tossed it into the laundry chute. She set the desired cleansing level and stepped into the cleansing bay, allowing the delicate lasers to clean and massage her tired body.

She had spent the previous evening – and almost every evening with Jeremy. He had run her through a multi-gravity workout then pushed her through yet another practice round of Command Tri-Polyhedrons. He placed several practice robots along the course, giving her yet more obstacles to overcome in her practice. She was bruised, a little sore – but after standing in the cleansing bay for a few minutes she was surprised how good she actually was feeling. She had been noticing that she was been recovering easier and faster from her physical workouts. She wondered why, when in the past she never noticed this level of improvement in recovery. Once the cleansing cycle ended she ordered an application of a light concealer make up on her face to cover her freckles and applied a light tan coloration to her eyes.

She emerged from the bay and put on a uniform top, matching skirt – both black with gold piping running down the front of the top and the sides of the skirt, space transparencies and medium height black uniform boots. Her hair was still growing slowly, but for now she was keeping it in a layered pixie cut to keep it out of her face while in her work out sessions. She rechecked her uniform to ensure it was fitted and properly set. She then slapped the communication device on her desk to contact the duty officer of the day. The holographic display on the wall showed an older black haired Blessed Beta Starship Captain answering her call. Jaime did not recognize this officer -- another of the many Blessed that avoided contact with the Normal members of the crew.

"Delta Starship Captain Jaime Bordeaux reporting for daily assignment."

The man looked at her with a confused look. "Bordeaux, I have not met you before. That name sounds a little southern."

"Only southern in France..." she said with a smile, while thinking, *"Idiot..."*

"Ah, well ok then. I suppose you are looking for a duty assignment?"

"No kidding dumb ass." She thought as she smiled and nodded.

He looked at his monitor. "Today's duty assignment for you is...Simulator."

"Sir, I have been on simulator duty for the past three weeks. Will I get to see the bridge anytime soon?"

"Well don't worry Bordeaux, after your simulator training you are scheduled to report to...laundry for crew supervision."

"Great...are you sure about that? This is not right that I have nothing to do but practice and babysit the laundry crew."

"Not in my hands Bordeaux." He immediately shut off the transmission.

She sighed and shook her head slightly in disgust before heading out of her cabin. She hopped aboard first one, then a second transport car that traversed the long massive tube of the ship's living connector. She got off of the transport and walked down a long hallway to the simulator section and to her pre-set session. Several simulator sections were available for bridge personnel to practice command and control of the massive space ark. Jaime checked in and was assigned a simulator for Normal crew. She wondered what the difference was between Normal and Blessed simulators. She figured the Blessed simulators probably let them win every scenario as opposed to the almost un-winnable exercises provided by the simulators for the Normal crew.

Fortunately, she had been able to use her knowledge of war and battle strategy to win and keep her score high.

She passed by a few simulator doors marked "Blessed Only!" She turned and looked at the door and wondered what would happen if she ventured in – but decided against it. She finally came to the simulator reserved for her, stopped and read the simulation instructions displayed on the screen at the door. This simulator was a bridge command simulation and would provide Jaime with a full mockup of the bridge with simulated working bridge controls. The simulator could be fully manned or filled with holo-mock ups of crew members, thus providing a full bridge crew.

Upon entering, she looked around the simulator – it was an exact mockup of the Starlight Bridge. There were five stations in a circle around a directional holographic image that could be selected differently for each of the bridge staff with the command chair right behind the control circle. The command chair would rotate around the bridge behind each of the stations, thus allowing her to see every action at every station. The command chair normally was positioned directly behind the helm, science on the right next to the helm station and followed by weapons control. On the left, the bridge engineer would sit and next to this position is the communications station completing the control circle.

All members of the bridge crew could see the Captain from their respective seats with the exception of the helmsman who was normally directly in front of the Captain with their back toward the officer – this positioning was given to provide partial autonomy to helm to pilot the ship without the Captain's direct command. There were eight-foot-tall crystal displays around the outside of the circular bridge that provided captured images of space all around the ship. Thus, one could use either the holographic or surrounding star screens to see the current situation in the surrounding space. A single door led to the bridge and on the actual bridge there was also a door to the Star Force Commander's ready room.

Sometimes she would take the various consoles for different scenarios so she could get experience at every bridge station. Today however, she chose to complete a Captain's bridge scenario. As she entered the simulator she noticed it was already fully staffed with a bridge crew. She sat in the command chair and pressed the activation code to start the simulation. She was given a battle simulation today – she thought at least it would be somewhat interesting. She linked her palm command sensor to the bridge command network – it disconnected itself from the socket in her palm and magnetically bound itself to the left arm rest of the command console, thus locking her commands into every station. This would ensure that no one could override any order she gave – it gave her complete and unconditional command and prevented any possibility of mutiny of the crew or loss of control of the craft. Her command console activated, providing a holographic display of various ships systems to her right and a holographic tactical analysis display on her left. On the console, several command function controls were available for her use to activate the various systems or procedures if the situation dictated.

A number of unknown vessels were detected on SCADAR and the simulated science officer announced their incoming formation. She looked at the formation of the ships and the trajectory at which they were approaching. She made no command as the craft approached. The ships were approaching fast and direct.

Jaime was surprised by a female voice that sounded out in front of her at the helm console. "So, Captain Holo – we going to do something, or just get smashed to bits by these ships?" Jaime peered over the top of the helm chair and saw that it was a real person in the simulator with her, although the person at the helm had not yet realized it.

She stood up and walked over to the helmsman and whispered into her ear "So, what makes you think that we will get smashed to bits? And what makes you think you have a holo Captain?"

The woman at the helm turned and saw Jaime, then gasped, stood up, and saluted. "My apologies Delta Starship Captain, I thought I was…"

"Alone? Ah, no. Now, could you quickly change course to 145.88 for me so we *don't* get smashed?"

The woman, without letting her eyes leave Jaime's, reached around her back to the helm console and without looking -- entered in the coordinates as requested. The bridge tilted slightly and the three ships on the view screen passed by without causing any damage to the simulated space ark.

"I am impressed Helmsman!" Jaime said as she looked over the young woman. She had medium length straight hair that was such a dark brown that it almost appeared black. It was parted on the left side which caused the hair on the right side of the part to drape across her forehead slightly but was cut in such a way that it did not impede her vision, although it did at times drape across her right eye. Her eyes were brown but one would hardly be able to notice through the vision adjustment contact lenses she was wearing. She had a round face with a very small chin and slightly fat cheeks. She wore some coverage make up to conceal the light blemishes of her youth. She stood a few inches shorter than Jaime at full attention and was slightly pudgy in the belly. She wore a simulated cotton grey casual outfit which indicated she was not on duty. She also noted she did not have a bead around her neck – she was Normal.

Jaime without looking away pointed at the view screen. "Umm, I think we had better start steering the ship? The next batch appears to be coming in at an attack vector."

She dropped into her chair, turned and began quickly entering steering commands causing the ship to quickly and efficiently steer a course allowing for full weapons to bear down on the three ships. Jaime nodded, then announced "Weapons, lock on the incoming alien vessels. Activate magnetic plate shielding and prepare to fire cannons." She waited for the ships to come a little closer then barked out "Fire all proton cannons!" The view screen displayed the simulated view of plasma bolts shooting out hitting two of the three ships. "Fire rail launchers." Shimmering bolts of plutonium shot across the screen hitting the last ship. "Steer around that if possible…" she had not even gotten the command fully out before the helmsman was moving the ship away from the nuclear explosions and avoiding any damage to the simulated space ark.

The lights came on and on the screen flashed the message:

"Simulator Mission 19884:
Difficulty – 68
Friendly ships destroyed – 0
Enemy ships destroyed – 3 out of 3
Ship damage: 0
Mission Score: 100
Rank: Normal 1st, Blessed: 1st, Overall: 2nd"

"A perfect score? I don't believe it!" shouted the young woman as she quickly stood and thrust her fist into the air in victory. She again realized she was not alone and quickly slunk back into her seat. "How did you know?"

"Know what?"

"That the first wave was not aggressive?"

"Simple for a former fighter pilot. They were at the wrong angle. I could see they were fleeing something else, not attacking us. We were just in the way."

"Oh wow, that was amazing!"

Jaime gave a small quiet giggle. "Helmsman, what is your name?"

She jumped out of her chair and once again stood back up at full attention. "Delta Helmsman Halley Cet" she shouted out while saluting.

"At ease Helmsman...please! Halley...the same as the comet?"

"Yes, my parents named me that because I think they wanted me to be a full-time astronomer. Instead they got a helmsman. I thought about changing my name -- or at least the pronunciation as I don't like to be called "Hal-EE". I thought about changing it to "Hail-EE". What do you think Delta Starship Captain?"

"I would stick with Hal-EE I think. There is something special about being named after a comet."

"Very well Captain, you know best...Well in any case, it was an honor to steer the ship for you Delta Starship Captain."

82

"Well, it is nice to meet a person who can actually steer a starship! Perhaps we can do this again? As, I have a feeling that I will be doing these simulations for quite a while."

"Very possibly Delta Starship Captain. I think that since we took off from Earth, almost every Normal bridge crew member has not seen any real duty."

She put her hand on her chin and rubbed it while thinking "I think you are right Halley." She looked the helmsman up and down again before suggesting "Perhaps we can meet up here on a regular basis? I bet we might become one good team. Perhaps we could find some others as we practice?"

"I am sure of that Delta Starship Captain. As a matter of fact, I may know a few who will want to join us. I just need to let them in on the time of our practice sessions. Let me make a few calls later."

Jaime nodded then looked at her command module. "Well, it will be a while before the simulator is ready again for another go at it. How about I buy you a cup of coffee? Release..." By giving the release command to the simulator and holding her left palm over the arm of the command console, the plate with her command chip wiggled loose from the holder on the arm and flew to her palm, rebinding itself with her hand.

Halley stiffened up again. "It would be an honor, thank you Delta Starship Captain!"

"Sure, but only if we are at ease during our break -- ok?" Halley responded with a smile and a nod.

The pair of women adjourned to the simulator break lounge. The lights were turned down low so it would be a place for relaxation -- there was a view screen on one wall, and a ship's status screen on the other wall. The room had three tables with four matching chairs each. There was a small Vendo-Matic on the wall near the entrance to the lounge. Jaime ordered two coffee flavored protein drinks and brought them to Halley who waited at one of the tables in the corner of the lounge. Halley took a sip of the drink, enjoyed the flavor and temperature and smiled as she sniffed the aroma of the artificial drink.

Jaime stared at the view screen across the room. The image of Mars filled the room with reds and greens. She never tired of looking at the planet. She wondered how her comrades down on the nearby planet were doing – the ones who stayed to try again to colonize. She had found it hard to survive down there during the war – but she made it and so did her fellow soldiers. She brought her mind back to the present and the spunky young helmsman looking at her with wide eyes and a small smile. "So, how did you get so good at steering a starship Halley?"

"I don't really know -- it just came to me when I was nine or ten I think. My father was an astronomer and worked at the Alliance Astronomy Institute. He would take me to work quite often and I would get to spend time in their simulator while he worked. They used the simulator to train navigators and he thought the simulator time would give me the ability to recognize stars quickly, but instead it gave me the chance at learning to pilot a spacecraft. I really never had to work at learning the controls of a ship – it just came so naturally and I knew I would have to be a pilot when I got older. After the war started, I volunteered to fly cargo runs in the war effort. I shuttled troops and supplies between Earth and Mars for a couple years until the South gave up the attempt at taking over space. Then I requested a position here on Starlight and I was surprised when they granted it."

"Really? Why would it surprise you?"

"Well, I *am* Normal after all and a little chunky too. However, I think one of the Blessed liked me at one time – I am not sure which one, but I am sure that is the reason I got here. I also think he must have changed his mind as I have never had anyone approach me. Probably because they realized I was a little heavier than they preferred once they saw me in person."

"What do you mean?" Jaime was totally confused by her comment.

"A bunch of us suspect that most of us Normals – women – were brought here for the pleasure of the Blessed. They do nothing else but flirt with us and try to order us to their rooms. They don't use our skills -- they just constantly try to get us into bed. It has to be the reason we are here – thankfully I don't seem to appeal to them. But quite a few of my girlfriends are constantly bothered. I take it you have been spared this?"

"I don't think any of them would dare..." Jaime hated to think that most of the Normal women were only brought on this trip to be sex toys of the Blessed – just thinking about it made her blood boil. "Actually, I do hope one of them tries." She smiled and rubbed the knuckles on her fist. "It would give me a good chance..."

She was interrupted by her command communicator. She tapped the small button behind her right ear and an image of Jeremy appeared on the view screen on the wall. "Jaime, I need you to come to the gym. They have just scheduled a game of Command Tri-Polyhedrons. We need to discuss strategy."

"Very well, I will be there in a few minutes." She tapped her command device to deactivate the image. "Well Helmsman, how about a rain check on the next simulation?"

"You've got it Delta Starship Captain. I will get some help for our next simulator session. Will you text me the time you wish to meet?"

"I will. Until next time..."

Halley gave her the traditional chest thump and the sideways salute with her right hand. "Go knock 'em dead Delta Starship Captain! I will be rooting for you."

Jaime turned and gave a small smile and a return salute. "Thanks, I might just do that..." As she turned and walked away she had the distinct impression she had just made her first female friend on this journey.

Starlight Flight Time: 33 days, 2 hours, 2 minutes

Jeremy Ponds:

When Jeremy arrived at the gym to meet Jaime and escort her to the arena, he was surprised to find that instead of just waiting for him, she instead had started lifting weights in high gravity. He was worried that by starting before he arrived she would be too tired to put up a good fight in the upcoming games.

"Jaime, what are you doing? You are wearing yourself out!"

She put down the weights and smiled at him. "This time I am right about this. I feel great!"

He noticed that even though she was sweating profusely, she was not showing any signs of fatigue. As a matter of fact, she was looking stronger than ever – her muscles were fully pumped and looking quite strong. He smiled and nodded at her. "You know, I think this time you are right. I don't know how, but you don't appear tired at all!"

"I'm not. I have been lifting and prepping and I seem to have more energy than when I started! Let me hit the cleansing bay for a moment and I will be ready. Go on ahead, I will meet you at the arena, ok?"

"Sounds good, see you in a few minutes." She waved and ran off toward the locker room as he walked to the arena where the game of Command Tri-Polyhedrons is to be played. The actual arena was much larger than the simulation he had set up for Jaime in the gym. The area was enclosed in a giant dome with spectator seating that surrounded the entire playing field. There were platforms and hanging loops on the inside surface of the dome – spots for jumping on and off the main game plane. The main playing field consisted of three long ramps that progressed up to the top of the dome where the victory basket floated eight feet above the final defender. At the top of each ramp was a flat platform – which is where the bulk of the offense/defense will take place. The ball will be launched from a tube at the very bottom of the playing field. The lowest level Captain is to stand at that position and will be given the first chance to run through the gauntlet, up the ramps to the top, while all other players are to attempt to stop them.

"Well, Jeremy Ponds! Some fool has taken you as their trainer? Say it isn't so!" Jeremy turned to find Faulkner Paulsen standing behind him. He is a Blessed, and is quite tall with a very well-developed body. His dark long hair was pulled to the back and tied in a ponytail. Like all Blessed he had a small bead on a titanium alloy chain – his was made of pearl and had the number "187". He had that smile on his face that made Jeremy's blood boil. He was smug and confident and why shouldn't he be -- after all, he was the trainer of Kip Gurrigan, the top Starship Captain whom to date was unbeaten. "Oh, that's right...that Normal girl took you on as a trainer. Sorry for you, she has no chance at all...no chance. As a matter of fact, I don't even know why she is going to try – after all, she is just a girl."

Faulkner finally took a breath long enough for Jeremy to simply say "We will see Faulkner, we will see..." Waving the Blessed trainer off, he walked away and found a seat near the bottom of the ramp where he would be able to fully watch Jaime in action.

The arena was now filling quickly and within a span of fifteen minutes the seating went from empty and quiet, to jam packed and loud. The crowd was already cheering and yelling out for their favorite Captain. Most of the crowd was Blessed -- however a few seats were allowed to be occupied by Normal humans. The crowd went into a frenzy when the announcer came on.

"Blessed Ladies and Gentlemen...Normals...it is time. Get to your feet and give a big cheer for the Captains of the game. Your Starship Captains! Come on!"

A door opened at the base of the dome and the thirty Starship Captains walked out. The first was Kip Gurrigan – he was wearing a tight-fitting outfit of gold sparkling spandex. His tight shorts showed off his muscular legs, buttocks and an artificially enhanced front crotch. On top, he wore a matching muscle shirt which was also selected to show off his bulging arms, chest and shoulders. He had his golden hair perfectly styled, wavy and flowing. His choice of outfit tonight offered him no protection in the event of any fighting, he however seemed to not care at all. He waved to the crowd and blew kisses to them as they cheered him on with shouts of "Kip! Kip! Kip!"

The rest of the Captains marched out wearing skin tight shiny black suits. Some had made modifications adding pieces of armor and various belts and accoutrements of decoration. Jaime was the last to enter the arena wearing only a plain black suit like the other Captains -- however she had added no decorations or additions. She was wearing dark flat heeled boots with soft soles and a matching dark belt. As she marched onto the playing field the crowd began screaming out boos and insulting cat calls. She obviously was not popular with the Blessed. There was one section that was cheering support however – the single group of Normals. Unfortunately, they were drowned out by the shouting and screaming of the much larger crowd of Blessed.

Jeremy inserted noise limiting earplugs. "Ah, much better!"

Jaime Bordeaux:

When Jaime entered the arena, she was stunned by the noise and rowdiness of the crowd. She expected the boos and even the catcalls, but was shocked over the noise level that they were generating. The Alphas and Betas had already taken their place on the first and second levels. The Deltas however were still hovering around the base of the starting ramp. Eight of the nine other Deltas were Blessed -- the one Normal Captain was not standing with the Blessed officers but instead stood on his starting position at the second position of the ramp. Jaime recognized the Blessed Delta officers – the number one Delta was Jarred Maltz, followed by Columbia Koss, Mort Torsis, brothers Bellevue and Baylor Blythe, Tipper Dars, Leopold Paulst and Jacob Smith. She had never seen the Normal officer before.

Jarred spoke for the group. "Bordeaux, word has it the Supreme Commander brought you in because you are a southerner and he wanted us to inflict pain on you."

"Oh really? I thought he brought me here to teach you just how stupid you really are." She gave him a smug look and slightly shook her head in disgust.

"You should know that you will not make it past the third position. We would suggest you drop the ball and save yourself some pain." They all were giving her growling noises and mean intimidating looks.

Jaime got right in his face. "You think so eh? Did you know that before I started flying spacecraft I was a soldier? I like pain, and I enjoy giving it, so please...try to stop me..." she rubbed her knuckles and gave him a light smile. The sneer across his mouth started to tremble as she continued to stare him down. She sunk her deep blue eyes into his dull green eyes and her nose was almost touching his sweating proboscis. Finally, he blinked – she smiled, winked, then defiantly turned her back to him and walked away. He gave a slight snort, turned and ran up the ramp. The other Deltas followed, bumping into the Normal Captain still maintaining his position on the ramp. She walked up to him and gave him a thorough looking over. He gave her a smile and said "Good luck, I hope you make it. But you should know they will cheat."

"Thanks for the warning, Delta Starship Captain?"

"Delta Starship Captain Allen James."

"Delta Starship Captain Jaime Bordeaux. Pleased to meet you. Perhaps next time I will try to soften them up for you – but not this time, ok? I have to knock you out to move up." He nodded in acknowledgement with the knowledge that he would have no chance against her.

The announcer came over the arena sound system at a volume loud enough to quiet the crowd. "Ladies, Gentlemen...Normals...our Alliance anthem." A mutilated form of the Star-Spangled Banner played over the speakers. The Blessed stood and sung wildly to the rewritten lyrics while the Normals simply stood. Jaime continued staring down the lead Delta Starship Captain now standing at the top of the ramp – he was returning the stare down back to her. She continued to give him a cold hard stare until he turned away. When he did not turn back and return the look – she knew she had him. The crowd went wild again as soon as the music ended.

"The Captains are in position -- the ball is ready to be launched. Are you ready crowd? Let's hear it!" Once again, the crowd went into a frenzy of screaming. "Remember, every person the ball carrier can get around and knock off the ramp will move that Captain up in the ranking. If they make it all the way to the top and can dunk the polyhedron into the basket, they win -- and will become the top Alpha Starship Captain. As a reward for winning, the new Captain will get their very own starship when one is built or become a governor of a colony planet. Now, isn't that exciting! Alright, let's start Command Tri-Polyhedrons! Launch the ball as our first Captain to attempt the ascent is Delta Starship Captain Jaime Bordeaux, let's hear it for her!" Only the Normals were cheering as the rest of the crowd was booing and throwing drinks onto the arena dome. The glasses and cups hit the dome, shattered and slid into a collection gutter at the bottom where they were removed out of the area. The acrylic surface of the dome prevented any of the liquid beverages from entering the playing field.

Jaime turned toward the tube that would launch the ball. A warning horn sounded and with a whump the polyhedron ejected from the tube at a high velocity and rolled around the base of the dome. Jaime ran out and grabbed the ball. A charge cheer sounded over the PA system and the crowd roared. She looked up the ramp – Allen was standing in front of her, arms out -- the other Deltas were huddled discussing strategy.

She started to run up the ramp and felt the gravity shift to below Earth gravity. She took advantage of the change by jumping and flipping over Allen. As soon as she landed she spun around and before he could turn she hit him with a solid roundhouse kick, sending him flying off the ramp. He hit the floor with a loud thud, but then sat up, looked at her and gave her a big smile. She returned the smile and turned up to face the next Captain on the ramp.

Jacob Smith gave about as little resistance as Allen as she walked right up to him and ducked one, two, and then three punches before using a leg sweep to put him on the surface of the ramp. "Bye, bye" she said as she applied a swift side kick to his shoulder flinging him off the ramp. "Two down..."

Leopold and Tipper immediately attacked her with flying fists and kicks. She ducked, avoided and blocked every attack they threw at her. She felt the ball start to shift weight – so she tossed the polyhedron into the face of Tipper. By using the former weight to toss the ball she was able to put enough velocity that the change in weight did not affect its speed. The ball was twice its former weight when it hit him squarely in the nose -- shattering it. He screamed as pain flowed along with his blood. As she caught the ball on the rebound she put an elbow into Leopold's face breaking his jaw. As to clear the ramp and end their suffering she rammed her shoulder into Tipper, then the other into Leopold sending them flying off the ramp. A score display panel in the arena showed the thirty contestants as lit stick figures – she was indicated by a green lit stick figure at the bottom of the display. Two of the stick figures indicating Leopold and Tipper dimmed and were replaced by bright red X's. The boos and jeers from the mob grew to an increasing crescendo for every Blessed she took out. Even more glasses were hitting the dome making the sound of the plastic against plastic impacts almost as loud as the voicing of displeasure from the audience.

The last five Delta Captains were now on her in a group attack. The gravity shifted even lighter and she used this shifting to jump out of the way of the first three attacking and landed between Mort, Bellevue and Baylor now lower on the ramp and Jarred and Columbia at the top of the ramp. She spun around, landed a quick upper cut to the back of the jaw of Bellevue immediately knocking him out – gravity took him down the ramp sliding on his back, unconscious. She then landed a front kick into Mort's chin and finally swung around using the ball as a weapon into the side of Baylor's face – stunning and knocking him down. With one lower defender, totally out of the game and the other two out for a brief moment -- she concentrated on the two above her.

She felt the gravity shift again as they were jumping in the air to take advantage of the lighter gravity. Unfortunately for them, the gravity changed to heavier than Earth standard. Columbia was flying in for a heavy landing, feet-first on top of her, when she fell flat to the ground and quickly shoved her foot up to land squarely in his crotch. The increase in gravity and the force of her foot caused his protective cup to crush turning the protective gear into a hard-pressing vice against his testicles. He screamed in agony as she shifted to the side, her leg still stiff and using the movement to throw him off the ramp – her foot still squarely lodged into his crushed jewels. Jarred was now landing to her side as she rolled Columbia off the ramp. He sent a fast fist to her face at the moment he landed. She swiveled her body and placed the polyhedron between her and his incoming fist. It bounced his fist back into his own face, smacking himself and sending him reeling back. The ball also rebounded into Jaime's face stunning her slightly. She stood up slowly to see Jarred bounding toward her face first. She stepped aside and pushed him with her free arm on past her and off the ramp onto the floor. He hit the floor with his head and passed out.

She had forgotten about the two below her for a moment and that proved to be a mistake as she felt the hard slam of a steel rod against her head. She wobbled slightly as she turned to see Baylor now rushing her as Mort was taking yet another swing. Her natural instincts took over as she fell onto the floor landing on her elbow while still holding onto the ball. This made her attacker miss and stumble over on top of her. She put her other hand out and stiff-armed him in an arc toward the edge of the ramp, but not enough to send him out of the game.

The two Deltas were swinging furiously at Jaime who was still propped on the floor of the ramp. She used her star fighter experience to wiggle and shift her body, thus avoiding their shots – one, two, three and a fourth shot missed – each time their open hands hit the ramp a loud metallic sound was generated as they were using hidden metal rods in their attacks. She misjudged one swing and felt the cold steel land against her rib cage. She grunted in pain as the weapon cracked ribs and caused internal damage.

She felt the gravity shift once again to a lighter setting. She put the ball onto the ramp, quickly flipping into a hand stand -- then using her arms flipped herself into the air while fighting off the pain of her broken ribs and avoiding the swinging steel weapons. She landed on her feet below her attackers, landed a hard fist into Mort's side returning the favor of broken rib damage, then grabbed the rolling ball and at the same time she swung her foot into the back of Baylor's knee, buckling it. She then sent a quick foot into his head as he was falling to the floor, then with another kick shoved him off the ramp. Mort was sliding slowly down the ramp and was now below her. He was in a fetal position as he could barely breathe. She gave him a light shove off the ramp onto the floor.

She did not even get a chance to turn around before the Beta hit her with a solid steel rod to the head – the blood began to flow from her mouth. Woozy, she attempted to spin around to defend but was pounded in the leg with a steel-toed boot from another Beta – but not even that hard shot could take down her muscular thighs. She then heard a thump like the sound of an energy weapon. At that same moment, she felt a vibration in her thigh – pain immediately followed while her leg gave out due to the fracturing of her femur. At the same time, she took yet another wallop to the head with a hidden weapon. This caused her to drop the polyhedron while she fell. She felt unyielding steel rods hit her at least three or maybe four more times -- one shot breaking her right arm. As she started to lose sight of reality she saw in her blurry vision Kip standing above her. He had dropped down from his top ramp position to give her one final swift kick breaking more of her ribs. Barely conscious, she saw him raise his fists in victory to elevate the frantic level of the crowd before picking her up above his head and tossing her off the ramp.

Time now seemed to exist in slow motion as the ramp fell away from her in frames of reality. She barely could hear the roar of pleasure coming from the crowd when she finally hit the surface of the playing field floor -- immediately losing consciousness as her head hit the hard surface.

She awakened to find Jeremy above her with a worried look on his face. He gave a slight smile as he realized she was somewhat regaining consciousness. "You put up a good fight, but now we need to get you to a doctor."

Somehow, she found the energy to grab his shoulder with her good arm and pulled him close to her. She whispered, "Only take me to a NORMAL doctor...no Blessed..."

"Don't worry -- I have just the person..."

Starlight Flight Time: 33 days, 5 hours, 15 minutes

Doctor Max Sollix:

Max was first surprised when Jeremy called him with an emergency that evening – secondly, he was surprised that the person he brought in was a Captain. He looked at the tall woman on the stretcher. He immediately discerned she had been extremely beaten as her face was covered with bruises from where heavy objects had struck her. He was very surprised that she was even conscious with the amount of damage inflicted on her body. Although he did not know this -- the Blessed had subjected her to massive amounts of damage in the Command Tri-Polyhedrons game that evening. He never watched the matches as he had no desire to be in a room with as many Frogspawn as filled the arena and he could think of no reason to watch the Tele-Vid of the event.

"Set her on the exam table please" he requested of the much larger Jeremy. The strong trainer hoisted her from the stretcher to the cushioned table. He turned on the exam light above her and leaned down to remove her outfit. As he moved in close he felt a strong set of fingers reaching around his neck, squeezing his throat.

A weak voice demanded "Show me your neck! Prove you are Normal!"

Jaime was squeezing his neck tightly with her left hand, but not enough to injure him. He gasped slightly and opened his tunic to expose his naked neck. She felt around and did not find any bead identifying him as a Blessed and she let loose of her grip on him. "Sorry, just had to make sure you were…"

"Normal? Of course, I am my dear. Allow me to introduce myself -- I am now your doctor. My name is Max Sollix. Now if I may…" He waved his arm over her broken body.

She let her left arm drop to her side. He finished removing her clothing and examined her. He found she had three broken ribs, fractures to her facial bones, a cracked skull, a fractured arm, and a shattered right leg. He looked at Jeremy. "She is a mess! This was all done in that game?" Jeremy nodded. He waved a hand scanner over her leg and his eyes opened wide from the results. "It appears as if she was shot in the leg with a sonic weapon!"

Jeremy looked at the scanner display then scratched his head. "That would explain why she suddenly went down. Despite what they were doing to her – she would have found a way to get the upper hand if they had not taken out her leg. I wondered why she suddenly fell like that. I knew they were cheating, but not to that extent!"

Max shook his head then started to put on a medical hat and mask. "Well, we have much work to do. We will start with healing the bones." He looked down at the barely conscious Jaime. "As far as healing is concerned, I do not do things the way Blessed doctors do. I will not use sealing lasers on you as they do not heal efficiently. Instead I will inject your broken bones with a special chemical substance I have invented that will mesh and bond with your bones to seal the breaks. It takes a little longer than using a sealing laser...but your bones will be much stronger and better than if I used lasers. Then I will use a vitality ray that I also invented that will start the healing process as your bones mend. This ray uses selected frequencies that come naturally from our sun – that is before the sun's rays became deadly on our home world. I have removed the harmful light frequencies and kept the light rays that heal and provide nutrition. It will not be painful after I finish the sealing and mending of the bones for healing – however, unless I put you totally out the mending process will not be pleasant. So, I am going to put you out – do I have your permission?"

Jaime looked up at the doctor. Even with the mask covering his nose and mouth, she could tell he was of advanced age. His eyes were green but the color had faded some over the years. She also saw the bags under his eyes -- he was not the normal age to be on this vessel her fuzzy mind assumed. But she saw the concern and honesty in his face and felt she could trust him. She nodded and he nodded back. He moved his mask down off of his face and gave her a kindly smile, like a grandfather to his granddaughter, then moved the hair out of her face, stroked it lightly and then put the mask back on and prepared to operate.

He prepared an anesthesia injection -- put monitoring sensors on her temples, her ankles, her fingers and one on the command sensor plate on her palm. A computer monitor came alive with the various readouts from the monitoring points. He made sure all of her vital signs were normal – he was surprised that she was actually showing the vital signs of someone in perfect health, not that of someone who was just almost beaten to death.

"Ok, here we go. We will talk to you in a few hours..." was all she heard as he administered the laser injection.

Max worked for hours on Jaime's broken body. He injected his fusion solution into every broken bone allowing the solution to find every crack and break within her bones. He monitored the medication with medical sensors – watching the bonding of the solution as he continued to work on the remainder of the breaks in the various bones. He was amazed with how her body accepted and utilized his formula so quickly – more quickly than he had ever seen before. He actually saw the mending process begin on her leg as he was finishing injecting the substance into her arm. Her arm was starting to bond as he finished up her face and skull.

Her leg bone was almost fifty percent bonded when he was finished and wheeled her into the vitality ray booth. The beams just increased the speed at which her bones healed. She awoke after an hour of the process. He entered the booth and looked at her vital signs. "You are showing perfect vital signs Delta Starship Captain. So perfect, that I have to admit, I am amazed at your rate of healing! Do you have any idea why you are so resilient?'

"Jaime...please Doctor...call me Jaime."

"Alright Jaime...you call me Max ok? So, do you know why you seem to heal so quickly?"

"No...no idea Max. But I can tell you I am feeling pretty decent now." She started to squirm as if she was going to try to stand. He put his hands on her shoulders, keeping her down. She was not as strong as she thought and she gave up her attempt to get up and off of the table after only a few seconds. He picked up the sheets she threw on the floor and placed them back onto her body.

"You have to rest. Your bones need to heal – I am going to trust you will lie here quietly until I tell you. We do not want you trying to use that leg until it is fully healed or you will fall and could re-break that femur. Ah, the vitality ray is about to fire again..." He put on his goggles then placed goggles on Jaime right before a bright light emitted from an array of tubes in the ceiling of the booth. The rays gave Jaime a feeling of goodness and warmth. She smiled and spread her arms as she tried to get even more of her body bathed in the soothing beams of filtered electromagnetic spectrum. She gave a slight sound of pleasure as the vitality rays shut down – a smile came to her face. Max removed his goggles and smiled back at her. "As you can see, the vitality ray is quite soothing. It will bathe you every twenty minutes during the healing process. I have programmed your goggles to give you any form of programming available while you lay here and rest. Just please do not move for the next couple weeks."

"Weeks? Max, I cannot be gone that long. I have to train. Also, who knows what they will do…"

He gave her a "tisk, tisk" and motioned to her to stop speaking. "The ship will be exactly as it was when you left and your rank will be the same. Now, stay in this position. I will bring you something to eat after you have had a few more ray treatments."

On the fourth day Max woke up and went to the infirmary first thing to check on his patient. He walked in and found Jaime pacing the vitality booth. He was shocked and furious. "What are you doing? You are not supposed to be on your feet!" he shouted as he entered the booth.

"I feel great!" she proclaimed. "I need to get back to work. I have training to do – there will be another match in a few weeks. I have to prepare…"

"Your bones need to heal!" He took his medical scanner and began to scan her. His eyes opened wide and he almost dropped the scanner when he saw the results. She was fully healed and was in perfect health after only four days in the booth. "This is impossible…"

"I really feel great, really! These rays made me feel better every time they fired up. Really, I do feel fine…"

"The instruments agree with you Jaime." He looked at his medical scanner once again then sighed. "Your bones are completely healed. Not just partially, but fully healed. And your bones are not showing any residual signs they were even damaged at one time. You are completely healed. I just don't understand…"

"Neither do I, but I do know that as of late, I seem to heal really fast. I have no idea why though."

"For once, I don't know why either. Well, the scans agree with you. You are in perfect health, please stop in once a day for a vitality ray treatment at least?"

Jaime smiled at her doctor. "I will, I promise. Thank you..." She got dressed, gave Max a big strong hug almost crushing his ribs, and then ran out the door.

He shook his head again while he looked at his scanner. "Amazing..."

The Ark of the Blessed

Starlight Flight Time: 40 days, 10 hours, 37 minutes

Boral Oldham:

He felt confident, but still his palms sweated profusely. He was nervous over today's pending test of the two propulsion systems – the Pulsar drive and the Graviton. The plan is to activate the drives as they finish their pass of Mars – using the Pulsars to provide the initial motion, then using the planet as a repulsion point and pushing away with the Graviton. They plan to then set the front of the craft in the opposing force hoping to attract the gravity field of the asteroid Vesta, currently a mere 100 million miles away. With luck, the pushing from Mars and the attraction of Vesta will help to propel the ship with minimal or no use of the ion drives.

If that test is successful, they would then test combinations of ion drives, Pulsars and the Graviton drive to propel the ship at much higher speeds -- maybe even to a tenth of the speed of light. The more they could use the Graviton the less they would have to burn fusion materials powering the ion drives – as these drives consumed the most energy to run. But before they could attempt these future tests, they must make it through this first hurdle. They were about to energize the external skin of the ship and he hoped it would not do anything inside to either the Blessed crew or the electronics of the craft.

He activated his voice enhancer and turned up the lighting above his head. "We are on schedule -- give me a status of the test preparations, Science Officer."

For this test, Boral selected who he thought would be the best person for the job at the science station. This person of course was Blessed – Bellevue Blythe. He had graduated from science school with Blessed degrees in gravitational and electromagnetic sciences and had worked with the engineering staff on the installation of the Graviton and of the magnetic Pulsar drives. He had come up with using Vesta as the test subject – who better to assist him with this testing venture.

Bellevue's jaw was still swollen and black from the last round of Command Tri-Polyhedrons – so he required a voice assistance device as he had problems opening his mouth and speaking loudly. He said through the device "The Graviton is primed, all loops are energized, repulsion and attraction targets are selected and programmed into the helm controls, the Pulsars are primed – we are ready."

"Alright, we are deviating from our straight-line course to do this – so let's get the show on the road shall we? Shut down the ion drives Helm, and bring us to a stop. Then activate the Pulsar drives for propulsion on my command." He waited until he saw the ion drives had completely shut down. "Helm, activate Pulsars."

The helmsman flipped switches on his control panel providing control to only the Pulsar drives. He then pulled back on the throttle stick engaging the new engines. The throttle stick provided power to the superconductor electromagnets in the rear of the craft. A small vibration shook the ship and became louder and more pronounced as the Pulsar drives started running at almost full speed. The ship suddenly began shaking and vibrating.

Boral became worried that the ship was going to tear itself apart. "What's the problem Bellevue? Should we shut down?" he yelled over the noise of the vibrations.

Bellevue held up a finger as if to hold any further orders, and then looked over his controls while he barked orders as best he could to the engineering section. "They are telling me to hold on -- they are having some synchronization problems but are hoping to have it under control in a few moments."

"I hope so, because someone will pay if I have to abort this test because of their failure. I hope we have only Blessed in engineering and not some Normal mucking up the works back there!"

"Blessed have manned the console, Sir. They WILL have it under control!" Boral nodded to him, giving them the time they needed – deep inside however, he was worried for his ship.

After a few moments, the vibration stopped and they were smoothly and quietly leaving Mars behind. The view screen showed the planet slowly moving away. After a few moments passed, Boral announced "Ok it is time to activate the Graviton – let's see if Mars will move us."

The helmsman once again flipped more controls to activate the Graviton and raised the power level to try to bring it up to the same level as the Pulsars. Boral heard the fusion reactors increase their workload as they began providing the electricity that would energize the large coils that surrounded the entire engine section. Once energized, these superconductive coils have the ability to turn the entire rear of the ship into a giant field coil that will then gather dark matter and eject it out the back of the craft. Ejecting the dark matter would then act as the repulsive force. The computers are calibrated to maintain the repulsive force away from the rear of the ship thus providing a push against the target s gravity field – in this case Mars. The Pulsar electromagnets are designed to push the craft enough to allow for the Graviton repulsion drive to kick in. Once the repulsion drive is functioning as planned they will kick in the coils that surround the command section and allow the computer to adjust the force so it is providing an attraction force against the gravity field of another body – in this case the asteroid Vesta.

The plan was that the ship would be propelled by the two forces at a rate of speed that will then take the stress off of the ion drives when engaged. With the stress removed, the ion drives would be free to run at a higher rate thus allowing for greater speed and fuel efficiency. It is hoped that in this test they will next be able to run without the ion drives and yet propel the craft at one-percent the speed of light. Any faster in this part of the Solar System would be dangerous. Once past the asteroid belt, they will slowly proceed to increase their speed. After they exit the Oort Cloud surrounding the system, then they would push the craft to faster speeds and eventually test the Subspace Crawler drive.

The lights dimmed as power was rerouted to the coils. The ship pounced forward, causing the bridge crew to gasp and look around waiting once again for the hull to break apart – but it never happened. Boral was slightly disgusted that his Blessed bridge crew would have any doubts that the ship would survive -- after all, the ship and its systems were designed by Blessed engineers. "I had no doubt that the invention they came up with would not only work, but work as impressively as it did. You should have more faith in your fellow Blessed!"

Jonathan Faraday:

He had been told to sit in the corner like a dunce. The Blessed engineers had decided that they were going to be the only people to touch the controls during the testing of the Pulsar drives and the Graviton system. Along with all of the other Normal engineers, he had decided to just sit and watch the show – they had nothing better to do. The Blessed told him specifically to sit in the corner, so be it.

He sat there and watched them running around in a panic. They had no clue about how to run the computer program that would energize the various fields and synchronize the pulsating magnets of the Pulsar drive. If they energized the wrong coil or segment of hull coiling, a few things could happen – from ejecting electromagnets to tearing the ship apart in a burst of explosive decompression. They were determined to take the credit for the design that they had no part in – and in the glory of the first test run.

Jonathan was content with this – he put his feet up on the console and adjusted the frame of his correction spectacles. He peered through the silver coated lenses of the glasses while using the built-in heads-up display to monitor the ambient temperature of the ship, the various flows of electricity, and while he was at it, set his glasses to also provide the heart rates of selected Blessed engineers racing around.

Kate Grayson walked up, pulled up a chair and sat next to him. "Think they will kill us?" she asked him in a whisper.

"Very possibly, very possibly…"

"Should we step in?"

"Well, you're the boss…but my opinion is we wait. We could kick on the recorders however. I could use a good laugh later should we survive this."

She smiled, reached over to one of the command consoles and activated the section monitors – this would be kept for posterity.

The Blessed engineers were madly flipping switches and checking readings. A large warning alert notified them that the helm was activating the Pulsar drive. Red lights began to illuminate across the entire control panel. Alpha Blessed Engineer Hilton Maxwell looked up at the pair with a worried look on his face.

"He's going to crack already isn't he?" Kate mused and Jonathan nodded.

They could hear the pulsing of the electromagnets in the rear of the craft as they started to vibrate. The clanking vibration was caused by the coils of the electromagnets which then forced the cores to pulse back and forth, which caused a magnetic pulse that started the initial propulsion. Once the Pulsar drive had been tested this would provide the initial thrust to the craft until the repulsion/attraction coils kicked in. It was also thought that the Pulsar drive engines could be used as primary thrust for much of the journey. But for now, there was a problem, the magnets did not sound right to Hilton -- he knew there was a timing problem.

Jonathan chuckled. "They have no idea how to synchronize the pulse magnets." Kate just shook her head in agreement without saying anything, but stared intently at the activity – she was a bit worried.

After a few minutes of flipping switches and trying various combinations of synchronizing the pulses Hilton put his hands on his head. "I just don't get it!" he shouted out. Finally, he looked over at the pair of engineers with a pleading look. Jonathan just pointed at himself and mouthed "Who me?" Hilton nodded with pleading eyes.

"No sorry, I am not smart enough to help, remember?" Jonathan said causing Hilton to give a pained look.

Kate stood up. "Well, I do not want to die – so I am going to help. Stay here if you want."

"No, no, I will help…" Begrudgingly he stood and ambled over to the control console and stepped in front of Hilton while giving him an annoyed look. "Alright Kate, Activating the L-14 synchronization program. In 30 seconds prepare to align the magnet pulses." Kate nodded and smiled.

Hilton received a message from the bridge to which he answered "We have everything under control, we will have the Pulsars synchronized in 30 seconds." He got a dirty look from Kate to which he returned a sheepish smile.

"Aligning the pulses now…" Kate announced as she adjusted the slider controls on the panel. The vibration immediately stopped and the clunking of the magnets turned into a loud but smooth whine.

Jonathan activated the magnifying function of his glasses to look at the superconductive temperature of the external coils from a display across the room – then checked the ships speed. "Ok, we are ready to fire up the repulsion system. Awaiting helm request..." After a few seconds, an annunciation chime sounded indicating ships speed as requested from the helm.

Kate entered commands into the computer. "Computer activation sequence initiated. Coils active in 10 seconds."

As the coils are energized, some sparks jumped from the hull to a few of the engineering consoles causing the Blessed engineers to jump – and the Normal engineers to laugh.

"Repulsion coils are active and engaged. Awaiting attraction request..." announced Jonathan.

After a few minutes the helm thrust request chime rang again, prompting Kate to order "Ok, let's kick in the attraction coils." Within a minute the fields in the front of the craft became energized and ready for attraction mobility at the order of the helm. A few minutes later the helm activated the attraction fields, pulling the ship faster out into space.

Kate raised her hand to Jonathan who slapped it in victory. Hilton walked back up to the console -- with a sneering face and head motion he indicated to both of them to step away from the console and return to their seats in the corner. They returned and sat down as Hilton announced on the command intercom "All systems functioning properly. We have done it!"

*   *   *

Jonathan only stayed in the Engine Room for a few minutes after the initial startup. The Blessed had not wanted him to do anything after startup – as a matter of fact -- they did not want any Normals around when Boral came down to congratulate them. He thought the best thing to do would be to retire to his quarters and work on his latest idea for an invention.

His quarters were in the connecting tube between the engine section and the command section, known as the habitat connector. Like all Normals, his quarters were on the lower decks of the connector – as far from Blessed comforts as possible. To get there he had to take a transport car across to the mid-point of the connector then take a lift tube down to the lower levels. He took out his computer gel and began to read a technical manual while he waited for a transport.

The car arrived and he was relieved to see that no one was on board. He stepped in, sat down and waited for departure. Right before the doors closed however, five large Blessed soldier ranks boarded the transport. They were shouting and laughing, and showing how obviously drunk they were. After a moment, the transport had begun its run -- the soldiers continued their laughing and pushing each other around. The car stopped again picking up another passenger then continued its way.

The group of rowdies finally turned and noticed him in the corner of the car. They walked over to him laughing and sneering at the much smaller and weaker engineer. He glanced up, and then returned his look to his computer gel.

"Well, look here...we have a little Normal. What-cha reading?" the large soldier ripped the gel out of his hand. "Aww, engine design characteristics. How sweet! You know there is no way you would even be able to touch the engines here, don't you Norm?" Jonathan did not say anything. "Hey Norm, I am talking to you!" He grabbed Jonathan by the collar lifting him in the air. Jonathan only weighed 110 pounds and did not cause a strain to the well-built Blessed soldier. He looked at the reflection in the small square reflective lenses of his glasses. "What are these?" He took the glasses off Jonathan's head and looked at them before tossing them across the car.

He now stared at Jonathan -- he noted the roundness of his face, his rounded cheeks, almost non-existent chin, his black curly hair and small brown eyes. "You know what I think? I think you are a geek that needs to be taught a lesson – that you cannot outdo a Blessed at anything...not even geeky engineering. Yes, you need to be taught that lesson – and I will be your teacher." He formed a fist and held it threateningly in front of his face.

Jonathan closed his eyes preparing for the beating when he heard 'You know what I think? I think you should quit being a bully and pick on someone that might be able to put up a fight and possibly kick your ass." Jonathan was immediately dropped to the floor. He opened his eyes to see the large man had turned around, no longer concerned with him. He instinctively backed himself into a corner. On the other side of the group of soldiers was a woman. She had reddish-blonde hair and matching eyebrows slightly darkened by makeup, plump lips pursed in a small smile, high cheekbones made-up to mostly cover, but still allowed for a tiny number of freckles to show through, and piercing blue eyes giving a look that would make a smart man retreat. Jonathan thought she was the most beautiful woman he ever set his eyes on. He was surprised to see she had Captain's insignias, but yet was Normal.

The brutish bald commander pointed a stumpy finger at her "Listen lady, I don't care if you ARE a Captain. You are not Blessed, and because of that you are not to interfere with us. I will put you down!" The other four soldiers grumbled in agreement while backing off just a little from their squad commander.

"Well, who am I to worry about rank?" she said calmly.

"Fine with me my queen..." She gave him a slightly confused look over his comment -- he attempted to take advantage of her confusion as he tried a sneak attack by throwing a wild punch to her face. She quickly shifted her weight, moving her body just a small bit, causing him to miss. As he spun around in his wild missing attack, she put a small open palm into his nose, shattering it. As his face flung up due to the force of the blow she applied a twisting punch into his solar plexus, then took his head and rammed it into one of the supporting posts of the transport car's handrails. He wobbled then fell to the floor – blood flowing from his nose down his face.

"Next..." she said as she motioned her fingers to the other four soldiers beckoning them to attack.

The four didn't attack however; instead they just stood petrified – not wanting to provoke the wrath of the Captain. Fortunately for them, the car was reaching the next station. As soon as the car came to a stop they grabbed their unconscious commander and ran out into the station not saying a word.

She watched them flee, then walked over and grabbed Jonathan's glasses and handed them to him. "Are you ok?" He nodded yes, but was still stunned – but he wasn't sure if it was due to the scene he just witnessed or her beauty. "I am Delta Starship Captain Jaime Bordeaux, what's your name?"

"Jonathan, Jonathan Faraday..." he put on his glasses and took in a good look at his savior. He confirmed her beauty in the back of his mind before he realized he had not said anything and she was giving him a questioning look thinking he was hurt. "Umm...thank you, thank you very much. I really don't know what

I would have done if you had not stepped in Delta Starship Captain."

She smiled at him and then put her hand on his small shoulder and squeezed it lightly – he thought she was going to crush his shoulder. "It was my pleasure Jonathan…although striking a Blessed like that might cause me to lose some rank" – she would end up losing two rank positions, from 1st Delta to 3rd. The car came to a stop as it reached the next station. "Oh, I need to get off here. Are you okay to make it to your stop?" He nodded and she smiled at him again. "Ok, I hope to see you again…umm, Engineer Faraday, is it?" she asked while looking at his engineering uniform.

"Yes, Delta Starship Captain!" He snapped to attention as his training kicked in – although this was one of the few times he wanted to show respect to a higher-up.

"Very well, take care…" she turned and gave a wave as she walked away.

"Wow, she has fists of steel and a heart of gold…" He let a large sigh escape his lips as he watched her walk away and exit the car.

The Ark of the Blessed

Starlight Flight Time: 43 days, 3 hours, 12 minutes

Boral Oldham:

He was sitting in his ready room with Kip Gurrigan, had his drink in hand and was reading a report. "She took out one of our most powerful soldiers. How did she do it Kip?"

The young Captain thought about it for a moment. A thought finally came to his mind and his face lit up. "Ah, she had to have caught him by surprise. There is no way a Normal could have done it otherwise. He must have had his mind on something else – perhaps her body? It is quite pleasant."

"Perhaps you are right – and that would explain why she has done so well in the arena too." He too was attracted to her and could understand being mentally incapacitated by her. He took another drink. "I always assumed that is why the Supreme Commander suggested her as our Normal female recruit…although the trouble she has caused now makes me wonder about his decision. I may have to contact him before we reach deep space."

Kip chuckled "I think we will be able to handle her from now on. We know her tactics – we know how to take her down – we will take her down. She will have to come to you if she wants anything else in life – status, command, a ship of her own?"

"I like the way you think. I guess that is why you are my Alpha Captain – my second in command, eh?"

Kip smiled. "I would suggest Sir that you monitor her movements and watch her training carefully. If they are planning something, we should know." Boral nodded in agreement.

Halley Cet:

She anxiously waited for everyone at the simulator. She had found the best of the Normals. She had looked for just the right amount of talent for the best bridge crew ever. She contacted each of them and invited them to practice with her. It took a lot of work to convince them to join her but she did it. Now, if only they would show up.

The simulator door finally opened. A short young girl with blond hair sheepishly peered into the room. She spotted Halley at the helm and gave her a small smile. She wore a blue casual uniform skirt, flat blue shoes, and matching casual blue blouse – no military decoration adorned her. Her blond hair was tied into pig tails which kept it off her lower head and neck.

"Lindy!" Halley shouted as she got up and ran to her and gave her a strong hug when she reached her. "I knew I could depend on you. Thanks for coming, I think this will be well worth it...someday."

The young woman blushed at Halley's boldness. "I was not sure. But I thought "What the hey, I am going to be spending most of this trip in a simulator anyway so why not spend it with friends?" So, here I am..." She looked around the empty simulator "So, where are the rest of them? You promised..."

"Don't worry, they will show I am sure." She was crossing her fingers and toes in her mind. "Take your spot for now and get things ready for when the rest show."

She nodded and walked over to the communications console, deactivated the holo-officer, and activated the console controls. She then removed a communication plug from the console and plugged it into a digital access port surgically implanted into the back of her neck. Through this device she would be able to monitor all communications throughout the simulated ship and still be able to listen to incoming transmissions from space and give verbal communication to the bridge staff. Her eyes lit up slightly as she began accessing all of the simulated communications.

The simulator door opened again and a tall thin man walked in. Like the others in the room, he did not have a bead, which indicated that he was a Normal like the rest of them. "So, did someone call for a Weapons Master?" His large toothy smile took a good portion of his lower face. He had green eyes, wavy brown hair parted on the left stiffly obeying some form of styling glue, a large protruding chin, large cheeks and medium sized nose with a small bump at the root also making it slightly wide at the same spot. He was dressed in a blue casual jumpsuit uniform – black belt around his waist, shooting star insignias on the top of the arms and two red epaulets on the shoulders with old style cannon medals indicating his skill in handling a ship's weapons systems.

Halley bounded to the young man and gave him a hug to which he gladly returned. "Ah Yuli, I am so glad you made it. We are awaiting the others – please take your station." He gave her a salute but then walked over to the opposite side of the simulator Bridge to the communication station.

"I am Yuli Capsain, and you my dear are?"

The blond looked up and offered a handshake "Lindy Light – Communications." He took her hand and gave it a light kiss – she immediately pulled it back slightly repulsed and returned her full attention to the communications console. He pouted slightly before walking across the bridge to the weapons console, deactivated the holo-officer at that station, sat down at the console, activated the controls, and put on the control gloves that allow him to fire the various weapons systems of the ship with small movements of his hand.

The simulator door had not even had a chance to close before an attractive Japanese woman appeared. "I hope I am not too late..." She was much shorter than Halley and had light brown hair parted in the middle that flowed out and down around the outline of her thin face before curling at the ends in the style of the popular Japanese bob hairdo. Almond shaped brown eyes and small nose and mouth. At only 17 years old, she was one of the youngest crew members on board the space ark. She wore her official black uniform – not a casual uniform like Halley or the others in the room – short skirt, medium black boots and black uniform tunic.

"Absolutely not Katsumi!" She guided her onto the Bridge "Everyone, this is Katsumi Ito – our Science Officer."

Katsumi politely bowed to everyone then walked over to the science station. Yuli eyed her proper manner and form before boldly asking "Japanese? I did not think the Blessed would allow any of your countrymen on board this ship?"

She did not take her eyes off the console while she activated the controls. "Some would say the same thing about letting a Russian on board. I might ask you the same question..."

"Touché!" He had always wondered the same thing himself – but would never admit it.

A familiar voice to Halley now filled the room "Looks like we are almost fully staffed Halley. Good job!" She turned to find Jaime standing at the simulator entrance. "No engineering officer?"

"I am still working on that..."

Jonathan Faraday:

He was running down the corridor on his way to an emergency repair duty. His communicator rang. "Damn, not again..." he looked at the device and rolled his eyes before answering. "Halley, I could get there a whole lot faster if you would quit calling! I am running as fast I can."

Halley had a look of real panic on her face "Jonathan, if you don't get here we are going to miss our training time. I have a very important group of people here and we need this simulator fixed now."

"Then why not put in a General Mechanical Emergency Case? Form 401. They could have someone down there much faster than it would take me to run there."

"No, you are the only one I trust to fix the console properly...I think you know why."

His eyes opened wide upon hearing that "I thought we agreed never to speak of things like that?" Halley smiled and nodded giving him a slight bit of relief in the panicked flush he suddenly felt flow over him. He knew she was going to hold that little bit of knowledge over his head forever.

He turned the corner and stopped for a second to catch his breath. "I'm almost there..." he said shutting off his communicator. A moment later he continued his jog, finally reaching the simulator lounge, then slowed to a stroll while he located the simulator that needed to be fixed. He found the proper portal, entered his access code, the door slid open. Upon entering however, he was surprised to find an entire crew and not any holo-officers – except the engineer. He realized he had been duped. "Ok Cet, what the hell is going on here? I told you I don't work bridge duty..."

"But I heard you were the best Mister Faraday..."

That voice, coming from the other side of the command chair – he recognized it. He looked at the command chair and saw

114

the same pixie cut, strawberry blond hair of his savior. She was dressed in a black vinyl uniform blouse and slacks that were tucked into matching boots. Her shoulders were adorned with the shooting stars of the ship's logo, the Captain's sun medals and the delta symbols of her rank. She immediately spun around and gave him that look with her deep blue eyes – that small smile on her face. He found his heart instantly melting at the sight of his savior Captain.

"Couldn't you give us just a little bit of your time? You might enjoy a little "bridge-time" – this could be a good group. Perhaps the best this ship's got. So, can I talk you into taking the engineering station? At least once – if you hate it, you never have to again...I promise."

"Sure!" he snapped out without even thinking. As he walked to the station he muttered "...what the hell am I thinking?" Lindy heard him and chuckled softly.

Jaime Bordeaux:

Halley stood and went around the room. Jaime made note of her dark blue slacks, flat shoes and gray tunic – she would have to improve her dress later she thought. "Captain, let me introduce you to your simulator staff. On Weapons, we have Yuli Capsain, your Science Officer is Katsumi Ito, Communications is Lindy Light, you know your Engineer Jonathan Faraday and I don't have to introduce myself."

She had a full bridge crew. She trusted that Halley picked the best of the Normals that she could find. Now she had to get them to function as a single unit. If they did know their stuff, this would not be a challenge – however, if even one of them had problems this would be a failure. No -- she had a good feeling about all of them.

She stood up from the command chair, walked around the bridge and gave each of them a handshake. "I am Delta Starship Captain Jaime Bordeaux -- it is a real pleasure having you as my crew for this simulator session. Let's see if we can kick some simulated bottom now shall we?" They all gave a cheer of acknowledgement and an official salute. *"Yes, this could work..."*

The door slid open to the simulator surprising even Jaime as the security locks should be up -- she secured them herself after the entire crew had arrived. To her surprise Max Sollix walked in. He looked around the room then gave a slight look of surprise.

"Umm, I appear to have entered the wrong simulator. I was told there was a medical emergency, but this appears to be the wrong room. My apologies Captain."

Jaime smiled at the older doctor "It is good to know that you are on the job...that is, in the event we do have an accident. I would trust no other to come to our aid."

He nodded, smiled and walked out of the simulator. Jaime got up and rechecked the security seal – it was in place. She pondered why it let him in, before passing it off as a misfire of the system – or perhaps he could override with a medical code. Returning to her seat, she placed her palm on the arm sensor of the command chair. The small plate wiggled out of her palm and slapped into the command slot on the left arm of the chair. This connected to the simulated ship's systems and gave her complete command of those systems. The ship simulation beeped and lights activated indicating that she now had full control of the bridge. "Ok, let's see what the computer can dish up for us..." she said as she punched in commands for the computer to select and activate a simulation.

The controls all released for the bridge crew, their respective consoles automatically moved to the center of the room around the main central holo-projector and the star screens placed all around the perimeter of the bridge became activated. Jaime's holographic console instructed her to follow a pre-defined course – she transferred the course to Halley's station. The helmsman followed the programmed course exactly.

Alerts came on at Katsumi's station. She gazed at the readouts and the sensor replies. "Delta Starship Captain, we have an incoming force approaching. I am counting three capital ships and about ten support vessels."

"Race?"

She studied the sensor readouts again "Oxtail..."

"What? Are you kidding? What Blessed wrote this scenario?" The crew gave a slight chuckle. "Very well, let's not take any chances. Engineer, activate the magnetic shielding. Weapons, open the ports, prime but do not fully activate the beams, load the rail launchers and have the star fighters on-line ready to go. Helm, be ready to kick up the Pulsars if we need a burst of speed and have the ion drives on standby just in case. Communications, see if you can pick up any Oxtail...chatter...or whatever they do and try to translate. Be ready all -- this does not feel right. Katsumi, give me a status of what weapons they have. What can you tell about their armaments?"

She looked deeply into the returns from the SCADAR scans "The front end of those ships are loaded with ports and I must assume those are some form of weapons ports. There is radiation emitting from every one of those open ports. I would venture to say that they are all active and ready to fire. I am picking up fewer emissions amidships and none in the back end."

"Ox, well that gives us something to work with. Communications, greet them." Lindy sent standard common greeting messages in every language in the computer database at multiple frequencies per second. She looked up and shook her head telling Jaime she was not receiving any response.

"Delta Starship Captain" Katsumi yelled out "we have targeting beams on us!"

"Kick up the Pulsars! Helm, take us away from the main force. Let's hope they follow us with their capitol ships – do not use the ion drives...yet." Halley followed her instructions quickly and efficiently while thinking how surprised she was at how cool in battle this Captain was – she wondered if Jaime was thinking it was only a simulation and was not worried? No, she knew that any loss would be a strike against her. She was just that good.

The three ships followed their ship while letting their beamed weapons fly – however they were much too far away to do any damage if by some chance they did hit against the energized shielded armor plating of the simulated space ark.

Jaime looked at the ships following them in the reverse view on her command display. "Ok, prepare all Star Fighters for launch on my command. Yuri, fire up the cutters, P-accelerators and Proton cannons – lock and load the rail guns. Helm, start to do a slow turn starboard. Let's hope they follow us..." As she predicted, the three ships started a slow turn in the same direction forming a small triangle pattern with one ship starboard and one in the lead on the port side and the third ship following directly behind the lead. "Good...on my mark, kick in the ion drive, turn starboard sharply and put us behind them. If I have guessed correctly, they will not be ready for us..." She spoke softly as if they were listening. Beams from the enemy ships continued firing at them. She waited another few seconds before ordering "Ok...kick it!"

Halley pushed the control stick on the ion drive nearly doubling the speed of the craft, then pushed on the steering control. As predicted the maneuver put them behind the three large ships. They were now directly at the rear end of the trailing ship on the port side – the blue glow of the large engines lit up the image on the view screen.

"Put us between those two ships Helm. Fire all weapons, now!" A flurry of red laser beams, multi-colored bolts, arcs of plasma, and radioactive shells shot across the screen as the ship fired all weapons into the rear of the first two ships. As she predicted, they were unprepared for this attack maneuver and did not have the defenses to fight back against a rear assault. "Keep moving up, keep firing everything we have. Do not stop 'till we see those three ships start to break apart."

Large burning holes started to form in the sides of the first two ships – as they moved, the pummeling of the weapons turned the thick hulls of the enemy ships into Swiss cheese. "Ok, launch our fighters. Helm, move us up to the lead ship now. Keep the weapons firing – time to take down this one's shields and finish this." A swarm of fighters was indicated on the various view screens that surrounded the bridge. Each one attacking the burning ships left behind by the simulated Starlight. The lead ship was already starting to show the results of the barrage – its engine section was already full of holes and burning, its engines were starting to sputter. "Ok Halley, take us to the port side of this one and finish it off."

A few more minutes of weapons fire and the engines of the lead ship were now totally down. The ship was now beginning to pound the port side of the Oxtail ship. For a brief moment, the Oxtail were able to fire off a few shots from the side ports and the forward guns – another minute of attacks from Jaime and her crew however stopped any random firing from enemy weapons.

"Order the fighters to attack the support ships once they are done with those two back there. Let's finish this bunch off." Lindy acknowledged her order. Within moments, the fighters had moved off the two burning capitol ships and were swiftly taking out the ten ships that had now started to flee. They could not get away in time and within minutes had joined the larger ships in becoming burning heaps of space rubble.

Katsumi yelled out "Delta Starship Captain, I am picking up a build-up of some type of energy in this ship. I suggest we move away…" Jaime nodded to Halley who activated all drives and at full speed moved the ship away from the burning hulk. A minute later, the ship exploded into a massive fireball. Sparks shot out of a few of the bridge consoles and the engines started to waver for a moment as the radiation affected their ion and magnetic outputs. Jonathan quickly made adjustments to the systems, which allowed the engines to compensate for the additional radiation.

Lindy called out "Delta Starship Captain, we are getting surrender messages from the remaining enemy ships. They are asking for mercy."

"So, they do speak eh? Very well, break off the fighters and recall. Keep the weapons charged Yuri. Halley, turn us around -- Jonathan, prepare magnetic attractor beams and be ready to pick up any survival pods." They all looked at each other in surprise – no Blessed Captain would break off an attack and pick up survivors. Jaime spoke up at their confusion "We are not like the Blessed – we will pick up survivors and see if we can make peace. They may have a reason we don't know or understand for their attack. Maybe we can take this unpleasant situation and make something good from it."

A half hour passed as they picked up survival pods and collected their Star Fighters. Finally, the situation appeared to be in control The screens went blank, the lights came on and the controls shut down. A message appeared on the center holo-display:

"Simulator Mission 189:
Difficulty – 94
Enemy ships destroyed – 8 out of 10
Enemy ships disabled – 2 out of 10
Ship damage: 1
Mission Score: 92
Rank: Normal 1st, Blessed 1st, Overall: 6th"

"Sixth? What the hell?" Halley questioned.

"Don't be surprised – we did not kill all of them" Jaime acknowledged.

Yuri spoke up "Captain, if I may suggest – if they see we keep giving mercy they will never let us on the bridge."

Jaime nodded in agreement to the Weapons Master "I know Yuri, I forgot that this was only a simulation – next time we will get first place and will wipe out all ships and survivors. There will be no reason for the Star Force Commander to keep us off the bridge – that is once I make Beta level one. But for now, enjoy your victory – great job!"

They all gave her a cheer and then began to congratulate themselves on a job well done. She dismissed them and one by one they disembarked from the simulator. Jonathan was still in the simulator after the rest of the group left. Jaime looked at the young man with questioning eyes. "Something on your mind?"

"Yes, Delta Starship Captain. I just thought you should know that I filtered out most of the people in this simulator run as I do not think we want the Blessed knowing that we had a full Bridge Crew." Jaime gave him a confused look. "They cannot know that a full crew is practicing together – they would never let us make it to the bridge otherwise. I will allow for each one of us to show up in each simulation. They will know how good we are, just not as a group. Please trust me on this Delta Starship Captain. I have been told it is for the best."

"Told by whom?"

"I can't tell you now. But you will discover it in time. I now know however, that you will need me and because of that, I offer myself to you as your Engineer."

"Deal!" she shouted out and offered him her hand. He lightly took it and she heartily shook it – almost crushing it. He breathed out as she let go – he grabbed, then rubbed his now sore hand. "I look forward to us working together Mr. Faraday" she said as she reached over and gave him a hug before leaving the simulator. He just stood there, blushed, and then gave a long sigh.

Starlight Flight Time: 44 days, 7 hours, 22 minutes

Boral Oldham:

Boral was in the command chair watching as they made their incoming approach to Vesta. He ordered Kip to take the engineering console and Bellevue the science station as he wanted his best men on the job. Today, they would test the full ability of the Graviton drive as they would slingshot themselves around hundreds of asteroids in the belt and finally shoot themselves toward Jupiter. If all went well, they would be pushing three percent of the speed of light as they left the belt. Jupiter would only be hours away.

He was personally going to pick the route – selecting various asteroids to use as sling points. He selected asteroids that he felt would give them the straightest line and the best velocity through the enormous belt and on to Jupiter. Using this new system, he felt, would help save reserves of nuclear fusion fuel that although was currently in plentiful supply, could become a rare necessity if the voyage to find resourceful planets became long as they ventured forth.

Bellevue looked over Boral's flight plan with a slightly confused look on his face. "Sir, I am a bit concerned with using M-543 as a reflection point. It is small enough that it may not be able to support our reflecting off it."

Boral gave the science officer an annoyed look "I think I have determined the best route to take…" he muttered. Bellevue said no more, only nodded.

The large crater-covered surface of Vesta consumed almost the entire image of the front view screen – and every second the image got larger and larger.

"Approaching our first reflection point Sir!" announced the helmsman.

Boral studied the holographic command display. "Very well, activate the shield plating just in case we hit some asteroid fragments and prepare for first reflection on my mark." He waited for the command display to indicate the ideal point. "Begin reflection now."

The helmsman began steering around the large asteroid as Kip began to shift the electrical pulses in the hull of the ship thus causing the polarity to also shift. This caused the ship to go from attraction to repulsion against the surface of Vesta. They could feel the jerking of the ship as it started to bounce off the gravitational field of the space body. Boral pulled a muscle in his neck as he was not expecting the initial bouncing.

"Now shifting to repulsion from Vesta..." announced Kip.

"Perhaps next time you could announce that sooner...and shift smoother!" Boral barked as he rubbed his now stiffened neck. Kip continued to stare at his console, refusing to look at his Commander for fear of any further verbal retribution.

The ship's speed had dramatically increased with the first slingshot maneuver. They were rapidly approaching the next target, a smaller unnamed ragged chunk of rock – smaller than Vesta but still at least a hundred miles across. The crew effortlessly shifted the gravity factors and repulsed onward. They headed to the next target – the smallest asteroid in their path, M-543. This was mostly a rock in terms of the asteroid belt – barely ten miles across and constantly spinning.

"Approaching our next reflection point sir – M-543" announced Bellevue.

"Very well...Helmsman, start our reflection navigation. Kip, begin the gravity shifting."

The crew reacted as expected. The helm began making a slight course adjustment as Kip began to shift the electrical impulses in the ship's coils causing the change in polarities. Suddenly the entire ship jerked as if being thrown across space. One crewman who was working on a control panel was thrown across the bridge and the rest of the bridge staff was hard pressed to reach their control panels as the sudden shift of velocity either pushed them over or far away from their controls.

"What the hell is going on?" Boral shouted out. There was shouting and screaming as the crew went through a moment of panic. "Calm the hell down and report!" he shouted out again, now using his voice enhancer.

Finally, Kip gave a status "Sir, when we repulsed against M-543 it broke away from its position. I suspect we actually weighed more than the rock. It just flew out of the belt! I am using the Pulsars and ion drives to give helm the ability to adjust."

Within a few moments, the ship regained its control – albeit, with some loss of reflected velocity. Boral examined his command readouts "Damn, we lost speed. How did you let that happen Kip?" The First Captain just shrugged his shoulders. "Can we get some speed by using another asteroid? I want to get us to Jupiter…"

Bellevue looked at his astrometric console. "Star Force Commander, I believe we can reflect off of a few more asteroids to regain speed and continue the path through the belt layers. We can then use Ceres as a final reflection point without deviating too much off of our current flight path. I am computing the course now…" He typed furiously on his console before announcing "Yes, we can do it. Feeding the coordinates into your console for your approval."

Boral looked at the calculations that the computer provided. He had no idea what the display was showing him. He just nodded and said "Do it…"

The helm was fed the new route and the helmsman followed the path provided by the computer. It took three days – a day longer than expected -- to bounce from one asteroid to another. Finally, an even larger planetoid was showing on the front view screen -- Ceres. As with Vesta, it was getting bigger by the second. This fly-by went exactly as planned – by the time they had made this final slingshot maneuver, the ship was running at almost three percent the speed of light without using their ion drives. In just a little over a day they would be starting their slingshot of Jupiter and trying to achieve an even faster speed by using a slight thrust of the ion drives.

Boral was pleased with the outcome of his test. He had a thought about that smaller asteroid – he turned to Bellevue "So, what happened with M-543?"

He studied his SCADAR then looked up. "Looks like we threw it out of the belt's orbit by trying to slingshot off of it. We sent it…somewhere…" Boral gave him a confused look. "It headed further into the Solar System…at this time I cannot be sure where, however. It could turn into a comet, or fall into the sun."

"Well, if that is all that could happen, then no big deal. There will be no more talk of that." Boral said smugly.

Starlight Flight Time: 46 days, 10 hours, 11 minutes

Jaime Bordeaux:

The reveille tone sounded once again waking her from her sound sleep. She got up, turned on the view screen – the gas giant Jupiter was now behind them as they made their slingshot of the massive planet. The colorful rings of the planet's atmosphere swirled as it circled the gas giant. Jupiter's big red eye swirled around the bottom half of the planet – Jaime stared at the swirling storm in total fascination as the planet quickly got smaller and smaller on the screen. The ship was now travelling at fifteen percent of the speed of light. She was sure the ship could probably move even faster, they just needed the guts to actually push it. In any case, they would be heading totally out of the Solar System quite soon – but not soon enough for her. Their path would now take them past the planet Neptune and then another slingshot providing a little lower energy speed to leave the system.

She set the cleansing bay, stepped in and took a relaxing laser shower and massage session. After she got out she applied her normal medium light application of concealing makeup, her tan eye make-up and her normal uniform suit. As every morning, she checked her uniform to make sure all was proper, and then activated her communication device.

The duty officer – a Blessed – answered and gave her the assignment for the day. Today's assignment, Simulator – no surprise, just like every other day. She then expected her normal assignment of babysitting the laundry, janitorial or culinary staff. Instead however, she was assigned a crew to perform cleaning duty in "The Pens". She had no idea what that was, or even where it was in the ship, but her curiosity was peaked somewhat and she was pleasantly surprised by having been given a different assignment.

She followed her normal routine – she met her unofficial bridge crew and ran through a simulation. This simulation involved several alien attack spacecraft while they escorted a flotilla of refugee carriers back to the Solar System. The crew carried out Jaime's orders expertly and the outcome was as perfect as any crew could accomplish – but still not enough to beat out the Blessed scores. Jaime had a feeling that no matter

125

how well they did they would never achieve that accolade – and maybe that was a good thing. As always, Jonathan selected only a couple of the bridge crew to show on the scoring and attendance records. Jaime was amazed with how adept his talent was for computer hacking and wondered what else he had already found or could discover in the ship's computers.

After the simulation session, she met Halley for a coffee and discussed the day's simulation activities with her. She found herself to be totally comfortable with her, and she found she really enjoyed the female companionship of this young woman.

She now headed to her next duty of the day – supervision of the cleaning crew in "The Pens". She consulted her command computer for the directions to The Pens. The computer created customized lighting that would change as she approached and would guide her to her destination. She got the strangest feeling as she followed the computer aided path that she was being followed. Each way she turned she felt someone taking the same path. Finally, she rounded a corner and stopped to wait in ambush. The figure rounded the corner as she anticipated and she grabbed the person tailing her.

To her surprise it was Jonathan. She gave him a confused look "What the hell are you doing following me?"

He looked at her with eyes peering above the small golden colored lenses of his spectacles, put a finger to his lips to silence her and then handed her something. She suddenly held in her hand a small wadded up object. She looked at the small object then unfolded it – it had writing on it:

"*Do not say anything -- meet at deck 43 area 177, 1744 hours. Please return and recycle*"

She looked confused at the message then looked at him. He smiled, then held out his hand. She looked at him again with even more confusion and he pushed his open hand to her again. She reread the message. "Ah!" she said quietly and handed it back to him before asking "What is that?"

He smiled and said "It's called paper. Enjoy "The Pens" – you will find them interesting..." he said as he turned and ran off.

Confused, Jaime shrugged her shoulders and continued her journey down to one of the lowest levels of the ship. Here a massive steel door separated her from her duty. The computer console verified she was in the correct spot. She touched the door control with her command palm pad and the door slid slowly open. The odor that accosted her nose was the most horrid thing she had ever smelled. She was not sure what the smell was, but it was awful. Still standing outside the door she heard strange sounds – noises from non-human creatures. Slightly disturbed, she slowly and cautiously entered the large area with her command weapon raised in a defensive posture. The door slid closed behind her with a loud clang – giving her a slight jump.

There were five men in the giant room ahead of her – all Normals. She relaxed her tense posture and walked to the group of men. They were her crew for this assignment. They were all in work jumpsuits and covered with filth. Upon seeing her, they all snapped to attention and saluted. There was one of the crew marked with leadership ribbons, she returned their salute then looked at the large man. "Mind telling me where I am?"

"Welcome to The Pens, Delta Starship Captain!" he snapped in reply. "This is where they have stored all of the animals that will be used not only as food for the Blessed but also as stock for colonization."

"Really, interesting…" she said as she walked up to one of the enclosures holding a large brown animal. It stood on four legs and did nothing but look at her, drool dripping from its mouth. She scanned the animal with the image collector of her command computer, but the computer did not return identification on the creature. She turned to the men and pointed her thumb at the beast "What is that?"

"Those creatures are called Cattle. They provide real meat and dairy products."

"Real meat and dairy…you don't say?" The man nodded. A memory came to her – one of when she was only five years old and the world was still a beautiful place. She remembered her parents taking her out into the fields of France, where cattle like these roamed and browsed. She remembered how excited she was to see these large creatures.

She reached out and was surprised that the brown beast did not move or give any reaction to her approaching hand. She petted it on the snout – it looked at her with dark thoughtless eyes. She felt the warmth of the creature and the softness of its short fur on its leather hide. She felt sadness in her heart as she petted the cow – she knew someday it would become some Blessed's dinner. She wished she could hide the thing away and keep it safe.

The young man continued "Over in those pens you will find animals called Horses, and then there are cages with animals called Chickens. The Supreme Commander had the wisdom to store these animals underground during the bombing. He granted a share of them to this mission."

"You don't say…" She looked around a few more moments and got a feel for the other animals in the pens before returning to her task. "Well, I think we are supposed to clean this place. Let's get to it!" The men snapped to attention, saluted again and began the work of scooping dung from the various pens, loading up carts and finally depositing the dung in disposal chutes to be shot into space. After they removed all the dung, the pens were cleaned with lasers, and sprayed with disinfectant.

While she supervised the cleaning, she was startled by the sound of screaming – one of her team was hurt. She and the rest of the cleaning crew ran to his aid. He was sitting on the floor, shovel in hand, beating the floor with the implement. He had his other hand wrapped around his leg – blood was oozing from two holes in his skin and dripping down the material of his pants. Jaime looked at the crewman confused, he simply pointed to the corner of the pen he was cleaning with his shovel. In that corner was a small beast with rounded ears, long pointed nose, fat body, and long thin tail. It also had a drooling mouth with a formidable set of sharp fangs. She put the fangs together with the injury to his leg and saw the connection.

She continued to stare at the strange creature until the crew chief answered her unasked question. "Damn space rat."

"Space Rat?"

"Yes, damn creatures somehow got themselves onto a rocket and lived on the starbase. Once this ship was completed they somehow got onto the ship. We have never been able to eradicate them. Don't get too close Delta Starship Captain. They have a nasty bite and the venom can be deadly!"

"Well, we need to get this man away and to medical treatment." She held up her arm and carefully aimed her command weapon at the beast. She fired and the creature

instantly disintegrated. After the blast she looked at her weapon – could she have actually fired a blast that powerful?

The crew chief whistled in amazement "Wow, I have never seen a Normal able to wield a command weapon in such a manner! As a matter of fact, I don't think I have ever seen a Blessed fire a beam as strong as that!"

"How many Normals have you seen with one of these?"

"One…" he gave a smirking smile then ran over to help his comrade up. With Jaime's permission, he escorted the man to the medical facility.

The rest of the crew completed the duties of the entire team. She inspected the area and nodded in acknowledgement of their hard work. "Good work, you are dismissed. Go get cleaned up!"

The men snapped to attention, saluted and quickly exited the large storage area. It still smelled, but it was much better than when she first arrived. Satisfied with their work, she too headed to the door and opened the large steel barrier. She turned around before leaving and took a good look at the animals and shook her head in amazement before closing the large hatch door.

She barely had time to return to her quarters and clean up before it was time for her to head to the meeting as specified in the message Jonathan provided. The meeting was to take place at one of the lower levels of the engine section of the ship. She arrived a few minutes before the designated time. This area was dark, as there was barely any artificial lighting in this section. The air was damp from the cooling coils that maintained the temperature of the massive engines located just a few levels above.

"Hello Delta Starship Captain…" said a man's voice in the shadows. She could not recognize the voice as it was being electronically modified.

"Who are you? Show yourself…" she demanded. She pointed her command weapon in the direction that she thought was the origin point of the voice.

"I think for now I will stay out of sight. However, trying to use your weapon down here would not be wise. Please, just listen for now."

Jaime realized the voice was correct – a shot of her electrical stunner in this area would probably cause a larger electrical discharge. This would more than likely kill her instead of incapacitating her target. She lowered her arm "Fine, so what is it you want?"

"First, I think you should know you are on this ship for a purpose that eventually will become evident to you. For now however, you will be told in a few days that there will be another game of Command Tri-Polyhedrons. They will wait until the last minute to try to throw you off of your training schedule. Be ready."

Jaime wondered why this person was telling her this "Why would you want to help me? None of the Blessed want me to progress any further and will probably kill me to stop me."

"That is probably true..." replied the man "however, we think you will be able to succeed – but you must move up with care."

"What are you talking about? As long as I can avoid their cheating, I know I could even take out Kip."

"You must not do that! At least not yet..."

"Wait I have heard that before. Why not yet?"

"Listen..." he paused to think about what he was about to say before continuing "the top Captain will get one of two things – either become the first officer of the Star Force Commander, or will be given a ship of their own. There currently is no way to build a starship and I don't think you want to become the Commander's First do you?"

Jaime nodded "No...hell no..."

"I didn't think so. So, for now do not attempt to take the top Captain position. I would suggest you make it to Beta rank one...then stop."

"Why only Beta rank one?" she asked.

"Because then you can pick a bridge crew and actually command this ship. The Supreme Commander's own wishes are that the top Beta be given the chance to command Starlight. He felt it would give them a reason to fight for higher command – thus promoting better Tri-Polyhedron events, which would make him more credits...like credits matter at all out here anymore. But you don't want to go any higher up the rankings, not yet – trust me on that."

She thought about what he said for a moment. "Ok, very well, I agree. Only Beta level one for now. You have my word on that Jonathan."

The voice laughed. "No, he is only the messenger! However, keep him around as he is very handy – much more than he is letting on. He will be an asset to you – one you can depend on. I think we have talked enough for now – until next time Captain."

She was surprised by his deliberate lack of official protocol when addressing her. She listened for a moment to try to hear his footsteps but he was too quiet – she could not hear anything of his departure. He was definitely going to be a mystery for her to solve.

Jonathan Faraday:

After he made his delivery he received an encrypted message on his hand-held computer. He was still on one of the lower decks. He found a place he knew was unguarded and unmonitored – a dark hallway just off of level Yellow 7. He ducked down the dark hall and activated the device, entered his personal code and then the special encryption key that would unlock the message.

"If you have delivered the message, report to engineering section 33. There is a package that will need to be delivered as we pass Proteus."

Jonathan destroyed any trace of the message from his device and hurried to the section as instructed. He found Kate Grayson there at the engineering controls. She turned and spotted him as he entered – a small smile came to her face as she realized why he was there.

"So, are you here for..." he nodded in acknowledgement "Good, then help me with the launch sequence – over there." She pointed to a control panel.

He looked at her, slightly confused "How long have you..."

He did not finish his question before she quietly said "Long enough. We are approaching Neptune. Prepare the probe."

131

He flipped switches and activated a view screen showing a small device with an ion engine attached. The device had a small payload area surrounded by a protective titanium alloy shield. "Probe is ready."

"We will be passing Proteus in one minute – launch at fifteen seconds on my mark...Launch."

Jonathan activated the sequence and the probe was quickly and quietly launched from a small hidden tube in the bottom back end of the engine section. The probe was small enough to not attract SCADAR or visual notice by anyone on the bridge as it sneaked off on its voyage. The ion engine kicked in and launched the probe to the moon of Neptune, Proteus. Quickly, it flew to the moon – then using the braking maneuvers of its engines, it efficiently performed a soft landing on the surface. Once safely on the moon's surface, the protective shell opened and a large antenna array was automatically erected and activated.

Kate received a signal from the probe on her console. "It has landed and activated. We now have our own private link to Earth!"

Starlight Flight Time: 65 days, 15 hours, 1 minute

Jaime Bordeaux:

She had been expecting this for a few days now. Command Tri-Polyhedrons was about to start in two hours. They thought that not telling her would cause her to not practice, to be off her game. They were wrong however, as she was even more prepared for this game than ever. Thanks to her advance warning, she had trained even harder and longer during her off-time. Jeremy had run her through every combination of polyhedron shape, gravity shift and robotic obstacle. She was readier than they could imagine.

As the ship made its final sling shot pass of the frozen planet Pluto and was now leaving the Solar System they were going to have one more game. She was going to have one more shot to move up in rank. She had no intention of losing. She wondered what they would attempt in trying to stop her this time. She also wondered why her mysterious informant also advised her not to try for the top spot – Rank 1 Alpha Starship Captain. She sat in the Captain's locker room pondering who and why was this person helping her. She heard the rowdy voices of the Blessed Captains behind her – they were making disparaging commentary about her chances. She chuckled to herself, knowing that many of them would be eating those words very soon.

"Delta Starship Captain, I wish you the best of luck" snapped her out of her thoughts. She turned to see who was addressing her as it surprised her to hear someone that actually sounded sincere. It was Delta Starship Captain Allen James, he had a small friendly smile on his face and an extended hand pointed toward her.

She stood and took his hand "Thank you very much Delta Starship Captain. I hope to make it up a few levels tonight – I hope you will advance some."

"I hope so Delta…" he glanced down and noticed that she was not dressed yet. He slightly gulped at the sight of her muscular freckled body. He considered her eyes -- she had no thought of modesty or shame. He regained his composure

"...Starship Captain. Perhaps we can celebrate our victories afterwards?"

"That would be nice, that is if we survive this and don't both end up in the Infirmary. I will look for you afterwards – but I had better get ready now." He shook his head yes without moving his eyes from her face, smiled and stiffly turned and walked away. She turned back around, but moved her head just enough to see him slightly turn and look at her again, thinking she might not catch him. She smiled slightly and laughed to herself.

She put on a tight navy blue stretch top, matching tight fitting shorts and finally half-height, flat soled, black acrylic boots. She had let her hair finally start to grow and it was now dangling over the base of her neck – she tied it into a tight ponytail which caused it to dangle slightly down the middle of her neck. She went to the mirror and checked her make up, then began her stretching routine.

More heckles and cat calls started assaulting her ears from behind as a group of Blessed Captains increased their attempted intimidation of her. She ignored them and began to stretch her long legs – putting the left one out in front of her and bending it while letting the right leg drift back. She allowed her arms to flow up above her head, stretching her shoulders and neck, then slowly let them fall back down to her sides.

"I suppose you think all that fancy dancing is going to help? You will be lucky to not get knocked down to tenth level Delta tonight!" It was Jarred Maltz again – he had all eight Delta Starship Captains and two Betas behind him backing him up. She continued her stretching, ignoring him. "Hey, look at me when I speak to you!" He reached for her hair to pull her around, but instead she spun around in her stretching position, grabbed his finger and bent it back fracturing it. He screamed as he felt the bone start to snap.

She stopped just before it totally broke and eased the pressure as she told him "I don't want you to miss any of the fun. Besides, you will have the polyhedron before me – good luck..." She turned and returned to her stretching while he ran off to get his finger mended before the match.

Ten minutes later, the chime sounded that indicated it was time for the game to start. She stood, once again checked her appearance in a nearby mirror and moved into position at the head of the Delta Starship Captains. She would lead the Deltas out into the arena after the Alphas and Betas.

As in previous matches, as soon as she entered the crowd began booing, shouting insults and throwing objects against the dome in vain attempts to hurt her with flying debris. She smiled and waved as if they did not even exist. She ran up the ramp and took her spot at the top of the Delta defense ramp. This would be her spot until she had taken out every one of the Deltas that could make it up to her – then it would be her turn. She looked up at the road ahead – a slight flat spot at the landing of the Delta ramp, then a switchback turn leading to the Beta defense ramp. A dark-haired Blessed Beta stood at the first spot rubbing his fists as he stared at her. He was shorter than she (as were most Blessed), had a short squatty nose, small sunken dark eyes, and a rounded chin. She recognized him – he quite often was on duty station. He was one of the Betas that gave her the lousy shit work that she has had to endure since this voyage began. He always enjoyed giving her those duties – now she would enjoy giving him some repayment for his kindness.

The announcer went through the rules of the game, the Alliance anthem was played again – only the Blessed stood and sang to it as always, and finally the warning horn sounded. Jaime put on her game-face, looked down the ramp, and waited. The ball was shot out into the arena -- the first to get a chance was Allen. He fought bravely – moving up to rank six before being ganged up on and beaten senseless with metallic bars hidden in the uniform sleeves of the remaining Blessed Deltas. She was happy he advanced a few spots – she thought he just needed more training. Perhaps she would invite him to join her and Jeremy later.

A few more of the Deltas tried to get past each other but failed. Jaime did nothing to help any of the defenders as she knew they would be her enemies in just a few moments. She had no desire to help any Blessed defend or advance.

The ball was launched again. Now it was Bellevue's turn and he grabbed the polyhedron and started up the ramp. He had a good head of steam as he took down the remaining four Captains knocking them off the ramp and out of the game. He came up to Jared who began swinging wildly at him. He managed to avoid every shot and surprised both Jared and Jaime who watched from above. He lashed out with a low leg sweep, followed up by a high roundhouse that caused Jared to wobble. Bellevue took the opportunity to finish up with an elbow to the face then a side kick – sending him flying off of the ramp and onto the hard floor below. He shouted in victory and held the polyhedron up in the air. The crowd went wild at this underdog's victory over the second position Delta.

He now looked at Jaime – breathing heavily and smiling like a wild man. Foamy drool dripped down from the corner of his mouth like a rabid dog. He analyzed his situation and began planning his attack. Jaime stiffened up preparing for his assault. It only took a few seconds after he caught his breath to charge her. The gravity shifted for him to lighter than Earth normal – he took advantage and jumped over her landing on the flat at the top of the Delta ramp.

"Now, just one good shot..." as he went down to land a forward kick into the back of her knees. He thought if he could get that one shot in, she would collapse giving him the advantage to take her down. He did not anticipate that she would use the lighter gravity as she jumped into the air, swung around and landed on his leg now extended in the missed kick. He felt the pain as she landed on his leg bone – he was not sure if it was fractured -- but it hurt. She then jumped off of his leg landing to the side of him. He looked up to his side to assess his situation when a small hard fist hit his jaw. He felt his jaw break and suddenly everything went black as she shoved him off of the ramp and onto the floor below.

Jaime grabbed the polyhedron – it was her turn and nothing was going to stop her. Even before she was able to turn and start up the ramp, the first two Beta Captains were upon her. The dark-haired Beta Captain made three fast swings at her – she avoided every attack, and then used the lighter gravity to backflip out of the way of the two attacking men, bouncing on one arm as she held onto the polyhedron with the other hand. They charged in pursuit and upon reaching her started attacking again. This time however, Jaime ducked out of the way of one attacker and put a fist into his ribs, then quickly jabbed him in his solar plexus. He immediately crumbled to the ground as she put a fast foot to his face, then grabbed his arm while he tried to catch his breath. Using his arm, she deflected a swing from the dark-haired task master. His hand hit the metal rod hidden under the sleeve of the game jersey of the downed Captain -- breaking bones in his fingers. He screamed in pain and turned, giving Jaime the time to swing the downed man's arm -- and the metal bar into his side, knocking him back while sliding the first attacking Captain off of the ramp and out of the game.

She then ran up to him, he had his back turned away from her as he grasped his hand. She turned him around -- tears were flowing from his dark eyes and he was crying like a little baby. She shook her head in disgust, bounced the polyhedron onto the floor and applied five quick jabs to his face. Blood began dropping out of his nose even before the polyhedron had completed its bounce off of the floor, into the air, and back into her outstretched hand. His tears flowed even more freely as he turned away from her, ran to the edge of the ramp and jumped off, eliminating himself.

Onward she fought, easily taking out the next seven obstacles to the top of the ramp – despite them ganging up on her. She now faced a very large and menacing first level Beta Starship Captain. She had never seen this person before, but he was very bulky, muscular and was much taller than she -- quite unlike most Blessed. His legs were like tree stumps -- large, solid looking and muscular. His arms were not much different -- muscular and fully flexed. Large chest and solid abdomen shook in and out with every huge breath he took. His long black hair dangled behind his muscular back in a ponytail. His face looked like it had been chiseled out of stone, wide nose, bushy black eyebrows shadowing his beady dark eyes sunken into an extended forehead, large mouth with pearly white teeth, and a pointed chin. She stood and analyzed what she would have to do to take him down. He just stood there rubbing his fists in anticipation and chuckling.

"Come my little bird, fly to me and take your punishment..." the large man softly told her while motioning with his hands.

She determined that she would be much faster than him and could outmaneuver him. She felt a shift to lighter gravity and with that change, made her move. With a leap of her strong legs she jumped to grab one of the dome's hanging loop handholds, with this move she could then maneuver to the flat on the top of the ramp – she hoped that getting off of the smaller angled ramp would be to her advantage. She was surprised however by the feel of a large hand that took hold of her foot, then swung her back down to the ramp surface. She was shocked by his speed as she felt her head hit the surface of the ramp.

She shook her head trying to remove the cobwebs as she felt him pick her up by her free arm, he flipped her around and wrapped his large arms around her. With a squeeze, she felt his flesh covered weapons constrict like a python on its prey – she felt her breath start to quickly leave while at the same time she found it almost impossible to refill her compressed lungs. She gasped over and over trying to regain precious lost oxygen, both while she attempted to hang onto the polyhedron and determine how to escape his death grip. He just kept chuckling in a low tone while he continued his squeeze on her torso.

In desperation, she lowered her head to her chest then with a quick snap, shot it into his forehead. She saw stars briefly but felt his grip quickly release as her head smashed into the bridge of his nose. He started to let go of her with one arm. She took advantage of this moment and reached up with her free hand and shoved her thumb into one of his dark eyes. He screamed in agony as he dropped her and reached up to rub his damaged eye. She fell to the floor, almost dropping the now changing polyhedron – she barely managed to keep the object from slipping out of her hands.

While he was concentrating on his eye, she landed a flurry of kicks to the legs, and punches to the abdomen – but they appeared to not do any damage. As a matter of fact, after her attack he stopped rubbing his eye and instead swung his large fist at her. She blocked the attack with her arm, but was sent flying up the ramp landing flat on her back, stunned. He charged her like a raging bull, snorting through his nose with each step of his huge feet on the ramp. As he reached her he jumped into the air, his body stretched out, arms flung wide open, legs stretched and open – he was going to body slam her.

Using only instincts, she put her feet up into the air to greet him hoping that the lighter gravity would be to her advantage. As she felt her feet touch the closing body, she also felt the change in gravity – it was now heavier. She pushed with all her might on the falling bulk – she could have sworn her legs would snap under the weight of the pouncing man. Somehow, she managed to get her feet on him just enough to start a pivot point with her legs as the fulcrum. Using every bit of strength her training had provided, she pushed his direction of travel toward the edge of the platform. He flew over her and hit the surface with a thud. Quickly, she jumped to her feet and found him half off of the platform trying to regain the breath he lost in landing. She took advantage of this brief moment and quickly slid into his hip sending the rest of his bulk over the side and down to the floor.

Even before she had a chance to realize she had won she felt pain in her head. A metal rod had hit her so hard she swore her skull was as soft as marshmallow. As she started to spin around, small specks began floating in her mind and in her eyes. She then saw one of the Alphas – she was not sure who, put a gloved hand to her leg. Intense pain followed as she looked down and saw her leg instantly turn black and blue where his hand had been. She immediately collapsed as her leg shattered and she felt a large boot kick her hip – she might have felt it fracture slightly but she was in such pain it did not matter. As she was kicked over the edge all she could think was "*Here we go again...*"

She regained consciousness once again in the Vitality Ray Chamber – feeling the warm and healing rays of the simulated sun.

Boral Oldham:

Boral turned off the monitor after the first part of the match – he knew the main event was already over. "Damn it!"

He thought about his situation – he now was forced by protocol to give this Normal Captain a commanding shift in the rotation. Because of her win, she would now actually command this starship and he could not do anything to stop it – not without causing a major breach in the Supreme Commander's rules. These rules were set up to give hope to the lower level Captains that someday they might make a command shift. He never thought that someone would actually be able to win and take advantage of the rules. He had even rigged the game by placing Vitally Embry into the top Beta Captain spot and yet, she was now the top Beta Starship Captain.

Now, he was forced to give this person a command and allow her to select her Bridge staff. He knew she would more than likely only pick Normals for her Bridge crew. They would more than likely blow up the ship with their incompetency, he figured.

"How can I stop it? There must be some way to stop it..."

He took a sip of his drink while he pondered his situation. Finally, a thought came to mind – he activated his communication device. After a moment, a voice answered "Yes, Star Force Commander?"

"I have a request of you. I want you to find some reason to either challenge or be challenged by Beta Starship Captain Jaime Bordeaux. After she challenges you, I want you to take her out and destroy her. I will stop the ship long enough for you to get the job done and I will do whatever it takes to help you defeat her. You are one of the best we have -- can I depend on you completing this task?"

The voice on the other end simply said "Of course..."

Starlight Flight Time: 82 days, 4 hours, 27 minutes

Jaime Bordeaux:

The reveille tone sounded once again waking her from her sound sleep. She got up, turned on the view screen – nothing but stars. They had performed their final slingshot and were headed out into deep space. Very soon, she would get to officially pick her Bridge crew and finally pilot the enormous starship.

After her now morning ritual – stretching, Tai Chi, and a session in the cleansing bay, she got dressed and verified her uniform was properly situated then called for her duty roster. The dark-haired Blessed officer gave her nothing unusual – simulator duty and cleaning of "The Pens" again. She now knew he was enjoying giving her that stench as a work duty – but that's ok, she would always remember how he cried right before he jumped off the ramp. In addition to her normal daily routine, she added a run and workout into her schedule for later in the evening.

She contacted her crew to meet at the simulator. She grabbed a light breakfast and wandered through the upper entertainment decks of the ship while sipping simulated coffee and nibbling on a scone. When she arrived at the simulator the crew had arrived (early, she noted) and were ready for their simulated duty. They were all dressed in their best Bridge uniforms – she was totally impressed.

"Good morning" she announced as she walked in. The crew all gave a courteous reply of "Good morning" and all saluted as she entered. "So, what's our simulation today Engineer?"

Jonathan looked at his console. "I think I have a great idea…I believe -- at least some of us will be with you on the Bridge soon?" Jaime nodded in agreement. "How about we see exactly what the Blessed train with today?" Once again, he looked to Jaime for permission.

She nodded her head again and smiled. "An interesting proposition. You can do that?" he nodded affirmation. "Well, let's see what always gets them those good scores, shall we?"

Jonathan entered control commands, disabling the tracking protocols of the computer then looked through the simulation files with "Blessed Only" access. He selected the highest rated scenario. "I think we have it. Difficulty rating 10 out of 10" he said as he typed the commands to load.

Jaime's command console brought up the scenario. *Defeat the rebel fleet, destroy the rebel leader.* "Well, this is an interesting one. Ok, we have a rebel fleet to take care of. Let's go right to battle status 1. Lock and load all weapons. Halley, be ready to quickly maneuver – I have no idea where we will end up. Science Station, SCADAR on full detail scan mode. Here we go..."

The scenario gave her the Starlight along with four other Alliance starships against a single large spacecraft. The enemy – a supposed fleet of Normal rebels flew the single ship against her fleet. This ship appeared to be a big blocky looking craft. Three large cubes made up the main sections of the ship and were connected by rectangular structure sections. This ship had no other real detail – some portals were evident, other than that no other outward exterior accoutrements.

Jaime shook her head. "You have got to be kidding me? This is what they think Normal rebels would build and fly? Did their simulator designer get lazy or something?" Jonathan just shrugged when she looked at him. "Very well, Katsumi give me a reading from SCADAR."

The young Japanese woman went over her virtual readouts examining all of the returns from the scanning radar array. "They have powered up their weapons, I count a fairly equal number of weapons to the Starlight – rail guns, cutter lasers and p-accelerators. Not much else, not even nukes."

Lindy called out "Beta Starship Captain, the other Captains are awaiting orders. As Starlight Command, you get to make all battle orders."

Jaime sighed "This is a cakewalk...very well, ships 2 and 3 use pattern D-18 and go in for a frontal assault, 1 and 4 do flip maneuvers to get in behind the rebels. We will take the heat and hope their weapons are not that powerful. Yuli, as soon as we are in range, let em' have it."

It was a powerful and quick battle. Jaime's instructions to the other craft took the rebels totally by surprise. Within minutes the rebel starship was reduced to a burning heap.

Lindy, listening on her monitoring channel got an odd look on her face before announcing "Beta Starship Captain, I am receiving a hail from the Queen of the Rebels. She wishes to discuss terms of surrender and pleads for mercy...this is odd..."

Jaime looked at her "What?"

"Beta Starship Captain...well, I think you just need to see it. Shall I put it up?"

"Absolutely, on the main holo-projector Lindy." When the image appeared on the middle holographic screen of the bridge main display, it caused Jaime to mutter "What the hell?" She stood from her command chair and stared at the image. A computer simulated image of her was being shown on the holo-display – she was wearing a light and airy pink dress with ruffles around the neck, puffy sleeves covering her arms and a large ruffle flowing down the front of the frilly outfit.

The computer simulated her own voice which called out through the bridge "Please Blessed Fleet, I the Queen of the Normal Rebel Fleet implore you to show mercy. We are defeated, whatever it takes I will provide. Please show mercy, I offer myself to you now."

Jaime stared at the image, fists tightly clinched and her jaw solidly locked as she held back the urge to blast the holo-projector with her command weapon. She now understood what all of the comments she had been hearing from the Blessed crew actually meant. Being called *My Queen* and the other quips about royalty by the Blessed – she now knew the source. She quietly said to Jonathan "Turn that shit off..." as she turned and left the now totally silent crew in the simulator.

Once outside, she walked down the hall briskly but then stopped to wipe some small tears that she was unable to prevent from escaping. She first slammed her fist against the wall, her head followed right afterwards at a much slower pace and came to rest on the cool steel. She tried to transfer her mental rage into the body of the ship. Finally, she found the ability to quell her rage and started light standing mediation. She began to control her breathing, and took long deep breaths to relax.

After a few minutes, she sensed a presence behind her – it was Jonathan. "I am sorry Beta Starship Captain -- I had no idea about the simulation..."

She gave him a light but weak smile "It's ok Jonathan, you did not know. However, we all know now just what the Blessed think of us. They think we Normals are not only weak and stupid, but rebellious. I sometimes wonder..." she stopped herself as she realized every place on this ship was bugged – at least she assumed that was the case in this hallway. He reached over and placed his hand into hers – leaving a small piece of paper. He gave her a small smile, then saluted, turned and returned to the simulator. She walked back to the main hallway then looked at the paper "*Meet me in section Brown 55, area 44 at 2253. Return and Reuse*" At least this time he was going to wait until she would be finished with her workout.

That evening, she took a transport tube to the lowest level of the lifestyle section of the ship – the cylinder that connected the engine section to the command section. In this connector housed most of the recreational facilities of the ship: gymnasiums, theaters, restaurants, lounges, parks, sitting areas, training facilities, and the polyhedron arena. In addition to these luxury-living areas, there were also slums in the lower levels. These slums housed the rejects of the crew – Blessed or Normal, it made no difference. These were either rejected crew members, stowaways or many other types of mixed vermin that did not want to be found. To get to this evening's meeting, Jaime was forced to travel through these levels to get to the area of the engine section for her meeting.

Originally, this area was to be a posh extension of the lifestyle section, where luxury lounges of various forms were to provide music and dance. Somehow, the area never got a good start – the fancy nightclubs and musical lounges showed up in the upper levels closer to the Blessed and instead this area now sported nothing but seedy bars and houses of prostitution. She was amazed that this level of poverty and degradation of life could exist on this starship, and only a few decks below the life of luxury and quality living. She quickly passed through the thoroughfare – a dingy silver metal corridor of filthy doorways with small signs indicating purpose. The whole hallway was stained and smelled of shit, piss, vomit, and other unspeakable odors. She hurried down the main passageway and down a side corridor. She walked quickly hoping to exit this section as soon as possible.

Three men stepped in front of her – she stopped and looked at the trio. All were dressed in shabby, dirty rags that she could tell were former uniforms. Based on the fit of the clothing, she determined that they had not been their original outfits, but they had found them in the refuse or stole them off some unfortunate soul.

The man in the center, wearing a filthy Alliance work jumpsuit came forward and looked at her with grey sunken eyes surrounded by wrinkled dark circles. His face covered with stubble, bulging red nose which indicated some form of substance abuse, thin mouth with rotted missing teeth that was still able to form a pathetic smile. "Well, look at this...a Captain...and a pretty one...all by herself!" he blurted the mangled words tainted by the stench of chemical abuse into her face. She was surprised he knew of her rank, and wondered what brought him here. She knew in any case she needed to get around these three and on her way.

"Out of my way, allow me to pass please." she replied.

The man on the left replied "Oh no, not until you have paid your toll.. "

The man in the center then spoke "Yes, I think you need to pay to pass...let's see what shall we charge?" His thin dried fingers began moving toward her chest. She quickly and easily slapped them away. "Oh, feisty, aren't we?" he said as the other two began reaching under their clothing.

"They're getting weapons!"

As the center bum reached out again for her breast she spun around and threw him into the wall. The other two had freed their weapons from under their clothing. Before they could take aim however, Jaime pointed her left arm, concentrated and fired the electrostatic shocker from her command weapon. The unit fired an arc of high voltage electricity generated by her own reactor enhanced nervous system which hit the first man. He immediately crumbled to the ground and violently convulsed due to the disruption to his nervous system. Quickly she aimed her arm at the man on her right and fired. He too began shaking and fell to the ground as she continued her electronic defensive assault. Realizing she was killing him, she stopped her attack and allowed him to just shudder on the ground. Finally, she turned and aimed at the leader -- the groper. She flexed to fire but nothing happened – the weapon refused to discharge.

The man laughed as he saw her attack falter. Slowly he returned to his feet while still laughing. "You don't get it do you? That won't work against me..." He opened the collar of his jumpsuit revealing a stained and tattered bead on a metal rope. "I am Blessed...your weapon will not harm me. They programmed it that way." He began a weak but consistent chuckling laugh as his confidence increased.

The quick roundhouse kick she placed into his face however provided much more damage than her weapon could ever dish out. He crumpled to the ground -- spit and blood flew out of his mouth and splattered on the wall from the force of her boot against his face. "I don't need a weapon to take you down. No man has ever gotten to me..."

She heard a thud behind her – as she turned a man fell to the ground at her feet. In his hand, an old large bladed knife. He had no shoes, which prevented her from hearing him sneak up behind her. *"He should have killed me? I was foolish and lost my concentration. But who took him out?"* Her question was answered by a laugh – a laugh she had not heard since Earth but totally recognized and remembered. "Eva? Is that you?"

"Hey, you didn't forget me? I'm touched..." The dark-haired woman emerged from a darkened doorway off of the corridor. She stood facing Jaime, slightly shorter than her. A big smile stretched across her large cheeks. Her bright green eyes stared deeply into hers as if they were trying to see directly into her mind. Her dark black hair now flowed down her back in waves of movement as she stepped forward. "I should have let him kill you. But then what fun would that be?"

"Well, I guess I should thank you..."

"Oh don't!" she interrupted "I only did that so I could soon have the pleasure myself."

"What is with you Eva? What have I done to cause such hatred in you?" Now her eyes bore into Eva's trying to see what was hidden in her soul.

"I just became tired...tired of all your little successes. Did you ever lose at anything? Oh wait, I guess you did – you finally were injured in battle. And even that brought you success, a Captaincy. Had I known you would get that I would have never shot you in the first place." The smile on her face was all the proof Jaime needed to know -- she was telling the truth. Jaime also saw that she was enjoying this moment.

As Eva told her what really happened, Jaime's blood heated to a simmer "You...you shot me? You shot at your own? I was shot by friendly fire? Friendly fire from you?"

Eva laughed again "Yes dear Jaime. I hid in the rubble with my ship electronically hidden from your scanners and when you cleared the field I fired the missile knowing you would avoid it, but not my beam. As a matter of fact, I knew your sensors would not even detect my firing at you – you were a sitting duck! I should have taken you out then..." Jaime's hard fist across her chin stopped her gloating and sent her to the ground.

Jaime was breathing hard with anger "I don't have time to waste with you" She activated her command computer and typed in a grievance request. "I have filed a grievance and will get revenge later. Trust me, I will have revenge..." she turned and ran off leaving her still sitting on the hard steel floor.

"Yes, you will get your chance my dear...and it will be your final mistake..." her cackling could be heard throughout the slum and almost all the way down into the lower levels of the engine section.

Even before she reached her destination her computer chirped. She activated it and was surprised to see that a reply to her request for grievance had already been answered. As a matter of fact, it was already approved and determined – a fighter duel to the death. *"Well, at least it will be interesting...but so quickly approved...hmm..."*

She reached the designated meeting spot as requested on the note. "Well, I am here." she called out.

"Hello Beta Starship Captain..." once again the voice seemed to come from everywhere, electronically disguised and indistinguishable from anyone she had ever dealt with. "I am glad you decided to make it. You will be getting your command orders very soon. Do you have your crew picked?"

"Yes, I think so. They are all good people, but I think you know that."

"Yes, as a matter of fact I know exactly who you are going to pick and we approve!"

"We?"

The man paused for a moment after he realized she caught his mistaken words. "Yes, you should know there are more than just myself – I am simply the recruiter. We have a network of people all working toward a common cause – a cause I hope to introduce you to in the future."

"Why not allow me to see you and meet the others? Don't you trust me?"

"If we did not trust you, you would not be here now. I think you know how the Blessed operate – especially after what you saw today in the simulator. They don't think very highly of you, do they?"

"No, not at all. I can't believe they envision me a as rebel! I have been loyal to the Alliance all my life..."

"And what has that gotten you?"

She thought a moment ""Nothing...nothing, but pain and sorrow..."

"And this is why it is important that you continue to work with them and learn what they're about. The Alliance is not the wonderful force you were trained to think and the Blessed are their spawn. Remember that..."

"I will now."

"Good. Now however, you have a more important mission – to get your crew and man the bridge of this ship. There is a very unique celestial feature out there – one that the Blessed have been too blind to see, but they are flying right at it. You must be prepared to investigate it and avoid it for all of our sakes. I can't tell you what it is, as we don't know ourselves – but something is there, we can tell based on gravity readings that it exists and it is not good, and we will be flying at it or near it. I will make the arrangements -- you will be on Bridge duty when we approach whatever it is. You will be able to determine what it is and make any appropriate course adjustments if needed."

"So, you can manipulate the schedule? Then that is why I got such a quick response."

The man paused again "Response? To what?"

"You know. My grievance against Eva – War Bitch. You got me the duel with her – to finally take her down once and for all."

"Duel? I had nothing to do with that." Jaime detected concern in the voice even with electronic masking. "I or any of us had nothing to do with approval of a duel...it's a setup. You must refuse this..."

"No, I cannot and will not! I have filed a grievance and accept the challenge willingly!" She thought how dare he try to spoil her one chance at revenge.

"Captain...Jaime...I think this is a way to get rid of you!" Jaime never heard the voice call her specifically by name in that manner and something familiar came to her when she heard it from him – even with the manipulation.

"I will be careful – and I will win. Don't worry."

"That is not my fear as you are the best fighter pilot we have ever seen."

"There he said "we" again."

"Please look over to your right -- you will see a small device." She looked as directed and in the corner, was a small device sitting on the floor. She walked over, picked it up and examined it. It was a small tube, no more than two inches long and half an inch in diameter and was composed of shiny polished stainless steel. It had a single button with a cover to prevent accidental pressing. She examined it with curiosity. "It will implant a secured communication device. You must implant it just behind your ear on the left side – do not implant it on the right as it would interfere with your Alliance communicator."

"What if I decide I don't want to join you and do not implant this? What makes you think I won't just take this to the Commander and have the Blessed crack your channels?"

"I don't think you would do that as I have some knowledge of you -- and I trust you. Also, if you don't use it within two days it will self-destruct into dust. No one will be able to do anything with it after that. We hope you decide to join us and use that, but if not, then nothing gained or lost. The choice is yours..."

"I will consider it then."

"That is all we ask. As far as your duel, I will not try to persuade you to change your mind. However, we will be on guard here watching out for you. Good luck and be careful. You had better leave now as the security surveillance system will be activating in one minute. Good night Captain." Jaime sensed the man behind the voice had left and was long gone down the dark corridors. She looked at the small device again, tucked it securely into her uniform pocket and quickly proceeded on her trip back to the civilized part of the ship.

Starlight Flight Time: 84 days, 15 hours, 38 minutes

Halley Cet:

She stood at Jaime's door, deciding if she should intrude. Finally, she built up enough nerve to ring the annunciator. Jaime opened the door and looked at her, wondering what she was doing at her doorstep. She was shocked to find that Jaime had already shaved her head in preparation of getting into her flight suit. She stood at the door totally naked and shaved and was totally unashamed or embarrassed by being naked – perhaps from her years as a soldier. Halley felt a slight rush of excitement and embarrassment over the sight of her Captain standing there. Jaime still had a look on her face, wondering what she wanted – an eyebrow would have been cocked at her if she had not shaved them.

"I wanted to see you before you went out..." she quietly said.

Jaime gave her a small warm smile "Come on in, please..." and stepped away from the door while she motioned her in with a welcoming hand movement. "Something to drink? Coffee perhaps? I cannot join you as it is best if I am totally clean of substances before my flight."

"Coffee, thanks. Actually, don't bother, I can get it..." She went over and ordered a coffee from the dispenser and brought it back to a chair at the desk while Jaime proceeded to put on her flight suit. She sat down and sipped on the hot coffee flavored beverage while she looked at the desk in front of her. There was a view screen showing a star field.

"It is the direction we are going...I never look back now." Jaime told her as she started checking every joint and seal on her flight suit. She ensured that the ribbing was glowing – indicating that it was fully and properly connected and that her electrical patterns were properly in tune with the suit.

Halley continued to look at the items on the desk – a display of her medals and awards, digital books of command and battle tactics, and a holographic image of a man. He was attractive and looked about the same age as Jaime. She stared at the person in the image while she wondered what type of person could capture her in such a manner as to cause her to keep an image of him.

Jaime walked over to her and looked at the image. "That was Dex...we were scheduled to be joined after we left Earth. However, he died during takeoff..." she picked up his image and stared at it. "He was the only man I ever loved...ever will love..."

"I'm sorry, this is not right to discuss at this time..." Halley just wanted to crawl out of her cabin as she was so upset that she brought up such a painful subject at a time like this.

"No" she interrupted "it actually is a perfect time. If she...Eva...had not shot me and made everyone think I was injured, I would not have left Earth...and Dex would..." she choked on her words slightly as a tear came rolling down her cheek. "Yes, this actually is the perfect time to discuss and remember. But you didn't come here to listen to me get all soft, did you?"

She shook her head slightly no. "Believe it or not, I think of you as not just my commander but also I think of you as my friend – as a matter of fact, you are my only friend. So, I just wanted to tell you that. When you are out there I will be hoping and praying for you."

"Prayer will not be needed. That god abandoned me a long time ago. No, just hope that my skill is still with me and that I will take her down." She sniffed and stopped the flow of tears from her eyes and stiffness came over her face.

"You know that is my wish for you. I want you to come back – I need you to be my Captain!" She jumped up and wrapped her arms around her -- tears flowing down her cheeks.

"Oh, my sweet Halley..." She lifted her chin and gave her one small kiss, then smiled at her. Halley now felt like melted butter in her arms -- and that tiny small sweet kiss stayed on her lips. At the same time, she could feel her pushing away -- she let go of her knowing she had more important things to do. "Thank you...now let me get ready. I will see you soon, ok?"

Halley walked to the door, turned and smiled at her "Go get her Beta Starship Captain! I will see you after the battle." She pressed the door lock and walked into the hallway. She felt confident, but was scared and shaking. She tapped on the left side of her neck. "Are you there? I am worried, is there anything we can do?"

A male voice on the other end said "The only thing we can do is to make sure that people on this side do not interfere or cheat. Can we depend on your help?"

"Of course."

"Then go to transmitter console 559 on level Red 23. It will be cleared so that only you will be able to operate it – and it will be secure." The communication was quickly cut off. She immediately ran off to her instructed destination. *"Don't worry Jaime, I have your back!"*

Jaime Bordeaux:

It felt good to be in a Wolf Pack Star Fighter yet once again. This time however, she would be killing one of her own – one that caused her so much pain and sorrow. She was ready -- to get revenge.

She wiggled and shimmied getting a feel for the craft and its response. She felt slightly disadvantaged as she only had a single craft and no pups, but her opponent would also have the same disadvantage of a single craft. It would be a true one-on-one battle – Eva had no chance, Jaime knew she would win.

She was taken by surprise by a voice coming over her comm system "Jaime, can you hear me?" It was Halley, somehow, she had gotten a secured channel on the ship wide communication network, or at least she hoped it was secure. As if reading her mind "I am told this is both secure and is on a tunneled channel protocol directed only so your ship can receive and decipher the protocols – don't worry, no one will hear us"

"How did you get that arranged?"

"There are ways to do pretty much anything here, I am told…"

"Well, I am not going to look this gift horse in the mouth then."

"Good! I hope you don't mind me calling you Jaime…I just can't be so formal in a situation like this…I am so worried. I promise I will call you Beta Starship Captain in public, ok?"

"Well, you are the one friend I have on this ship, so I don't know why not."

"You don't know how wonderful that feels to hear you say that. Wait, Eva is now out there."

Jaime looked around the ITC for her opponent's star fighter but she was not showing up anywhere on her scanning radar or on her visual display. She swiveled all around to view the star field but she could not see any sign of Eva and her craft. "Where is she?"

After a slight pause, Halley shouted "Jaime, we think they have her ship's signature stealthed! You won't be able to see her on your displays, but she is right behind you -- six o'clock and Z level zero!"

"Shit!" She made a quick downward lunge, just as Eva's beam weapons shot out barely missed taking her out in one swoop. Jaime rolled upwards and around in a loop, then pulling a barrel roll coming in on Eva's side. Using only visual targeting she fired her P-Accelerators singeing Eva's tail section – a quarter of an inch more and the battle would have already been over on the other side. Instead, Eva pulled a similar loop but instead of rolling back into Jaime, she took an opposite route away from her – concealing her location once again.

"Oh my dear Jaime, I am a ghost – you can't see or hit me!" Eva said on the open comm channel laughing in that hideous manner after her announcement.

"Jaime, she is coming back up behind you – will be in firing range in a matter of seconds...currently at five o'clock Z negative fifty-five." Following Halley's coordinates, she once again rolled the ship around and away from her blasts just in the nick of time.

"Damn, I can't pursue her if I can't see her!" Frustration filled her voice as she looked around for her opponent but she could not see the black ship against the darkness of outer space.

"If there was some way to light her up, then you could get a fix on her. In the meantime, I will just have to give you positions."

"Find her position quick...Halley?"

"Nine o'clock Z ninety."

"Right" she said as she steered her ship in a rounding maneuver to keep her out of range while she tried to think of a plan. She saw the massive starship ahead in the star field display and came up with an idea. She quickly flew to the back of the ship and then guided her ship behind the massive engines of the space ark. They were in standby mode but still giving off heat and light – the light was what Jaime found to be important as she made a quick ninety-degree turn away from the rear of the ship. Turning in her pod she saw the outline of Eva's ship in the glow of the exhaust – she had caught up and had maneuvered in behind her again. The outline was just enough to tell that she was almost in a perfect position to fire.

"Chaff times five – pattern eight" she shouted. With this command Jaime released five rounds of atomic chaff in a blossom pattern. The chaff capsules ignited as soon as they left the launch tubes and exploded into bright meteors of light right in front of Eva's ship – causing her to be temporarily blinded and at the same time the fiery objects struck her pod taking out most of her front sensor array. She was now almost as blind as Jaime – the scales were now balanced.

In the time it took for Eva to regain her presence and her vision, Jaime had sunk slightly below Eva's ship and performed a total reverse maneuver putting her into a firing position. Now that she had the advantage, she flexed her fists and let loose a full barrage of cutter photon beams and rail projectiles. Eva, still clearing her vision did not see the attack coming. The assault caused the frame of Eva's ship to split into five separate pieces – each piece, including the part of the ship with her pod began flipping in an uncontrollable tumble. Eva screamed as she felt the burning of the ship as it was ripped apart. She was barely able to eject her pod from the ship frame before it exploded. The explosion sent her pod even deeper into space and away from the starship and possible rescue. Using small emergency thrusters, she was able to stop the pod from tumbling and finally brought it to a dead stop in space. She curled up into a ball inside her pod and waited for the final blow from her opponent – but it never happened. She activated her marker lights hoping it would help her find and finish her. However, after a minute she realized that her opponent was not attacking.

"Jaime, why aren't you firing? I would not hesitate..."

After a moment Jaime stopped her star fighter directly in front of the floating pod and finally answered "I don't need to fire and take you out. No one will be rescuing you. You are stranded out here and that is a much better fate. Taking you out would be much too quick and painless – I want you to remember my anger for a long time. If you were smart you brought a suicide injector..."

Quietly she answered "No...I never carry one..."

"A real shame for you then... Enjoy your new home in space." She turned her ship and headed back to the Starlight.

"Jaime, you really are leaving me? Jaime?" She started quietly sobbing. "Good-bye Jaime...I'm sorry..."

"Sorry? Do you really expect me to believe that now, that you are sorry?"

"It doesn't matter now, but you should know I was only carrying out orders..." she whimpered.

This peaked Jaime's interest "Whose orders?"

"It doesn't matter now I guess. I was only following orders from..." Nothing.

"Eva? Shit!" She switched channels to her connection to Halley "Halley, what happened to Eva's comm channel?"

After a moment of checking, she replied "Looks like they are blocking her."

Jaime flew a little farther then stopped her craft – her anger was quickly subsiding. Finally, she admitted to herself while softly saying "Shit...you are going to regret this Bordeaux..." as she turned her craft back toward the stranded pod floating in space.

"Jaime, what are you doing?" Halley cried out.

"I can't do it. I can't leave her there. I will not stoop to the level of a Blessed."

"She was the reason you lost Dex. This is your chance to get your revenge."

"No, she was only the tool. Dex died doing his job. I can't do it – I can't leave her out there alone. She would not do the same, but I can't...not if I want to live with myself."

She flew around and shot a grapple anchor onto Eva's pod and began dragging her back. As the ship came into view she noticed that it appeared the magnetic pulsar drives where engaged.

"Are they leaving me? It looks like the engines are firing up!"

"One sec..." Halley answered. "Yes...yes they are trying to leave. We thought they might do this. No problem, we will have the engine malfunction occur in just a second." Within moments the pulsar drives stopped and the ship slowed down to a dead crawl once again.

Jaime smiled at the efficiency of the sabotage that this group was capable of performing. "Great, I will be there in just a moment...and remind me to never trust any of my ships with you..." Jaime stopped her announcement when she saw a warning light on her computer heads-up readout. For some reason, the living gel inside her pod was starting to die. She looked down at her feet and the gel was turning from clear to a murky red color. At the same time, she started noticing it was getting harder to breathe. Every cell that died in the pod was one less creature providing atmosphere to her.

The fighter was getting closer to the space ark but the gel was dying just as quickly. The pod on the grapple line added drag causing her not to be able to cruise at full speed. She pressed the engines to accelerate even faster than full speed as the landing hangar approached closer and closer. For every mile she progressed, thousands of gel cells died. Her breathing was getting harder and harder.

"Jaime, are you ok?"

"I can't talk...wastes air..." she said gasping between words. She stretched her body out and grasped for the opening of the landing deck on the underside of the massive ship. The engines slightly increased, but her ability to control the ship was beginning to fade at the same pace as the dissipating precious oxygen as the gel died.

She barely brought the craft in on its landing struts but then lost control and it slid onto its side as soon as it penetrated the environmental force field and atmosphere filled bubble of the hangar. Before the sliding ship came to a complete stop, she ejected the emergency hatch which allowed the now dead gel to flow freely out and at the same time expelled her from the pod. She rolled onto the hangar deck like a rag doll – barely missing being crushed by Eva's pod still being dragged by the now unpiloted ship. She tumbled and rolled until she came to a full stop. She pulled her helmet off, tossed it to the side and gasped while she tried to take in as much air as possible, and struggled to prevent passing out. The crew rushed in along with Max. He gave her additional oxygen to help her body get the needed gas into her bloodstream. At the same time, Max examined her and found numerous bumps and bruises but no broken bones.

"Max, you are always around when I need you..." she finally said with a panting voice.

Max smiled and nodded as he continued to give her oxygen. "And you always make my job easy as you seem to magically recover." This time was no exception as she immediately started to feel better the moment the fresh oxygen entered her lungs. Of no surprise to Max, her body was already healing the bruises right before his eyes. He made no outward notice to the remarkable healing of her body.

At the same time, a crew opened up the pod in tow containing Eva and was helping her evacuate the dead container. She removed her helmet with tears in her eyes. As soon as she was able, she stood and went to check on Jaime. The oxygen had done its work and she was awake and alert. She looked at Eva who extended her hand to help her up. After spending a moment to check all her body parts, Jaime shook her head negative and stood on her own and stared at her defeated opponent. Eva's flight suit's collar was open revealing a numbered bead on a wire. "Blessed?"

"Not anymore..." she told her as she walked over to a toolbox and retrieved a cutter. She put the cutter up to the wire. "There is nothing blessed about me or them...you showed me mercy even though you had the best reason in the world to kill me. They would not have done the same and I cannot and will not do it anymore."

Before she could cut the thin wire however, Jaime grabbed her hand and urged her to drop the cutter. "If you really mean that then don't do that. Not yet at least."

Jaime let go of her arm and she obediently dropped the cutter to the floor. "You beat me squarely, and then you spared my life and saved me. My life is yours now Jaime...Beta Starship Captain. I am now loyal to you..." She saluted and offered her hand.

Jaime still refused her hand and instead put her face right into Eva's "Then tell me who…the name!" she softly ordered.

Eva shook her head no and whispered "Not here, not now…"

"Well, then later it will be. As far as loyalty, we will see… only you can prove that. Right now, everything you say is a pack of lies to me."

Turning to Max she nodded and he acknowledged her with a similar nod. Jaime turned her back on Eva, and left her standing alone on the flight deck. Eva turned to the departing victor and once again saluted her as she whispered "You are tough as steel but your heart beats the warmest of blood, Beta Starship Captain…"

Max looked at Eva and shook his head in amazement before saying as he walked away "Looks like she passed…"

Jaime went back to her cabin, removed her flight suit and plopped herself onto the bed. She pondered what had just happened and why they tried to abandon her. When that plan with Eva failed she was sure they tried to nullify her by killing the pod's gel. She stood back up and walked over to her uniform hanging in the closet. She reached into her pocket and took out the small tube device that she was given earlier. She sat it on the table and just stared at it.

After an hour, she finally picked it up, looked at it again, then put it to her skin just behind her left ear and pressed the button. A brief jab of pain, then her mind suddenly felt like it had opened to a giant community. She could swear she heard voices -- hundreds or maybe even thousands of voices.

Suddenly, one solid voice was present in her head – it was like this person was in the same room, loud and clear. She realized it was the recruiter, or at least his synthetically disguised voice. "Hello Jaime, we are glad you decided to join us."

The Ark of the Blessed

Starlight Flight Time: 105 days, 2 hours, 30 minutes

Boral Oldham:

Boral looked at the computer readouts from the battle that just occurred. Once again, his operative failed in eliminating her target. Not only that, but after Jaime had beaten Eva the crew failed to start the engines on time to strand her in the middle of the vastness of space. Even sabotaging the pod to kill the gel did not remove this pain in his side. Now, he realized he had no choice in his next decision. He pressed the call on his computer console. A moment later, Kip was announcing himself at his door.

"Kip, no matter what we do – she keeps coming back to haunt us. Is the ranking correct? Did she gain top Beta Captaincy spot? Are we sure?"

"Yes, unfortunately Sir. She gained top Beta Starship Captain during the last tri-polyhedron event."

"Well, I have to maintain order and consistency in my command. Dammit!" He stared at his computer console for another moment trying to figure out any option. He tapped on the table before saying "And finally the Supreme Commander's orders have been provided by the computer – we are to head to Alpha Centauri and colonize or conquer if possible. If not, move to the next suitable system as selected by the computer." Kip raised an eyebrow. Boral continued to look at the duty roster "What to do with her.." he thought for another moment before he finally mumbled "Shit…put her in the rotation for bridge command."

"Very well sir."

Kip turned to return to the bridge to carry out his orders but before he could get to the door Boral barked out "Put her on the late shift, I don't want to see her on my Bridge. Let's hope she does not blow up our ship during that time."

Jaime Bordeaux:

It took a while, but Jaime was finally able to get to sleep. Ever since she inserted the communication device into her head she had been unable to shut off all the various conversations. She was unable to separate any single discussion, all she heard was just a jumble of talking. The only voice able to directly communicate with her was that of her mysterious electronic man. He told her that after an adjustment period of a few weeks her brain would shut out any of the extraneous communications and she would soon be able to control the communications between herself and the others in the network. He was correct, the voices finally did fade, and she was able to start drifting off into periods of light sleep. Even her light sleep was disturbed at times however, as small electrical connections were made between the communications device and her brain.

What little sleep she did get that night was over within a couple hours, as her reveille alarm announced it was time for her to start her daily routine. She rolled out of bed and walked over to the sink, splashed some water on her face, and looked in the mirror. She moaned as she realized she looked like death warmed over. She felt a slight pain in her ear – when she lifted her hair and looked she had a small red bump on the top of each of her ears. Staring at the two bumps for a moment she determined she had somehow contracted some type of infection. She figured Max could fix her up and would stop by to see him later.

She ordered a cup of coffee and sat at the computer console at her desk. A message was already waiting for her. She assumed it would be her normal daily routine of simulator then some disgusting clean up task. Instead her eyes lit up as she read the duty roster for the day.

"Report to Bridge at 2200 hours for command duties. Make sure you have selected your Bridge crew from available staff, contact and order them to report for duty at same hour. All other tasks for day have been discharged to other command staff."

She totally forgot about her lack of sleep as she immediately became alert. She realized she had so much to do. She needed her crew – finally. She reread the command to report to the Bridge then shut off the duty roster and instead queried for the available crew listings. She hoped that her crew had not been noticed and taken from her. The long list of names were returned from her query and were listed on the screen. She began to scroll through the enormous listing of available crew. She realized after a moment a pattern in the listing, they were all Normal -- there was not a single Blessed in the listing. All the better she thought as she would not want one of them on her Bridge when she was in command anyway.

"Come on, come on…where are you…" she spoke to the listing hoping to find even one of the people she was used to working with. Finally, her eyes lit up as she found a name – Cet, Halley. "Yes!" She continued searching the list until she found everyone she wanted – Yuli Capsain, Lindy Light, Katsumi Ito, and even Jonathan Faraday. She felt truly lucky this day. As she requisitioned her Bridge staff she felt a slight buzzing behind her ear from the new communication device. She touched it as she spoke "Yes…"

"Jaime, did you get your assignment. Find your crew?" It was her mysterious electronic voice.

"I think you know the answer…"

"We do, but I just wanted to hear it from you."

"Then yes, and yes I got every crewperson I wanted. Am I to thank you for this?"

"Only for making sure your crew stayed under the SCADAR – we did not want a Blessed discovering them and stealing them from you, or us."

"Then I thank you."

"Tonight will be a big night. Not only for you, but for all of us. I have to tell you that when you come on shift you will see a bright light in space. Our scientists have determined that we do not want to get near it."

She crinkled her forehead "Why not? Why not examine it?"

"We think it may be a danger to the ship. This is why your shift occurs when it does. You will get on duty in time to take control and steer around that anomaly. We don't want to find out what it is. It appears to radiate a gravitation force – although a small one. It is enough to worry our scientists. Scan it with SCADAR, but do it from a distance, ok?"

"Very well, I will trust you on this one." She felt the connection fade in her implant. With a smile on her face she ordered her cleaning, and today – no makeup, she was going to look totally natural and *Normal*. She got dressed, called Jeremy and headed directly for the gym. He was already waiting for her when she arrived. She noticed he also had cut his brown hair, beard and moustache extra short. She wondered why he had changed his looks.

His eyes lit up as she approached "Hey, you look great with freckles! I forgot you had those hidden...and I hear you finally got the command order, didn't you?" He now had a large grin on his face.

Jaime stopped and just looked at him. She wondered if perhaps he was part of this mysterious group of Normals that have joined together to make sure this ship gets to deep space. "How did you know?"

"Jaime, this ship is big – but not so big that good news does not travel fast. Besides, I just saw Jonathan who told me you sent his orders."

"Wow, that boy gets around, doesn't he? Already telling everyone eh? Well, good enough. Jeremy, I need another good workout to get me primed for tonight. Care to throw the kitchen sink at me?"

He considered her request for a moment. "Well, let's not throw sinks. However, I think I have enough training robots and moving weights to do the trick. I will make this the toughest workout you have yet experienced. But Jaime, afterwards I want you to stop by Doctor Sollix's office for a pre-flight check ok?"

She gave him a puzzled look "Really?" he nodded in acknowledgment "Ok, you know best when it comes to my body." She remembered the welts on her ears – it would be good to have him look at those anyway. They then started the workout – Jeremy kept his promise, it was one of the toughest workouts Jaime had ever experienced.

Max Sollix:

Max was prepared for Jaime's visit and was waiting for her at his desk when she rang the annunciator. He pressed the door entry button and stood up while motioning her in.

"Jaime! Come in, come in. I thought it would be good to give you a quick check up and a vitality ray treatment prior to your taking the Bridge for the first time."

Her eyes lit up in surprise "You too? Is there anyone who doesn't know that I am commanding the ship tonight?"

He chuckled "Relax, Jeremy called me while you were on your way here. Now come, place yourself on the medical scanning table for me please."

She jumped onto the metal table and let her hands relax on each side. "Max, take a look at some small growths on my ears while you are at it, ok?" He moved her head to the side and carefully looked at the small red bumps on the tops of her ears.

"Hmmm" he mumbled while trying to figure out what was causing the bumps.

Jaime looked at Max's sideburns while he looked at her ears and commented "Max, are you coloring your hair?"

"Now of course not, why do you say that?"

"Well, I swear some of your grey is gone...I think you are fibbing. Have you met someone?"

He chuckled at her assumption and continued his examination. After giving up on determining the growths, he swabbed a small sample from her ear then activated his medical scanner while he analyzed the images on the screen. Jaime noticed a slight concerned look on his face as he examined the images of the inside of her body on the screen. "What's wrong?"

He continued to stare at the image viewer while speaking with a slightly distant voice "Oh nothing, just making sure everything is in order..." he face came back to reality "...and it is! Ok, up with you my dear. Let's get you a vitality ray treatment then you had better get a little rest before you report. You will want all of your strength tonight."

She followed his instructions and entered the ray booth. He activated the soothing beams that provided healing and rejuvenation of her entire body. While she bathed in the invigorating beams he tapped on a small communication device behind his left ear, while at the same time examined the hair on his sideburns in a mirror on the wall – they had turned from grey to their former dark black color. When his communication connected, he began giving his report.

"This is interesting. Her nervous system – the implants in her nerves have somehow expanded and grown. Her nervous system is now completely hyper-energized. Her body somehow duplicated the superconductive materials and expanded the network, thus now her entire nervous system is now more powerful than any other human-being I have ever examined. The amount of energy and information she can process through her body is amazing. In addition, the communication implants have already fully matured. When I first examined her, I found a couple percent of genetic pairs that were active that shouldn't be. Now, there are 15 percent more active pairs – we have always considered these gene pairs to be junk, but in her they are active. Because of all of this activity, it appears as if she is actually becoming more youthful and stronger – she has some mysterious growths on her ears also. Who knows what else is going on in there – more and more of her genes are being activated the farther from Earth we travel. This along with her recuperative powers…well, I don't have to tell you what this means to Normal humans. If her body is any indication, then yes, we have a chance at survival."

Starlight Flight Time: 106 days, 21 hours, 50 minutes

Alpha Starship Captain Leopold Muldoon:

It was almost the end of his shift and he was tired, all he was doing up to this point was waiting for his replacement. An hour ago, he spotted a small bright light directly ahead and ordered the helmsman to steer the ship close to the object. He was curious to discover what it was – he hoped it was something valuable that he could load aboard. If he was correct, he might find some new power source – one that would give him great power and wealth. All he needed to do was capture it before the next shift, but it was farther away than he thought and it looked like the next Captain was going to get their chance at the prize.

"Damn, we are not going to make it before shift change, are we?" he asked the helmsman who turned and simply nodded no. "Increase speed – kick the ion drives up a notch. I will personally pay for the fuel once we capture that power source." The helm acknowledged and pulled the speed control farther down increasing thrust and moving the ship closer to the bright blinking object ahead. "Just a few more minutes are all we need now…" He looked at the science officer "Anything else coming in on SCADAR?"

The young Blessed officer looked at the readouts on his console again. "No Alpha Starship Captain. I am getting no indication as to what that is out there. It shows on the screen, but SCADAR is not showing anything -- it shows no mass, no volume, nothing!"

"Fine, fine… Come on ship, faster…faster…we have to get there!"

Behind him he heard the bridge door open. He turned to find a Normal bridge crewman – Halley Cet in full bridge uniform and beaming brightly as she headed to the helm position. She tapped the helmsman on the shoulder to relieve him. The helmsman turned and looked at Leopold, awaiting his command that would release him from duty.

"Normal, your Captain has not arrived. No station will be released until then."

"Then begin releasing them Alpha Starship Captain as I am here." Leopold turned to find Jaime Bordeaux now standing right behind him. Her crew had also arrived – all Normals. Each of them took their positions behind their on-duty counterparts awaiting the release of control from the on-duty Captain.

He looked her up and down before saying "You're kidding, right? The Star Force Commander actually gave you control of this bridge shift? He must have eaten something bad to make that kind of mistake. He would never give control to a Normal – and a girl at that!" He did a double take with a slight look of revulsion "What, what is wrong with your face?"

She gave him a confused look "What do you mean?"

"Your face, it is covered with dark splotches. Do you have a disease?"

She slightly rolled her eyes, barely keeping herself from committing insubordination. "Alpha Starship Captain, those are natural and called freckles."

"You should have them removed. Now as far as the Star Force Commander actually giving you a command shift..."

Jaime looked at him, and then at the holo-display – the blinking object in space was getting increasingly closer. "Perhaps we can discuss my ability to lead later...like in the arena? For now however, would you be so kind as to release the command to me so my crew can take over?"

Leopold looked at his command display, they were so close. He had to remain on duty just another minute. "No, I don't think so. I don't think I will ever relinquish command to a Normal."

"Alpha Starship Captain, first of all, it is the hour for my command. Second, have you noticed you are steering the ship dangerously close to an unknown object?"

"Ah, so the truth comes out!" He jumped out of the command seat and looked up directly into her eyes. "You want to make the discovery so you can take the glory and profit from it. Admit it! No, I will not be releas..." His rant was stopped by the sudden jerking of the ship as space itself opened up and swallowed them.

Jaime Bordeaux:

It happened quickly, the small bright blinking object no bigger than a light bulb suddenly opened up and swallowed the enormous starship. The ship lurched and began accelerating – sending Leopold flying across the bridge as he had not activated his personal gravity stabilizer field. Jaime who had activated her unit as soon as she entered the bridge, stood steadfast. As always, a Blessed did not follow standard operating procedures and was now lying on the floor unconscious.

The bridge was in a state of confusion and panic, as all of the Blessed officers were in shock over the sudden change in space. The holo-display showed streaking flashes of light as the ship moved farther in. The Blessed bridge crew sat in their chairs just staring, or crying, or glancing across their consoles trying to figure out what to do.

Halley looked at Jaime, then at the helmsman just sitting at the console sobbing. Jaime nodded giving her permission to Halley, who took the man, spun him around and pushed him out of the chair. She left him curled up and sobbing on the floor as she took control of the ship. She looked at the controls for a moment then called out "Beta Starship Captain – I cannot take control of the ship as the former Captain still has lockout command."

"Shit!" she said as she looked at the command chair – his command palm plate was still magnetically embedded in the left arm rest of the chair's console. Until he releases command, she could do nothing to save the ship. She jumped out of the chair and ran over to the unconscious Captain. She dragged him over to the command chair, supported his back, set him up and held his left hand up to the command chair. "Alpha Starship Captain, you must release the ship!"

She lightly slapped his face to bring him into a semi-conscious state. Finally, he slightly opened his eyes "What?" he said in a groggy, confused voice.

"You have to release command of the ship – otherwise we are going to die!"

"What?" he said again.

"Oh, come on…" she said in frustration "release the ship to me, now!"

"What? Release? Release what?" That was all he needed to say, the bridge command computer heard and recognized his weakened voice giving some semblance of the release command. The chair beeped and she held his left palm up closer to the chair. The command palm plate wiggled, and then flew out of the socket in the chair to his hand and then bonded into his palm.

"Finally!" she said as she dropped him back to the floor – he gave out a slight "ugh" as his head hit the hard metal floor again. His eyes rolled back into his head and he passed out again. "Oops…"

Not wasting another moment, she jumped into the command chair and placed her palm onto the command control on the left arm rest. A second later the small metal plate embedded in her palm wiggled loose and left her hand integrating itself with the command console. The command display cleared and then displayed *"Welcome Beta Starship Captain."* The rest of her crew took their respective seats in an equivalent manner as Halley – forcibly.

"Give me status, Helm?"

"We have ion and pulsar drive control -- we can increase or decrease our speed. We have nowhere to steer however, as this is some sort of tunnel, I don't think trying to turn around would be wise. I suggest we stay on a straight-line course through it and hope for the best."

"Very good… Science?"

Katsumi examined her readouts "It is some sort of gravity well – but the forces inside appear to be increasing against us. It looks like it is starting to actually push against us."

"So, can we use that opposite force to allow it to push us back out?"

"No, we can't do that Beta Starship Captain!" Jonathan yelled out from the engineering station.

Now turning to the young man, she queried "Why not?"

"Everything is indicating that the force to push us out is not there. I suggest we instead increase our speed and fight the opposing force. It is not forceful enough to prevent us from gaining speed. I suggest we push our way through this."

She looked back to Katsumi. She looked at her console again and nodded yes. "Very well, increase our speed Helm."

Jonathan yelled out "Beta Starship Captain, may I suggest that we activate the repulsion coils. It might help us to resist this gravity force against us."

Without thinking she called out "Do it!" Jonathan activated the field coils surrounding the ship causing a very slight bubble of force to repel the gravimetric forces formerly pushing against the ship.

Katsumi called out "Beta Starship Captain, a large opening is showing on SCADAR and there are objects inside the opening. However, there is something not right as I am getting massive gravity readings also ahead. I think I see another opening on the opposite side however. We might try to increase our speed and attempt a run at that opening."

Jaime connected to her science console and looked at the readouts from SCADAR. "I agree. Halley, kick the ion drives to maximum."

Halley scrunched her forehead slightly as she knew the engines had never been put into full thrust output. The thrust would put the ship to near light speed – however with the gravity forces, she was feeling she now thought that perhaps the ship might instead tear itself apart. Nonetheless, she closed her eyes for a moment and pulled fully back on the ion drive thrust control while whispering *"Come on, stay together..."*

The ship zipped into a massive void at the end of the tunnel. Light came from all the cosmic forces that swirled around the outside of the huge void cavern. Around them they could see large alien vessels floating around the enormous void space. Halley smoothly maneuvered around the strange looking vessels. The ship's repulsion field continued to hold which allowed the ship to float by many of the disabled vessels – however, about halfway through the void the ship began to buck and pulse in its forward movement.

Jaime looked at her readout. "Jonathan, we are losing it. Turn up the power on the coils."

"Beta Starship Captain, if we do that we will burn them out."

"If we don't, it might not matter! We might end up like those ships out there. I really don't want to spend the rest of my life here please."

"You have a point..." he applied full voltage to the coils surrounding the hull of the ship.

The ship began to glow from the heat, but the forces attempting to keep them in the void were repelled enough to permit the ion drives to regain enough thrust to sling them to the small opening in the opposite side of the void. Within a moment they were entering another tunnel – forces once again battered against the ship. The battle between the engines, the repulsion forces of the ship, and the gravity flow within the tunnel were tremendous.

A high-pitched noise began emanating across the entire ship, causing everyone aboard to cover their ears in pain. On the bridge, computer equipment began overheating from the strain being placed on it to maintain the voltage flow within the coils. The temperature across the ship was increasing and the crew was beginning to pass out from the heat. Jaime was beginning to think they were not going to make it when just as quickly as the thought entered her mind, the forces against the ship began to subside. She looked over at Katsumi "Is the force against us weakening?"

"It appears so Beta Starship Captain!"

"Jonathan, turn down the voltage!" He immediately followed her orders. The high-pitched squeal subsided and the temperature began to go down.

"Beta Starship Captain..." it was Katsumi, "there is something ahead – directly in our path."

"Shit, now what?" She looked into the holo-display – something large and dark was in their path and appeared to take up the entire gravity tunnel.

Halley was manipulating her computer controls as she examined the large object in their path. She adjusted the maneuvering controls on her screen, taking measurements and marking spots on the object. Finally, she turned to Jaime and called out "I think we can squeeze through..."

"Really?" Halley shook her head yes. Jaime looked at Jonathan who just shrugged his shoulders. "Well, what choice do we have? Go ahead..."

She took the control stick and powered down the ion thrusters. A planetoid was blocking their path and all Halley could find was a small canyon creating an opening that she thought – hoped -- she could pilot through. She guided the speeding ship skillfully toward the opening. Her computer console showed an outline of the trench ahead all in green – her confidence grew. She turned the ship sideways and completed her approach. Sweat rolled down her forehead as she stared at the navigation monitor while she steered. Suddenly, the console turned red – it had missed a measurement in the trench and a hidden overhang was now visible. The ship would not fully clear the only opening in the object. She quietly whispered "Damn, we aren't going to make it…" Jaime's eyes opened wide upon hearing that.

Two digital chirps inside the bridge, then two explosions in front of the ship caused the opening to quickly enlarge allowing for the ship to barely pass through. Both Jaime and Halley, surprised, let out a large gasp of air as the ship passed, albeit barely, through the trench and into open space. The sounds of thousands of rock fragments pinged across the hull of the ship. Finally realizing that they somehow made it, Jaime queried "What the hell just happened? I thought we were done for…" She looked around the room.

When her glance came upon Yuri, he simply gave a cocky look and flashed the smile of a cat that just ate the bird. He held up his hand with the fire control glove and then gave thumbs up. "I hope you did not mind if I widened the opening Beta Starship Captain…" Still slightly shocked, all Jaime could do was shake her head in the negative. His toothy grin became even bigger.

Lindy mumbled "He is going to be impossible to work with now…" she stopped speaking as her communication port became completely active. She was totally quiet for a few seconds before calling out "Beta Starship Captain, I am getting comm calls from all over the ship. Everyone is in a panic…including the Star Fleet Commander…"

Still slightly dazed, she mumbled "Aw damn…that's all I need…"

Jonathan manipulated his computer console "I have locked down the bridge logs Beta Starship Captain – no one will be able to manipulate them." She gave him a nod and a slight smile.

Now fully back to reality, she quickly stood up and called out. "All stop!" She looked at the star screens around the Bridge "Now, where the hell are we? Give me a celestial fix please."

Halley looked at her navigation console for a moment before saying "I can't. I am not seeing any familiar fixtures."

Katsumi also looked at her science station, then looked at Jaime, and shrugged "I cannot get a fix either. I don't think we are anywhere near where we were a few minutes ago."

"Not a single recognizable star or constellation?" Both of the women shook their heads no, with worried looks on their faces.

Jonathan called out "Beta Starship Captain, I think you should look at the ship's chronometer…"

She looked at the flight time on her console:

Starlight Flight Time: 0 days, 0 hours, 0 minutes:

Jaime walked up to the forward star screen. In front of the ship, a strange colorful nebula floated in the distance. She turned and looked at the rear star screen which showed the planetoid they just avoided. The small light of the gravity tunnel, if it was there, was hidden behind the planetoid. In every other direction she looked, space was packed with stars. She ran her fingers through her hair as she wondered out loud "Where the hell are we?"

Day 0

Boral Oldham

He awoke by being thrown out of bed and onto the floor. To add insult to injury, he was then tossed into the wall with a sudden shift in the opposite direction. Boral was definitely not happy, and he knew why – it was because of "her". That damn woman was in command and had done something to his ship. He needed to find out what she had done – but he needed to see in person. As soon as the ship appeared to have settled down, he quickly got dressed and ordered priority transport from his cabin to the bridge.

When he arrived, he found Jaime standing at full attention along with Alpha Starship Captain Leopold Muldoon. Leopold had a smug look on his face. The younger Blessed Captain clicked his heels at attention when he walked onto the bridge. Boral walked in and looked at him – a small trickle of blood had flowed down the right side of his forehead and into his blonde hair. He did not know the blood existed until Boral took out a hankie, wetted it with his saliva and cleaned up the little dribble of dried blood from his skin.

He then stepped back and looked at the two Captains. "Now, would someone mind telling me what the hell just happened?" he screamed out. Behind him he heard the bridge door open and in his peripheral vision saw Kip enter the Bridge. The young Captain walked over and shoved Jonathan away from the engineering console and began to work his way through the computer records.

Leopold stepped forward "Star Force Commander, this…woman…took over command and as soon as she did she ran the ship into some bright light. I think she was after riches and reward – despite my recommendations against getting near the phenomenon. Well, as soon as she hit it I was thrown across the bridge and was rendered unconscious. I do not know what happened after that. I barely just awoke!"

Leopold stepped back, and Boral took a step forward and put his face as close to Jaime as he could – he detected a very pleasant smell on her that made it hard to keep his aversion toward her at that proximity. He forced an angry scowl as he looked up at her. "So, you got greedy and put the ship – my ship --

into danger for your own personal gain? I will have you spaced for this Bordeaux!" He motioned for two of his personal guards, who stepped forward and each took one of her arms. "Alpha Starship Captain, will you show us the evidence on the computer records?"

He looked at Kip who gave him a pained look then shrugged his shoulders. Boral returned a questioning look. Kip sighed and activated the holographic record of the events that had just taken place. Boral watched with a confused look as he saw Leopold run the ship into the gravity well and then witnessed how Jaime and her crew had found a way to not only prevent being trapped in the void, but were also able get the ship out of the well and around the planetoid blocking the exit.

"Alpha Starship Captain Gurrigan, have those computer records been altered in any way?" He knew the answer without needing to ask. She did it to him again, he was sure.

"No Star Force Commander…the records had been locked preventing any alteration. This is the actual record of events."

Boral sighed quietly. "Very well…" He looked at Leopold "After I dismiss you, you will be confined to quarters until I figure out what to do with you. Definitely your entertainment privileges will be revoked!" Jaime cringed at the light treatment and Leopold gave a small nod before looking down at the floor like a beaten dog. "Kip, do we have any idea where the hell we ended up?"

Kip looked over the navigation records "No idea yet Star Force Commander…"

"Star Force Commander, Alpha and Beta Starship Captains…" it was Katsumi at the science station "I think you may want to see this." She activated the main holo-display in the center of the bridge – a probe was doing a fly over of the planetoid that was blocking the gravity well.

"Who ordered that probe?" Boral yelled.

"I did Star Force Commander" Jaime replied. "As per Command Regulations 1 dash 3 Section 38 Chapter 77 Order 4 hash 4-0-3, my Star Force Commander! "Upon entering an area that is unknown, and a planetary body or bodies exist in the area, the Starship Bridge Commander will immediately launch exploratory probes." I have followed that order my Star Force Commander" she called out. Boral looked at Kip again – he nodded acknowledgement that she was correct.

"Um, Star Force Commander...I think you will want to see this part of the flyover..." Katsumi announced in a shy quiet voice.

All of them turned and looked at the image again. It showed the surface of the planetoid littered with the smashed and broken bodies of various starships. None of those ships had been as lucky as Starlight. Kip's eyes lit up "Star Force Commander, I believe there is a goldmine of raw materials and possibly alien technology down there. We could build at least one more starship from all of that junk!"

Jaime felt a slight buzz in her left ear followed by a voice "We have to get over there – the technology could be invaluable!" she slightly nodded. She also wondered how they were able to know what was transpiring on the bridge. She now suspected that this group of Normals she had joined was much more than met the eye.

Boral rubbed his stubbly chin still thinking of Kip's suggestion. "Hmmm, I believe you are right Kip..." he looked at Jaime, then at Leopold. "Yes, you two...gather your crews and pick any others you will need to run salvage on that rock. I will be rid of you, and while you salvage, we will explore this area and perhaps even test out the ship. Get to it!"

Jaime saluted and then held her left palm out and ordered the release of command – her command module loosened from the arm of the command console and magnetically flew to her hand embedding itself back into its metallic cradle. She then turned and nodded to her bridge crew who followed close behind her to the bridge door. Leopold followed suit, quickly leaving while he had the chance. Boral watched Jaime's backside walk calmly away from him – her scent was still blurring his thoughts. Once his thoughts cleared, he looked at Kip. "Launch a location buoy – we don't want to lose Leopold. I think it is time we tested out the crawler, don't you?"

Kip gave him a huge smile. "Yes Sir, Star Force Commander! I will begin preparations!"

Jaime Bordeaux:

She put the call out for volunteers as soon as she returned to her quarters. She cleaned up and by the time she was getting dressed she found that she already had a full list of recruits for her salvage team. She put on her space uniform and headed out to the launch bay. She was surprised to find that all of them were already waiting in the launch bay by the time she arrived. She had her bridge crew of course, but she was surprised to find about hundred others including Max, Jeremy, and Delta Starship Captain Allen James.

She stopped and looked at the three men standing at attention. "You guys, what do you think you are doing?"

Max answered, "I think it is obvious Beta Starship Captain – we have volunteered to go on this mission."

She got close to the three men and whispered "You do realize that they could possibly leave us here and not come back, don't you?"

The three men nodded. Max got right up to Jaime's ear and whispered "I don't think we are worried. They will not leave us...there is too much valuable material down there...good material for us to use if they did not return. Besides, we know the risks."

She gave a slightly surprised look, then smiled and put her hand on his shoulder and nodded while whispering "So, how many are in this little cabal?"

He tapped on the communication device on his left ear, smiled and simply said "Most that are here..." she looked at Allen who gave a slight nod of acknowledgment. Just a few feet down from him Halley looked at her with an amused look – beyond her Jonathan looked at her and winked. Surprised, she scrunched the skin of her forehead trying to clear the bit of confusion as to just how many were hooked into the Normal communication network. Max reached up, touched her forehead and softly said "Stop wrinkling your brow...it will become permanent."

She gave a slight chuckle then turned and continued down the line of men and women. She stopped at Jonathan and said "So, who is going to keep this ship together if you come with us?"

"The Chief Engineer is a Normal, Beta Starship Captain – she will take good care of the ship and make sure it gets back in one piece."

She sighed, then called out "Well, alright everyone...determine what we need – atmosphere generators, shelters, tools, assembly robots, equipment...get it on the ship, then put on your spacesuits and board the transport." She heard footsteps behind her and turned to see Leopold standing behind her along with about fifty Blessed and another fifty Normal workers.

"All Normal, eh? Good, we need the labor…I take it you are ready and were just waiting for me to arrive?" Jaime made no indication whatsoever. "Very good…" he tapped some instructions into his command module – a list showed up on a holo-display on Jaime's module "Here is a list of supplies that I require – have your Normals load them onto my vessel. Afterward, you may board your vessel…Oh, and take my Normals with you. I would prefer they do not ride with us."

"Very good Alpha Starship Captain…" she acknowledged with a tight jaw. She looked over his list – totally incomplete. She then looked at the complement of Normals he selected to accompany him. "Come on, figure out what you will need, let's get it loaded and then you can board our ship."

All the Normals worked with amplified energy as they were excited to be finally getting off the ship for some exploration. While the Blessed watched, the Normal crew spent the next three hours loading the two transport ships with a myriad of items for survival that they might need to live, and manufacturing tools to salvage whatever they could from the derelict spacecraft that were now lying on the planetoid that was blocking the gravity well. They then put on space suits and boarded the gray colored transport vessels. Jaime walked around and inspected her transport vessel – it was slightly bullet shaped, had small fins on the sides, top, and at the rear. Slots in the sides of the craft allowed for wings to be extended when flying in the atmosphere if needed. The rear of the craft consisted of a large crawler drive as it was sub-space capable, also a set of ion drives for normal space. The front of the craft flattened out from the top slightly where the pilot's compartment sat. On each side of Leopold's craft, a Blessed had painted two large lightning bolts in yellow and in red paint were scrolled the words "Thunderclap of Death" – on her ship painted in pink letters "The Rebel Queen".

Jaime called out to Allen on her communication device "As soon as we get to the planetoid, get out there with a crew and remove that…" Allen looked up, cringed at the sloppily written text and gave a hearty nod.

Within three hours the two medium sized transport vehicles were ready to leave the space ark. She personally piloted her transport vessel with Halley as copilot. Over the ship-to-ship communication system Starship Hangar Control announced, "Thunderclap of Death, Rebel Queen, prepare for launch – Acknowledge."

Jaime ignored the controller and instead replied "Transport 359-Zulu, ready for departure."

The two craft left through the rear launch bay of the ship and made a straight line to the planetoid blocking the path that would return them to their known space. In the distance on each side were two sets of two identical planetary bodies making a total of five planetoids. She wondered if each of them was blocking a similar passageway. She made an orbit around the top of the large body then travelled down the other side and slowly passed by the bottom of the dead giant rock – avoiding any orbits around the circumference of the planetoid as they did not want to find the gravity well with the transports. Katsumi scanned the surface as they circled to both evaluate the wrecks and to search for the best spot to setup a base camp – Jonathan stood behind her watching the readouts. Finally, she and Jonathan found a suitable spot on the lower pole of the blockading rocky body. Jaime carefully and skillfully landed the transport craft onto the exact spot specified by the pair.

Over the space communications channel Leopold announced "We have selected a spot on the top pole of this rock – send our workers over, would you? We need to get unloaded as soon as possible."

"Damn him" she muttered. "Allen, would you and Jonathan organize the unloading of the ship. As soon as all is off-loaded, and you are setting up base camp I will fly his crew up there." Allen acknowledged her command and gave a quick snappy salute. He and Jonathan went about their tasks.

Three hours later, the ship had been emptied of its cargo and Jaime flew the fifty Normal crew members to the northern camp. When she arrived, she noted that absolutely nothing had been done. Their transport ship still sat fully loaded as the Blessed were not about to do any menial tasks -- after all, that was why they brought the Normal crew. She bid the Normals the best of luck, offered assistance if needed, then took off and flew back to the southern camp.

Upon returning she circled the site of the camp and was amazed at how quickly everyone on her team had chipped in to get the camp set up. The team already laid out and filled the large inflatable bubble that would be used for living and organization of the salvage operation – it looked like a large white slug laying on the dead surface as it inflated. She received a report that Allen and Max were already out scouting around the area. She looked down from the circling ship -- the ground was littered with the masses of dead spacecraft. She was not even sure how many ships had crashed there as it was too many to count. In the distance, she could see a blinking bright light – the gravity well. She would make sure everyone stayed far away from that area.

She decided to pick a spot between some of the relics to land the transport in hopes it would conceal the ship slightly – just in case someone was to stop by. She was not sure why she felt the need to conceal the ship, but she had a nagging feeling. Upon landing she put on a clear helmet which sealed around her space suit, opened the transport hatch, lowered the loading ramp and found she was greeted on the ramp by Max who had just come out of one of the wrecks. He waved at her and she felt the now familiar buzzing of what she had decided to call *"Norm-Comm"* behind her left ear. She flexed her jaw slightly to activate the device.

Max had the tone of voice and excitement of a young child experiencing his first time in a candy store "Jaime, you won't believe this place! There is technology everywhere just waiting to be removed and studied. We are going to learn so much by being here. I honestly am glad they decided to leave us Normals here. The question is...how much of this can we take and hide?"

"Hide? You do not want to tell everyone about our discoveries?"

"Think about it Jaime...Do you want Star Force Commander Oldham to have everything we find?"

"You have a point..."

"Glad you see what I mean..." she could almost detect the smile in his voice. "In any case, some of these wrecks will only provide raw materials – but a few of them may actually still be active!"

"Beta Starship Captain…" it was Allen on the standard communications channel. "I found a cave. We may be able to seal and pressurize it."

"Very well Delta Starship Captain. Grab Jonathan and a few people and see what you can do. Do not spend too much time if you cannot make it suitable for us. We have way too much to do, and Starlight will not be gone that long."

He acknowledged with a simple "Roger that."

"Jaime…" Max called out on Norm-Comm again "we may want to consider exploring the other rocks in the area. There could be even more things to discover – perhaps take a scout craft from Starlight?"

She took a step down off the ramp and stumbled on her first step as she left the artificial gravity generated by the ship. She realized she had to adjust to the low gravity, so she took her first steps on alien soil slowly. She looked up into this new unknown galaxy that she was about to explore. In the distance, she could see two of the other planetoids – she wondered what secrets they were hiding. In the other direction, she could see Starlight and beyond that a colorful nebula along with billions of stars – more than she could ever remember seeing from her Solar System. As alien as this new galaxy appeared to her, it somehow also felt so familiar.

Day 15:

Max Sollix:

They had now spent two weeks on what had become lovingly known as "Stopper" -- named for the way it blocked any access to the gravity well, which had been given the nickname "Devil's Throat". Their time there so far had been quite productive. During their exploration, they had found a large complex of caverns. These caverns were solid and deep – which allowed for pressure doors to be installed. That in turn provided a secure place for installing the atmosphere generators which pressurized the caves and converted them into viable living spaces. They would then seal more areas of the caves where they could set up the shops that would allow them to salvage gear and materials and store those finds from the wrecked starships. Once materials were salvaged and manufactured into usable parts, sections of the new starship could be assembled and moved out onto the surface. Those sections could then be taken into space to be assembled into their final configuration.

This particular day however, Max had been kept busy by his trained profession. He had received many complaints ranging from skin irritations to growths. Most of the work team had been complaining about the same small skin irritations on the tops of their ears. The irritation was the same complaint that Jaime had recently come to him regarding. Along with the irritations, Max had noticed that everyone who had complained about the irritation had also started showing the same small bumps on the top of their ears. The skin growths were what was concerning to him – as a matter of fact, Max himself noticed the same bumps on his own ears when he woke up that morning. He was now worried that perhaps this was some disease native to this galaxy. Or perhaps this particular area of space might be toxic to humans. What was also distressing was that he had not heard of any reports of these growths on any of the Blessed – thus it could be a disease that was only affecting Normal humans.

Max was searching his computer looking for anything that might give him a clue to this disorder when a call came in on Norm-Comm. It was Delta Starship Captain Allen James. "Max, do you have a few minutes?"

"Sure, do you have a medical emergency or problem?"

"No, actually we found something. We are not sure what to make of it – since Jaime was called back to Starlight, perhaps you can shed some light on it? We are in salvage ship A-5."

"On my way..." he already had his pressure suit on as he had been making some house calls that morning. He snapped on his helmet and exited the cavern habitat via the nearest air lock. He only had a short distance to jump/run to the location of that particular ship.

He arrived and entered the air lock. He was surprised to find that the ship still held its pressure and was filled with an oxygen-rich atmosphere. He removed his helmet as he received another Norm-Comm message from Allen. "I will activate a beacon and meet you half way" he replied. Allen activated the beacon and Max used the small increasing beeps in his ear to guide him through the winding corridors of the alien vessel. The ship was devoid of any other life as the entire crew had died long ago – only a bony skeleton here and there littered the passageways.

He came upon Allen about halfway to the ship's bridge. "Max, this ship is a gold mine of technology. The engines appear to have been damaged when the ship crashed, but otherwise the ship stayed intact. Unfortunately for the crew, their food supply ran out."

Max nodded and noted another pile of bones on the floor. He stopped to examine the long set of dried bones stretched out in the hallway. There was a burn mark on what appeared to be the creature's elongated head – a blast mark from a weapon he surmised. "This one has been shot. What do you suppose went on in their last days?"

"I would suspect that they started attacking each other in a fight for the remaining food scraps. There are bodies like this all over the ship. Only three had remained on the bridge. Fortunately for us, their power systems were able to survive better than the crew. This ship is still fully powered and if it weren't for its lack of engines, we could take off in it right now. Jonathan has found an interesting field generator, we have the physics team looking at it and we hope to soon have an idea of what it actually does. Jonathan thinks that perhaps it will generate an electrical or magnetic field – possibly for protection. I am sure they will figure it out soon. We have also found some devices we think might be weapons. Oh, and look at these..." He handed Max a small metallic ball – no bigger than a shot for a bb gun. Just placing it in his hand, the force of the weight against his skin and bone almost broke his hand with some form of high gravity. Max groaned under the strain of the small ball in his hand. "Yeah, that was my reaction to the first time someone handed me one of those. They seem to have some sort of built in ultra-heavy gravity field in the metal. Who knows what we will be able to do with those...we found a case of 'em. Ah, here we are – come in here Max..."

They approached an open door that led to a room off the main corridor. A few feet ahead at the end of the corridor, Max saw a large entrance leading to what looked like might be the bridge. Allen motioned him to step inside the smaller entryway. Entering the room Max could see that the room was designed for the purpose of living – albeit for an alien form. From the decor and size, he surmised that it might even be the Captain's or Commander's living quarters. On one wall was a structure that Max assumed was for resting – it was indented to support a being with a large long head who also had thin arms and legs. On the opposite wall sat what appeared to be some sort of command console and a wall sized viewing screen – now deactivated. In the corner furthest from the door, Jonathan was huddled in front of a storage bin. Inside this bin Max saw several stacked closed containers. These containers were each about three feet long by two and half feet tall, and the same amount deep.

"What did you find?" he asked.

"Well Max, each one of these is a stasis chamber – and every one of them is active." Allen replied.

Max rubbed his chin "Interesting, I wonder what's in 'em?"

"Well..." Jonathan mumbled.

He looked at the young man "Please tell me you didn't open one...you didn't did you?" Jonathan now had a guilty look on his face as he gave a very small nod of acknowledgement. "Oh god, did you release something?"

"Fortunately for him he didn't – it is in stasis" Allen answered. "However, what he did find inside, I think you will find interesting." He reached for the latches on one of the boxes.

Max reached out and stopped Allen's hand from unlocking the case "Allen, one mistake has already been made and you were lucky. Let s not press our luck with alien life!"

"You need to see this...it is *not* alien..."

Max gave a confused look "What?" Allen opened the box -- a deep blue light filled the room as he opened it. When the lid was fully raised Max peered into the case and gasped. "Is that what I think it is?" Allen nodded yes. "My god, I thought all of these died in the bombing..."

Jonathan asked "So, what do we do with them?"

Max rubbed his chin again. "Can't leave 'em here. I think they are safe – they are still in stasis anyway. Take them back to the habitat."

Jonathan gave a big grin "I was hoping you would say that!"

"Now Jonathan, don't even think about shutting down the stasis fields!"

He gave a whining "AWWW..." then shrugged his shoulders "Ok, I will not deactivate the cases."

"Good boy!" he said, then looked at the open box again "So, the question is...how the hell did they get onto an alien ship and why did they take them all the way out here?"

Jaime Bordeaux:

A small shuttle had come down to Stopper to pick her up and return her to Starlight. She was not sure why, all she was told was that the Star Force Commander wanted to see her. She arrived at the space ark and was immediately escorted to his quarters. She rang the annunciator and was surprised to be greeted by a casually dressed Boral Oldham.

"Ah, Bordeaux...come in, come in!" He motioned for her to come in. His quarters were lavishly decorated and dimly lit. He was dressed in a green satin shirt, slightly open, exposing his hairy chest. She noted that the hair on his chest was turning quite gray. He also sported a baggy pair of black casual pants that were bound at the ankles showing his white socks and soft soled black slippers. "Here, please sit. Make yourself comfortable..." He motioned for her to sit on a fully stuffed, black, faux leather couch -- she obediently followed his suggestion and now really wondered what was going on.

He went to a built-in bar on the other side of the large living cabin. He took out a bottle of clear liquid and poured the fluid into a shaker, added ice, shook the concoction, then poured it into two glasses. He walked back and presented her with one of the glasses. She suspiciously eyed the fluid in the glass. "Don't worry, it is not poisonous. It is an Earth delicacy beverage – slightly alcoholic and very tasty. It is a potato derivative that is distilled into a beverage called Vodka. Try it, you will enjoy it. I insist..."

She sniffed the liquid and smelled the light but strong aroma of the drink. He took a sip then motioned for her to follow suit. She put the glass to her lips and took a small sip. She curled her lip slightly as she tasted the pure alcohol on her palate.

"Good, isn't it?" she said nothing "Now, down the hatch...to your health." He raised his glass at her and motioned for her to follow. She took the glass and gulped it down – it almost made her gag. She felt the warmth of the fluid drift down her esophagus and into her stomach. A moment later, she began to feel the effects of the alcohol in her head. She was surprised how quickly she felt it enter her mind. She now realized why he had summoned her here this evening – and wondered how she was going to get out of this without killing him. He took her glass and poured another of the chilled drink and handed it to her. "Have another...relax. I thought that perhaps we should get together, talk and get to know each other better. I thought it might help in forming a partnership of cooperation." He motioned her to follow his lead and belt down the second glass of the toxic fluid. She did as instructed, and again felt the almost immediate effect in her head. Once again, he took her glass and poured yet another round of drinks.

Feeling the effects, she started to worry. *"Damn you, I know what you are trying...and I am not sure how much more I can drink and keep my sanity..."* Her head was already spinning, and her vision blurred slightly. Through fuzzy vision she saw him hand her another glass of the venom. Again, he motioned her to follow his lead and gulp down the mind-numbing fluid. She belted it down and felt her worries and inhibitions start to wane – she wanted to fight it, but was unable.

"So, Jaime...you don't mind if I call you Jaime, do you?" he said as he plopped himself down on the cushy sofa almost sitting on her, and now so close that she felt his body heat on the few sections of her exposed skin. She noticed him bring his face up to her shoulder and he sniffed. The vodka burned in her belly and her mind, making her head numb and preventing her normal thoughts. He whispered, "I don't see any reason we can't be friends...or maybe even more?"

She gulped as she felt him start to put an arm around her. Her mind was too confused by the liquor to come up with a plan – for the moment. What happened after that moment she was not sure -- but she suddenly noticed that the feelings of wooziness in her head were fading from her brain as quickly as they appeared. Within another minute she found her mind had totally cleared. She was then able to logically think about her situation and come up with a way out of this without losing her commission or face charges of murder.

She then got an idea she needed to test "Boral...may I call you that?" he nodded and raised his eyebrows "I think that I like that Vodka. May I have some more?"

He got an evil smile on his face, jumped up as quickly as his fat legs would allow and made another shaker of the chilled vodka drink. He quickly brought it back to her, poured a glass and handed it to her.

"I hope you are going to join me? This stuff makes me feel happy and free and I do not want to feel so free all by myself..." she said with a playful small grin on her face. He reached for his glass and poured himself a matching amount of the drink. She held the glass up and tapped his glass with it, then belted the swill down. A moment later, she felt the effects shoot to her brain – then immediately fade.

For the next hour, every time he started to get close she would ask for another drink and insisted that he join her. Thinking he was making progress, he obediently obeyed her request.

In a slurring voice he finally said "I...I really can...can't believe you're still...still drinking? May I...I tell...tell you how beautiful you are?"

"Tell me with another one of those wonderful drinks, hmm?" he poured them another round from the shaker and then belted it down without even waiting for her. "Now, what was it you were saying?" He looked at her with crossed eyes, gagging slightly as the last drink hit his belly. He waivered while he sat next to her, then began to wobble, and finally fell into her lap unconscious. Using one finger, she pushed on his shoulder until he fell to the floor. He lay on the carpeted floor snoring with the volume of an ion engine at full throttle. She walked to the door and opened it. The guard looked at her with surprise. She nodded behind her "He couldn't handle his liquor I guess…" The guard chuckled and smiled slightly, then motioned her to follow him back to the shuttle.

On the way back, she pondered on this latest one of many changes she had been experiencing. She wondered how she managed to recover from the effects of the alcohol so quickly. She also wondered what else she would discover as she seemed to be changing more and more with each day she spent in this new universe.

Day 30:

Jaime Bordeaux:

Work had progressed quite well since they arrived on Stopper. Many items of technology had already been found and were being studied by the Normal scientific staff. From the reports she received from the Normals at Leopold's salvage camp, they had not been as fruitful in their salvage operations. So far, they had only found usable metals and building materials at the top of the planetoid. She assumed that the top side of Stopper had already been picked clean of technology. All the better she thought, as everyone on her team was worried to let the Blessed have any of the new-found technology without first seeing what threat it posed to themselves in the long run.

It was this morning that Max, Allen, and Katsumi had come to her with a proposal. Yesterday Katsumi had sent out a probe from the base that found a wealth of un-salvaged spacecraft on one of the other nearby planetoids, deftly named "Bung". In addition, the probe had showed that there were systems of caverns within that planetoid body that had the capability to house a large-scale salvage and manufacturing operation. They added that this cavern was large enough to allow for the building of spacecraft. The spacecraft that could be built within the cavern could be large enough to house many Normals – allowing them to break away from Starlight and the Blessed – she now understood that this was the true reason for their fate in going on this mission and for being there.

Allen had asked to take the transport and a few of the work crew, to go out and explore Bung and verify that it had the capability to house this hidden base. They suggested that they transport over while Starlight was away on an upcoming mapping mission. During the few days, the ship would be gone would be just enough time to get over there and set up an initial base. From there, they could work in secret, setting up savage operations and beginning the process of putting together a ship – a ship for Normals. Jaime agreed that this mission was a worthwhile risk and had approved it.

She took another sip of her coffee while she looked at the view screen in the mess hall of the salvage base. On the screen was the image of Starlight floating in the distance as it orbited above the planetoid. A moment later, the ion drives on the craft lit up and the ship zoomed off -- now only stars filled the view screen display.

She tapped on her Norm-Comm "Allen, put together your exploration crew and take what you need. We are set up enough to give up half of the crew. Go find something for us."

An excited Allen replied "Very good Beta Starship Captain. I won't disappoint."

She tapped her Norm-Comm again "Halley, get the transport ready to take Allen and his work team. He will give you the location and details en route. Take the southern route – do your best to avoid the SCADAR from Leopold's base."

Within a few hours the ship was loaded and on its way.

Allen James:

Allen was very excited at the prospect of exploring another of the planetoids that formed the half-circle of unnaturally set rocks – all blocking the openings of gravity wells. He was headed to the farthest away planetoid that had been code named "Bung". Bung was located next to Plug and then Stopper -- where the Devil's Throat that led to their galaxy was located. On the other side of Stopper was Cork, and finally Lid.

The fly-over surveys of Bung had showed not only a wealth of available salvage in the form of crashed spacecraft, but also a large network of tunnels that could be transformed into facilities for the conversion of raw materials and salvage into starship parts which could then be assembled into starships.

It took an hour at low sub-light speed to get to Bung. The proximity of the five planetoids prevented higher speeds between the bodies by the transport craft. It was not a problem however, as Halley was piloting the craft and was very careful to avoid detection by the other base at the top of Stopper.

He had taken twenty other Normal crew members to assist with exploring and setting up a base camp on Bung. He hoped that within a month they would be in full salvage and manufacturing mode. He just hoped the smelting and manufacturing robots they had completed and had taken with them would be up to the task. The robots had been redesigned by the science staff at the base on Stopper to be more efficient and almost self-sustaining. That would enable the humans to spend more time exploring the wrecks and collecting salvage for the robots to work with.

By the time Halley had landed the transport onto the surface of Bung, Allen was about out of his mind in anticipation of setting up a camp and getting work started. Through the viewports of the transport, he could see the heaps of wrecked spacecraft along the backside of the planetoid. Just looming along the surface of the back of Bung blinked the always hazardous gateway, another gravity well. He wondered where this particular well would lead, if one were to enter.

It took them three more hours to unload the supplies and another hour to get the equipment to the cavern that had been scouted out and would soon become their base of operations. He felt so at home here – he was not sure why exactly, but it felt very comfortable.

Once all the equipment was set up, Allen assembled the salvage crew and immediately went out to the nearest wreck. This particular ship was completely dead, but appeared to have a wealth of raw materials – identifiable forms of titanium alloys, strong and capable of becoming spacecraft fuselage or in this case, pressure doors for the caverns. These materials were quickly gathered and transported to the smelting robots. As the smelters completed their task, the materials were moved to the manufacturing robots which would then start to form the pressure doors that were to be installed.

That first night, the crew stayed in the transport while the robots worked tirelessly without needing food or oxygen – only a skeleton crew was needed to maintain the program and direct the robots in the building and installing of pressure doors within the various cavern openings, based on computer generated plans and diagrams.

Allen and the rest of the crew awoke that next morning time segment to the return of the overnight work crew. He quickly ate a small breakfast, put on his spacesuit and went out to inspect the work. As he had hoped, the robots worked both efficiently and precisely on the installation of the pressure doors. All that was still needed were for the atmosphere generators to be set up and activated. He personally directed a crew in that task and within a few hours the first amounts of atmosphere began slowly filling the caverns which would provide a future home for him and his team. It took a full eight hours of constant operation to get the caverns fully pressurized and capable of sustaining life. Since they started pressurizing the caverns, they had been as lucky on Plug as they had been on Stopper in finding precious Malatite, the element that provided the atmosphere generators with the raw materials needed to consistently keep the air clean and fresh inside the caverns. It was another sign that felt to him like this had been the correct decision – coming here was definitely the right thing to have done.

After ensuring that the pressure doors were holding, and the new habitat was properly holding air, he bid Halley farewell and watched as the transport headed back to Stopper. He wondered how long he would have here before they would have to leave to return to Stopper, and eventually to Starlight. He knew they could not stay here forever as they would discover them to be missing and eventually come looking for them. Their hope was to source enough material to create a high-speed scout craft, list one or two of the Normal staff as lost, via accidental death, and send them on their way.

These "lost" Normals would then explore and find someplace where Normals could escape the Blessed on Starlight and settle down. To find a world where they could build a new civilization of humans, not poisoned by the Supreme Commander and the Council – where no Blessed could interfere with their growth as a civilization. They just had to find that place and become strong enough to fight the Blessed should they come after them. That was the plan from the start – they just had not expected to be executing the plan this far from home, but anywhere that they can lay their heads in comfort and safety would have to be home.

The short-term objective – find raw materials, build or find engines, obtain whatever technology was hidden there, and get that first ship built. He thought it would take at least a month before they would make progress – but day two found Samuel Stave with a discovery in his hands. The young man was totally out of breath as he reached him, he had long dropped his space helmet upon entering the habitat to save energy, which allowed him to run faster.

Allen looked at him curiously as he panted trying to catch his breath. In his arms, he carried a six-foot anti-gravity case. "Sam, what's got you in such a hurry?"

Sam took a few more breaths and set the case down. "Delta Starship Captain, you have to see this…" He flipped the switches on the case to shut down the anti-gravity generators, and once the case settled on the ground he quickly unlatched the five buckles on the case and quickly whipped the case open exposing a large plastic tube. The tube glowed with a low purple tone.

Allen peered into the tube "Have you checked this? Is it dangerous or a hazard to us?"

Sam shook his head yes, still panting "We have, it's giving off no radiation hazardous to humans. At least not right now…"

Allen looked at Sam and read his face. "Ok, there is something else going on…what else do you have to tell me?"

"This is exciting – it's what else we found…an engine…a really powerful and fast one!" He could not hide his excitement.

"Ok that explains your excitement." This news excited him too. He had expected to find some great technology, but he never dreamed that it would be this quickly. They could have a ship built before they even needed to leave Bung. He gazed back down at the glowing tube "So, what do you think this is?" he asked.

Sam also returned his gaze to the tube in the case and locked his gaze on the almost magical glow it emitted as he slowly told Allen "Well, we think it is a weapon – a powerful one…if the science guys got it right."

Day 33:

Boral Oldham:

He stared at the command console, his palms sweating. He moved his fat thumb to his mouth and softly chewed on the fleshy mass.

"Star Force Commander, we are almost ready..." Kip called out from his position standing next to the engineering station.

"Very well...Helm, has the computer formulated our navigation points?"

The young Blessed helmsman called out "Almos...Yes, Star Force Commander -- it has completed its computations. We are ready to go!"

"Very good, Kip are the sub-space rams ready?" Kip nodded in the positive. Boral paused and bit his thumb again before dimming the bridge lights, turning up a bright light on himself and announcing, "Very well, power up the crawler drive, prepare to punch a hole into sub-space."

A loud whine came from the rear of the ship as the massive sub-space crawler drive began to engage. In the front of the ship a light crackling sound began as the sub-space ram beams began powering up.

"We are ready Star Force Commander. At your command..." Kip yelled out over the whine of the engines. Even from the front of the command module, the large engines in the rear of the ship filled every nook and cranny with their loud whine.

Boral rubbed his palms against his slacks then looked around the room. The crew was just waiting for his order to move the large starship. Most of the Blessed crew were sweating and nervous in anticipation and fear. No one had ever tried this before – they were scared. He stood and looked at the main star screen at the front of the bridge. "Very well, activate the ramming beams..." The crackling beam projectors became as loud as the whine of the engines and Boral could see the glow from the beam launchers as they built up the power to punch a hole in the fabric of space. Suddenly he activated his voice enhancer and yelled out "Stop! Shut down all drives and beams!"

Kip reached over the engineer and quickly flipped the switches to instantly kill the drive system. "What happened, my Star Force Commander? What's wrong?"

"Kip, there was a sound in the engines I didn't like. It did not sound right. Who is the Chief Engineer on duty?"

Kip looked through the duty roster on his command computer. "Kate Grayson...a Normal."

"Damn! Well doesn't that just figure! No wonder the engines didn't sound right! Get her replaced with a Blessed engineer, tune up those engines and let's get ready to try it..." he stopped and thought about it for a moment "some other time..."

"Star Force Commander? Sir? Some other time?" Kip queried.

"Yes, I was thinking why risk the pride of the Supreme Commander's fleet. Don't you agree that perhaps we could find a better ship to test the drive?"

"Ah, of course my Star Force Commander! Very wise indeed!"

He thought for a moment before asking Kip "The medium transports have been fitted with a smaller version of the crawler drive, haven't they?"

Kip consulted with his command computer "Why yes they have, Star Force Commander!"

"Very well, do we have any command officers assigned to any of those craft at this time?"

"Yes, my Star Force Commander...Alpha Starship Captain Leopold Muldoon and Beta Starship Captain Jaime Bordeaux."

"Ah, perfect! They are both already in space! Send...Bordeaux...she will test the engines."

"Very well, my Star Force Commander, I will send the command order immediately!"

"Yes, perfect indeed..." he could not help but let a small smile slip across his fat lipped mouth. She somehow avoided his attempt to make her his own the other night, which had left him lying on the floor with nothing to show for his efforts but a hangover -- this would give her what she deserved and would give him his revenge. After all, if she died in sub-space then all the better.

Jaime Bordeaux:

She and all of her salvage team had watched the attempted crawler drive test on their telescopic monitor. She had seen the drive fire up, the ram beam prepare to fire, then nothing.

"Damn, he went coward..." she mumbled to herself.

"What do you think happened?" Halley asked her.

"I am not sure..." she decided not to disclose her true thoughts 'perhaps a system failure?"

"I really doubt that" Jonathan let slip. Everyone looked at him, he blushed slightly and then added "Listen, Kate Grayson is the Chief Engineer and I know she would have that system in tip-top shape "

"Perhaps, but I would not let your opinions out in any other group but this one. I would like you to NOT be spaced, ok?" Jaime scolded him. He blushed and, nodded in acknowledgment. She smiled at him before turning back to the screen. "I still don't get it – if there is no way they could have failed, then why abort?"

"Beta Starship Captain, Command Line Order for you..." Lindy said from the communication console. "Shall I tunnel it to your module?"

Jaime nodded at the young blonde who securely transferred the message to her command module, which then projected a small hologram in front of her curious face. She read the message, and her jaw tightened. "Damn that coward!"

"What's wrong Jaime?" asked Max.

She loosened her jaw enough to tell him "That damn coward...he has ordered me to use the crawler drive on the transport to validate that it's safe before any Blessed use it."

"Shit..." Max replied "when?"

"Immediately, as soon as I can get into the craft and take off. They're obviously thinking it's a suicide mission."

"I'll go too, Beta Starship Captain!" Halley yelled out.

"No Halley, it is too dangerous!"

"I disagree, Beta Starship Captain. If anything, you are going to need a good helmsman. I AM the best..."

"She's right Jaime" Max interjected "she could be the person that keeps you alive in subspace."

"Those engines will work" Jonathan added "I worked on the design myself. You both will be quite safe, Beta Starship Captain!"

"Alright...get your flight suit on. We leave immediately." Halley, upon hearing this, had a huge smile come across her small mouth. She instantly ran off to suit-up and to prepare supplies for the trip.

"Beta Starship Captain..." Jonathan called out causing her to turn around to face him "we have a new scanning device we would like to install onto the ship – for testing."

Jaime looked at him "Really? Did you invent this too?"

He tilted his head, not quite sure how to answer "Well...I found the initial device in one of the wrecks and modified it to emit what I think will be a useful scanning beam. I think it will work – it should give you a detailed information stream of whatever it is focused on -- and when placed into passive scanning mode it will map any stars, planets, or features it picks up. If it works the way I think, then we will get a good mapping of this part of the galaxy."

"Well, if you can get it installed quickly..."

"I'll have it installed in just a few minutes. I had already modified the fuselage of the ship to accommodate it...just need a few minutes..." he turned and ran off, excited to test his new invention.

She smiled at the young man and gave a small laugh. "Well, I had better get ready too!"

"Wait, you might need this also..." Max held out his hand, in his palm was a small interfacing chip.

Jaime looked at the chip with curiosity "A computer chip?"

"It is a gift from one of the alien ships. The computer techs just broke the encryption and figured out what it is – it has over one hundred thousand languages. What's odd, is that it also has Council Standard English...makes you wonder doesn't it? In any case, they told me that the on-board computer can utilize this. Have one of the techs hook it into your communication console and tune the console to your Blessed communication module frequency. It will use the computer to interpret the language if it is recognized, and in turn will transmit translations to you. If you speak through your transmitter and have an external speaker, it will translate English to whatever language it has been translating...allowing you to communicate two-way. If this works as we expect it to, it will be hard to give up to the Blessed. We have made a few copies for ourselves already."

Jaime held the chip and looked at it before tossing it into the air and catching it in her fist. She then smiled at him. "Thank you, my friend. Wish us luck!"

Max put a hand on her shoulder "Jaime, one thing to know about subspace. The scientists think that the forces in there will keep you weighted down to your seats. You might want to be prepared for a long flight with your gluteus glued to the seat. Be careful and may you return safely to us." She put her hand on his, smiled and nodded before quietly walking off.

Halley Cet:

Halley did not want to admit it to Jaime, but she was excited to try the new drive. They would be the first, and she was about to see a part of this new galaxy that no human had ever seen. She was already in the transport doing system checks and validations when Jaime arrived.

"I think someone is more excited to try this than I am..." Jaime said as soon as she removed her space helmet. "Are you that confident in this drive?"

"I am!" she said as she continued to check switches and controls on the helm. "We are about to be the first...and we will see and experience who knows what? Do we have any idea where we are going Beta Starship Captain?"

"Call me Jaime when it's just the two of us...no, no idea yet. They said they will give us our destination as soon as it is selected, and we are off Stopper."

"No matter, we will make it." she said confidently – or so she hoped.

After a few more installation checks from Jonathan, who was outside working on the new sensor beam array. He then confirmed that the new array had been installed, tested, and was ready to go. He gave the following instructions over the Norm-Comm as he looked through the window on the side of the flight deck – "Ok, it is hooked up to the forward holo-screen. There also is a computer command module installed in cabinet C-8 that will record and analyze all scans as they occur. Halley, you will be able to sift through the various scans by using the selector on your star drive control. Beta Starship Captain, you can use your command module to select any scanning image or data display and have it provided to your command console at will. I also had the translator chip installed into your ship's comm system – just in case. Good luck you two – come back to us safe."

"Thank you, Jonathan, we will see you soon." Jaime said with as much confidence she could muster, as she gave him a small salute through the window. "Alright Halley, take us up and do an upper orbit while we await orders."

Halley fired up the ion drives and blasted off. She put the ship into an orbit that passed over the Blessed camp in the north, and then returned over their camp at the south pole of the planetoid. After a few minutes, a message came over Jaime's command module. She displayed it onto her command holo-display. They had picked a star system that they believed had habitable planets based on recent astronomical images. They estimated the system was about a parsec away.

She acknowledged the order "Ok Halley, I loaded the destination into the computer. Go ahead and start the formulation for sub-space entry and exit."

Halley sent commands into her helm computer then sat back. "Now we wait. It will be a few minutes for the computer to formulate our entry and exit point and the launch velocity of the chaser."

She tried to look patient, but she found she could not maintain her excitement as she wiggled in her seat in anticipation. Jaime smiled and put her hand on her shoulder "You really are excited to do this aren't you?" She nodded her head quickly.

What seemed like an eternity to her finally passed and the computer provided flight paths, entry points, and speed estimates to her navigation console. "We've got it – ready to go!"

Jaime sighed "Well ok, fire up the engines and put us into position for insertion into sub-space." Her Captain was not as excited.

Halley fired up the ion drives again and within just a few minutes had the ship at the specified spot as determined by the computer. She made a small adjustment in the alignment of the ship, used navigation jets to slow, then placed the ship into a dead stop. "Here we are Jaime. We are ready to go."

"Very good, fire up the crawler drive – prepare the battering beam and prepare for insertion."

Halley followed her orders immediately, which filled the ship with the sound of the crawler drive. The drive was a singular engine design and was much smaller than the ones used on the space ark, but was still powerful enough to send the ship into a tear in the fabric of space and then into the void between the folds in normal space. She then activated the beam in the front of the craft. As it had on Starlight, it crackled and glowed as it prepared the powerful beam.

She nodded to Jaime that they were ready. "Engines are high by five, beams are ready to fly, my Beta Starship Captain!" she yelled out over the whine of the engine and the crackling of the beams.

"Ok, hit it…" was all Jaime had to say. Halley engaged the beams – they shot out a short distance from the craft and seemed to just dissipate into the area of space directly in front of the ship. Suddenly space just seemed to tear apart as the beam created a maw in the fabric of the known universe. The hole was just the right size to shove the transport through. The beam shut down and then a small particle was launched into the hole – it disappeared into the reddish glow of sub-space. After a moment, the beams fired again sending a bolt of energy that was swallowed up by the hole.

"Chaser is launched and on its way. Door Marker is launched – and here we go…" She pressed on the engine speed control and the large engine slowly propelled the ship into the glowing opening – which quickly sealed shut as soon as they entered.

Day 41:

Jaime Bordeaux:

The entry into subspace was hard on the pair of pilots. The crawler engine slowly pushed them into a place where nothing existed. They were slowly moving between two layers within a folding in the fabric of space. Flashes of reds and whites appeared all around them, as random particles that entered with them spun and danced in the void between the layers of the real universe.

After the initial shock of entering the void, Jaime was finally able to let out a slight moan of discomfort. "Ugh...I think I see why the crawler engines are set to move us so slowly..."

Halley too, was just coming back to reality after the shock of entry. After a moment, she understood what Jaime had just said, before finally replying "Yes, had we used the ion drives in here we would have been crushed. They figured that out during the unmanned tests." She looked over her navigation controls "Ah, there's the chaser, it's just ahead of us. We'll be able to keep a bead on it. So far, so good..."

The chaser was a particle of antimatter that was launched into the tear in space right before the ship entered. It had a mass light enough, that when launched, allowed it to travel relatively quickly through subspace, while providing an object that would be easy to detect in the void. Thus, by placing a reverse nuclear signature on the particle, they were able to distinguish it from the other vagabond particles that may have slipped into the area of subspace with them. The navigation console found and easily followed the particle as it moved at a slightly faster rate of speed toward its final destination.

They endured the pressures of the subspace void for two long days. During that time, they barely moved – it was too hard for them to get up. Food packs near their chairs and portable waste disposal units kept them from having to get out of their seats. Jaime found that even with her well-developed strength, she was not able to get up and move around. She decided that she was determined to get strong enough to not only get up in subspace, but also to do a workout here someday.

The chaser stopped at a pre-determined position in the void – its energy was calculated to deplete at just the right point to mark where the ship was to tear a new hole, and return to normal space. The particle left a slight residue marking the exit point. An extra pulse of the battering beam that was following the particle slammed into the spot where the chaser died out, leaving a scuff mark in the fabric of space – a door marker for the ship to find. As they approached the marked spot, Halley activated the battering beam again and allowed the force of the ray to tear a hole back into normal space using the force of gravity. A small tear formed and as the ray began to spin and form a vortex, it opened the tear wider and wider. Finally, the pair could see the stars of normal space – Halley activated thrust on the crawler drive again and pushed the ship out of the tear, returning them to the normal universe at the spot in the galaxy where they had hoped to arrive – or at least they hoped that was where they ended up.

The new scanners immediately began shooting beams out to measure any navigational features they could find. Stars, systems, planets, and moons were studied by the pulses of energy. The computer that Jonathan installed accepted and utilized the information being returned from the scanners. As the computer analyzed the data, an image of that area of space was displayed to Halley on her navigation console. She studied the holographic image deeply before finally announcing "Yep, we are exactly where we should be – Jaime, it worked!"

Jaime reached out and took her hand and shook it lightly "You did it...you were the first to pilot subspace. You did an excellent job." Her admiration for her skills made Halley brightly blush.

Halley fired up the ion drives, and the pair proceeded to their destination. The system had been designated A-1 as it was the closest to the Devil's Throat. It had seven planets orbiting a bright yellow sun. The first three planets they travelled past were frozen and totally unsuited for humans to even temporarily inhabit. The fourth, third and first planets were all in volcanic phases. The surfaces of those three planets were massive eruptions of molten elements. What atmosphere did exist was a mixture of waste gasses that were pure poison to a human, which hardly mattered as the temperature of the heated gases would first sear the lungs of anyone who dared to breathe what little air there was. Only the second planet showed a surface that could sustain human life. They took the craft into orbit around the planet close enough to see down into the clean world.

The planet looked like heaven to the two women as they looked down from orbit. They saw lush forests of greens and pinks, blue lakes, green oceans, and white flowing clouds that travelled across the planet. The scans reported that the atmosphere was a perfect mixture of nitrogen, oxygen, and trace gases. There were no traces of poison in any of the readings and the planet appeared to have no signs of civilization – no cities, villages, ruins -- it was perfect.

Jaime looked over the readings again. "I just can't believe a planet this perfect is uninhabited..." she stared out the view port at the planet below their orbit. "Just seems too good..."

"Come on Jaime, this galaxy is full of star systems and planets. Wouldn't it be our great luck if we stumbled upon a perfect place the very first time?"

"Yes, and that is what worries me. Why is it so perfect and yet it is so near the gravity wells?" She rubbed her forehead while she thought about it a moment. "Ok, I can't think of any reason not to head down there..."

"Yes!" Halley cried out as she began to calculate landing vectors, while Jaime scanned the SCADAR readings for a suitable landing spot.

Within moments she had the craft in a descent angle and was burning through the atmosphere -- the shield plating of the ship taking the brunt force of the air-caused friction. Fire danced around the ship like magical fairies as they cut through the upper layers of the planet's sky. Once the flames subsided, Halley flipped switches that activated motors which extended wings on the sides of the craft. The ship became less of a bullet and flew soundly and smoothly through the air.

Jaime continued to monitor the SCADAR as Halley skillfully leveled the ship and slowed its descent. While still staring at the readouts on her holo-screen, Jaime finally called out "There! There is a lake by a large forested area -- land by that lake, on that nice flat spot. We can sample the water and the plant life there." She was now showing her excitement – a smile was on her face; her blue eyes were open wide. She had not seen anything so beautiful in her adult life. She had not seen such a clean and beautiful place since she had been a little girl living on a farm in southern France. Her mind was filled with excitement at the possibilities.

Halley skillfully landed the craft just a short distance from the calm waters of a small lake. The ship made a pitch before front facing jets caused the ship to come to a complete stop in midair. Thrusters fired from the bottom of the craft and kept the ship hovering above the ground, while the wings retracted back into the body. Then, Halley gently set the craft onto the surface of this new world.

Jaime activated the advanced sensors that once again began their work as soon as the ship landed. Additional air samples were taken, drills were lowered, and soil samples removed, SCADAR and sensor beams scanned for life forms, but none were detected in the nearby vicinity. They searched for any hazards they could think of – airborne bacteria and potential pathogens. Finally, after an hour of checking and rechecking, they could not find any reason to keep the hatch closed. Jaime stood at the door with Halley close behind. She rubbed her palms together in anticipation, and then pressed the button to open the hatch.

The smell of fresh clean air slipped past the hatch and entered their noses – the two took a deep wonderful breath. As the hatch continued to open, the warmth of the planet's sun hit their faces and caused both of them to close their eyes for a moment. They squinted to see the world in front of them as their eyes became accustomed to the light. A ramp extended out from the hatchway and lowered itself to the ground below.

Halley was about to run down the ramp when Jaime grabbed her arm with a strong grip. "No, first we check the plants. We don't want to step on something that might hurt or kill us."

The young girl gave a pained frustrated look, but then took out her area scanning device and waved it over the grass at the bottom of the ramp. Then she took out a probe and touched the grass with the rounded end of the long metallic sensor. "Nothing dangerous detected." Before Jaime had a chance to react, she stepped out into the green blades of grass.

"No!" Jaime called out, but it was already too late – she was already several steps off the ramp and in the long waving grass.

Halley put her hands down in the grass and waved it back and forth. It felt soft to her palms and she bent down and sniffed the growing plants. Never had she smelled anything so natural and beautiful. "It is wonderful!" She looked down toward the lake

"I am going to go take a sample of that water. If it is safe, I am going to jump in. I hope you will join me Jaime..." and she ran off down the hill.

"Oh, to hell with protocols..." Jaime sighed as she slowly stepped down off the ramp, then gave up and set a pace to quickly catch up with Halley already at the lake. After a few feet down the slope, she stopped, turned and activated her command module to close the hatch door, keeping anything that might want inside the ship on the outside. Then she continued down the slight slope to the edge of the lake where Halley had her sensor probe in the water to determine its safety.

After a minute of waving the probe around in the water she checked the readout "It is perfect water. We will want to filter it as there are microorganisms, but otherwise it is fresh and pure!"

Jaime used her mobile SCADAR to check the lake for any life forms. There were some small fish but nothing else. "Ah hell, you only live once..." she said to Halley as she dropped her backpack, deactivated the seals on her flight suit and peeled off the tight black outfit before diving head first into the cool clean water. Jaime's head came back above the surface -- she let out a big puff of air and then let out an exuberant laugh and shook the water off her head as she bobbed up and down on the surface. She looked at Halley and motioned her to jump in.

She was totally taken off guard by Jaime's actions. She had never seen her let loose of her professional manner like this – but she liked what she was seeing from her Captain and her friend. It had not taken any further coaxing for her to quickly remove her clothing and jump in. The two women laughed, splashed and completely enjoyed the moment and environment of this private paradise.

They played, swam and splashed in the water for over an hour. Finally, they came back to the shore and both lay down on the soft tufts of grass. Jaime smelled the freshness of the clean air – the grass gave off a slightly sweet smell. Clouds slowly rolled by in the sky above. She turned her head and saw Halley staring at her. "What?" she asked.

"Nothing, just enjoying this moment... Thanks for letting me come along."

Jaime reached over and gave her a soft kiss on her plump lips – Halley tasted the sweetness on her lips and melted inside as Jaime told her "No, thank you for convincing me to let you drive. This has been the most peaceful thing I think I've ever done since we left Earth. I have not felt such happiness since…well, since I was on the starbase with Dex."

Halley looked at a small ring on a chain dangling from her neck. "You still really miss him, don't you?"

"I do…still" Jaime turned and looked back toward the sky "I am not sure I will ever get over him not being with me. Until now I had been so full of anger over his death. I just held it inside and let it build – only releasing it when the Blessed deserved it or when I was in the arena. But for the first time, my soul feels at peace since he passed."

Halley turned toward her and looked at her while she stared at the sky. Jaime's hair was pulled back behind her ears – revealing a growth on her ear. "Jaime, how long have you had that growth?"

Jaime self-consciously pulled her hair over her ears, embarrassed "For a while now – I am not really sure, but it has grown. At least it is not sore anymore. Doctor Sollix says I shouldn't worry about it, but it is making my ears look very strange. I may have him cut the growths off – I hope it is not actually cancerous."

"I hope not too…" she said as she brushed her hair behind her ear revealing a similar, albeit smaller growth. "I think many of us have these – do you think this galaxy is killing us? I am a little worried, even though I feel fine."

"I feel fine too…so, let's hope that it is not hazardous being out this far in space. I am not sure if we can ever go…" she stopped speaking suddenly and looked to her right. She sat up and focused her vision out into the forest that was about two tenths of a mile from the lake. She could have sworn she heard something from that direction – although she was not sure how she might have heard something that far away. Finally, she caught a glimpse of an animal – it appeared to be grazing on the grass right at the edge of the forest. She reached in her backpack and grabbed her scanning computer film, aimed the hand-held sensor, and scanned the creature.

The computer analyzed the creature -- it beeped and clicked while it performed the analysis. Jaime looked at the screen while waiting for the result. She glanced back up to look at the creature, but it was no longer there – instead it was in a different area of grass, much closer than before, perhaps only a few hundred feet now. She could get a decent look at the creature from this distance – it stood on four legs, was covered in a layer of short tan colored fur, had a dark nose and two dark blank eyes, small tail and two large tear-shaped, fur covered ears that seemed to be pointed in their direction while it grazed. Between the creature's ears were a pair of antlers that had two small forks on the end.

The computer signaled its analysis was ready – it validated Jaime's observations about the creature. Halley peered over Jaime's shoulder to read the computer's analysis. The computer came up with the closest match it could find in historical Earth zoology records. It indicated that the closest match it could find is that of a Deer of the early twenty first century. "A Deer...hmm"

"What's a Deer?" Halley asked.

"An animal that roamed parts of the Earth prior to the Great War. The computer says it was a grazer – it ate nothing but plant materials. It was not intelligent and was used as food by humans for years. But they are all gone on Earth now – but this one appears to be very similar to an Earth Deer." Jaime looked up and the creature had vanished. "Well, it appears this one is gone now too..."

The pair got dressed, had a meal, found some wood, started a fire, and then watched the sun go down. Halley had gone back to the ship and started the new advanced sensors in mapping the stars from the surface. When she returned, the two lay in the grass, feeling the fire warm their skins through their flight suits as they looked up at the multitude of stars in the clear dark sky.

While staring up at the millions of stars, Halley pointed at a small bright spot "that is the nebula near the Devil's Throat, I am sure of it."

Jaime looked at the spot and nodded "I have no doubt you are correct about that." She stared up at the dark sky watching the blinking stars before finally saying "If it weren't for the other Normals, I would just say let's stay right here."

They continued to stare into the sky for hours before fatigue finally set in and they fell asleep in the comfort of the soft grass.

The next morning Jaime awoke, and slowly sat up. She stretched and looked around at the landscape now being lit by the yellow light of morning. She decided to take an early morning run while Halley continued to sleep. She quickly ran to the edge of the forest, stopped to consider the dense stand of trees and then she ran into the forest. As she ran, she looked around but saw nothing that she felt was a threat – only a few of those deer. They seemed to almost ignore her when she ran by them – only grazed and followed her with their large ears. After running for a mile into the forest she realized that it seemed to continue on and on, and decided it would be best to return to camp.

Upon returning, she noticed that a few hundred feet from their camp now stood five of the deer-like creatures – once again they stood there and nibbled on the soft tufts of grass while their enormous ears pointed in their direction keeping a constant vigil on the two humans.

Halley now stirred and looked up at Jaime "Good morning! Up for another swim before we get to work?"

Jaime turned her attention away from the grazing creatures and smiled at the younger woman "Sure, sounds like a terrific way to freshen up." Once again, she beat Halley in removing her flight suit and jumping into the clear chilly water. She screamed and laughed as the icy water shocked her body – Halley was close behind although she was not as quick to jump into the freezing water.

They played in the water for a while until the cold of the water started to soak into their bones. Exiting the water, they returned to the spot in the grass where they had set up their camp. Jaime looked out and noticed that the herd of deer had gotten much larger – at least fifteen that she could see, and they were also much closer. They were now only a hundred or so feet away – still they seemed to offer no threat – just grazed, occasionally looked up and chewed while staring in their direction. Their mouths moving up and down and side to side as they slowly ground the tender grasses into a liquid pulp before swallowing the tender plants.

They let the sun dry their naked bodies. While drying, Jaime took out her computer film and started typing up a task list "Well, I suppose we really need to do some real work. We should take a survey of the forest over there, test the soil, write some reports, and maybe even study the deer."

Halley was also studying her computer as she pondered "I wonder what those deer…" her thoughts were interrupted when she noticed a shadow blocking the sun on her body. When she turned and looked up from the computer she found herself face to face with a pair of dark black eyes. The dark blank eyes were staring deeply into her eyes. She reached behind her to tap Jaime on the shoulder.

Annoyed by Halley's tapping she snapped "What Halley?" and turned. Seeing the creature right next to them, she jumped up and stood ready to fight. Her quick movements startled the animal causing it to jump a few feet back – but then it stopped and took a step back toward the pair. It then continued to just stare at them. Seconds later, twenty additional creatures came bounding through the grass and surrounded the pair of naked humans.

"They don't seem to be afraid of us. Should we be worried?" Halley asked. Jaime shrugged but readied her command weapon, just in case. She wished she had gotten dressed sooner as standing naked in front of these creatures made her feel vulnerable.

One of the animals suddenly let out a high-pitched squeal followed by a few grunts and honks, surprising the two women. Jaime still had her communication device on her ear and through that the computer picked up the sounds and routed them through the translator circuit that Jonathan installed on the ship. Seconds later their communicator circuit transmitted in a male voice three words "What are you?"

Day 46:

Allen James:

The smelter robots had been working full-time since they arrived on Bung. After two days, they had found enough raw materials to begin building the frame of their first ship -- a scout ship. The plans had already been drawn up by the Normal designers months ago. The plans had been programmed into the builder robots that had been working constantly and they were already completing the frame of the scout ship. Jonathan had shown him the design for the small craft – it would support a crew of two, and the design had been modified to accommodate one of the new high-speed ion engines that they had found on one of the alien derelicts. He was really surprised that no one had cleaned this planetoid of the valuable materials in these wrecked spacecrafts.

He looked out through the viewport into the assembly cavern where the robots worked without the need of food, sleep or atmosphere -- constantly and tirelessly they worked, without so much as a break. At this pace he estimated, the ship would be assembled in a matter of days. After that, it would be only a matter of another week to put together computers and controls for the inside of the new craft – then it would be ready for a test flight.

He turned and walked down a long hallway to a steel door – entered a combination and unlocked the door. He walked in and found Jonathan and the science staff working on one of the two engines that they had been able to remove from one of the wrecked starships. This particular spacecraft had smashed head-first into the planetoid when it had attempted to escape the gravity well. Fortunately, the front of the craft took the brunt of the impact and spared the rear engine compartment and the two ion drives. Jonathan was sure these powerful engines could propel a small craft faster than light speed. If it worked, they would be able to explore this galaxy while the rest of the Normals survived aboard Starlight. Once a suitable planet was found, they could return and find a way to break away from the grasp of the Blessed and become an independent race in this new galaxy.

"So, what do we have?" he asked Jonathan.

Jonathan looked up from the guts of the engine. Pieces and parts were sitting in an organized manner in different areas of the room. The engine Jonathan was working on was being dissected piece by piece – each piece being cataloged and analyzed. "I think we have determined all but two of the control circuits in this engine. If we are correct in our analysis, then we will be able to create and attach controls to this engine. I think we will have a working faster-than-light-speed ion drive very soon – maybe even by the end of the week!"

Allen could see the excitement on his face. He had full confidence in this young man. He had been told about the true genius that this man had hidden inside his small skull. His story was so typical of many Normal humans in the Alliance – discarded and ignored. Allowed to do the work and create the inventions the Supreme Commander and the Council needed, but were then disregarded once their tasks were completed. For once, he was doing something that would make a difference – and Allen was glad he too was part of this effort.

Jonathan took a wiring laser and made a few stiches into the alien circuit board – looked at his work, then smiled. "We have it – we can use this circuitry and control it through our navigation systems!" He looked at Allen "We need a test..."

Allen rolled his eyes and ran his fingers through his straight brown hair. "Oh boy...How soon?"

"As soon as possible – tomorrow...today...now?"

Allen laughed then activated his Norm-Comm to contact an engineering crew and commanded "I need a crew to set up a test platform ASAP!"

Jaime Bordeaux:

"What are you?" was again translated from the squeals and snorts of the deer standing in front of her. It tilted its head as if trying to determine what she was thinking.

Finally, she answered "I am a Human being...from Earth." It took a few seconds for the computer to translate and return the message back to the deer.

The creature tilted its head from one side to the other as if trying to get multiple views of her face and head. Finally, it snorted and squeaked to which the computer translated "One moment..." Its antlers glowed slightly and finally it considered her

216

eyes with a pair of black eyes and to Jaime's surprise said "I have learned your language. I can now communicate in your rudimentary vocalizations. You are called Human? Where is Earth?" He spoke with a male voice; his diction was very distinct and proper as if he had spoken the language all his life.

Jaime was still a little taken aback. She thought a moment, then answered "That is a little difficult as I am not exactly sure myself right now. However, there is this gravity well…"

"You came through one of the ancient passageways? You are not supposed to be here!"

Frustrated, Jaime replied "Well, if there was any way to get back then we might try – but there isn't, so we are stuck here."

A slight glow emanated from all the antlers of the deer standing around the pair of women followed by a moment of silence. She assumed they were communicating amongst themselves. Finally, he said "Of course. Somehow you made it here, and since you are standing here that must be the truth." He looked her up and down then commented "How can you survive without fur?"

Jaime looked down and realized that she was still naked. She slightly blushed and replied "Well, we do wear protective clothing. However, you kind of caught us by surprise. May we get dressed?"

"You might have weapons hidden. How can we trust that you will not attack us? We do not know your motives after all…"

Jaime turned and pointed her command weapon toward the lake and shot a small burst into the water. "I have been armed the entire time. If I was going to hurt you, I would have by now."

She could have sworn she saw a smile on the deer's lips as he nodded to one of the other creatures in the circle. This animal turned and pointed its head toward the lake – its antlers lit up and an arc of power formed between them. Then a bolt of plasma emitted from the arc and landed in the lake – it sizzled and boiled from the force of the plasma blast. "As you can see, we were never in danger – you may put your protective coverings on." As the pair put their clothing on, the lead deer continued "I would like to introduce myself, I am Oomha, leader of this patrol. You are on the home world of the Flaybah. We welcome you here as guests."

"Thank you Oomha" Halley replied.

Oomha turned to Halley and looked her up and down. "You are colored differently...you have red indentions in your facial skin instead of brown dots and you have a different scent. Are you also Human?"

Halley wanted to die as she realized he was speaking of the blemishes on her face, but instead simply answered "Yes, we just have unique features, but we are both human."

He looked back and forth again at the pair of women. "Something is not right..." They looked at him confused. "I just referenced your race and you do not match..." Oomha turned and waggled his head in their direction. Around from behind the circle of deer came five multi-legged creatures – they appeared to look like giant spiders. Jaime counted six legs – three to each of the sides and an appendage on the back of each creature. These appendages had some form of sharp clawed fingers that wiggled threateningly. The front of the creature had multiple eyes and a gaping mouth with a set of sharp teeth. It appeared that the creatures were wearing a bluish-colored armor – she was not sure if the armor was attached naturally or applied.

Jaime got a little worried and looked at Halley who also had a look of concern on her face. She wondered how they would know what a human even was. Oomha took a step forward putting his nose right up almost touching Jaime's face – his dark black eyes stared into hers as he sniffed the skin of her face. "You are not who you say you are..." He moved his nose around her face taking large sniffs of her scent. Finally, he moved his nose to the side of her head and sniffed her hair. He reached up and raised his front hoof and moved it to the side of her head. Small finger like appendages emerged from the surface of the hoof – he ran the small fingers through her hair moving it to the side, exposing her ear. He looked at her ear, then moved his nose in and sniffed the pointed growth on the tip of her small ear. He took a step back, nodded to the multi-legged creatures – they in turn took a step back and folded their legs underneath their bodies as they lay down onto the grass. "My apologies -- however, you said you were human...and you are definitely not. Have you checked with your medical experts lately?"

Jaime scrunched her forehead in confusion. "I am not sure what you mean? We are human..." he shook his head no. She touched the tips of her ears and wondered what was changing both in her and her fellow Normal compatriots. She shrugged her shoulders before saying "Well, we used to be then…"

Oomha once again had a smile on his small mouth. "Now that we have cleared up that confusion, allow us to show you our civilization. Come, our habitation grouping is not far…" he nodded his head in the direction of the forest as the bulk of the creatures went bounding off in various directions – jumping away on springs of four legs. The spider creatures gathered around the group and escorted them along the way. As they walked, Oomha continued "We have flourished on this planet for a millennium. Our leaders decided that to keep our race thriving we must venture out and expand our civilization. As we went out however, we discovered as you are now finding out that we are not the only beings that live in the galaxy. As logical beings, we eventually joined the Star League Coalition and signed the agreement to not expand farther than the three-star systems we currently inhabit. This is not a problem however as we have learned that we can control our population to prevent over utilization of our worlds."

Jaime stopped and looked at him "You're spacefaring?"

He nodded "Of course, what intelligent civilization is not?"

Jaime looked at Halley "I think we're not as lucky as we thought. We may be exploring a long time before we find a home…"

Day 70:

Jaime Bordeaux:

The Flaybah habitation encampment was much farther than Jaime expected. After two days, they still had not reached the entrance. She wished she had moved the ship closer instead of walking the entire way since she would then have to walk all the way back to get the ship and fly it to the encampment. The walk provided the pair of women with an opportunity to get a feel for this planet they were visiting. They walked through lush green and pink forests, giant conifer and poplar-type trees stood strongly in the ground making their way up toward the sky. Multi-colored vines almost blocked off the sun in places as they travelled up the large trees. They heard various sounds of the different fauna that inhabited the forested area. They admired the beauty that was all around them as they slowly walked.

"We did not anticipate that you would be so slow in mobility.. " Oomha told her as they walked.

"It's no problem – once we get there, I will head back and move the ship closer."

"Very well, I will have my mate give the coordinates for a good landing spot once we arrive."

She nodded in acknowledgment to the fawn-colored creature leading them on.

Three more hours elapsed before the group reached a large cavern entrance in the side of a large cliff face. Oomha stopped and lifted his hoof, pointing toward the large entrance "This, is our home – one of many inhabitations that occupy our planet."

"Oomha...don't you worry about showing us all of this?" Jaime queried.

A smile formed on Oomha's face "Why would we worry? You don't appear to be a threat. We have analyzed the weaponry on your ship – accelerated light beams, proton accelerated emitters, plasma arcs and radioactive projectile guns – we did not see anything that should concern us."

Jaime was shocked that they were able to determine every weapon on her craft in such a short time and with such accuracy –

and that they had the ability to do such an evaluation without even boarding the ship. She also wondered just how advanced this civilization really was – were they that much more advanced or did they just understand space weaponry and knew they could fight it out with humans?

They were led inside the large cavern. Artificial illumination brightly lit the enormous cavern and sub-caverns – it appeared as if the sun actually shone inside, yet they were completely underground. They ventured at least three miles into the depths of the habitation – the caverns opened into a large communal area and along the exterior of that area were numerous smaller tunnels that extended out from there. These smaller tunnels eventually turned into streets which opened onto smaller open cavern areas that formed city-style neighborhoods. As they walked further, doors and windows lined both sides of the streets. Jaime assumed they had entered a residential area. Finally, they came to a set of double doors, well-appointed with golden symbols and images. "This is my habitation – and I welcome you to enjoy my hospitality" Oomha told them.

Jaime looked at the ornate door, turned to the young buck and smiled "We would be honored to be your guests."

The door opened, and a smaller deer stood at the opening and looked the pair of women up and down. This one had two small nubs on its head instead of the antlers like on Oomha's head. The two nubs began glowing at the same time as Oomha's antlers – Jaime realized they were communicating.

Finally, Oomha turned to Jaime "This is my mate Jaedar, we are prepared to take you in. Please..." he motioned to the two women to enter.

"Please join us and be welcome in our habitation" Jaedar spoke. She used the same perfect English as her mate. Her voice imitated that of a female – Jaime assumed it was to give the two a familiar female type of their race. "I will start formulating some food that will be both nutritious and palatable to you."

They entered the home and were surprised by the roominess of the living space. There were multiple rooms that adjoined the main living area in the center of the habitation. Jaime noticed that every side room was wide open to the main space – there would be no privacy while staying here. She leaned close to Halley "better throw away your modesty while we are here..."

Halley looked around the room and saw the mounds of straw that lined the floors of the side rooms and realized those were the sleeping quarters. She realized what Jaime was telling her and gulped "I see what you mean. Well, I will just remember that we are living with deer...what about the bathroom?"

"One step at a time" she replied, "Let's figure out the arrangements and get the other details as we move forward..."

Oomha walked to one of the side rooms and nodded his head toward it "Jaime, this will be your sleeping den and Halley you will take this one next to Jaime's."

"Very kind, thank you" Jaime replied. She stepped into her den and looked around – the room was full of a straw material, she looked at it skeptically. Finally, she bent over and ran her hands through the fibrous material – she was surprised that when her hand touched the material it softened up into a satin-like feel. She turned and sat herself down onto the bed of hay -- it turned instantly soft and comfortable. She nodded her head and gave a look of positive acceptance. She heard Halley give an astonished gasp as she too realized the comfort of the straw bedding material.

That evening they gathered in the central area for a meal. Jaedar served the meal to the two women in phosphorescent blue bowls which maintained the warmth of a brownish thick paste held within. The two Flaybah sat across from them and browsed on a plate of twigs and berries. Jaime looked at the thick paste and gulped – it looked like waste material – totally inedible. She was worried that it might not agree with their systems or worse, kill them.

Jaedar sensed their concern. She looked at them, gave a deerish smile and said, "Don't worry, I made sure it was safe and I am sure it will agree with your physiology."

Jaime gave her a sheepish smile, then took her eating leaf and scooped a small amount onto it. She sniffed it, but could not smell anything from the paste-like material. She slowly put it to her lips then took a small amount in her mouth. She swished the thick food around on her tongue, looked at Halley, and then back to Jaedar. She finally smiled and said, "It's delicious!" The young doe gave a slight sigh of relief.

Jaime took another bite while Halley took her first taste. Halley raised her eyebrows in surprise then looked at the thick brown paste in the leaf while she chewed. After she swallowed she said, "It does not look palatable by human standards, but it is quite good."

"Would a different color help?" Jaedar asked.

"Perhaps pink?" Halley said jokingly.

Jaime gave the young woman a look, then said "No, it's fine the way it is. Thank you for your concern."

They ate their meals, Jaedar then provided some sweet waters for the four of them to sip as a dessert. Once again, Jaime was surprised by just how delicious the glass of clear fluid tasted. She took another taste of the sweet fluid and considered her situation before saying "Oomha, I will need to get back to my ship. I should fly it here for the remainder of our stay." She then thought for a moment with a look of concern on her face.

Oomha saw the look and returned a curious look with his dark black eyes – he could tell she was worried. "What is it Jaime?"

"Oh nothing..." she concealed the worry she felt about what she would have to report when she returned to Starlight.

That evening they were allowed to freely wander the habitation. Halley was lying on the straw in her room when Jaime decided to take a walk. She found that all the Flaybah were friendly, and seemed not at all surprised or worried to find alien beings wandering around their encampment. She found the entrance to the habitation and wandered out a short distance from the large cavern opening. She considered the night sky and stared at the millions of stars.

Halley snuck up and sat beside her while she stared into the dark sky. "What are you thinking?" she asked her Captain.

"Oh Halley, I'm worried. Worried about what will happen when we return. The Blessed will review our ship's logs, and will realize there is a world for the taking here. They will come here guns blazing I fear – and I fear for the lives of our new friends."

"Me too...I wish we could hide our visit here" the young girl confided.

Jaime sighed and continued to stare into the starry sky – not recognizing any of the constellations. "This universe, it is so strange and different. It shouldn't be, but it is. I look up and feel so lost. I don't recognize any star clusters or patterns. But at the same time I feel very at ease here. I don't understand the conflicting feelings I am having…"

Halley nodded while staring into the sky "I know how you feel. It's creepy that it feels right, yet it is totally unfamiliar…yet it is familiar. I don't know how to describe it."

The pair heard the clopping of hoofs behind them. Jaime turned to find Oomha standing in the distance, not wanting to eavesdrop or disturb them. "Jaime, the encampment may be totally safe – but out here we still have some wild animals. You may want to come back inside."

Jaime sat up and looked at the young deer. "I suppose you are right. Besides, it's been a long day and I'm feeling a bit tired."

She stood up and walked over to Oomha, Halley quickly followed. She looked at the young buck for a moment, looked back up into the sky again, then turned to him and stared into his eyes. Finally, she felt comfortable enough to say to him "I'm worried Oomha. I somehow must delete all the records of our visit here, and I'm not really sure how to do it so that suspicion is not raised. How do I explain the time we spent here and how do I account for that time in our ship's logs?"

"I think I can help Jaime" said Jaedar, as she approached the group from the encampment entrance. "I am a computer expert and I looked at the scanning logs of your ship. Your computers are of a primitive singular binary nature, not a challenge at all. We can manipulate the file structure easily enough."

"What?" Halley blurted out. "What do you mean primitive singular binary? These are our culture's most advanced computer systems."

"They may be your most advanced dear…but they are really not very evolved. We Flaybah for example use a triple dimensional binary code for storage and processing of data. We know that there are other races that can compute to an even more complex level than us. Please, I say that not in insult – we have all had to grow and find that there are others that are more advanced than ourselves. Please do not think me as rude..."

"Of course not Jaedar" Jaime interjected. "It would be ignorant of us to not think that we are behind in many categories of technology and advancement." She thought of the Blessed and how arrogant they were and how that arrogance was going to be the doom of them all. She knew they could not find out about this world. "I would appreciate any help you can offer – thank you."

"Now, shall we head back to the habitation?" Oomha said as he nodded his head in the direction of the entrance.

The four walked back toward the habitation. When they reached Oomha and Jaedar's habitation space they all had another glass of the sweet water beverage and went to their respective sleeping quarters. Jaime lay down on the soft hay, closed her eyes and quickly fell asleep – and for the first time since they left Earth, the dead pilot did not even partially invade her dreams.

Day 75:

Boral Oldham:

The SCADAR showed something out there. He looked at the returns, but they were so inconclusive. Despite how little of the readouts he understood, he could figure out that indeed *something* was out there.

"Damn peculiar..." he scratched the thin hair on the side of his head, moving the long strands from one side, across the bald top to the other side of his wide head. "Get me Kip at the construction site!" he barked.

Kip Gurrigan had been at the space dock for the past two weeks, he had gone there to oversee the progress of the Normal workers who were building his ship. The construction robots had been working tirelessly day and night – retrieving materials from the lower salvage camp and piecing them together out in space as prescribed by Blessed engineers and designers. The ship was finally taking shape – it was a smaller version of the Starlight. It had the same pyramid command module, connecting tubular structure and an engineering section that had a smaller bank of ion drives and sub-space crawler.

Kip appeared on the command hologram. "Kip, what is your progress. We have something on SCADAR that concerns me."

"We are way ahead of schedule, my Star Force Commander!" he snapped out. "The structure is complete, we have engines installed and are putting together the power plant as we speak, Sir." His smile faded slightly as what Boral was about to tell him started to sink in "So, what is out there?"

"I just don't know Kip. But it appears to be moving on its own power, so it worries me."

"What do you suggest we do my Star Force Commander?"

He thought for a moment then snapped his fingers. "Engineer, can we attach cables to that craft?"

The engineer ran numbers through his console and nodded yes.

Kip interjected as he read the figures on his command hologram. "Ah, a tow?"

Max Sollix:

Max watched the view screen as the transport robots worked. The robots were moving materials from the assembly cavern out into space to the construction dock platform where they were then left so that assembly robots could use the materials where needed. All was going well, and the ship had taken shape quickly.

"It is really going well, isn't it Doctor?" Katsumi said as she came up quietly behind him and gave him a slight start.

"Oh, yes Katsumi it is...for what it's worth." She gave him a puzzled look. "I really hate doing this for a Blessed to command, this should be for us."

"It is not time. Not yet..."

He looked at her and realized how right she was, and smiled. "Yes, of course – not our time... Yet."

"Besides" she interrupted "we really don't want to explore space in *that* do we?" He turned from the view screen and gave her a questioning look. Without him saying anything, she answered with "Our designs are much better..."

He chuckled, knowing she was right. "Yes...now that you mention it, I do not want to be caught dead in..." he turned to point at the ship being built but instead stopped in mid-sentence as he saw Starlight come up and over the partially completed ship. Suddenly it attached multiple cables to various sections of the new craft and to the attached space dock. "What the hell are they doing?" A moment later, Starlight slowly began to move – taking the new ship and the construction dock with it. "Damn, what the hell are they doing? Where are they going?" he turned to Katsumi "Quick, recall the transport robots – we don't want them lost out there!"

Katsumi quickly sat down at the command console and commanded the return of the robots. She looked at the base SCADAR returns – her almond eyes opened wide as she read the output of the scan analysis. "Doctor, there is something coming..."

He looked down at the scan readings. "Shit!" He turned and looked at Lindy who was sitting at the communication station. "Tunnel me to Captain James!" he ordered.

A moment later a tunneled protocol communication band was established, and Allen James appeared on the monitor.

"Allen…" Max said excitedly.

"We see it too Max." he said calmly. "Listen, we're battening down everything -- recalling all robots, shutting down all production, and closing the space doors. I suggest you do the same."

"Good idea…" he nodded to Katsumi who began to enter the recall codes for all robots. Lindy began sending communications to all personnel who were either in the ships being salvaged or out on the manufacturing docks, instructing them to immediately return to the cavern base.

"Max, I also would suggest you power down as much as possible. We have no idea what this object is and what it's capable of doing. We've been able to get a visual on it however, and it definitely is a ship. Take a look…" he switched his view screen to the SCADAR visual imaging. On the screen, a white ball shaped object with a featureless rectangular block attached to the rear which made up the craft, was moving quickly toward their location. "It appears to be headed your way Max. Do whatever you can to hide and protect yourself. We'll be following suit…James out."

Max turned back to the view screen that was showing the departing starships. "Damn those cowards. Well, that explains what they're doing – turning and running. Leaving us for dead…"

"Should I call the other base?" Lindy asked.

"No, at least not on regular channels – no need to warn the Blessed they had left. Can you warn the Normals over there?"

"I think so…" Lindy pulled the plug from one of the base's sub-space antennas and plugged it into the communication port in the back of her neck. A slight pulse of space energy was sent from the cable into the port, giving her brain a slight numbing jolt. She faltered slightly, then looked pale and wobbled in her chair as if she was going to pass out. Max started to run to her side to assist, but she waved him away. She quickly shook the cobwebs out of her head before saying, "I will handle getting a message to them Doctor." She pressed the Norm-Comm device embedded behind her ear and started to transmit "*All Normals hearing this message. An unknown craft is headed our way. If possible, seek shelter and avoid being out on the surface of the planetoid. Do not respond, only comply.*" She repeated the message for five minutes before discontinuing the message and unplugging the antenna to prevent detection.

Max heard Lindy's initial message and nodded to her, then turned back to the science station. "Ok Katsumi -- shut down power. Leave only minimal life support and oxygen generation. Let's try to look as much like a dead rock as we can – and let's hope we survive this…"

They watched as the ship approached, then it slowed to a crawling speed in an orbit around Stopper. Now with the ship much closer, they could see the details of the craft on their monitor. Its front section looked like a giant golf ball – dimpled and white. Each dimple appeared to hold some form of antenna array. The golf ball section was attached to a dull rectangular block – no portholes or windows were visible on either section. The rectangular section showed no features whatsoever on the dull silver colored block of metal. There were no visible exterior propulsion systems attached to either section, but Max assumed it must have had some engines on the back side hidden from their view.

"Did you get enough images?" he asked Katsumi who nodded in acknowledgement. "Then shut it down. We do not want any imaging or SCADAR emitting from the base. Shut it all down now."

"Now what do we do?" Katsumi asked as she flipped the virtual switches shutting down almost all systems within the base.

Max put his hand on her shoulder and quietly said "Either think lots of positive thoughts…or pray…"

The room went dark along with the rest of the base. He thought they had taken as many precautions as they could, and he hoped they would be able to hide and not be noticed. A moment later however, his fears were realized, and his confidence was blasted down with the force of the beams that began hitting the surface of the planetoid. The ground shook and rocks fell from the ceiling – one hitting him in the head, taking him down, and knocking him out.

Jaime Bordeaux:

Two days of running and fast walking had returned her and Halley to the transport ship. They had been accompanied by two of the Flaybah and eight of the multi-legged creatures that Oomha called Fletchvar.

The Fletchvar were soldiers that the Flaybah used, as they did not personally partake in physical violence. The relationship they had was amazing to her – the Flaybah provided space protection to the Fletchvar and the Flaybah's dead and criminals became a food source for the Fletchvar. The Fletchvar therefore, provided cleanup of the dead, a deterrent to crime, and ground based protection in the event of an invasion. They had a perfect balance of nature on this planet. Jaime was amazed by the way these two lived in harmony and peace.

When they arrived at the ship, they found it in perfect condition – just the way they had left it. Despite the knowledge the Flaybah had of the technology on board, they had not even come near it. Their advanced scanning could peer right through the hull and investigate the entire system and thus they had no need to go inside. She was shocked that they were even able to identify weapons systems that were off-line and shut down.

A two-day hike only took twenty minutes to return via the air. They invited the two Flaybah chaperones to return with them – however they refused saying they preferred to use the journey back as physical training time.

Upon their arrival at the habitation, Jaedar was waiting and met them at the landing bay. She wasted no time boarding the ship. "Jaime, I will reprogram your computer now -- this way you will be able to leave at any time and there will not be any record of your visit with us. You do still want that, don't you?"

"Of course…there is no way I want anyone from the Alliance discovering your planet."

Jaime detected a smile as it formed on each side of Jaedar's mouth. "Good! Then I will interface and begin…" She lowered herself to balance on her hindquarters, separating her small fingers from her front hooves. She reached into a saddle pouch strapped around her neck and pulled out a small disk with a wire attached. She placed the disk on top of the computer rack and then pulled on the other end of the wire causing it to separate – a cap appeared on each of the wire ends. She placed each cap on one of the nubs on the top of her head – the same spots where antlers grew on the males. A glow emanated from each of the small bumps causing the disk to glow with the same green tint. A moment later the disk emitted an image – the image showed various levels of machine language code. Her dark eyes scanned the lines of binary for a few moments before she said "Good, this will not be a problem!" She turned and looked at pair of women "Jaime, the habitation chief wanted to meet with you – this would be a perfect time. I will have the records changed within the hour. Oomha is outside and will take you to him."

Amazed at the ability of the young doe, she simply nodded and walked off the ship. As promised, Oomha was waiting at the bottom of the ramp "Follow me please…" He guided them to the center of the habitation where a large dome sat in the exact center of the facility. "This is our hub of government. You will be meeting with the current chief of the habitation. Every year, we elect a new chief based on the competitions earlier in the season. This chief is Mobor – not the brightest leader we have had, and he is gruff, but don't let it bother you. He likes to push his weight around, but I doubt he would do that with you."

They entered the giant dome and were led to a large audience chamber in the exact center of the dome. At the back of the chamber sat an older looking Flaybah with an enormous rack of antlers. His dark eyes opened wide when the three entered the room. Oomha held his head down in respect while announcing "Leader, these are the two humans from the spacecraft. I present Jaime and Halley of the planet Earth."

The large buck stood and looked at the pair of women before saying "Hmm, bipeds…" He took a step forward and looked at Halley, then Jaime "Which one of you leads?"

"I do, as I am the Captain. My name is Jaime…"

He interrupted her in mid-sentence with a loud heavy voice "Prepare yourself!"

Before she had a chance to understand his instruction, Mobor rushed to her and flung his head – his antlers glowed and created a force that threw Jaime into the nearby wall. "What the hell?" she yelled out as he began rushing her again.

Oomha yelled out "No my Leader, they do not understand!" but Mobor would not back down as he accelerated toward her.

He bent his head down for another flinging attack, but was stopped by the power of two hands wrapped around his antlers. Her position was just right to keep his neck from having freedom of movement – she managed to hold him in place. His eyes became as large as dark saucers as she held him. When she felt he would not attack again she let go of his large antlers and took a step away from the large beast leader.

He shook with rage, but stood his ground – Oomha also was looking at the two of them, surprised and shocked. Halley looked at Oomha and then at Mobor "What?" she asked.

"She, she *touched* me!" Mobor cried out. "Why did you do that? What type of barbarian are you?"

Jaime looked puzzled "What? You attacked me?"

"Jaime..." said Oomha "we do not touch when we spar..."

"When did I agree to spar?"

"I was testing your strength and prowess, but discovered you are a barbarian!" Mobor yelled out.

"I did not know, I'm sorry..."

Before she had a chance to say anything else, Mobor's antlers lit up like a pair of green neon bulbs as he charged her again "Take this barbarian!" he yelled as he charged.

Jaime reached out again, but this time she somehow managed to leverage the large beast up and over her head – and yet she never noticed feeling him on her hands. He landed against the curtained wall with a large crash. He huffed and snorted as he slowly picked himself up and prepared for another charge when something held him in place – he was totally immobile. He looked to his side and saw Oomha standing next to him – his smaller antlers glowed an even brighter green than the older leader.

"Enough, Leader!" he cried out "They are our guests – we should treat them with respect. She threw you fair and square that last spar – she bested you! Do you want it to get out that you were bested by a biped?"

Mobor was shocked by not only losing to Jaime -- but also from being held by this smaller, younger buck. He was speechless. He finally stopped struggling against the force holding him and nodded his head in agreement. Oomha's antlers stopped glowing and Mobor was released. As he slowly returned to his mat all he could mutter was "Remove these biped barbarians..."

Oomha nodded at the pair to follow him. They left the dome quickly and quietly. Jaime, still confused by the events was dumbfounded. Oomha finally spoke once outside the building. "Jaime, I was glad you were able to defend against that last attack – I could not have gotten there in time."

Jaime scrunched her forehead in confusion "I did not do...anything..."

"Well, nonetheless" Oomha continued "nothing else will be said about his behavior or your ability to best him. It would cause a scandal that would force a recall election. The habitat would be in political chaos.

"But Oomha, I saw you hold him! You were as strong as he was for that time."

Oomha looked around hoping no one heard her "I will ask you never to say anything about that. Many of us younger bucks know we can best a leader type – however, we do not as we do not wish to be in a political position."

Halley chuckled "Some things never change with younger people of any race..."

Before returning to the ship, they stopped at Oomha's quarters for a quick meal. Jaime found their food was now colored pink. Jaime cringed at the new color of the food and Halley giggled. Once finished with their meal, they returned to the ship and found Jaedar waiting for them. "I have reprogrammed your historical records. Now your computer will show a visit to one of the other planets as being this planet. It will appear to not be habitable and will conceal your visit with us."

Jaime thought for a moment then smiled at Jaedar while saying "I guess we have no more excuses then – we have to return to our kind...return to our starship."

"I hope you and Halley will someday return to visit us." Oomha said. "Should you ever need our assistance, our race will be happy to help you. We have a powerful star fleet and if needed we would fight by your side."

"I have not seen any signs of a fleet Oomha." Jaime interjected.

"Perhaps when you leave" said Jaedar.

Oomha brought his head close to Jaime's ear and whispered "Jaime, I could be fed to the Fletchvar for what I am about to tell you – as we have strict laws regarding helping of lesser races…" Jaime gave him a disgusted look for that comment "My apologies, it is the consensus amongst the habitat. In any case, I should warn you – avoid any contact with two races…the Og and the Mayoola. They are both ancient races and dangerous. Even we Flaybah are fearful of them."

Jaime gave him a smile and a nod "I will, thank you. Also, please be aware that there are humans who are not like us…"

"The Blessed…yes, I remember."

"They will bear the flag of the Northern Alliance…they are not to be trusted."

Jaedar hearing this, questioned "But, if we cannot trust anyone from your Alliance…how will we know when it is you returning?"

Jaime thought for a moment. "I'll tell you what. If it is us, we will identify ourselves as Human – not Alliance."

"But you are not…" Jaedar replied causing Jaime to give her a puzzled look.

Halley, unable to control herself any longer reached out and wrapped her arms around Jaedar "Thank you for everything!" she then unwrapped her arms from the surprised Jaedar and then wrapped them in the same manner around Oomha, before releasing her embrace around him and turning to head up the ramp.

Oomha gave a slight chortle at Jaedar's surprise "They seem to enjoy physical touch…" Jaedar just nodded her head in agreement as the two humans waved and walked up the ramp.

Within three minutes the pair of women were launched and headed back to outer space. They left the atmosphere and did a short orbit prior to engaging the ion engines to achieve apogee in preparation for the two-week journey out of the star system and to the sub-space insertion point. Halley looked at the SCADAR returns and was shocked by the readings "Um, Jaime...there is something on the port side...something really big!"

"Hmm?" Jaime mumbled as she casually turned to look out the left star screen. Her eyes opened wide as she saw an enormous ship headed toward them from behind one of the planet's moons. The ship was cigar shaped and pointed on each of the ends. She estimated it to be at least twice as large as Starlight. It was a similar fawn color to the Flaybah's fur. The ship was covered with portal windows -- bright lights emanated from these portals. At the front of the ship were a large set of antler-like metallic structures that jutted out into space and appeared to be feeling the space in front of the craft. Each of the antler structures glowed a soft green just like Oomha's velvety head appendages. There appeared to be hundreds of launch bays and thousands of various tubes and openings that Jaime decided had to be weapon launchers.

On the transceiver circuit, they received a message. *"Human vessel, this is Battle-Buck Marcole. We will escort you out of the system at which point you will be able to use the faster than light propulsion system of your ship. Safe voyage."*

"Roger that Marcole – thank you for the escort." Jaime replied. She looked out the star screen again at the enormous craft for a moment before turning to Halley and quietly saying "The faster than light propulsion system of our ship..." she shook her head lightly before she turned back and once again looked at the Marcole "We are definitely out-classed in this galaxy...Flaybah, Og, Mayoola...definitely out-classed..."

Day 90:

Jaime Bordeaux:

When the ship finally reached the subspace tear it slowly coasted out on just a hint of crawler drive power. As they moved at a crawl from the tear, the two occupants recovered from the trip through the area between the layers of known space.

Jaime recovered first and began to get her bearings while Halley recovered at a much slower rate. The ship cruised on auto-pilot while they regained their presence of mind. Jaime looked over the SCADAR readouts – nothing was in the area.

Halley shook her head to clear the cobwebs "We really need to find a way to handle that better..." Jaime nodded her head in agreement while continuing to view the readouts. "Is something wrong Jaime?"

"No, I thought something didn't look right – but it must have just been our exit from subspace. Ok, let's fire up the ion drives and..." The proximity alarms interrupted her orders as they blared out urgently of the pending emergency. "What the hell?"

Halley immediately stopped the motion of the craft and the two women considered the view screens for some sign of a foreign object, but could not see anything.

Over Norm-Comm Jaime heard a familiar voice – one that for a moment to Jaime, was too familiar. "Beta Starship Captain Bordeaux, I presume?"

"Who...? Captain James?" she replied.

"Yes, it's me Captain."

She looked at the star screen perplexed "You are coming in so clear, like you are right next to us. But I see no ship..."

"Ah, my apologies Captain – one moment." A moment later the two women saw a set of starship marker lights off the starboard side of their ship, but they could barely make out anything but the lights. "Is that better?"

Jaime squinted to see the craft on their side "No, not really – we can barely make out anything about the ship you are in. What is that?"

"Let me move the ship to the front so you can activate your running lights on us."

Jaime activated the running headlights and a moment later saw a black spaceship move in front of their craft. It was shaped like the head of a trident -- the two outer cylindrical sides curved in to meet each other like a horseshoe – each side starting in a sharp tip which curved in toward the back of the craft where they became wider at the point they met up toward the rear of the ship. A single engine took up most of the rear of the vessel and two smaller ion drives sat on each side of the larger engine. All three engines faintly glowed with a slight greenish-blue light as they sat in standby mode. Coming out of the front of the curved main horseshoe body, a center fuselage was attached. It was round in the rear, but flattened out into a shape that resembled the head of a flat worm at the front. Two small view screens were mounted at the front of the head of the craft. The ship was coated in a black-colored material – Jaime assumed that since their SCADAR did not pick up the vessel, the coating must make the ship stealth to not only the scanning radar but other types of sensor scanning devices. The ship itself was quite small – she estimated it only had enough room for two people to pilot it and live for any extended period.

Jaime was stunned by what she saw. "Crap Allen, did your team build that?"

"We sure did Jaime! Quite a piece of work, isn't it? We named it the Blackbird after the spy aircraft of Earth in the 1960's. If you didn't notice, it has a special stealth coating that repels all SCADAR and many other types of scanning beams. This ship is a scout ship, it was built to be fast and elusive – it was built to explore."

Jaime shook her head in amazement. "You built that in the time we were gone?"

"Yes, and your crew on Stopper was building a craft for the Blessed – until the attack."

"Attack? What attack?"

Allen's voice became stiff as he described the attack on the base. "Some unknown craft just came in and attacked. Starlight took the new spaceship in tow and ran off – Max was able to get a warning out to the Normals on Stopper, but we have not heard anything from them since. Once the invading ship left the area we did a fly-by in the Blackbird but saw no activity. Sorry, I don't have anything better to report Captain."

"Then we had better head back and see if anything is left of the base. Are you headed back with us?"

"No, we're taking the Blackbird out to explore. We decided while you were gone that we needed to go out on our own and try to find somewhere we can live. We must get away from the Blessed"

"Who's with you?"

A deep voice interjected into their Norm-Comm messaging. "Geologist Buck Strong, Beta Starship Captain."

"Very well..." she sighed slightly at the thought of losing this pair of good men. She thought for a moment before asking "How do we explain your disappearance?"

"We think that you could list us as missing in the attack. They will have no record of who was where, when..."

"Very true. They really don't have many records of us anyway. The one advantage to being a second-class creature, eh?"

Allen chuckled "Yes, indeed! Oh, Jaime – can you stop at Bung and pick up Jonathan and a few of the others? They will need to get back to Starlight with you. I have assigned a small group to stay there and work. They too will show as missing in action after the attack. It worked out well that the attack came, and we were able to remove some of our people from the crew manifests. Well, if everyone on Stopper survived that is..." He stopped, not wanting to shatter any hopes Jaime might have had for survivors – he was pretty sure the base was decimated. "By the way, did you have any luck? Did you find a planet for us?"

"No, nothing we would want to, or could inhabit. There are tons of intelligent life out here, Allen. We met one such race, the Flaybah. I will download our advanced scans only – everything that the Blessed will see has been modified so they will discover nothing about them." She thought for a moment, then added "If you do head that way, be sure to introduce Geologist Strong to them – I think they will enjoy meeting him"

Allen chuckled slightly knowing that Jaime in her dry way was telling some small joke. "Will do, Captain. Well, drat! I was hoping that you might have found something and saved us some time. All right, then I guess we will have to head out and find something ourselves."

"Allen, there is something I need to know...your voice for a moment when you first contacted me...well, it sounded familiar but not like you."

"I don't know what you are talking about Jaime. Can you describe further?"

The sincerity in his voice put her mind at ease "Never mind. Good luck – go find us a home!"

"Aye, aye Captain. Now, watch this...you're going to be impressed!" The two ships moved in opposite directions slowly. Jaime and Halley watched as the small black ship slightly lit up, then blurred and disappeared right before their eyes.

"Shit, they have faster than light drive!" Halley shouted out.

Jaime just nodded in agreement for a second. "Yes, and with that we have a chance..."

After a few hours of flight time they arrived at the five planetoids that blocked the passageways to the other galaxies – one of them being their own galaxy of origin. They stopped at Bung and picked up Jonathan and ten other technicians who were no longer needed at the secret facility. Jaime wished she had time to tour the facility, but she was in a hurry to get to Stopper and look for survivors.

Jonathan ran to the pair of women as soon as he boarded and first gave Halley a big hug – then to her surprise, saluted Jaime. "Great to see you Beta Starship Captain!" he announced.

Jaime smiled and reached out and gave the thin young man a squeezing hug. He blushed and looked at the ground. "It's really good to see you too Jonathan. So, I saw the fruits of your labor– Blackbird is a beauty."

Jonathan glowed with pride. "It is the first ship of our own design. We were fortunate to find all the materials we needed. Stealth coating – still not quite sure what it is, but the chemists will figure out the composition. The super light titanium frame, and the RFS."

"RFS?" Jaime queried.

"The engine, we think it is faster than light. We will know more when Blackbird returns. We also hope that by the time Blackbird returns, we will have the full schematic and will be able to reproduce it. Right now, it is only one of two."

Jaime shook her head in amazement "I just can't believe how much you have accomplished while we were gone! I wish we..." her thoughts were interrupted by a very weak voice on her Norm-Comm channel.

"Captain?"

Jaime was about to speak to the voice in her left ear but then it finally occurred to her who it was. "Lindy? Is that you?"

"Yes Captain..."

Jaime was in shock – how could she have been speaking with her, she was way out of range for Norm-Comm. "Lindy, are you on Stopper?"

"Yes Captain."

She was so far away and, yet her communication signal sounded as if she was right outside the ship. "Can you tell me how you are doing? Is everyone there alive?"

"I don't know...there are no lights, the power is out."

"Ck Lindy, we're nearby and are headed out to get you. We will be there for you very soon." She turned to Halley "Fire up the drives, we're leaving now – they need us." Halley immediately obeyed her command, secured the hatches and activated the ion drives for immediate departure. Jaime pointed at Jonathan to take his chair, and she sat down in the command seat. As the ship lifted off she felt a slight burning sensation in her head – right behind her left ear – in her Norm-Comm device.

Leopold Muldoon:

The attack had come quickly – he was outside the enclosure when the ship arrived. From his vantage point a mile away from the enclosure he could see the large golf ball shaped ship as it emitted thousands of small laser-like beams. It tore through the fabric of the enclosure and shredded it within seconds. The transport ship was blasted just as quickly. He had ordered it to take off, but not soon enough – it was obliterated in seconds.

A good Blessed pilot was lost this day, along with at least another twenty or so Blessed. After the ship had destroyed their base, it headed right toward his position, blasting at anything or anyone that moved. To his fortune, he was out looking for a device that he had spotted while doing a SCADAR survey of the planetoid. He had been wandering toward its location with two Normals that he brought along to carry the device back to base for analysis. When the ship approached, he sent the Normals away from his position while he hid. His plan worked, and the ship pursued the Normals and blasted them while it lost track of him as he hid in a deep crevice.

Once the ship left, he returned to the base only to find most everyone was dead. He managed to locate two Blessed and an assemblage of Normals who were still alive. Somehow, the Normals had been able to scatter and avoid detection by the attackers. He wondered how they had gotten away – something to think about another day. The ones left alive were all in space suits and were rummaging through the littered remains of the habitat looking for surviving people and equipment.

His heads-up display indicated a ship was landing on the bottom of the planetoid – Bordeaux had returned after surviving her trip into sub-space. He tapped on his communication device tunneling the beam to two Blessed who were looking through the rubble. "You two…" they both stopped and snapped to attention. He looked around and spotted a toolbox that survived the assault. "Grab those tools and follow me!" he barked. They followed obediently and the three headed back out, away from the destroyed habitation. He knew that if Bordeaux had returned she would be arriving there shortly to pick them up. He needed to find his treasure and return before that happened.

After a ten-mile low gravity trek through the grey passageways of rock that lined this part of the surface of Stopper, they came to a flat section. "We are almost there…" He told the pair as they started a hop-style walk toward a glow that appeared at the end of the flat, no more than another mile away. When they reached the end of the flat, they came upon a large, golden, egg-shaped device. A red stripe ran around the top of the device. There were five legs on the device – each one had been drilled into the solid surface of the planetoid. On the top was a control panel of some form – there were no writings on the panel, only various blinking lights and indicators. The device gave off a slight hum that pierced their space suits and rang in their heads.

"Yes, here it is...my deserved treasure..."

Lindy Light

It was pitch black – the air was stale, and filled with dust and smoke. There was enough air to breathe, but the floating particulates made it difficult, and caused her to cough on occasion. She did not move – as staying flat on the ground and not moving seemed to make the most sense. She had been able to get a message to the Captain – she really was not sure how, but she had. Her head pounded as if someone had taken a boot and stomped repeatedly on her forehead.

She wondered if anyone else was alive. She heard no one else in the room – neither Max, or Katsumi were making any sounds. She did not even know if they were still there. When the attack started, what few lights that had been left on, went out. The cavern started to crumble, and rocks fell onto them. After that, she had passed out and until now could not remember anything that had happened -- what that attacking ship had done or the possibility of how many of her friends were now dead.

A noise, she heard it in the distance. She wondered if the attackers were now inside the habitat, on their way to finish the job. Her fears increased, and tears welled up in her eyes, she struggled to keep them back. She bit her lip to keep herself from sobbing – fearing that her crying would alert the approaching attackers. She thought to herself, if she could get up and find a weapon – something that would protect her and anyone else that might have survived.

Lights were suddenly moving in one of the corridors in the distance, they were moving toward her. She tried to move but whenever she tried, she felt a stabbing pain in her leg. She almost cried out from the pain, but bit her lip even harder, silencing any cries that might give away her position to the invaders. The footsteps were getting louder, they were getting closer. She put her face down toward the ground and hoped they would go away, but they did not. They were now even closer and were almost in the same room. She found a rock next to her hand and slowly she reached over and grabbed it. She would pummel anyone who tried to take her – she was determined to take someone with her when she died.

She heard them enter the room – not a word was said. Seeing the light through her eyelids, she could tell they were shining their lights on her. She played dead, hoping they would ignore her and move on, but they didn't. She felt something touch her – an appendage. Without looking, she swung the rock in her hand toward the alien hoping to strike it. A hand stopped her in mid-swing. The hand was strong, but not large and she could have sworn she felt five fingers.

When she swung the rock, it made her move her legs, which caused excruciating pain. She cried out and opened her eyes. Her hand was being held by her Captain. Jaime was stopping her hand from striking her while at the same time trying to get her to lay her head back onto the ground.

"Take it easy Communications Officer" she said.

In the background, she could hear Jonathan's voice. He was yelling out something about finding gray cases and samples. She could tell he was franticly trying to find people to help. She winced in pain as the nerves in her legs fired another jolt – letting her know she was still injured.

Once the pain in her legs subsided she gave a slight sigh and the best smile she could muster. Jaime stroked her blond hair and tried to calm her. She felt another hand on her – she allowed her eyes to crack open slightly and saw Max hovering over her. He was waving a medical scanner and preparing medications for her.

"Max...you're alive..." she barely squeaked out.

"Of course, my dear – it is going to take a lot more that an alien attack to take me down. Now Lindy, I am going to have to sedate you so we can put you in a splint and get you aboard the transport. We will get you all fixed up once we arrive back on Starlight. Do you understand?" All she could do at that point was nod – he had given her the pain reliever and a nod were the only move she could now manage through the drug induced calm.

She woke up with Max turned away from her – they were still in the habitat. He looked at her curiously and said, "You're awake?" he gave her another shot, putting her back into her slumber.

She awoke, this time inside a pressurized stretcher. She peered through the canopy window with foggy eyes but could barely pick out the pair of men carrying her through the vacuum of space toward the transport vehicle. She was taken into the air lock and into the pressurized environment of the ship. The seal was released – letting out a slight hiss and then the top was removed. Max was once again looking at her, scanning and waving a flashlight into her eyes. The ship shook suddenly, and Max almost fell on top of her. She heard Captain Bordeaux in the distance shouting something about the planetoid shifting and take off was to be immediate. She slightly picked up on the communication channel traffic and heard something about diverting to Ultimate.

Max looked toward the cockpit then back down at her with a confused look on his face "I can't believe you're back again." He prepared yet another injection "Okay, this time I will knock you out and you will not wake up for a long, long time." Another shot and she was out again.

She had no concept of the passing of time. However, this time when she awoke, she was in a well-lit area. As the fuzziness cleared, she realized it was the hangar deck of a starship. Her eyes cleared a little more and saw a face staring down at her. It was a man, and from what she could tell, he was young, and very handsome. He stood above her with dark-eyes staring into her face. He had a large, glowing, toothy-smile bounded by his broad cheeks, and a very distinct pointed chin between strong jaw bones. Topping his face were locks of wavy blonde hair perfectly situated and held in place by some form of styling solution. Around his neck was a platinum medallion, indicating he was Blessed.

"So, we are awake, are we?" her mouth was too dry to speak, she just nodded. "Well, I saw them cart you in and I just had to stop them, so I could look at your gorgeous face." She managed a light smile. "Well, I won't keep you from your appointment with the doctor. However, when you are healed up I would like you to join me for an evening of dinner and perhaps a visit to the club?" She gave a look of confusion. He read her facial expression and smiled. "I am Kip Gurrigan, Captain of this ship – The Ultimate. I welcome you aboard my vessel. Until we are together and staring into each other's eyes…very soon…adieu"

She finally realized who he was as he walked away with a light bouncy step. He was wearing a tight, black uniform tunic, and in an unusual combination – a vinyl kilt with a slight tartan pattern in a lighter shade of black. Gracing his legs, he wore a pair of dark black boots, and on his hands, a matching black forearm length set of gloves.

The Blessed attendant leaned over as Kip left and whispered "He has picked you – you are very lucky…"

She slightly smiled, still a little out of it from the drugs that were slowly clearing from her head. A moment later, Max appeared above her and looked down into her eyes. "How?" he shined a flashlight into her eyes again. "You should have been out for at least another eight hours with the amount of sedatives I gave you." He scanned her again and prepared another mist injection. "This time I will up the dosage even further – I have to have you out, so I can work!" Another shot and she blacked out once again.

Leopold Muldoon:

The device hummed and glowed as he stared at it. "Yes, this is it – the treasure we have been looking for!"

One of the Blessed soldiers looked at it, and then at Leopold "What is it?"

"Who cares – it is made of gold! It is treasure, and it is mine!" He looked at the lights on the top of the humming unit. "You there, touch it."

The soldier looked at him and then pointed to himself, questioning the order. Leopold replied by nodding his head in a visible way through his helmet. The soldier began to breathe heavy quick breaths as he cautiously reached out and extended a finger toward the side of the device. Slowly his finger moved near the beveled surface near the top – finally barely touching the gold surface – nothing happened. He gave a large sigh, fogging up the helmet of his suit.

"Bah, I could have told you nothing would happen! I just wanted to make sure there was not an electrical short." Leopold barked as he reached out, shoved the soldier to the side, and placed both hands on the glowing device. He rubbed his hands along the sides, examining the surface. The side of the device was smooth with no distinguishing features – except five legs that extended out of the device and into the surface of the planetoid. Although the legs were drilled into the surface, he felt they could somehow be removed from the rock.

The other soldier spoke "Sir, I just received word that they have a shuttle at the base to take us back to the ship. They are ordering us back now."

"BAH!" he spat out "Not until I get this loosened up and transported back. No one is leaving until I am done here!" He stared at the blinking lights and buttons on the top of the device again "So, which one is it?" he pondered as his fingers lightly traversed the control panel. His fingers finally slid across a red button with a white light above it "This has to be it..." he said as he depressed the button.

The five legs suddenly began to unscrew from the surface and then retracted into the body of the device. The lights on the top extinguished, the glow stopped, and the hum discontinued. The center of the device that was firmly embedded into the surface was now breaking away from the crust of soil holding it in place. It started to float up – Leopold grabbed it with two gloved hands and brought it in toward his chest like a large child. "Alright, let's head back..." he said as he quickly turned and headed back in the reverse direction. The two soldiers quickly followed in tow.

A slight earth tremor caused the trio to slightly lose their balance. Leopold extended an elbow to steady himself on a large rock without dropping the device. A moment later, the shaking stopped, and they continued their steady pace back to the shuttle.

Over his intercom, the shuttle contacted him "Sir, are you on your way back? We are experiencing a few earthquakes here. We are not sure how much longer we can stay here."

"We are on our way back -- you will stay where you are." he barked.

They walked for another tenth of a mile, when the ground shook again – more violently this time. At the same moment, their bodies suddenly felt very heavy and Leopold found the device was becoming extremely heavy.

One of the soldiers looked up "Shit!" was all he could say.

"What is it, Minion?" he asked, then noticed he was looking up. He allowed his gaze to venture into space and was shocked by what he saw – the stars were slowly spinning. "What the hell is going on?" Suddenly, the ground of the planetoid shook violently once again – sending him to the ground.

The shuttle called again. "Sorry sir, we are leaving while we can. Good luck to you – we will return and pick you up if we can…"

"Wait!" one of the soldiers shouted out as he stood and started to run as fast as he could toward the location of the shuttle.

"Stop soldier and help me with this – follow my order!" He looked at the other soldier who was looking confused as to what to do. "You there, help me with this!" He aimed his command weapon at him in a threatening motion.

The soldier looked ahead to where he could see the shuttle slowly lifting off the surface of the planetoid, and then looked back at Leopold. "Screw you…" he said as he reached out with large arms and shoved Leopold, causing him to fall to the surface – the device landing squarely on his chest.

His breath was knocked out of him by the force of the device landing on his chest – every second the device sat on him the heavier it got. His head hit the surface and his eyes looked straight up into the sky – the stars were spinning even faster now. The soldier who had just knocked him down was now standing above him – rage boiling in his eyes. "You…you caused this. You are the reason they left us – you piece of shit!"

"Help me up!" he ordered, despite the soldier's insolence.

Instead of helping him up however, the soldier reached down and pressed the red button, activating the unit. "Maybe this will fix things" he said as the device started to hum. The legs popped out of the side of the device and the pointed tips began to spin. They lowered themselves into Leopold's arms and legs securing them to the surface of the planetoid, the fifth arm of the unit barely missed his helmet as it drilled into the ground next to his head. His suit self-sealed, which stopped oxygen from leaking where the legs had drilled into his body. The blood gushing from his injuries was beginning to fill the arms and legs of the inside of his suit. The device became even heavier, and slowly began to crush his chest – he was barely able to cry out in agony.

The soldier laughed maniacally as he quickly lost his mind to the panic of the situation. He started to run, but was knocked to the ground by a quick shift of gravity.

Leopold watched the stars spun around and around before the spinning suddenly stopped, and his vision was now filled with the sight of space opening like a giant maw. Stopper was sucked into the Devil's Throat and as it moved, the device pressed against his chest tighter and tighter. Had he survived any longer, he would have been totally crushed by the increasing weight of the device. Fortunately for him, he and Stopper both disintegrated into small fragments of matter under the force of the gravity well.

Boral Oldham:

"What just happened" he asked his science officer.

He looked at his SCADAR readouts and scratched his head before softly saying "It's gone...the planetoid just drifted into the Devil's Throat..."

"Communications, did our shuttle get out of there?"

The communications officer got on and spoke for a moment with the pilot before reporting "Yes, my Star Force Commander. Everyone got off except for three – two soldiers...and Alpha Starship Captain Muldoon...Sir."

"Muldoon? Damn! A waste of a fine officer." He stood and gave a salute to the viewport where Stopper once sat, before yelling out "He is conquering the heavens now! Hail our dead Blessed one!" All the bridge members stood and repeated the same salute and repeated the same words as Boral before returning to their duties.

He wiped a small tear off his cheek and sat back into his command chair. "Well, I guess now we have nothing stopping us from going home. Shall we set a course Helmsman?"

The science officer interjected "Sir, we know we barely made it through the Throat to get here. With our current knowledge of the forces in there, I do not think we would make it."

Boral looked at the officer and scratched his chin "So, how did we get here? Aren't there any records in the computer?"

"Nothing that would give us an indication of a way to make it back through? We could ask Beta Starship Captain Bordeaux ..."

"Ask, are you kidding? No...I have a better idea. Communications, get me Bordeaux." A moment later, Jaime's face appeared on the bridge display. "Bordeaux, I am tasking you with figuring out how you got through the Devil's Throat and testing that theory yourself. Use whatever expertise you Normals may have and get a ship prepared to send you back. I want you back on the Starlight immediately working on this problem. Star Force Commander, out!" Jaime barely had time to give a facial reaction and a nod of acknowledgement before he disconnected her. "There, either she will figure out a way to get us home or she will be dead. Either way, she will be out of my hair – perhaps permanently." He smiled in satisfaction of his idea and slightly shook his head in the positive.

"Sir..." the science officer spoke up "The computer has traced the course of the ship that attacked us and has determined its point of origin."

Boral raised an eyebrow "Really? So, we can find their home world?" the science officer nodded in acknowledgment "In that case, we will have a change in plans. Helmsman, how long to formulate the path into sub-space for arrival at the enemy's home world?

The helmsman entered various points into a mapping console and then waited for the computer to estimate calculation time before he replied, "About eleven days, Star Force Commander."

"Eleven days? Why so long? It only took Bordeaux two hours for their course calculation"

"It was a much shorter course sir – which takes a lot less time for the computer to formulate" he replied.

Boral sighed "Very well, start the formulations and set a course for the attacker's home world as soon as possible. Communications, cancel the order I just sent to Bordeaux. Get me Alpha Starship Captain Gurrigan on the Ultimate." A moment later Kip appeared on his holo-screen. "Kip, we are formulating a sub-space insertion to attack the enemy's home world. In the meantime, find some shit duty for that Bordeaux to do on board your ship. I have no desire to see her until I am ready to send her through the Devil's Throat – and if she somehow dies doing her work duty...well, so be it. We will find someone else to work on the Throat problem."

Kip nodded "Very well my Star Force Commander. I am sure I will have something special for her to accomplish on board."

"Excellent" he replied as Kip closed the communication line. "In the meantime, get everything ready for battle – very soon we will be going out for revenge."

The Ark of the Blessed

Day 100

Lindy Light

He arrived promptly at 1900 hours as promised. He rang the annunciator and she answered to find the most handsome man she had ever seen standing at her door. He was so well dressed – wearing an Alliance black waistcoat. Buttons and gold lace flowed up each side of the long lapels that hung from his neck to below his matching gold belt. Over his heart was the insignia of the Alliance and the Order. Below the jacket was a white ruffled shirt and below the belt he wore a tight pair of space nylon tights that ran down to a knee-length pair of black boots. His hair was in perfect order; blonde waves flowed from the left side of his head to the right – perfectly trimmed, almost non-existent sideburns, and that glowing set of white teeth. She nearly melted at the site of this god-like apparition standing before her.

"Hello Kip..." was all she could say.

He looked her up and down. She was wearing a yellow semi-transparent top – a lacy material that flowed over her chest, partially exposing her breasts. Below her bare, well-shaped belly, a yellow chiffon skirt flowed over her hips and wrapped around her shapely legs, but had a split in the front that allowed a slight exposure of leg when she moved. She had put most of her blonde hair into a fishtail bun that gave her a sexy look, but still provided cover and concealment of her communication port.

He licked his lips as he told her "You are absolutely scrumptious my dear! I have an exciting night planned for us. First, dancing at The Posh – it is the nicest dance club on this ship. As a matter of fact, I designed it myself. Then, reservations for dinner, does that sound appealing?"

She took no time to answer, "What are we waiting for?" She extended her arm and he lightly took it and walked her to The Posh. Kip had designed this club to his own exact specifications. It was a perfect place to dance and mingle. She sipped on non-alcoholic beverages while he enjoyed light Vodka drinks during their rest breaks between dances. Hardly a word was said between them while they enjoyed the music, and moved their bodies to the rhythms and the excitement of the club. They danced for hours, and afterward they moved on to the Captain's dining hall which had been specially prepared for them.

Within minutes of their arrival a meal of fresh vegetables, cheeses, and meats was presented. Lindy enjoyed the vegetarian food but refused the meat. He looked at her peculiarly "You don't like the meat?"

"I don't eat meat, or simulated meat protein, for that matter. That type of protein disrupts my communications processing."

He looked at her strangely, then he replied "Well, that is a shame as it is quite good. But, to each their own, I guess…" He took a large cut of meat, and slowly put it into his mouth. He chewed the meat slowly to give extra effect to Lindy of his enjoyment of the food. She found it repulsive to watch him eat in such a way, and wondered why he was acting in such a manner after she had told him of her food preferences.

"Lindy…" he interrupted her thoughts "you appear to be quite healthy. I have this…well, it is strange…but I have this phobia of unhealthy people. I wonder if you would mind if my personal doctor gives you a quick scan? It will not be invasive at all. I just want to make sure you are not carrying any germs that might be harmful. Pretty please?"

She looked at him and he was staring back at her with big, goofy eyes, giving her a begging look. It made her laugh slightly – he returned a slight giggle also. She nodded to provide her permission. The doctor came up behind her, and waved his medical scanner over her. He read the results for a moment, then looked at Kip and nodded, which caused him to smile.

"How about a drink, hmm?" he waved to the waiter who brought two glasses of sparkling beverages. "I am assuming you will not join me in an alcoholic beverage?" Lindy shook her head, no. "I thought not, so I have had a sparkling fruit beverage prepared for you. I think you will find it scrumptious!"

He tipped the flute of sparkling beverage at her and she tipped hers in return. He clinked his flute against hers, and took a large sip of the beverage, then gave a look of satisfaction. She put the glass to her lips and took a small sip. The sweet fruit did agree with her palate – however, there was a slight bitterness in the aftertaste that she found slightly repugnant.

"How do you like it? It is the essence of an old Earth fruit – the peach. I had it squeezed of its essence and then fermented into a sparkling beverage."

"It's quite good…" she told him, slightly lying while thinking about the aftertaste.

He tipped his glass again, and motioned for her to join him in taking another drink. "Now, please eat." He waved his hand over the many plates of food spread out in front of them. "So, tell me, how do you like this? Is this a life you would like to live? I could arrange it, so you could have this life and not ever have to work."

"Well, it is very nice but in some ways, I do prefer the challenge of going to my job and doing what I have trained for. Doing the job I had my communications port implanted for."

"Well, that is all good…" he replied "but I think you have a different destiny. You know that we Blessed take Normal women as mates, don't you?"

Lindy gave a weak smile but found it hard to control the slight quivering of her lower lip. She now had a feeling that perhaps she had made a terrible mistake by joining him.

"I think you were meant to find me here, and to spend time as my mate. I think tonight you and I will make beautiful love together, and we will even have children someday. What do you think of that idea, my sweet Lindy?"

She had enough "I think this was a mistake, if you will now excuse me I must call it a night." She stood up, and placed her napkin on the plate in front of her. "Thank you for the lovely evening, but I have to prepare for my next shift…I…" she began to feel something strange happening to her. The table in front of her began to pulsate, and the room began to spin.

"Oh, I think not my dear. I think you will be staying with me tonight. It is meant to be this way – you are a Normal, and Norm women are meant for one thing, and one thing alone – procreation. You will service me this evening and you shall bear me a child. Why do you think we brought so many of you? Blessed do not normally have baby girls – thus, you Norms are required for not only our pleasure, but to be the vessels for our seeds."

She felt two strong pairs of hands grab each of her arms. The doctor came into her blurry field of vision holding a large injection device. He pressed it to her neck and began to slowly fill her arteries with drugs.

Before she passed out Kip told her "You should be honored. You will be producing one of many strong children for me this evening."

*   *   *

She was not sure how long she had been out, but she awoke to find her body naked and electronically strapped to a bed. Kip was on top of her enjoying himself in his unwanted pleasure of her. She began to sob, which caused him to look down at her face.

"Dammit, she is waking – put her out, now!" she heard, as she saw the doctor appear in her blurry vision. A moment later, she felt another dose of the mind-dampening fluid enter her bloodstream.

She awoke again after a time, finding the doctor hovering above her again – running his medical scanner over her belly. Through fuzzy eyes she saw Kip standing at the edge of the bed waiting in anticipation. The doctor finished his scan and looked at Kip before motioning no to him.

Kip was furious "Fine, if I cannot have a child with this one, then perhaps one of the other Captains can." He motioned into the darkness and several men approached – all were wearing Captain's uniforms, at least for a moment. As soon as they approached the bed they began removing their clothing. She began to shiver in fear as they stripped down and looked at her with hungry eyes.

She began to sob and cry. Kip looked at her with disgust "What is she doing awake again? Put that bitch out. I do not want to hear her anymore..." he ordered, and she once again felt an injection blank her mind.

She started to become conscious and was able to see one of the men on top of her scratching her skin and causing her almost unbearable pain. She felt pain in other parts of her body as well. She started to cry, and mumbled a plea for them to stop the torture. The man hovering over her looked at her before saying "Shit, she's awake again! She's going to need another shot." He rolled off her, and turned her over. He moved the hair away from her neck, then laughed before saying "Hey, Xavier I think I found a hole that's perfect for you!"

She heard laughing, and then one of the men shouted, "Screw you, Fitchburg!"

She heard the first man reply, "No, screw this!" and the room filled with laughter.

Once again, the doctor came over to her – he had a confused look on his face. "I don't get it – I gave her a large enough dose to put out an elephant for a week..." He sighed, and then reached down and gave her yet another shot.

She awoke sometime later – Lindy was not exactly sure how long she had been there. The restraints had been removed however, and she was now alone in the room. She was still naked, her body was bruised and battered. Every orifice on her hurt and felt dirty. She had a horrible taste in her mouth. When she sat up, she felt something odd at the back of her neck. When she reached around and felt her communication port, she found it too was soiled – they left no part of her body pure.

On the nightstand, her computer sat and blinked with a message notification. She sobbed and moved slowly to avoid any additional pain while she reached over to pick up her computer. She activated the message – it was an automated notification of a change in assignment. She was to report to Alpha Starship Captain Fitchburg Griggs for communications duty on the next ship to be built. She would remain on one of the planetoids with Griggs until a new ship was constructed.

She slowly got up, and with small movements made her way to the cleansing bay. She activated a real water shower – damn the cost to them – then soaked her abused body until the water limiter shut the shower down. She then laser cleaned her teeth and mouth – even after three cleaning sessions, the lasers were not able to remove the taste fully from her dry mouth.

The whole time she cried as she cleaned up. After a while however, she found she had ran out of tears, and was able to dress and make herself presentable enough to leave the quarters. Outside were two guards who escorted her to the space dock where she was immediately loaded onto a shuttle and sent to one of the planetoids. She tried to send out a message to any of her Normal crew mates, but her mind was still too numb to properly use her Norm-Comm. As the transport left the ship, she could tell all feeling and emotion was fading from her, leaving her an empty shell. There was nothing left inside of her -- except the hatred she now had toward the Frogspawn. She looked out the portal of the transport as Ultimate quickly faded into the distance – leaving behind all her friends, sending her into a lonely life as a slave and prisoner of the Blessed.

Day 105:

Kip Gurrigan:

"What duty do we have her doing?" Kip asked of his First Officer.

"Just what you requested, air lock cleaning and maintenance, Alpha Starship Captain."

"Good, good. Find her and activate the monitor on her."

A moment later, her image was projected onto the bridge's main holo-screen. The image showed Jaime cleaning corrosion from a circuit board inside one of the many air locks aboard the ship. The air lock door was open and locked toward the inside of the ship. "Wow, that is dangerous work wouldn't you say?" Kip asked his First Officer, who nodded in acknowledgment. "Would be bad for her if that air lock malfunctioned while she was working on it..."

As he leaned forward and looked at her working, the image began to break up into static. "Fix that image, and prepare to flush that air lock."

Jaime Bordeaux:

Cleaning the air lock circuitry was not fun work for Jaime, but it did provide a way to ignore the pain she was feeling that day. She stopped her cleaning again and tapped on her Norm-Comm "Max, are you going to be here soon? I really could use some help."

"I'm almost there – a minute at the most..." he replied.

As promised he did arrive within a minute. In one hand, he held a glass of water, in the other, two small pills. "Here take these first, then I want to examine you."

She took the pills and swallowed them, washing them down with half the glass of water. "Max, what the hell is wrong with me? I've been having nothing but pain in my head and in my ears all day! As a matter of fact, I think my Norm-Comm is acting up. I feel like I'm transmitting without even touching it."

"Really? Stand up and let me scan you in that case..." he motioned her upward with his fingers on one hand, and lowered his other hand to assist her to stand. She placed the half-drunk glass of water on the floor of the air lock, and with his assistance, stood up. "Come out here into better light" he suggested. They stood in the hallway and he ran his scanner up and down her body – taking extra time to scan, and look over her head and brain. "Odd...Jaime, we will need to replace your reactor I think..."

She looked at him and scrunched her forehead. He put his fingers on her forehead and rubbed the skin until she relaxed her forehead muscles, then he continued his scan of her neck. "I think it's breaking down. Typical Blessed technology you know. Nothing to worry about, will only take a minute to replace. No rush, see me about it when you can. You will probably just find that your command weapon will not function properly until we replace that reactor." He then moved his hand toward the side of her head and moved the hair aside, exposing her ears. He noticed a second growth was now forming in the middle of her ear along the back rim. This small growth protruded out and back away from her ear as if it were a small piece of fabric blowing in the wind. The growth on the top of her ear had also moved toward the back and away from her ear.

"What are those, Doc?" she asked "they have not hurt until today. They have grown quite a bit too, haven't they?" Max nodded, in agreement. "Great, if it weren't bad enough we're trapped here with the Blessed, but now there is something going completely wrong with my body."

"Jaime, how do you know that this is wrong? I have not been able to determine that there are any negative aspects or side effects, of either these growths or any of the changes you have been going through. As a matter of fact, most of the Normals have begun to have some of these same changes. So, what makes you think that this is bad, hmm?"

"Damn it, Doc! How can you look at this in a positive light? We're changing and who knows what we'll become! Quit being so damn upbeat!"

He pointed to the glass of water sitting on the floor of the air lock "Jaime, when you look at that, what do you see?"

She turned and looked and without thinking said "A half glass of water, why?"

"Empty or full?" he quickly queried.

Just as quickly she replied "Empty..."

"Well, I see that as a half full glass of water. See, I try to look at everything in the positive light. Much better for one's mental outlook."

"I still think it's half empty..." she quipped.

"Well, although a positive outlook is good for me – I bet some pessimism is probably good for a leader like you."

"I'm not much of a leader as I only have a small crew, and no ship."

"Not yet, it will come...it will come. Once again – be positive!" He looked down at the glass again. "If you think about it Jaime...it really is completely full. It is full of water and air...which means the glass is full. So, there!" he raised his head, proudly beaming.

Without warning, the air lock door quickly slid closed and the air was instantly emptied from the chamber as the exterior door slowly opened. She looked down through the window first at the control board she was cleaning – the display indicated that the air lock was still safe and secure. She then looked down at the glass -- the water had flash-frozen, and was evaporating quickly.

"What the hell just happened, Jaime?" he asked in a whisper as he looked at the controls, still showing green.

She looked at the monitoring sensor up in the corner of the hall "I would say that someone wanted me in there – I'm just not sure how come they triggered that malfunction so late." She looked at the glass and pointed to it – Max lowered his eyes and stared at the almost empty glass as the remaining water evaporated into the vacuum. "There, now the glass is almost empty. Still want to give me a lesson in positivity? I'm positive the glass is empty..."

She turned and left Max in the hallway staring at the glass that was now moving in the zero gravity with the last of the escaping air. He watched as it floated out into deep space. He raised his left eyebrow while considering his thoughts. An idea came to him, he raised a finger and turned to tell Jaime his thoughts, but found she was long gone.

A moment later claxons filled the hallway, followed by Kip announcing "All crew, prepare for insertion into subspace. We are going after our attackers, revenge will be ours! Stand-by, this is a fifteen-minute warning."

Jaime ran back to Max still in the hallway. "Max, we need to get everyone ready. They will find it hard to move. They will need supplies nearby and places to relax while we travel through sub-space. We have little time, come on!"

Halley Cet:

She received the message over Norm-Comm – all Normal humans were to find others they could bunk with for the duration of the trip through subspace. She knew what this trip would be like, so she decided to find Jonathan and spend the days travelling with him. Besides, she had things she wanted to talk to him about – he would be a captive audience.

She contacted him via Norm-Comm and arranged to meet him in one of the communal areas near the food dispensers. When she arrived, she found he had been joined by two other Normal engineers -- Georgie Hayson and William Jergens. All three crew members were sitting around a table playing poker. Jonathan saw Halley and motioned her over.

"Halley, join us. Hope you brought credits…" he said as he waved her to a cushioned seat at the round table and tossed a deck of cards at her to deal.

"Of course, however, I don't think I will need 'em…" she said as he began to deal out five cards to each of them.

They stared at their cards for a moment, then Georgie broke the silence "So, what did you find out there Cet…any life?"

"Actually, yes. We found a very advanced civilization – the Flaybah."

Jonathan's eyebrows arched up in surprise "I did not see that in the logs."

"Did you check the advanced scanning logs yet?"

He shook his head "No, not yet…"

"Then that is why you have not heard about this yet. The standard logs have been purged and manipulated. I'll take three cards…" she selected three cards and put them on the table.

The three engineers each put a single card down as a discard, then stared at her as she gave each of them a replacement draw and then dealt three cards for herself. William asked, "They are advanced enough to change the computer SCADAR logs?"

Halley shook her head yes. "My god, what type of creatures are they? What do they look like? Much more advanced than us I bet..."

"Actually, they are deer..." she looked at her cards "I bet one-thousand credits."

The three immediately unfolded and activated their computers and looked up the definition of a deer. They stared at the output without saying a word. Then almost simultaneously, they slowly set their computers down and stared at her. "Those fuzzy animals are the advanced civilization the Flaybah?" Jonathan said. "Do you really expect us to believe you? I think you are pulling our legs!" He picked up and looked at his cards "Just like your lousy poker bluffing skills...I raise you five-thousand credits." Georgie and William folded.

"No, I'm totally serious about the Flaybah. They are like the creatures called deer on Earth before the bombs – except they are intelligent, and more advanced than us. They have a large fleet of powerful starships, and live on many planets. Five-thousand credits, I call."

"And they have powerful enough computers to manipulate our computer logs...oh, sure. Ace-high flush, beat it."

"Yes, they do. As a matter of fact, their computers use a three-dimensional binary number system – and they told me there are races that can compute in binary numbers of even more dimensions than them...so chew on that." She placed her five cards down face up – Seven through Jack, all of hearts "Straight flush, thanks for the credits."

"Damn!" Jonathan muttered right before the claxon sounded indicating the insertion into subspace. "Here we go..."

Georgie settled into the soft cushioned chair and leaned her head back into her headrest before she muttered "three dimensional binary numbers...hmm." Jonathan looked at her and nodded – he was thinking about that also.

Halley looked at Georgie and smiled *"That's right, you all think about that..."*

The Ark of the Blessed

Day 110:

Jaime Bordeaux:

Jaime and Max shared the past five days in the Normal health clinic that was set up on board the Ultimate. During that time, she learned a lot about what he had discovered regarding the changes that she and other Normal humans were experiencing – Max included. He told her about the junk DNA strands that now were becoming active and manipulating their bodies. The first change they all seemed to be experiencing were the changes to their ears. Who knew what other changes were occurring that none of them could outwardly see or feel.

Perhaps one of the changes that they were now discovering was their unique ability to adapt to subspace. It seemed the more time they spent in between the layers of normal space the easier it was to live in that environment. By the time they had exited from the tear in space near the enemy's home system, they were moving around the ship normally. They also found that Normal humans were the only ones who could do this. Every Blessed they ran across while wandering the ship had been the total opposite – unable to move and close to death.

After floating in normal space for over an hour without any activity, Jaime decided to go up to the bridge and find out what was going on. When she arrived, and opened the bridge door she was hit with a horrid stench. The smell made her to recoil back away from the bridge doorway out almost into the corridor. When she recovered from the initial shock of the smell, she was able to venture farther into the bridge to discover what was causing the smell.

All the bridge personnel were Blessed – each and every one of them were unconscious and covered in various expulsions of vomit, shit, and piss. She concluded that they became unconscious the moment they entered sub-space and had lost control of all their bodily functions.

She called Max up to the bridge and had him check Kip's condition. Then despite her better judgment, she had him revive him. He slowly regained consciousness and finally through fuzzy eyes looked up at Jaime.

"What...what the hell?" he mumbled. He then looked down and saw his soiled uniform and almost gagged on his own stench.

"The trip through sub-space was not kind to you." Max interjected.

"I thought perhaps you would like to take a moment to get cleaned up before we wake your crew?" Jaime asked.

He slowly stood up "Yeah, and clean this mess up before I get back." He waved his hand across the soiled command chair and stumbled into the Captain's command quarters.

As he walked out of the room, she called and requested a cleaning robot, and then had Max awaken the rest of the bridge crew. Many of them threw up upon being roused, making the bridge an even bigger mess. More cleaning robots were called in to help.

A few hours passed while Blessed all over the fleet were awakened and recovered from their first journey into subspace. Jaime felt it was lucky that they left subspace at a far enough distance that they avoided detection from their enemy's sensing systems. They would have been sitting ducks had they appeared in the middle of the system, which the Star Force Commander had originally suggested.

Finally, with the bridge cleaned up and the crew fully recovered, Kip returned. He looked around the bridge inspecting the quality of the cleaning. "It is acceptable..." he said to Jaime.

He activated a tunneled communication with Boral on Starlight and put it onto his command holo-display. "Sir, we are ready for the attack. Do you have a plan?"

They noticed that Boral was still a mess and needed to clean up. He rubbed his stubbly chin for a moment before announcing "I am thinking their weaponry is inferior to ours based on their attack of our bases. I think we should be able to take them on in a frontal attack – eliminate any starships sent to intercept us, and then obliterate the planet with smart bombs."

"Sounds like a royal plan!" Kip replied.

"Sounds like a stupid plan to me..." Jaime thought.

Kip looked at Jaime and barked "Bordeaux, you go to the sub-bridge and assist with the Alpha on duty there. From there you will be able to watch how we Blessed conquer lesser races."

he then pointed to Max "Your doctor however must leave all bridges – no other inferiors are to be on any bridge during a battle."

Max held back his desired commentary and instead smiled, nodded at Kip, and then turned and left the bridge quickly.

Jaime also left the bridge and immediately went down to the sub-bridge – a backup bridge in the event of a catastrophe during battle. The sub-bridge was housed deep inside the command module of the ship. Although it was only meant to be a backup bridge, it was as fully capable to perform battle and emergency maneuvers. On duty was Alpha Starship Captain Bellevue Elythe.

She looked at him and then noticed his Alpha insignias, and gave a quizzical look. He beamed before saying "I was granted an emergency promotion, so I could help Kip. Now, sit over there." He pointed to a vacant chair at the science station.

She tightened her jaw before turning, and taking her seat. She looked at the holo-screen – a very small planet appeared as the ship approached. It was smaller than Earth's moon but was covered with a small ocean and several green continents. She could see many cities dotting the landscape.

Over the communication system Kip began barking his orders. "All stations, prepare for attack. Open the weapons ports, energize all beam and particle weapons – load the rail projectors. Look sharp, here they come."

The holo-screen was showing a small armada of ships as they approached. They had a similar configuration to the single ship that attacked the bases on Stopper – white balls with numerous dimples being pushed by a single grey rectangular engine section.

The communications officer of the sub-bridge announced "Alpha Starship Captain, they are receiving a message from the enemy fleet up in the main bridge. Shall I put their message up for us also?" Bellevue nodded yes.

On the screen was a large bulky humanoid. He had two eyes, a nose and a mouth like a human, but his features were very primitive. He had stringy brown hair that flowed around his face like a monkey. He had a fur lined collar and some sort of leather uniform jacket. What surprised them was that under each of the creature's shoulders was an extra arm – each arm acted independently of each other, allowing for multiple motions simultaneously. The creature began to speak in a foreign tongue. The translation computers began to work at interpreting the message that was being broadcast, but were unsuccessful in finding any interpretation.

Jaime tapped her Norm-Comm, bent down as if to check her boots, and softly said "Jonathan, capture this transmission and run it through the interpreter computer on the Rebel Queen." The science officer thought she was speaking to him, but since he was busy concentrating on studying the incoming SCADAR readings, he missed what she said – which she hoped he would. He quickly gave her a quick stare as to inquire what she wanted -- she just gave a quizzical look, and shrugged her shoulders.

"Screw it, we are getting nothing from that message" barked Kip over the bridge system "they are obviously quite primitive. Begin the attack – focus our weapons on the ships on the left, Starlight will take out the ones on the right -- Proceed."

The enemy ships fired first with a salvo of some form of particle beam which had minimal effect on the electrically charged hull plates. Kip yelled out attack commands, and Jaime heard various weapons being fired throughout the ship. On the holo-screen and with the returns from the SCADAR readings, she could see that the enemy fleet was quickly being destroyed. A tear came to her eye as she saw the carnage that the two ships were imparting to the fleet of outclassed starships. Within a matter of minutes, they had already obliterated the defenders – their home planet was now vulnerable to the will of the Supreme Commander.

Over the communications system she heard Boral calmly give the order "Fire smart bombs – take out the population of this planet. We will take it for ourselves after we eliminate this primitive race."

She heard the launchers indicating that smart bombs were being sent to their targets on the planet. She watched the holo-screen as they headed toward their assigned targets. She really did not want to see the extinction of this race, but she also knew she had to watch – she needed to never forget the lack of humanity in the Blessed. The bombs made their approach toward their targets, but before they could enter the atmosphere they exploded. It appeared that the planet was protected by some form of force field. Boral ordered another salvo, also having the same effect.

The channel was quiet for a moment. Boral then requested a tunneled communication with Kip. A minute later, the ship was being maneuvered into a new position pointed away from the planet. Jaime, now confused, looked at the science console and tried to determine what they were up to. She heard the subspace rams being fired up. *"Are we abandoning the capturing of the planet?"*

She then looked at the angle of the ship and the position of Starlight and felt a sinking feeling in her gut. "Tell me they're not going to do what I think they are going to do" she said. The science officer looked at her and shrugged his shoulders.

The beam fired out from Ultimate and began shattering the fabric of space. She then saw a second beam hit the same spot – it was being fired from Starlight. She looked at the console and saw that the force of the beam was being turned to maximum, and that the width of the beam was set to its widest setting.

The idea of what they were up to struck her like running into a brick wall "No!" she shouted out. Bellevue turned from the holo-screen and looked at her. "They can't do this – they are sending them into oblivion!"

"Shut up Bordeaux, or I will have you removed!" he said as he aimed his command weapon at her "Remember, this will fire at YOU, unlike your weapon. Do not make me use it..."

Frustrated, she slammed her fist on the science console as she looked at the holo-screen. The rip in space was enormous now and the ship was backing away from the tear. She looked at the SCADAR and saw the planet approaching the tear quickly as it travelled in its normal orbit.

She hoped that they had miscalculated the maneuver -- that the planet would not fit or would miss, but that was not to be the case. The communication channel started receiving a broadcast from the planet – another of the primitive looking creatures was screaming over the channel, she assumed it was more a plea for mercy than an expression of anger. A second holo-screen was activated on which she saw the small planet slowly squeezing into the now enormous tear in space – at the same moment the images on the screen being received from the planet were now starting to distort as subspace began effecting the atmosphere and gravity.

Tears welled up in Jaime's eyes as the planet entered the rift and was sucked into subspace, at the same moment the creature on the screen gave a scream of pain as the image faded, along with the planet. "What the hell are you? You can't be human..." she muttered.

Bellevue looked at her quizzically before saying "No, we are Blessed...we have conquered the first of many civilizations and have proven our superiority in this galaxy. Now leave this bridge." He pointed at the door.

She wiped the tears from her face and removed any sign of expression as she fought to regain her composure. She stood, pulled on her uniform top to straighten it out, then calmly walked off the bridge – all the while staring into the eyes of Bellevue, giving no expression but at the same time burning her brilliant blue eyes into his subconscious. His shoulders slightly shook with nervous energy as she left the room. When she was far enough away she heard him give a slight nervous chuckle.

As soon as she left the sub-bridge she contacted Max via Norm-Comm "Once we get back to Plug, we need to find a place to live, and I need a ship to command. I will not sit on this ship of murderers any longer. Even if it means we will have to make one of the salvaged ships operational, we will leave. I will not accept anything else. Do I have your support?"

"Of course, Jaime. We will back you in every way."

Jonathan announced himself while cutting into their conversation "Umm, Beta Starship Captain..."

"Call me Jaime on this channel Jonathan – at least until I can get an official command. What is it?"

He cleared his throat nervously before he continued "We were able to analyze a portion of that transmission from the enemy planet."

"Great, what did they say?"

"Only this...'Revenge on your race will be swift and complete. Your defiling of our space a second time now requires a total annihilation of your race by the powerful Og.' There is more, but we still have to decode it."

Jaime stopped and turned to put her fist against the bulkhead wall -- her head followed, and rested against her closed fist. She closed her eyes and thought for a moment, remembering what the Blessed just did to this entire planet before she replied "The Og, great. This is trouble and I mean big trouble. The Blessed just stirred up a hornet's nest as this was one of the two races we were warned about. Thanks Jonathan. Max, get everything prepared, it is time for us Normals to get out on our own."

The Ark of the Blessed

Day 116:

Allen James:

It was large, jagged and pitch black. It was so dark, and it blended into space so well that they almost ran into it – only by sheer luck did the sensors pick up the asteroid in time for them to avoid hitting it.

This was the fourth object that they ran across in the brief time they had been wandering around this galaxy. Three of the objects were planets that could support life, and now this asteroid – it was devoid of any sort of atmosphere and it did not orbit any sun. It would not support a single life form in its current state, but for some reason Allen decided to search it thoroughly. It measured one-hundred miles in length and was composed of an unknown black glassy rock. The sensors indicated that it was generating a light internal gravity. Allen piloted the craft around and around the large freely floating body.

"What exactly are we looking for?" Buck asked.

"I'm not sure – but whatever it is, I have a feeling we will find it...whatever it is, that is..." he replied.

He activated the high intensity illuminators to visually scan the surface, while the sensors probed the surface electronically. After four hours of searching, he finally found what his gut was had told him was there – a large cave-like opening in the surface. "There, we need to go in there!" he shouted as he began maneuvering the craft toward the entrance. Buck shook his head in confusion but then helped to maneuver the craft into the opening.

The entrance was two miles wide but was almost invisible due to the dark color of the asteroids' mass. With external illuminators running at full and SCADAR and scanner beams running along the walls, they finally found a shelf on which to land. The craft lightly touched down on the surface and immediately the pair donned spacesuits, and ventured out into the depths of the dark cave.

Allen looked around with full illuminators from his suit "You know, with some candles, this place could be quite cozy and nice."

Buck tapped a small geologist's hammer against a small black asteroid fragment laying on the ground while running a hand-held analyzer over the rock. "Cozy? Really? This place is made up of almost nothing other than this black material. It's nothing we have ever seen before – and it appears to be impervious to anything we have. In other words, impossible to cut, melt or use."

"No, I have a feeling...there's something here we can use...not sure what though...keep looking."

The geologist stood back up and hopped to the wall nearest the ship and shined his light on the wall. A bright shiny vein of gold shone from between two vertical layers of the black material that made up much of the cave wall. "Well, there's gold in here" he said as he continued to read his hand scanner. "I'm also picking up titanium and other metals that we could use to build...actually, quite a bit of it. Too bad it's encased in this rock – there will be no way to mine it out of this stuff."

Buck took out a laser torch and began to melt some of the gold for collection. To his surprise the black material merged with the melted gold and came pouring out onto the floor in front of him. "What the hell?"

"What? Did you find something?" Allen asked.

"Yes, but it's odd..." Buck replied, "This black material only can be removed by melting the gold." He looked at the puddle of molten black asteroid rock. He took out a spatula and took a small sample. It cooled as soon as he scraped it onto the spatula – leaving the now cooled drops of gold remaining, but now embedded into the black floor. "Interesting – the gold seems to melt this black material but does not merge with...it leaving it separate." He examined the small pancake of black asteroid material "Wow, this stuff is hard as diamonds again! I wonder..." He took a small piece of flexible plastic out of his geologist's bag and molded it into a little cup. He pointed the laser torch at the gold in the wall again. It melted and dripped into the cup, the melted black rock followed closely behind by the dripping gold. He allowed it to cool then turned the cup upside-down, allowing the separate gold and asteroid material to fall out and drop onto the ground. "You know Allen, I think you're right – there is something special on this rock...the rock itself. I think we can use the metals in this asteroid to mine the asteroid itself – this material is so hard, but by using the metal we can mold it and form anything we need. Tools, projectiles, or spaceship parts – all being as hard as any material we currently know. And who knows...we might find something that will merge with this element to create an even stronger alloy of this stuff!"

Allen picked up the cup shaped piece of asteroid rock and examined it. "Damn, I knew it! Okay, gather samples and get them to the ship – we need to get back and report this!"

They boarded the ship and left a marker buoy which could be activated when they were within two light years of the asteroid. They fired up the engines and started to exit the cavern. Just as they were about to leave the cavern however, a large ship appeared in front of them in a flash of light – this large ship now blocked their exit. Allen looked at the enormous ship – cigar shaped, brown colored, two large antler-shaped metal projections pointed out from the forward moving end of the craft.

Over their translation circuit they received a message "Alien vessel, you are trespassing in Flaybah territory. Identify yourself immediately – we have the legal right to destroy you."

Allen activated the transmitter "This is Captain Allen James. We are Human, I believe you have met our race before…"

"Activate your visual transmitter…" the voice replied.

Allen activated his viewer as instructed revealing a creature that looked like an Earth deer – a large set of antlers adorned his tan colored head between his large tear-shaped ears. Large black eyes glared into the view screen. The creature looked Allen up and down as thoroughly as he could. Finally, he said "Turn your head for me."

Allen did as he was instructed, and the large black eyes got closer to the screen as he visually examined Allen. The Flaybah Captain noticed the two growths on his ear. He pulled back and asked, "What did you say you were called?"

"Human. We are also known as the species Homo-sapiens" He replied.

His antlers were glowing the entire time they communicated – however for a moment Allen noticed a slight increase in the glow, before he was asked "Are you Blessed-Homo or Normal-Homo?"

Allen gave a slight chuckle before answering "We are Normal – of the species Homo-sapiens."

"Well, I do not think you are Human or Homo or Sapiens" the deer replied -- Allen chuckled lightly again. "No, you are something else. But you say you are Normal – you are not lying to me about being Blessed, are you?"

Allen quickly shook his head negative "Oh no! Absolutely not...we are Normal – not genetically manipulated or enhanced!"

"Then we know of you, and are your friends. Welcome to Star System Three of the Flaybah. I am Grazeel, Commander of this battle buck – The Marcole. May I inquire as to where have you explored?"

"Here, let me send you the three planets we found. Perhaps you could shed light on their habitability?" Allen said as he transmitted the scans and data collected regarding the three planets.

Grazeel looked at the data and shook his head in the negative "No, two of those are inhabited despite what your scans show you – going there would be to declare war. The other – Zebulous, is not compatible to your species. What about this asteroid -- do you have an interest in this body?"

"Well, we did – but it belongs to you." Allen replied.

"We have no use for it. If you are truly one that travels with Jaime, then you may have it."

Buck's eyes opened wide "You know of Captain Bordeaux?"

Grazeel turned and looked at the other human "And you are?"

"Geologist Buck Strong, Commander"

Grazeel's eyes opened wide and Buck could have sworn he saw a smile on his long face under his black nose "An excellent name!" he cried out.

Buck smiled as he remembered "Jaime – Captain Bordeaux told me you would say that..."

Lindy Light:

Every night since she had been transferred to Plug, she had been raped – usually by Fitchburg Griggs, but sometimes by some other random Blessed officer. This morning she awoke after what had become her normal ordeal, feeling sick to her stomach. She ran to the waste disposal unit and vomited. Her greatest fear began taking over her thoughts, and was confirmed by the daily visit by the base's doctor – she was pregnant with the child of a Blessed. She had hoped that they were all sterile, but obviously one was lucky enough to somehow impregnate her. Now she would have to live with the outcome of this never-ending nightmare – a half-Blessed child. She was amazed at the speed at which she got the morning sickness – it seemed to come along with the growths on her ears. One of her rapists would be happy this morning, but she could care less which one – she wished they would all die of some random illness.

The more she thought about it, the more she found herself hoping to miscarry – she did not want to have this child, and knew it would only grow up to be a freak. It would be the mix of a real human with a genetically modified Blessed and who knew what the outcome of that mixture would be.

She cleaned herself, got dressed, and then did her normal work routine – communicating with the various teams who were working out in the vacuum of space. She would move orders and communiques from one team to the other. She would use her Norm-Comm whenever she was able to help her Normal compatriots in the obtaining and hiding of advanced technology. When something was found, she would guide the Normal teams in helping to conceal the tech in nooks and crannies within the planetoid. The Blessed would never find any of it, if she had her way.

Today however, Norm-Comm picked up something she had not expected to hear – the voice of Allen James. "Hello...is Jaime there?"

She looked around to see if she was being watched before replying "No...she is still on Ultimate... the new Blessed starship."

"Lindy is that you?" he asked. "Where are you? Nearby?"

"Yes Allen, it is me... but I'm on Plug... where are you?"

He paused for a moment, absorbing what he just heard, before replying "Well, you're not going to believe this...but we are at least three light years out from your position."

"What?" she shouted before calming herself – looking around hoping no one had heard her. "How can that be?"

"I have no idea, Lindy. We were just on our way back when I could sense you on Norm-Comm. I decided to try to contact you since you seemed to be on the circuit and here you are! So, you tell me – how are you receiving me?"

"No idea, but I've noticed as of late, that I'm able to communicate a little further every day. Just the other day I was able to contact the team on Bung. Are you on your way here?"

"Yes" he replied "and if Jaime arrives before us, you must tell her she needs to make Alpha. We found the perfect place to live and build a ship."

Day 131:

Jaime Bordeaux:

The Ultimate was adrift for three days before the automated medical bay awakened the head Blessed doctor, who in turn awakened Kip and then the rest of the Blessed crew. That delay was aided by Jaime and Max, who reprogrammed the computer to wait two days before activating the awakening program. From there, it took an extra day for the doctor to finally recover and start his task of awakening the rest of the crew.

Also, what the Blessed did not know, was that Normals were no longer affected by subspace. The five days of travel for the Normal crew were spent clearing computer logs, reprogramming Blessed computers, and preparing for their eventual departure from the main Blessed fleet.

As soon as they came out of subspace, Jaime received a message from Lindy – Allen had found a place to live and build ships. He had also found three planets, but none were deemed habitable. Jaime had Allen send the coordinates of the three unsuitable planets to Lindy, who then converted them into false reports from Blessed deep space probes. If her deception worked, the Blessed would allow her to have the asteroid while they went off to conquer and colonize the other three planets.

Now all Jaime needed was for Boral to read the probe reports.

Boral Oldham:

It was too good to be true – the deep space probes had found three suitable planets for colonization – there was also some random asteroid. He knew with these planets he could construct new starships and build a massive fleet. With this fleet, no force in this new galaxy could defeat the Blessed.

He read over the probe reports again. "Perfect!" A large, rare smile graced his aging, tired face – he had not had news this good since they had accidently arrived here.

He activated a tunneled communication to Kip. "Eureka Kip, not just one – but three planets worthy of colonization! Who would have guessed that this would happen so quickly? We have shown our superiority to lesser races, and now we have three planets on which we can raise a race of superior Blessed beings."

Kip smiled "It is a wonderful day my Star Force Commander. So, we will be building ships here then?"

"No..." he replied "Let's see what progress they have made here. Then, we can take whatever materials and technology we have left, and build more ships once we have colonized."

"Sir, you do realize that with us building more ships and having planets to colonize we will have to allow for some of the lesser Captains to move up in rank. It is the only way we can promote to provide commanders of new ships and governors of our colony planets according to the law."

Boral rubbed his chin in thought "Hmm...Do you suspect that Bordeaux bitch has a chance to move up in rank?"

Kip nodded "Yes, I fear that. She has taken down most of the lesser Captains. I think she might make it if we have another contest. Is there any way around the Supreme Commander's rules?"

"No" he replied. He thought for a moment then snapped his fingers and opened his eyes wide, "I know, we have the right of substitution, do we not?" Kip nodded in agreement. "Yes, good...then we use substitutes in place of the lesser Alphas...ones that can beat her. Along with hidden advantages, there will be no way she can win. Yes...prepare the contest. Make it occur in five days – give our Captains plenty of time to recover from sub-space. Yes..." he smiled, content with his ideas.

"What if she does win though?" Kip asked softly, hoping not to anger his Commander.

"If she does win...? I think you overestimate her chances." he stated, before looking at the probe report. "But just in case, I am sure there is something crappy we can find to give her..."

Day 136:

Halley Cet:

Jaime had asked her to come by and help her prepare for the games. She found that to be very unusual as in the past she had always gotten ready alone. She arrived at her cabin and rang the annunciator.

Jaime answered wearing a bath robe and her hair was tied in a large knot at the top of her head "Hi Halley, please come in!"

Halley followed and was directed to a chair next to Jaime's dressing table. She turned and looked at her with a quizzing face "You can do hair braids, can't you? I seem to remember you being able to do that. Please tell me yes..." she now had a pleading look "I can't do this by myself."

"Of course... I have done hair braids for quite a few of the girls onboard" she boasted. She looked at the dressing table and noticed a small container, a box of steel flexible loops and a head band. She looked quizzically at the strange items.

Jaime untied the knot which allowed her long locks of reddish blonde hair to fall to almost her waistline. Halley was shocked at how long it had grown. "Good, let me tell you what I need then. Once my hair is braided I will need this head band placed so it will not fall off – I think you can see why..."

Halley had not noticed, but the growths on Jaime's ears were now at least an inch long and protruded back and away from the back rim of her ear. She now had three growths and between them, flaps of flesh had grown and formed what looked like small wings. "They remind me of the god Mercury...he was the messenger god" she said softly.

"I didn't know you knew about ancient gods..." Jaime said as she activated her computer and queried this mythical entity. The image showed the Roman god with his wide brimmed hat adorned with large wings. "Damn, you're right..."

She stood up and looked closer at them – wanting to touch them. "Can I?" she asked. Jaime nodded, and she extended a finger and lightly touched one of the fleshy wings.

Her light touch caused Jaime to giggle slightly. "So, as you can see, I have something to conceal...but I need to get my hair, so it will stay out of my face and allow me to fully fight."

Halley turned the side of her head toward Jaime and moved her own hair back exposing three growths moving back and away from her ear "I think I understand about hiding things..." The two laughed for a moment, then she told her "Just tell me what you want Jaime." She picked up a brush from the dressing table and began to run it through Jaime's long hair to prepare it for braiding.

Jaime put her hand up to stop her for a moment "You know...I have an idea..."

Jaime Bordeaux:

She examined her hair after Halley finished – a sparkling blue, plastic strap, high on the top of her head created a high ponytail, which allowed her hair to flow out and down her back. From there the ponytail was braided tightly with four knots, spaced apart every few inches. Each knot was a tightly packed ball of hair, bound by a metal pony loop, which would keep the braids tight, and allowed the ponytail to swing freely out of the way if she needed to move her head quickly. The sparkling dark blue headband was securely placed around her head in a way that it would not slip off or down onto her face.

She had put only a very small amount of make up on for this game. Her freckles were quite visible, and she knew the Blessed would be totally repulsed by them. She had put on her game outfit – sparkling, and a dark blue that matched her headband, a tight top that exposed her midriff, and a small tight pair of matching polymer shorts. To finish the outfit, she put on a tight matching pair of boots – with high stiletto heels. She jumped up and down after putting on the boots – the heels flexed and expanded as needed to provide her with cushioning and stability during the game. Halley wished her luck and then left. She checked herself in the mirror again -- all was ready. She stepped out into the corridor and headed down toward the gamer's locker room.

On the way her Norm-Comm buzzed inside her head -- it was Jeremy. "Jaime, I hope our final training session last night helped. We had not had much time together, but it looked like you had kept up your training, I think you are ready."

"I'm ready, thanks." She concentrated on the tone of his voice "Jeremy, are you ok?"

"Nothing I can't handle. I may be hiding out for a while – I will find you later though, so don't worry. See you soon." He cut off communications before she had a chance for further inquiry. She wondered what kind of trouble he was in, and made a mental note to find and help him.

When she arrived, it was almost game start time. Every Blessed Captain was in the room, yelling and shouting to psych each other, and work themselves into a fighting frenzy – that was until she walked in. All noise in the room came to a complete halt when Jaime stepped into the room. She looked at all of them while she walked through the room, and simply said "Good luck boys…" as she headed out into the arena.

The crowd had already filled the arena and became a screaming, howling mass as Jaime walked out and looked up. As soon as they saw her, bottles and other items of garbage started to be thrown, while at the same time they hollered obscenities, and booed at her. She looked up at the angry crowd, smiled and waved before calmly walking up the ramps to her position at the top of the Beta Captain battle platform.

The crowd reacted by going even crazier – starting fights with each other and finding bigger items to throw at the dome. At one point, one of the Blessed had managed to wrench their seat free from the metal clamps and heaved it at the dome, smashing into hundreds of bits as it hit the protective field. Jaime hoped that the Normals had listened to her and Max, and had not showed up – their lives would be at stake if any of them were up there.

A moment later, the Blessed Captains made the gaming march onto the field of play and stood in position to be recognized. The crowd cheered and urged their favorite Captains onward to victory. Finally, they ascended the ramp and took their positions. A couple of the Alphas bumped into Jaime as they passed and felt nothing but a steel hard shoulder – she did not move an inch. The others growled as they passed in a vain attempt at intimidation – Jaime maintained her motionless stance.

Finally, Kip walked up to her on his way to the top position. He stopped and looked her up and down before saying, "You know, you have no chance. If anything, I will stop you from getting to the basket. I have done it in the past and…"

Jaime cut him off, "and you will never do it again. Take your position and prepare to lose, Alpha Starship Captain." Not once did her head move from pointing straight ahead nor did her eyes turn to look at him. She ignored him from that moment as if he was not visible. Kip huffed a deep breath through his nose, and stormed up to the top of the ramp.

As always, the anthem of the Supreme Commander and the Order was played, the announcer worked the crowd into an even bigger frenzy, and finally the ball was launched starting the game. Jaime knew she had a few minutes as every Delta would have to make the attempt, then the Betas would get their chance – that is when she would need to get busy.

She was surprised that the lowest-ranked Beta was taken out by one of the Deltas – he however was defeated by the next Beta. One by one the Betas attempted to get past each other and one by one they were defeated by the next in line. Jaime found she had nothing to do – that was until Jaridan Hinds' turn. She remembered him from the last time she fought here – large and muscular – he had a frame that could replace Atlas for a break in his duties of holding up the Earth. He had massive tree trunks of legs, a large tight breadbasket, and muscular heaving chest that helped to hold his enormous jackhammer arms to his body. She swore he had gotten even bigger since the last time they had fought.

She tightened up her body preparing for the attack. She reminded herself that if she could not beat him, then there would be no way she could defeat all the Alphas – and she had to beat the Alphas. At that moment, she was the one hope for all the Normals. Her abilities tonight was going to provide the means for them to get away and establish themselves in this galaxy – either that or face extinction at the hands of the Blessed.

He punched his right fist into his left hand and rubbed his it while smacking his lips at her. "Well, we meet again my little birdie. This time it will be different..." he bent down and picked up the polyhedron. The moment he did that Jaime rushed in, and while his head was still lowered, packed a quick stiff boot to his chin. The force of the blow sent him flying back, his bulky frame hitting the lower platform with a loud crash – the back of his head hitting the solid surface of the platform, dazing him further.

"Sorry, but you can't get in my way" she said as she jumped down from the ramp and quickly applied the toe of her boot to his temple. Spittle flew out of his mouth and his head flung wildly to the opposite direction of the blow. He could not focus on anything at this point – his large hand removed its grip on the polyhedron. Jaime felt the gravity lighten as she grabbed the strap of his large silver muscle shirt. She bent her knees to get just the right force from her legs, and then flexed and swung her body in a quick circle while using the lower gravity to swing the large man at the same time. She let go of the strap sending him sliding across the floor, then off the platform.

Grabbing the polyhedron, she turned and began walking up the ramp to the top of the Beta section as she now mentally prepared herself for the next challenge – the Alpha Captains.

First a gravity change – back to normal, then the first five Alphas attacked in unison. She recognized them, kind of. She avoided hidden metal bars and structural disruptors as they wildly attacked. She realized that she had never really gotten to know any of these five as she pressed the disruptor of one attacker into the leg of another, sending him down in pain, and then quickly pushed the two of them off the ramp. She also realized that she did not even know any of their names as she quickly sent the last three flying off the ramp using a flurry of punches, kicks, and tripping moves.

She took a moment to catch her breath while she looked up to identify her next obstacle -- Bellevue Blythe, the "emergency promoted" Captain. He had sweat dripping down his forehead – she knew he was scared, and she did not blame him. She walked up to him and gave him a small smile while saying softly "Jump now and save yourself the pain. Otherwise I'm going right through you."

"You think me a weak fool!" he yelled as he quickly began swinging in a wild flurry of fists and kicks. Jaime quickly and easily repelled each attack by swinging her arms up or down to block each fist and high kick attack, and by wiggling her legs and knees to block any low kicking attacks – it almost looked like she was performing a dance while avoiding his attacks – a thing of beauty. After allowing him to attack for six seconds, she moved in and landed a quick twisting punch to his jaw, quickly snapping it once again. Bellevue moaned in pain, and instantly began wobbling like a top losing its spin.

Jaime shrugged her shoulders at him and said, "Sorry, but really – you are still only a Delta..." as she swung around and landed a roundhouse into his shoulder – dislocating the joint and sending him mercifully flying off the platform.

She now looked up the remaining ramps and looked at the final four Captains that waited above her -- Jarred Maltz (another emergency promotion), Fitchburg Griggs, one Captain she had never seen before and finally Kip standing at the top. She wondered about that third man, who was he and what were they up to? He did not look like much of a fighter.

The gravity shifted again as she marched up to take on Jarred and as she approached he lashed out with fast swings of a downward swinging stiff arm – hidden metal she assumed as she avoided all the quick wild swings. He then reached out trying to grab her arm – sonic structural disruptor weapon, she assumed. She avoided his grab and instead grabbed his forward moving arm and at the same time put her foot out in front of him. She pulled him across her outstretched leg using the heavy gravity to send him falling face first. At that same moment, the gravity shifted again, and she grabbed his arm with her free hand and started swiveling on her other foot, which started to send him into a momentum swing. She held on as she swung him around and at the point when he had swung a full ninety degrees, she let go – the momentum flew him across and off the ramp.

She confidently began walking further up the ramp to the half way platform – Fitchburg was waiting for her. He put up a little better fight than Jarred – managing to place a fist into Jaime's solar plexus, which made her gasp for air for a moment. He took advantage by grabbing her arm and swinging her onto the floor. He then raised his foot high with the intent to smash a large foot into her head.

She felt the gravity increase again as she saw the foot smash coming and slightly moved her head out of the way of the oncoming extremity, which caused a loud thump on the floor of the platform. She let her head softly rest back down onto the ramp, which he saw as an opening for another foot attack. He struggled to raise his foot high for a fatal blow. She quickly crunched both knees into her chest, while putting her heels into the air, thus avoiding his foot moving over her. She put everything she had into a quick upward movement sending her sharp heels deeply into his crotch while his body was in a heavy gravity motion downward. The force of her incoming feet and the downward gravity force became too much for the hard shell of his protective cup, which collapsed inward and subsequently crushed his valuable jewels. She immediately pivoted him and pushed him onto the floor as the gravity shifted again. She followed this move by a kip-up, bringing her to be standing over him. She shook her head as he writhed in pain below her "a common male mistake opening up that weakness..." she said as she put her heeled boot in his side and pushed, sending him sliding over the side of the platform.

She turned to the next Captain – the one she did not recognize at all. As she measured him up she realized he was nervous and shaking like leaves in the wind. "Are you sure you want to do this?" she asked him.

He looked at her and with a weak nervous voice simply said "Substitute."

Over the loud speaker she heard the announcer call out "The next opponent has called for a substitute. An Alpha can call for a substitute in the event they are ill or for some reason are unable to continue. Now who will substitute for him?"

A hatch opened in the ceiling of the dome and a platform came down carrying the substitute. A man stood on the platform in a wide foot stance, his crossed arms in a show of confidence. He was wearing a tight pair of maroon stretch pants, matching colored crossing bandoleer-like pieces of plastic material with a silver buckle connecting the two pieces of fabric together, being the only cover for his bare chest. His arms had no covering which showed off his large muscles. He rounded out his costume with silver boots and a matching maroon-colored cape with a large upward facing collar. On his head, he wore a helmet – the front hid his face in a reflective silver material and the back was of a polymer colored in the same maroon color as his outfit.

Jaime stood in shock as the man stepped from the platform, and exchanged places with the nervous Captain. He raised his arms to the audience for approval and the crowd went wild in appreciation. He turned to her and all she could say was "Perfecto?"

"Surprised Jaime? You shouldn't be – this is my chance, my chance to redeem myself. I am just sorry you have to be the subject for my redemption."

Still in shock all she could say was "What?"

He gave her no time to continue her questioning as he lashed out with a vicious swinging punch to her cheek. She fell backwards down the ramp and rolled, finally stopping herself. She quickly did a kip-up to get herself standing, then rubbed her jaw and cheek. He rushed in for another attack but this time she was ready and blocked every attack he threw at her.

"I see you have kept your skills up since the days we sparred Jaime" Perfecto commented.

"I just don't know why..." she said as she gave a false tell of a punch which she followed with a low leg sweep. She caught him with the sweep just right, and he began falling forward. She moved around behind him and grabbed his cape and started to swing him toward the edge of the ramp. He figured out what she was attempting however, and released the clasp on his cape sending both flying in opposite directions.

He stood up and turned toward her. She looked at him and her eyes opened wide in shock. Around his neck was a platinum wire with a bead. She saw the number "25" imprinted on the bead. "Blessed...you? I don't believe it!"

"Believe it. I was spurned by the Blessed most of my life – but now, they are giving me a chance to regain my status and join them. All I must do is defeat you – and I will defeat you. After all I am Perfecto and I know all too well how you fight Jaime."

For ten long minutes, the two former friends went back and forth – punching, kicking, blocking, and firing verbal barbs at each other – but still ended up in nothing but a stalemate. After another exchange, they stood and looked at each other (Jaime assumed he was looking at her through that mask) while both of their chests heaved in long deep breaths trying to draw in valuable oxygen.

"You cannot defeat me Jaime – I know you and your moves much too well. Please, jump off now and end this. I really do not want to hurt you..." he said as he moved in for yet another attack.

At the same time, the gravity shifted lighter and Jaime took advantage of the change by jumping high in the air, flipping upside down, putting her free hand on his shoulder and flipping over him. On the way down, she spun her body around while flipping her head quickly and sharply causing her ponytail to fling out, and smack Perfecto on the side of his helmet. The force of her hair hitting his helmet created a crack in the hard shell. She flipped her head the opposite direction forcing the ponytail to slap the opposite side of the helmet. The now cracked helmet broke into pieces when hit by her ponytail the second time. Pieces broke off including the silver faceplate – falling to the ground, exposing an ugly and mutated face.

There were tubes that ran around the sides of the helmet and were inserted in his nose for feeding. A third larger tube went into his mouth for assistance in breathing. These tubes ran to the metal unit on his chest which had mechanicals and provided this assistance. The mask helped to form a seal which allowed him to use the tube for breathing. He gagged causing the air tube to be expelled from his mouth. He started choking as he developed breathing problems without the assistance of the device. Jaime determined that the mask also provided vision assistance as he seemed to be almost blind without it.

The crowd went silent in shock as they witnessed the ugliness that was their Blessed champion, Perfecto.

Using his half blind eyes, he searched for his mask – reaching, hands out and feeling for the curved piece of plastic.

Jaime stepped on the mask and looked down at his grotesque face. "What happened to you? You are Blessed..." She could not stand watching him trying to hide his ugliness and slid the mask back toward him.

He reinserted the breathing tube into his mouth and placed the silver mask against his hideous face and held it with his hand. He took a few deep breaths before replying. "I was genetically enhanced like every other Blessed baby. They expected me to be one of the best manipulations ever – but they were wrong. Instead they turned me into – this! I was rejected by my Blessed brothers and I put on this mask and joined the ranks of Normals in the advancement of our Supreme Commander. I had hoped fighting for the cause would give me favor again with them. All my life I have tried and failed to gain back their favor – but I was always too ugly and imperfect. This was to be my one chance – but I failed now, I cannot continue."

Jaime picked up the other broken pieces of his helmet and placed them back in their proper place and allowed him to remove his hand from his faceplate. The helmet vacuum sealed enough to hold together on its own. "Do you want to continue?" She reached her hand out.

He took her hand, and used her assist to stand up. He reached out and placed a hand on her cheek and rubbed it softly before saying "No..." then quickly turned and jumped off the ramp.

"Thank you, my friend," she whispered before moving on to her last opponent – Kip.

He waved a finger at her as she boldly walked up the ramp to face him "Now, now...let's think about what you are about to do." She gave him a confused look. "You are about to fight the greatest Alpha Starship Captain in the fleet. Are you sure you want to do that?"

She rolled her eyes at him before punching him in the solar plexus. He collapsed and bent over for a moment while he caught his breath. Then just as quickly, he recovered and jabbed a quick steel rod into her solar plexus, thus returning the favor. She slightly bent down while she absorbed the blow and the pain, but then she replied his punch with a quick roundhouse kick into his side.

Kip felt a rib crack from the force of her kick, while at the same time he felt the gravity change lighter, which allowed him a little float time to get away and determine his next move. Unfortunately for him, Jaime had also taken advantage of the lower gravity to quickly jump up, flying past him and landed a few feet away which allowed her to wind up and deliver a hard blow to his face.

Fortunately for him, she did not break any bones – however, he had a visible red bulge on his cheek. "Damn you! You hit my face you bitch!" he cried out. He reached out and tried to grab her hand but was only able to grab the pinky finger of the hand holding the polyhedron. He fired his concealed structural disruptor, splitting the bone underneath the skin. She cried out in pain while he held on, trying to grab more of her hand. She swung her head quickly around, sending her long ponytail flinging into his head and face. This time his cheek and part of his skull caved in from the force of the blow. He fell, face first onto the floor almost blacking out. He managed to shake the cobwebs out of his head enough to get off the floor and onto his knees.

He looked at her and managed to mumble out "How did you do that?"

"That is my secret weapon…" she whispered to him before giving him another swift roundhouse – this time to the shoulder. The force of the blow sent him sliding toward the edge of the platform.

Right before he fell off however, he barely managed to call out "Substitute…"

The hatch opened again in the top of the dome and a golden figure jumped out and landed with a loud thump onto the platform. Jaime shielded her eyes while the figure landed with the assistance of booster jets – but once she lowered her arms she saw Boral standing in front of her in a powered battle suit.

"This is as far as you go…" he shouted out. "You will earn Alpha status and I will grant you a ship -- eventually. You will build a garbage scow for yourself and you will command it – but that is it. You will not win, and you will not be given a capital ship or a planet to govern. You will not be given another chance at the game – it ends here." Then, using the power of the suit he placed a quick blow to her chest sending her flying down the ramp.

He just stood at the top confidently with his hands on his hips while she regained her breath from the attack. She stood up and took a moment to regain her composure. She examined the suit – it was gold-colored plastic composite armor with a glowing exoskeleton that was powered by a reactor in a glowing dome of opaque plastic on the back. The suit appeared to have no weapons, but did have a computer that provided battle tactics to Boral on his heads-up display. The suit had a half-helmet that covered the top, sides, and back of his head, had a screen across his eyes for the heads-up display and was open slightly below his nose, as this suit was meant to operate in an atmosphere. The suit was limited in operation time by the fuel in the reactor. Jaime wondered if she could out survive the reactor – she had her doubts and now wondered how she was going to get through this.

She ran up and engaged Boral, sending a flurry of punches, kicks, sweeps, and checks hoping to find some weak point. The computer in the suit analyzed every move she made and indicated to Boral what to move and when, to avoid every attack. Finally, he sent another shot to her chest which flew her back down the ramp again.

"Time to end this" he said as he hurled down the ramp at her. She slid out of the way of his charge, while at the same time she stuck her foot out, tripping him onto the floor. He suffered no damage, except his pride. He stood back up and charged up to her sending down heavy fists of steel and plastic. She barely managed to wiggle back and forth to avoid each attack. Finally, she grabbed his leg and drew herself between his legs, then shoved herself away from the attacking machine.

While she slid away, he lifted his arm and fired his command neural disruptor. A heavy bolt of plasma flew out from the wrist device and squarely hit Jaime in the chest almost knocking her unconscious. She went down on one knee and tried to shake the cobwebs out of her head. Fortunately, her advanced quick recovery kicked in and her mind and body regenerated enough to continue the fight.

"What? How?" Boral shouted before rushing in for another attack.

She stood up and immediately was caught by a punch to the shoulder. She almost dropped the polyhedron while flying further down the ramp. As she stopped her slide, she felt the ball start to change its form – spikes jutted out from the blobby surface and became suddenly stiff and sharp. She held onto one of the spikes with a now bloody hand as it cut into her skin. While she was trying to gain control of the polyhedron, Boral walked up behind her without her realizing his position on her. He picked her up by the arm that was holding the polyhedron and dangled her like a ragdoll. He laughed as he played her like a puppet – she was unable to escape his increasing grasp and she let out a slight squeal of pain as he continued the pressure on her arm from his suit-enhanced hand.

He lifted his other hand and raised it in front her face "I have decided that even a garbage scow is too good for you. It is time that you perished playing this game – it happens occasionally you know. Now let me give you -- the finger!" He extended his middle finger and activated a servo which extended a small sharp blade. He chuckled then shoved the blade forward toward her head – she moved just enough to avoid having the blade hit her in the face. The knife edge slipped under her headband slicing it off – the blue plastic fluttered to the floor.

Boral looked at her now exposed ear and a look of surprise and shock came over him. "What the hell are you?"

Jaime smiled at him and simply said "The future…" as she slipped a rotating punch into the small opening under the visor of his helmet. She felt his teeth cave in beneath her rotating fist and his head snapped back. He released the grip on her arm, allowing her to fall to the floor – landing on one foot and cushioning the fall with her other leg, going down onto a single knee. He screamed out in agony while at the same time spitting out fragments of his formerly attached teeth.

To her surprise, for just a moment she heard something through her Norm-Comm. It was fighting the transmission blocking properties of the dome, but it was coming through, albeit barely. It was a simple message *"That is an Alpha 7 battle suit. It has two weaknesses and you just found one of them…"* The signal was quickly blocked again, and the channel went quiet. She thought about what she was told and looked at the now screaming Boral. He was fighting off the pain in his face and mouth – bobbing up and down and slowly turning around in circles. She knew she would not be able to place another shot there, so she scanned the suit looking for something else – that one other weakness.

"There, that has to be it!" she thought as she spotted what she thought was the other weak point. She moved up directly in front of him and gave him a jab to the sternum. This of course, did nothing through the hard shell of his suit. It notified him of her presence however, and activated the battle mode of the computer, giving him instructions for attack. Despite his pain he bent down and swung a fist – Jaime moved to the side to counter the downward attack, while once again reaching her arm between his legs and pulling herself through. The suit began to calculate a counter move but before he had a chance to react, she took the polyhedron – still cutting her hand with one of four sharpened spikes, and rammed the spike opposite the one in her hand into a slight gap in the armor between his calf and the heel of his foot. The spike sunk deep into his Achilles tendon, slicing it – blood shot out of the fold in the armor, splashing the thick red fluid all over Jaime's blue top.

Without the connective tissue of his leg and with the intense pain that now radiated throughout his body, he fell to the floor face first. He reached back and grabbed his now damaged leg and cried out in pain. Jaime stood up and looked down at the now pathetically crying man. She then swung her head around and planted her ponytail across the plastic bubble that held the suit's reactor. The flaying hair smashed the dome into bits exposing the power plant – it hummed and churned while continuing to provide power to the suit. She swung her head around again, sending the hair into the gap formed by the now broken dome. The ponytail hit the reactor and cracked it – she stepped away from Boral and watched as the reactor sparked and sizzled before finally burning out. Smoke spewed out of the opening as the remains of the reactor melted the plastic armor against his back.

She pulled the polyhedron out from his bloody ankle and started to slowly walk up the ramp. She noticed how quiet and peaceful the dome had become – the crowds of Blessed were stunned at the loss by their leader, and were not making a single peep. She strolled across the final Alpha platform and to the basket at the back side of the flat area.

Boral somehow fought off the pain enough to yell out "NO, you cannot do that. You will disrupt everything. You have to keep the order…"

"Order?" she yelled out. "There is no order here – you are the master of chaos. Winning this will change nothing in this universe that we are stuck in…" and with saying that she slowly reached up and held the polyhedron in the air. The ball sensed its proximity to the basket and slowly returned to the shape of a ball. She made a small jump into the air and dunked the ball into the basket.

A horn blew indicating success, and the lights returned to normal. A crew rushed out and tended to the injured Boral while Jaime slowly walked down the ramps, and out of the arena.

Max met her at the door of her cabin. She smiled at him and nodded for him to follow her in.

He began tending to her injuries but found that most of her wounds had already begun to heal – he was no longer surprised by this. "So…Jaime…as you know, I normally do not watch the matches. However, tonight's match was so important I decided to turn it on. Mind telling me how a simple knot of hair could do that much damage?"

She walked over and took a small container from the dressing table and opened it. Then she loosened one of the retaining loops holding the lowest knot of hair together and a small metal ball dropped out. When the ball hit the floor, it created a two-inch-deep dent in the titanium plate from the force of its landing. She picked up the ball and held it for Max to visually inspect. "It's a heavy gravity pellet. Jonathan found it in a weapon on one of the alien derelicts. Thought it might be useful –it was! I will say, I was surprised to have cracked the reactor dome on the suit – it must have been a flaw in the material."

Max looked at the small pellet in amazement "Hmm, I remember those. Well, you made it...you won. He'll have no choice but to grant you a ship and maybe even a colony. For now, your job is done."

She nodded in agreement. Her job for the moment was done, but she knew the real work was just beginning.

Day 140:

Boral Oldham:

He grabbed his cane and slowly pushed himself out of his chair. He was still healing from the wounds provided to him by Jaime during the game. The doctors worked for hours repairing his damaged Achilles tendon – they are still not sure he will ever regain full use and walk normally again. Also, when Jaime smashed the power reactor to his Alpha suit, it melted the plastic armor plate – which bonded to his skin. He now has a large circular gold plate embedded into the skin of his back. If all of that was not insult enough, he had been suffering through the reconstruction of his damaged teeth and mouth. He had a lot to hate her for, however there was one thing more that made him totally loathe her -- she was the winner of the Command Tri-Polyhedron contest. That meant that by the laws set forth by the Supreme Commander of the Earth he was obligated to grant her a reward.

He sat and looked at the various possibilities for rewards as determined by the computer. The computer compared the returns of the deep space probes to the alien navigation charts found in one of the wrecks. Based on those charts and the returns, the following list was presented:

1 – Governorship of the planet Dorellious 3, soon to be conquered by the Blessed.

2 – Governorship of the planet Qeek, also scheduled to be conquered by the Blessed.

3 – Governorship of the planet Zebulous, currently uninhabited.

4 – Captaincy of the next capital starship.

5 – Command of a base on an asteroid floating in sector "B'.

He looked at the planets and the probability of successful colonization. No, those would not do – neither would it do to give her a capital starship to command. If he gave her a ship, it would have to be the worst piece of shit ship in the fleet. At the same time, he did not want a scow like that even near his fleet – as a matter of fact he did not want *her* near his fleet. He needed something or some way to be rid of her – the fifth option seemed like a good possibility.

He read over the reports of the deep space probe. The asteroid was just floating in space nowhere near any planet or star system. The reports from the probe also indicated there were no life forms for food, minimal materials and the projections showed no possibility to colonize or live on the dead rock. He smiled as he determined it was perfect for her.

He also needed to be rid of any kind like her – she had turned into a mutant with those ears and he knew there were others like her. He thought they would not be hard to find – just look for the mutated ears. His plan was perfect – gather all the mutated Normals and that pain-in-the-ass woman and send them off to the dead rock floating in space. Give them barely enough supplies and equipment to survive for the next year and let them go off and die.

Kip was down on the planetoid supervising the construction of the next starship – he could not send him for this duty. Boral's puffy black and blue face also precluded him from finding her and sending her off to oblivion – as he could never be seen in this state. So, he contacted Bellevue Blythe instead "Captain, I have a job for you."

"Yes, my Star Force Commander!" he shouted back as best he could over the communication system since his jaw was still healing from the game.

"You remember how freakish that woman Bordeaux looked during the game, don't you?"

"Oh yes..." he replied, "how could anyone forget what a monster she has turned out to be!"

"Good. Then I want you to go through the fleet and catalog anyone else that has turned into a similar freak" he ordered. "I am sure they will not be hard to spot. Spread the word to all Blessed to be on the lookout for these freaks. When you locate them, gather them up in a common spot, and give me a count."

"I will do as you order, my Star Force Commander!" he snapped in reply and disconnected.

Jaime Bordeaux:

Max looked over Jaime with his medical scanner for a long while before announcing "Well, I don't know how your body does it, but you are once again completely healed!"

Jaime smiled "Just be glad it heals that way – otherwise you would be way too busy with me always being in here!"

"It's your active genetics my dear – genetics which seem to be changing in all of us...you are just quicker than we are. Or, are you the catalyst?" Jaime shook her head no. "Well in any case they were right in recruiting you."

"Who?" she asked.

"Our group – the group you are a part of was originally a splinter group from the People Against War."

"The terrorists? I can't believe that!"

"Jaime, you know we were not terrorists. That is government propaganda. If anything, we were the only thing keeping the planet together. When we realized that there was nothing more we could do on Earth, we split away from the main group and headed out to space. As the Blessed were being sent out on this mission, the group decided to join as Normal workers would be the best way to get aboard and get us out here. Recruiting you was the best thing we did after that. Besides, if we had originally told you were part of P.A.W. would you have joined us?"

"No, I would not have joined – you are correct. If I had not experienced everything the Blessed have done so far, I would still think you – or at least your group, were terrorists. But I do know better now, and I am glad to be part of this with you. So, in that case I must assume you were the person I kept meeting until I joined?"

Max shook his head no "You met with the recruiter. I am only the administrator – I push documents."

"Then who is the recruiter?" she asked.

"Someday they will tell you – when the time is right...along with others in specialized positions."

He smiled, and scanned her again "Perfect health again! I'll be out of a job if more people end up just like you!" He thought for a moment. "That brings up something I've been thinking about. We've had to start creating prosthetics for quite a few of the crew to hide their ears. I have been finding it harder and harder to keep up with the demand!"

"Is all of the crew being affected?" she wondered.

"No, and that is the other odd thing I have to consider..."

A tone from the annunciator interrupted their discussion – it was Jonathan at the door. He rushed in as soon as he saw Jaime. He tried, but was unable to speak as he had been running down the length of the starship. "Alpha Starship Captain...Jaime...Blessed troops have started gathering up anyone they find that is showing the ear changes as you...as me..." he managed to tell her between gasps of air. Jaime looked curiously at him and he looked up at her and removed a cover from the back of his ear. Once removed three growths popped out – a small amount of skin was forming between the growths. "Many of us are getting these – the Blessed are seeking us out. We're being rounded up and taken to the hanger deck."

She scrunched her forehead then rubbed her chin thinking about the situation. "Hmm, what do you think Max? Think they're hunting down us Normals that are changing – think they want to eliminate us?"

Max thought a moment before answering "Well if so, they'll be coming for you. After all, every Blessed knows about you by now."

Jaime's communication device began ringing in her right ear. "Ah, almost on cue! I would suspect they are going to round me up now?" She tapped on the small box on the back of her ear and listened to the message before turning it off. "Yep, I have been ordered to report to the hangar deck."

"I can watch the hangar and make sure the space doors don't open" Jonathan chimed in.

She put the back of her hand on his chin to raise his face and smiled at him "Thank you. I appreciate you watching over me." She started to head for the door then stopped. "Jonathan...someone gave me a clue as to how to beat Boral in the game. It was a female voice, but I don't think it was Lindy. Who was it?"

"Ah!" he replied with excitement "That was the communication expert I found. I could not find Lindy to break through the jamming and warn you, but I found another to get you that message. I'll have her report to you if you wish to meet her."

"Yes please, Jonathan, have her meet us on Blue 12 at the lift. I wish to meet her before I get to the hangar deck. Never know when you might need an emergency communication sent to all Normals." She motioned to him "Come on…"

They arrived at deck Blue 12 where a medium height, thin, brown haired woman was waiting for them. She had her hair pulled back and tied into a low hanging ponytail. She had high rounded cheeks, a plump jaw line, and large lips adorned in red lipstick that when she smiled showed large but appropriately sized front teeth. She had a small up-curved nose, deep brown eyes and thin brows that matched the color of her hair. Jaime also noticed that she was wearing the ear prosthetics – she was concealing the changes. She was dressed in a communication officer's black uniform dress with a set of uniform flat shoes. She snapped at attention when she approached and saluted "Alpha Starship Captain, it is so good to see you in proper health!"

"Please at ease…" she looked the young lady up and down before continuing "I am told I have you to thank for getting me that information?" She nodded in quiet response. "Then thank you. What is your name?"

"Communications Officer XOXO Otterdon, Alpha Starship Captain" she replied.

Jaime looked at her confused "X-O-X-O…or is it pronounced Soso?"

"Actually" she replied "it is X-O-X-O. However, most people call me Otter instead – short form of Otterdon."

"I can't call you Otter!"

"If not, then it is Communications Officer X O X O…that is my name. My mother wanted to just give me hugs and kisses and decided to 'grace' me with that name. It has been kind of a curse all my life, but it is who I am. I really do like and prefer being called Otter."

Jaime sighed "Well, then Otter it is…" she looked at Jonathan 'Have we ever heard anything from Lindy?" Jonathan just shook his head in the negative "Well, then I need a communications officer. Based on your help getting through the jamming, I have a feeling you are qualified to do the job. Am I correct?" Otter nodded yes. "Well, then would you like the job?"

"Absolutely Alpha Starship Captain!" she almost shouted.

Jaime held a finger to her mouth to quiet her, then smiled "Welcome aboard – although we really don't have a ship yet...and somehow I don't think we are going to get one soon..." She rubbed her chin while contemplating things. "Okay, go with Jonathan and when I figure out what's going on, I will contact you two. Now off" she said as she brushed them away with a flick of her wrist.

She opened the bulkhead door to the hangar deck and found two-hundred other Normals standing around with a contingent of Blessed soldiers guarding them. Bellevue was standing with the guards – his jaw once again wired partially shut so it would heal. He cringed slightly when he saw Jaime walk in, but managed to stiffen to attention and salute her. She walked up to him and he handed her a message chip. She put the chip into her command module and read the orders:

"You have been granted use of the Rebel Queen, enough supplies for a year, three manufacturing robots and all of the Normal humans that are showing signs of mutation – as a work crew. You are to proceed to the coordinates below and colonize. The Starfleet Commander expects for you and your mutated humans to build a starship capable of assisting the Supreme Commander's fleet in the conquering of this galaxy."

She closed the message "Well, I guess that's it then. We're out of here." She looked around at all the faces awaiting her command. "Okay, we have been granted equipment and supplies. Load them onto the ship and get prepared to get underway." She pressed her standard communication device "Max, get to the bay – we're going on a trip." She then reset the device and contacted Jonathan "Come on down and bring Otter with you."

"Will do Captain" Jonathan replied, "Will we be returning anytime soon?"

"No Jonathan. Get whatever you want to keep, and get it aboard."

"Roger that... I just have some cases to bring along. Be right down."

"Alpha Starship Captain?" Jaime turned and saw Katsumi and Yuli approaching.

She gave them both a smile, and then each a light hug. "What are you two doing here?"

Yuli replied as he turned his head "Well Alpha Starship Captain, it appears we have earned our wings..." To Jaime's surprise, there were the same three growths jutting back from the helix of his ears. Between the growths were the same thin flaps of skin. Katsumi pulled her hair back exposing the same configuration.

"Well, I'll be..." was all she could say. "Very well, welcome aboard. As soon as we are told how many more are coming along we'll be heading out. Get the ship prepared with needed supplies and stand by."

An engineer stepped up – his ears only had two small growths, but Jaime could tell a third was forming. "Alpha Starship Captain, where are we headed?"

She looked at him, and smiled before saying "Anywhere is better than here. But in any case, where we are headed is where we want to be." He looked at her confused, but then nodded and walked away to prepare supplies.

After two hours, five hundred people with the same affliction had been rounded up and loaded onto the Rebel Queen. Behind those five hundred were another thousand – Jaime suspected there would be even more behind them. They would have to make quite a few trips to get them transported.

The Rebel Queen was cleared for departure, and exited the Ultimate. They turned and headed away from the two ships to clear for insertion into subspace. Jaime was at the command station and Halley was flying the craft. Halley prepared the calculations for insertion into subspace.

Out the blue, Jaime heard Allen on Norm-Comm "Jaime..."

She pressed on her Norm-Comm implant and replied "Allen? Where are you?"

"We are about a light year ahead of you on the way to the new base. We have additional supplies and materials from Bung to get us going. We took a chance that the Blessed would be as predictable as they normally are, and we were right. The base will be close to being habitable by the time you arrive."

Jaime took a second to absorb everything he said before replying "A light year out? How?"

Allen chuckled "Not exactly sure – but my Norm-Comm range seems to have improved...I bet yours has too. See you there."

"Wow..." is all Jaime could say. Halley turned to her and looked confused. "Allen...he's able to communicate from over a light year away."

Halley looked even more confused "When did you talk to him?"

"Just a second ago..."

"I didn't hear you speaking..." she said as she activated the subspace crawler drive. She opened the ship wide communication channel. and announced "Prepare for insertion into subspace. Here we go..."

Max Sollix:

Five days of sub-space brought them to a point in the galaxy that no one aboard the Rebel Queen had ever seen before. After doing a quick check of the passengers and finding none of them suffering ill effects from subspace, he proceeded to the flight deck -- Max had to see where they were. Jaime and Halley were busily looking over scans and reports identifying their position in the galaxy, while also attempting to locate the new base of operations.

Over Norm-Comm he heard Allen calling "Hello Rebel Queen. You are two minutes away from asteroid base. Activate your advanced scanning equipment and look for a black spot in the readouts. SCADAR will have an almost impossible time locating the asteroid, so do not depend on it or you might run into us!"

Max looked out the front facing image screen "I don't see a thing..."

He saw Halley slow the ship down to a crawl, then pointed to a spot on the edge of the screen. "There, look just to the right of center."

He looked and saw nothing but a black spot on the screen. The spot looked jagged and was shaped kind of like a football. He heard Allen announce, "Activating docking lights…" as six red lights appeared in the middle of the black spot.

He heard Jaime reply "Roger, we see the landing beacons…approaching base now. We will do a loop around before entering the bay."

As the ship moved around the surface of the dark rock he could see small shiny reflections in the rock which he assumed were materials that would be used for the ships. In the middle of the asteroid he saw a crew working outside on the surface. There were two men in spacesuits running a piece of equipment that appeared to be a laser to melt out a vein of the shiny element. *"What is going on there?"* he thought.

"They're fixing a flaw in our base…" replied Allen. Max shook his head wondering how he anticipated his question. Allen continued "we're mining out the titanium, melting the space element and filling in the gap formed by the missing metal with melted space element – thus making the surface of the asteroid stronger."

"Oh…" replied Max which caused Jaime to give a slight chuckle.

As they circled around the asteroid they broke orbit and flew slightly out away from the surface before turning the ship around, and flying straight toward the beacon lights. Two large doors were now open between the six beacon lights. Jaime activated running illuminators as they slowly entered the dark cavern.

Halley found the landing bench and softly set the craft down on the solid surface. They all donned spacesuits and walked out onto the dark surface of the shelf. Jaime looked around but could not see a thing in the darkened cavern. She turned and saw the stars disappearing as the large hatches closed shut, sealing them into the heart of the asteroid.

As soon as the doors latched shut the cavern lit up with the light from thousands of illumination devices. They now were able to see the large cavern – the wall on the other side so far away that she could now understand how a large starship could be built in there.

Over Norm-Comm Allen announced "See, just needed a few candles to make the place home!"

They could now see the pressure doors leading to the air lock, which then led to the living and command center – currently the only air-filled area of the base. They passed into the air lock in groups of twenty-five at a time. Once the bulk of the crew was safe inside the pressurized zone the equipment was unloaded for installation and activation.

"Welcome to the base, Alpha Starship Captain" said Allen.

"Thank you" replied Jaime "but let's keep it to Captain for now." Allen nodded.

Max looked around in amazement. "How have you done this so quickly Allen?" he asked.

Allen gave a small smirk before replying "We had help…" and turned to a hallway where a creature emerged. He recognized the tan colored creature based on Jaime's description of an Earth deer. "Jaime, I think you remember…"

He was cut off by Jaime who rushed up and gave the deer a light hug around the neck. "Oomah! I would recognize you anywhere! Thank you for all you have done in getting our base set up."

The deer appeared to have a smile on his face – or at least that is the way Max interpreted the look. Then to his surprise the deer answered in perfect Alliance Standard English "We Flaybah have been more than happy to help our Normal friends. You are in Flaybah space and are totally welcome here while you build your fleet."

"Fleet?" Jonathan asked.

Allen answered, "Yes Jonathan…I think you will want to see this…" and guided him to a holograph projector where when he activated it, showed the blueprints for a starship.

"Is that what I think it is?" the young man asked. Allen nodded his head yes and a large toothy smile came over Jonathan's face.

"Well, what is it Jonathan? Or do I have to guess for myself as I have no idea what the hell you're looking at…" Max called out.

The starry-eyed engineer took a second and finally replied "It's the plans for a ship. Not just any ship -- but a Dragon-Class Star Cruiser."

"This is good?" he asked.

Jaime replied "Oh yes, my friend. If we can build this, there will be no Blessed starship that can stop us."

The Ark of the Blessed

Day 300:

Boral Oldham:

Another wave of Og ships came in for the attack. Boral heard and felt the shocks as their weapons hit the charged hull plates. They were causing minor damage, but were not penetrating the thick armor – there would be dents to remove and repairs to be made, but so far, they were no worse for the wear.

He shifted in his command chair, as his leg was bothering him. He shifted again slightly, then barked out "Send the fighters in to take out their bombers, prepare for counterattack against their capital ships" He then activated a tunneled communication to Kip "Kip, how is it going?"

Kip came up on his command holo-projection. His bridge was filled with smoke and Boral could see that there were some computer consoles that were damaged. Kip pressed some commands into his console before replying "I had a computer go sour on me, but we are still going strong. It will take a lot more than what they are throwing to beat Ultimate!"

Boral rubbed his forehead while he thought for a moment. "Okay, once we are done, let's see how things are going down on the salvage base. I think we need that new design in our fleet. Kip, take the ships on your left flank and through the center and we will take out the ones on the right. Ready to finish this?" Kip smiled, nodded, and then disconnected.

As ordered, Kip took the Ultimate directly between the two attacking groups of Og battleships. The golf ball shaped ships fired multiple bursts of particle beams at the charging craft. The beams hit but did not penetrate. Kip returned fire with every gun available to him -- the first salvo took out ten of the attacking ships. The next barrage took out the other five.

Boral followed suit on the five remaining ships on the right side of the battlefield. He waited until all ships were at point-blank range then opened fire with a flurry of plasma cannons and cutter lasers. He followed that up with a volley from his rail guns. The plutonium shells hit the golf ball shaped command sections and exploded, taking out the remaining ships from battle.

He watched as the Wolf Pack Fighters cleaned up on the enemy streamer fighter and bomber ships. Within five minutes there was nothing left of the attacking Og fleet except floating rubble.

With a smile on his face, Boral issued the next set of orders "Okay, recall the fighters and send out the salvage crews. Let's get some materials for another ship. Victory once again belongs to the Blessed!" Cheers filled the bridge on both ships.

He activated the main holo-display and contacted Plug. "Star Force Commander to construction base. We protected your ass once again. Tell me you have something for me."

The reply from Plug was simple and short "By the end of the year…"

Day 365:

Boral Oldham:

Another day of therapy and still he had weakness in his leg. He was realizing that between the damage to his leg and the plate embedded into his back he would always have memories of what Bordeaux had done to him. He would be reminded of his embarrassment and defeat at the hands of a Normal woman.

Fortunately, today was also a day of a victory – a new ship has been completed on the planetoid Plug and was to be presented to him. Thank god, he had a staff of competent Captains – it helped to make up for the actions of the mutinous Jaime Bordeaux he thought, as he boarded a shuttle to view and to tour the new craft.

The shuttle took him to the starship, now in polar orbit around Plug. The ship was not like either Starlight or Ultimate – it had a innovative design. The ship's command and control section were shaped like a Native American arrowhead -- flat and wide in the back with side edges coming to a sharp, thin point at the front. The middle of this section was wider at the top and became an almost sharp thin edge on the sides. Attached to the back of the command and control section was the propulsion section. This section was a rectangular body that contained a crawler drive in the middle toward the rear. On the two sides of the engineering section were pylons that connected to two updated ion drives – providing the closest to light speed of any craft so far.

He viewed the ship as the shuttle pilot gave him a visual tour. He marveled at all the various gun ports – he knew this ship was built for battle, and for victory. "I have seen enough, get me aboard."

Kip met them at the dock and took him for a tour of the interior of the ship.

"An impressive ship, Kip. Are you taking command of her?" he asked.

He shook his head "No Sir, this ship was in line to be captained by Alpha Starship Captain Griggs, Sir."

"Well then, in that case I would like to take her out personally for her maiden voyage. Will there be a problem with that?"

"I do not see why there would be. Where shall I tell the bridge to head?"

He smiled at his younger Captain "I have a perfect place to test this ship. I will give the coordinates when I get up to the bridge."

Year 1 plus 5 days:

Lindy Light:

Despite her being very tired and weak from the pregnancy, Lindy still insisted on working. She needed the work to keep herself from going insane and to keep her away from her forced husband and the father of her child as much as possible. Her plan failed her today as she discovered that Griggs was not going to the new starship. Boral was on his way, and the younger Captain was told that he would not be needed – so he would be staying down on base.

Fitchburg, being told not to go to his ship had made him even grumpier and meaner than normal. He went to the command center as soon as he had gotten the message that he was not needed up on the new ship. He had also decided to give his freak wife and soon-to-be mother of his child, whatever grief he could today. She knew that his abuse would be his way of making him feel better about his pitiful self.

He entered the room very slowly – still damaged from the game all those months ago. He walked up and looked at her while she worked the communications console. He flipped her hair back revealing the very large wings that jutted out from the back of her ears. Then he looked at her face – her blonde eye brows had also changed today as they had moved slightly upwards in the middle creating a slight point. All of this had come on quite quickly – quicker than most Normals. She had figured it was due to the pregnancy and the growth of the baby. It was now only a month away from being due and she constantly felt it moving and kicking. She refused to allow the doctor to tell her the sex or anything else about the small mixture of Normal and Blessed genetics growing inside her.

She glanced up at him, his reddish-brown hair had been shaved extra short today. His large nose was flared, and he was looking down at her with a large sneer. "You disgust me" he told her with a stern voice "I cannot believe that a creature like you is the only thing that I have successfully mated with. Why is it that I can only get a freak like you pregnant?"

"Are you sure I'm the freak? Besides, what makes you think I'm any happier about being a mother to a child created by rape? You disgust me, you're worse than a pig – you're not even anything that resembles human, you are nothing but a space rat."

"I ought to strike you where you sit for that tone, you bitch! You will not speak to your husband like that!" he raised his hand to her, then changed his mind "Ah, you are not even worth it."

She heard a slight pop and felt something. Fitchburg heard a noise like a leak and looked down and noticed liquid on the floor "Ack, you gross whore...you pissed all over the place. Are you that scared of me?"

She had felt the liquid dribble down her legs and knew what had happened. Although she had wished it was only a dream as it filled her with dread. She looked down at the puddle, and then felt the pain in her belly. He looked down to see what was happening -- she reached up and grabbed his collar, twisted it, and pulled him forcefully down to her face. She somehow had found a strength he had never experienced before, and she was choking him. Her breath was like fire in his face and her dagger piercing eyes actually frightened him as she said in a stern and gruff voice "You fucking moron...my water just broke and I'm about to have your baby. Get your idiot Blessed doctor– now – It's early!" She felt pain in her belly again and let go of him, then screamed and collapsed onto the floor.

Jonathan Faraday:

It was his off-time – the first in a week. He was excited to get back to his recently constructed quarters for a deserved rest. They had been so busy in the science labs – he had come up with the perfect alloy for the frame of the ship. The staff – to his embarrassment – named it "Faratainium". He declared that it was named after his grandfather. They had also figured out some of the weaponry that they had found during salvage operations, and were making these new weapons operational. Halley had given the computer experts some food for thought regarding three-dimensional computing, and they were hard at work developing that technology. All of this was happening while at the same time they were now well into the construction of the new starship. He was exhausted -- however, before he was going to be able to close his eyes and sleep, he needed to check on his special packages.

As soon as he arrived at his quarters, he quickly walked over to the storage closet and opened the doors. Inside were the grey cases that he had been protecting all this time. He had not had a chance to look at his precious items since they had been moved from the Ultimate, and he so badly wanted to check on them.

He rubbed his palms together and took a breath before dialing in the combination to unlock the top case. Upon entering the last number, the case unlatched, and he heard a change in pressure in the case. The noise took him by surprise as he figured the case should be at the same air pressure as that of the asteroid base. He was now worried as he slowly opened the case to peer in.

He worried about what he was about to find – would the creatures be dead, in a state of decomposition or something even worse? He took a deep breath then quickly opened the lid on the case. What he saw shocked him even more than what he expected.

"What the hell?" he said out loud as he peered into an empty container. He opened the other nine cases – all empty. He thought about looking around the cabin for them, but the alarm claxon gave him something even more important to worry about.

He started to head out the door when he could have sworn he heard crying – then for just a moment he forgot what he was doing. The claxon rang out again and just as quickly, it all came back to him – he bolted down the hallway to the control center.

Jaime Bordeaux:

She was awakened again by screaming and crying – she thought she recognized the voice, but had no idea where it was coming from. After a while, the crying changed – it sounded almost like a baby to her. Then she felt something in her head, something reading her thoughts – but only for a moment. For that moment however, she forgot what she was doing or even where she was. After all that occurred she found it impossible to get back to sleep, so instead she activated the lights in her quarters. She looked around at the dark walls that made up her room. She got up and walked over to the desk, and turned on the computer. She looked at various requests and requisitions, and she rubbed her head.

She turned her head away from the computer and activated a holo-image of Dex. She stared at the image of her dead lover -- her eyes welled up, and she felt a tear dripping down her cheek. It seemed like so long ago that he had died – but at the same time it felt like only yesterday that they were still together. She still missed him. "Oh Dex, this is so not me...I'm not an administrator...I need to be out there in space, not delegating work and providing supplies to a colony! Oh hell..."

She turned off the image and wiped her eyes. She took a moment to meditate, and regain her composure – she had work to do and did not have time for this sorrow. She stood up, and put on a casual uniform. She decided to walk down to the control center – maybe watching the work being performed would help her to relax.

She wandered the many cut corridors of the asteroid base. The electrically stimulated illumination panels running at only half power created a twilight feeling as she walked. She strolled through the various areas where laboratories were quietly running all the time – she stared through a window at a computer running a programmed simulation on the fatigue of a new metal alloy. This alloy was produced by the mixing of the various elements with the unknown black material that made up the bulk of their home. Finally, she reached the control center – she entered to find a skeleton crew manning the various tasks for the projects that ran day and night.

Two projects have been going simultaneously – the mining of the asteroid to expand the base This provided building materials for the first starship of the Normal fleet. The Normal scientists had found a way to mine the diamond hard asteroid element using molten gold. The gold allowed for cutting of the rock, which then was tossed into a vat of more molten gold. The gold melted the black space rock which could then be separated from the gold, and made into an alloy by adding titanium and other elements. This new compound was then formed into struts and plates, that were then molded and fashioned for the various components of the new ship. The gold that cut the material was then reused to cut more space metal, which then created even more building materials.

From the control room, she watched as space-suited Normals worked along with assembly robots in the construction of the engineering section. The ship was coming along fine -- struts were put into place forming the structure of the ship, while curved plates were being installed onto the completed frame simultaneously. The construction robots worked constantly and tirelessly, even when the human counterparts rested. She gazed at what was going to be *her ship* -- it was going to be one hell of a powerful ship she thought.

She glanced across the vast cavern that made up the construction bay of the base, and looked at the enormous solid black door that had been constructed to protect and conceal the shipyard dock. While at the base, she had not had that much to do – except wait for her ship. Yes, she had administrative chores – decisions to be made, determining allocations of resources across the base, and all sorts of other duties. But it was not her -- she even wondered why she was thrown into this position. There were plenty of other people who would do a much better job of running this base. After all, she was a starship Captain or at the very least a good fighter pilot. In a ship, out there in space was where she needed to be – she just had to be patient.

The proximity alarms took her away from her inner thoughts. "What the hell is that?"

Allen joined her within a few moments of the alarm going off. "Allen, check the probe beams. What's going on?"

"A ship has just appeared from a subspace tear. Getting a focus on our probes for an image..." he said as he frantically worked at the scanning controls.

Oomha ran in a moment later – his small antlers glowing with the now familiar green aura.

Jonathan ran in and joined Allen at the science station controls. He whispered "Allen, they're gone!"

Allen looked at him with disgust "You opened the cases and let them escape?" Oomha gave the pair a surprised look.

Jonathan shook his head no "What if they are still on Ultimate? They'll die there!" Before he could say anything else the scanning probes began to provide information about the starship outside their front door. He looked at the returning readings of the probe beams before whistling, and commenting "They actually did it..."

"Did what?" asked Jaime.

"Built that design..." the young man replied. He brought the image of a ship on the screen. The main section had an arrowhead shape with a dual engine configuration in the engineering section. "That" he said, "is a Hammerhead-Class Battle Cruiser – Blessed design."

"Blessed?" Jaime replied "What are they doing here? It has not been a year." She looked at Allen who had a blank look on his face "Allen, you ok?"

The blank look faded and for a moment he looked around as if trying to remember what was going on. "Umm..." he looked back down at the scanner console "I don't know..." Allen replied slowly then continued in his normal pace "but they must have found a way to recover from subspace quicker as they are already moving toward us. I don't see any weapons from the probe readings, but that does not mean they aren't targeting us."

"Can they damage us?" she asked.

Jonathan replied "Only if somehow they hit one of the external veins of gold. We have not gotten all of them removed and filled."

Jaime scrunched her forehead "Umm, what will that do?"

"It depends on which one they hit and how hard" Allen answered. "If they hit one with a direct laser they might melt the gold, which then would melt the space metal. If that happened it might melt other parts of the asteroid which could then cause a pressure shift and an explosion of the atmosphere into the vacuum. It would not be pleasant for sure. If they are typical Frogspawn, it would probably take them one hell of a lucky shot to start that scenario – but I really don't want to take that chance."

"Okay, so do we have any defenses active yet?" both of the men shook their heads no. "Ahh, so what do we do? I'm not really a base commander -- I should be in a ship. We have no weapons, correct?" they both nodded their heads yes "Okay, no offense, no defense...I'm open to suggestions."

"Well...hope that they have not improved their weapons or found alien technology that is stronger than what they currently had when we left, I guess." Jonathan answered. "If they still have standard Alliance weaponry then we just have to hope they do not hit one of the gold veins. If they have found new tech – well who knows. This is all assuming they're not here for a social call."

Oomha's antlers glowed brighter.

Jaime ordered "Let's find out. Send out a hail...tell them welcome."

Max rushed into the control center "What's going on...and who the hell is crying that loudly?" They all turned and looked at him like he was crazy. He shook his head as if saying *"Never mind"* then looked at the holo-display at the ship now approaching. "What the hell is that?"

"Nothing good..." Allen called out "they've just opened their weapons ports." The ship moved closer to the base. Allen's eyes opened wide in surprise as he yelled out "Charging weapons... firing! Shit, hang on!"

End of book I.

Next: Ark of the Blessed II -- The Metamorphosis of Normal.